What People Are Saying ...his Book

"A fascinating [historical fic... ...ount of the sharp end of espionage during a crucial part ...

Professor Jeremy Black,
Historian a...   of *Rethinking World War Two*,
War and Technology: Air Power, and o... ...00 military and political histories

"A fine account [historical fiction] focused on ... three important facets of World War II: the Battle of the Atlantic, ... intelligence, and the race to develop atomic weapons."

Gerhard L. Weinberg,
Professor Emeritus, University of North Carolina
and Author of *A World at Arms: A Global History of World War II*

"In April, 1941, the German surface raider *Atlantis* sank the Egyptian passenger liner *Zamzam* in the South Atlantic. In this cleverly conceived novel, Carpenter uses that event to construct a tale of diplomacy, espionage, atomic secrets, and peril on the high seas."

Craig L. Symonds,
Professor Emeritus, US Naval Academy and Author of
NEPTUNE: The Allied Invasion of Europe and the D-Day Landings
and *Decision at Sea: Five Naval Battles that Shaped American History*

"Novelists enjoy ... having their characters interact with historic figures. Carpenter places his protagonist Commodore John Braithwaite aboard the true-life freighter *Zamzam* on a perilous voyage in 1941. The fictional Braithwaite operates under orders from genuine superiors including William Stephenson, 'The man called Intrepid.' Ensuing events will leave some readers wondering where fact ends and fiction begins."

Barrett Tillman,
Military Historian and Author of
Enterprise: America's Fightingest Ship,
Whirlwind: The Air War Against Japan,
Dauntless: Novel of Midway and Guadalcanal,
Hellcats: A Novel of the Pacific,
and numerous WWII fiction and non-fiction works

RESURRECTION OF
ANTIMONY

S. D. M. Carpenter

Clovercroft Publishing

To Linda,
with love and admiration.

Resurrection of ANTIMONY

©2016 by S.D.M. Carpenter

Ship photos courtesy of the World War II Valor in the Pacific National Monument, Pearl Harbor, Hawaii and the U.S. Naval War College Museum, Newport, Rhode Island.

Independently published by the author through Clovercroft Publishing, Franklin, Tennessee

Published in association with Larry Carpenter of Christian Book Services, LLC of Franklin, Tennessee

Edited by Kristy Callahan
Cover Design by Suzanne Lawing
Interior Layout Design by Adept Content Solutions

ISBN-10: 1942557574
ISBN-13: 978-1942557579

Printed in the United States of America

PART I
TANGO ZAMZAM

CHAPTER 1
TENNIS MATCH

Nothing delights the British quite like the prospect of a hopeless situation.

The Ford convertible lurched to a stone-crunching halt in the gravel driveway of the venerable Oak Crest Club, bastion of New York's elite for over a century and miles from the frenetic hurry of the city, the perfect place for the powerful to conduct their business—political, social, or financial. Barren cherry trees, not quite ready to bloom in their pink and ivory splendor, ringed the circular drive. Magnificent oak trees, planted by the original club membership, lined the road in from the highway like Guardsmen on parade. Here and there stood saplings, replacements for the aged trees culled by nature's own pruning and thinning. The driver had received a call that morning requesting he be there at 2 p.m. for tennis. A smartly-dressed valet gripped the chrome door handle and, smiling broadly, swung open the door. The retired Royal Navy man stepped onto the white, rain-washed gravel that crunched under his flawlessly polished shoes.

"Good morning, Sir. Welcome to Oak Crest."

Commodore John David Fairchild Braithwaite nodded. The valet bounced into the driver's seat and the car slowly rolled away as Braithwaite stepped up onto the foot-worn, black marble steps through the ornately carved portico into a wall-to-ceiling oak- paneled foyer. Over the mirror-sharp, polished parquet floor lay an antique, deep burgundy rug. Portraits of former members lined the foyer stoically gazing down at all newcomers.

An elderly black man dressed in club livery greeted Braithwaite with the perfect comportment and formality required of such a place. "May I help you, Sir?"

"Yes. Commodore Braithwaite."

The porter checked the leather-bound appointment book sitting on a brass podium. "Ah, yes, Commodore Braithwaite. Please meet Mr. Stephenson at Tennis Court #2. I believe he is there now." He reached under the podium and pressed a hidden button. Within seconds, another black man raced into the foyer and snapped to attention, chin held high. "Please show Commodore Braithwaite to the Gentlemen's Locker Room. He will be playing tennis with Mr. Stephenson this afternoon. Please follow William, Sir, and have a good match."

"Thank you, I shall." Braithwaite followed the porter through the multiple corridors covered with past members' portraits. With each room paneled in a different oak variety, the guide explained that whenever a tree toppled on the grounds or had to be cut down, cabinet makers made new paneling. The main dining room, only partially paneled, awaited the fall of another red oak. The custom appealed to Braithwaite's sense of tradition and stability. The sparkling white locker room smelled of rubbing alcohol, disinfectant, and shaving lotion. A courteous attendant presented the RN man a note.

"John, old man. Please check in Locker 2110. You will find a kit. I'll be on Court #2. The helpful man at the counter will see to your needs. See you in a bit. Bill."

No locks hung from any of the light green metal doors. No club member would ever dream of nor would any employee ever dare to disturb any belongings. The locker contained everything the smartly-attired tennis player needed—a top of the line racket, fashionable togs, and three fuzzy balls. Few details ever missed his host. Braithwaite chuckled and loosened his tie. He spotted a floor length mirror and walked over, racket in hand. Vanity perhaps—or wishful thinking—*by God, he still looked fairly good for a middle-aged chap*. His hairline had been receding for some years, but he still sported a good head of dark brown hair, full and wavy in a casual way. Gray streaks around the temples gave him a distinct air of authority complimented by a crisply-trimmed mustache. On active duty, he never had facial hair, but since retirement three years earlier, a trim little mustache seemed just the thing. He had seen the actor wear one—*what was his name? Ah, yes, Dick Powell—carries off the mustache so damned effectively. Why not? He didn't have to be drab all of his life. Then when Alice died ... Alice died.* The Commodore softly padded the tennis racket handle in the palm of his left hand as he stared at the tiled floor. *Since Alice died.* Such a useless death—a sailing accident that final blissful summer before the war. He had retired early to spend the last years of his life with his love, consuming her day and night. They had no children. Every time he returned from the sea, there she stood, loyally waiting. But in their twenty years together, while he went from Naval Intelligence Officer extraordinaire to command of a destroyer, then a light cruiser, and a battleship, and finally as a squadron commodore, they had really only spent a few precious years together. God bless those rare years of shore duty. A tear welled up in his right eye and rolled down his cheek. He looked back up at the mirror. *Well, old sod. Be grateful for the years you did have together and honor her memory.*

The war erupted only a few weeks after the accident. He barely had time to bury the dead, but what a godsend for a grieving man. The day after the Polish invasion, he briskly marched into Admiralty and volunteered for recall to active duty not really caring in what capacity. He would bury himself in the war effort—balm for the wound. The Second Sea Lord recommended him for a Mediterranean command. However, the man in the office below the First Sea Lord's, Rear-Admiral John Godfrey, Director of Naval Intelligence (DNI), got him first. So be it. His field work in the First World War had been nothing short of spectacular. It earned him promotion to commander, the Victoria Cross, and the Distinguished Service Order. In spite of having been out of intelligence field work for twenty years, Godfrey requested his assignment to Naval Intelligence Division (NID) immediately. He had held high command before, but NID needed him. Very well. That is where he would make his home for the war's duration. And, although as was usual for a Commodore First Class, when he retired after his last squadron command, he reverted to the actual rank of captain, all who knew him simply referred to Braithwaite as "Commodore."

At fifty, of medium height with a strong aquiline, Anglo-Saxon nose and facial features, big-boned, but not overweight, he kept up his physique through as many games of tennis, rounds of golf, sailing, and riding as the demands of work permitted. He had long, strong fingers, which complemented his sports endeavors. And, of course, with the ever-so-jaunty, closely trimmed mustache, he appeared every bit the attractive, elegant, graceful, aristocratic British gentleman. Many a young London lady and, more recently, New York, swooned over this attractive older man. In truth, he could have his pick, but the memory of his Alice stayed too fresh, too tender. He buried her body, not her soul. No—too soon, if ever, and much too painful. He avoided the youngsters and concentrated on his work.

Braithwaite strode through the passageway out into the porch leading to an arbor formed of winding grape and ivy vines interlaced over white-washed frames and beams. White enameled wicker furniture dotted the marble tiled patio. At the center of the arbor, a bronze Greek maiden's vase poured out a trickling fountain. A few people, mostly matronly types, sipped cool drinks, chatting and playing bridge on the warm wonderful March day. There is a reason why the rich and powerful are the rich and powerful. They drove the engines of commerce and industry in the early spring of 1941 from the high rise skyscraper offices of Manhattan, not here in the sunny country playing cards and sipping cocktails. He stepped out into the sunshine. He loved spring after the gloomy, dull stinginess of winter. The sun felt good on his face. He placed his racket and tennis balls on the flagstone walk, bent down, and retied a shoelace—it just wouldn't do to lose a shot due to unsteady shoes. Up ahead a yellow sign indicated Court #2. On the immaculately groomed grass court, he noticed a metal sign with brass letters that read: "MR. STEPHENSON V. COMMODORE BRAITHWAITE." *Nice touch.* On the bench sat a short but muscular, powerful man. Bill Stephenson played every game, approached every problem, tackled every challenge with the same dogged tenacity and immense energy. Braithwaite admired this in the younger man. Like often attracts like. He saw in Bill Stephenson a mirror image of himself.

"Hello, worthy competitor!" Braithwaite shouted, raising his racket high in the air. He had actually never played tennis with Stephenson, but presumed him to be a skilled player since he did everything else so well.

"John! So glad you could make it. I trust I didn't interrupt anything important today," Stephenson responded.

Interrupt indeed! When Bill Stephenson summoned, one came.

"Wonderful day, eh?"

Simply put, Bill Stephenson, codenamed INTREPID by Winston Churchill himself, the most powerful spymaster in the world, controlled every aspect of British intelligence, counter-intelligence, and special operations in the New World from the Rockefeller Center offices of British Security Coordination or BSC. Under his command as the war dragged on came the counter-intelligence department (MI-5), the foreign intelligence gathering MI-6 organization, and the Special Operations Executive (SOE, also dubbed the "Baker Street Irregulars"). From BSC's special training base, Camp "X," in the Canadian forest, INTREPID sent out field agents to work with partisan and resistance groups and to conduct field operations against the Axis. Under the guise of a Passport Control Officer, a relatively minor Foreign Office functionary, INTREPID directed his empire with the winking complicity of the U.S. government. The confident, cheery smile belied the incredible responsibility laid on him for Britain and the Commonwealth's survival. William Stephenson, World War One fighter ace, Canadian entrepreneur from the harsh plains of Manitoba, and a founding father of the BBC, proved the perfect selection for the post as the world's greatest spymaster.

Braithwaite's first duty at NID had been to analyze the German Navy's surface threat to the unarmed merchant vessels in their dash across the North Atlantic. He tried to "get into the minds" of his German counterparts and anticipate their actions. He did this job until late 1940 when it became apparent that the U-boats represented the primary threat. The lack of a serious threat from the German surface fleet may have been somewhat credited to his work, but deep down, he knew that the German Navy remained reluctant to commit its scarce surface resources to the fray. Ever since Jutland in 1916, the German Navy had avoided any general fleet action with the Royal Navy. The admirals in Berlin preferred to send out commerce raiders, either warships disguised as merchantmen or the small, but powerful "pocket battleships" to snipe on the fringes of the maritime traffic routes. Ships such as the infamous and deadly effective Raider 16, the *Atlantis,* disguised as neutral merchantmen, accomplished the most destructive work. Given the lack of sustained, aggressive surface action against the convoys, he grew edgy in his role. When Bill Stephenson's BSC geared up in New York, Braithwaite talked Godfrey out of one job and Stephenson into another. At BSC, Braithwaite coordinated counter-intelligence efforts, a huge task and paramount to the war effort. Britain must remain alive until Hitler blundered, or the natural ally, the United States, came into the war. The Germans had more informants and agents on the New York waterfront than any other place in the world. These men had one mission—reporting shipping movements back to Berlin. The end result of this intelligence gathering might well be a torpedo slamming into the thin hull of a ship carrying vital supplies to Britain. So why play tennis today? Something tingled in the air. He would play along.

Double fault. The ball whizzed past his ear. *The man is good.* Braithwaite would have to be better. 15 LOVE. He raced to the baseline. His backhand swing struck the blurred ball directly in the racket's center. Strings hummed. *Good shot! Too late, Stephenson.* The ball bounced off the grass a full two feet from his outstretched racket. 40-30. The lob came down directly at his eyes looking as if it would take off his nose. He whirled about bringing the racket up as he leapt backward. Kawwhang! Service. The ball pitched in the air. The racket came down propelling it towards the lime dust outline across the net. *Fault. Damn! An inch at most.* Chalk dust caught in a breeze drifted over his opponent's court. Across the way, the man shifted his weight side to side, leaning forward, a gladiator, exhausted but ready. Sweat poured off Braithwaite's brow and dripped onto the grass below. Wiping it off with the back of his hand, he lifted the ball and squeezed, then tossed it. The racket crashed down, spinning the ball across the top of the net. *Too slow, Mr. Stephenson. Advantage, Mr. Braithwaite.* And so it went, minute by minute for almost two hours. And then, the gladiator succumbed.

The Commodore slumped into the wooden bench at mid-court, his exhausted arm still clutching the racket. He could barely see through the rivulets of perspiration running down his face dropping off into mid-air from his long, aristocratic nose and firm chin. The racket, his weapon, dropped to the grass below. This game of tennis—a battle of nerves, of muscle, of strategy, of endurance, and of heart played out on the elegantly appointed #2 Court in the oak woods—perfectly illustrated the mettle of both warriors.

"You're testing me Bill. Why?"

Stephenson continued to towel off, staring into the woods as if the question had never been asked. He draped the towel around his neck and looked at his watch. "What do you say to a late lunch? The shrimp salad here is extraordinary."

The head of BSC requested a table in the far corner of the patio, partially screened from the sun by overhanging ivy. A breeze fluttered the vine leaves overhead, bouncing sunlight off the wicker table, creating a mesmerizing pattern of light and shadow. Braithwaite chose the chicken salad instead of the shrimp—a man of the sea to be sure, but he didn't particularly enjoy seafood. It had the crisp, pungent flavor of nutmeg and garlic. The waiter cleared the dishes and brought two tall club sodas with a lime twist crowning the frosty glasses. Stephenson discouraged alcohol during working hours.

Braithwaite suspected just how much working had been going on this after-noon. INTREPID leaned back in the antique wicker chair, which creaked and groaned.

"John, how much do you know about nuclear fission?"

An odd question. "Precious little, I fear. I am aware that several nations, the United States, Britain, and Germany included, are bent on harnessing that energy for some sort of doomsday weapon. Why do you ask?"

INTREPID leaned forward and arched his head close to Braithwaite, al-though it wasn't necessary with the nearest person well out of earshot. "We have received good intelligence that Dr. Enrico Verdi, the émigré Italian physicist now working on the U.S. project in Chicago, has booked passage for South Africa. London fears Jerry may attempt some sort of prejudicial action."

The Commodore shifted his weight. He took a long draw of the cold drink more as a pause to formulate his response than anything else. "I see. What is the source of this intelligence?"

"CHARLEMAGNE."

Braithwaite leaned back and nodded his head. *CHARLEMAGNE. Of course, first rate source—someone highly placed in the Reich Foreign Office.* "So what are our friends up to with Dr. Verdi, the mad scientist?"

"Essentially this. We have nurtured rumors of a special weapons facility in South Africa over the past several months. We have hinted that it is a heavy water extraction plant. And that stuff is necessary for nuclear fission."

"And there is none."

"Correct. We threw this bone to confuse them while our actual research and development carries on elsewhere. A small thing, but this is a race we cannot lose. *Abwehr* is apparently sending a man in to track Verdi in hopes of discovering the facility. It makes perfect logic—American physicist known to be working on atomic research suddenly makes a trip to South Africa. Why? Obvious to the Germans. Their response? Put a man on his tail, follow him right to the plant, follow up with a sabotage raid. End of enemy's atomic research."

"But there is no atomic research plant. So why a trip to South Africa?"

"To visit his brother, a mining engineer in Pretoria. They haven't seen each other in years. Jerry wouldn't believe that, however."

The waiter arrived with another round of club sodas. INTREPID signed the card and thanked him. Braithwaite sat quietly, mulling over this intriguing bit of news.

"Why were you testing me today?"

"I heard you were a fair tennis player. I just wanted to see if you were really that good." The impish twinkle in Bill Stephenson's eyes gave away the lie. The Commodore swirled the ice and lime twist around in his glass.

"You are a bloody awful liar, Bill Stephenson."

INTREPID chuckled. "I suppose so. No good for field work, eh!" He breathed out slowly and wiped his still sweaty brow with a linen napkin. "The truth, John, is that we want you to accompany Verdi to Africa. To be a nanny, if you will."

Braithwaite jerked back as if struck by a lightning bolt. He dropped the swizzle stick. "Good Lord! You're not serious!"

"Perfectly serious. I have my doubts, but Godfrey wants it. He is somewhat adamant about it, actually."

"Why me? I haven't done field work in over twenty years."

"Precisely. Which may be an advantage. Whomever Jerry sends wouldn't ever guess that we would send a middle-aged agent. You are not a known entity in the present game. You're also close in age to our bird, so you should be able to strike up a friendship with Verdi while not arousing either his suspicions or the German's."

"I see. Why the tennis game?"

"I had to be sure you were fit. Fit in the sense of endurance. You obviously are."

"And?"

"I had to gauge your competitiveness. I needed to know how you reacted under stress and challenge. Let me say that I have had grave doubts about this entire matter. Field work is for supple young men. You are a brilliant intelligence officer, but I had to be comfortable that, shall we say, age has not been unkind."

"And the verdict?"

"I am going to send you unless you object, of course."

Object? Object? You must be bloody joking! A field assignment! He had never again hoped to get another. It made his blood fairly boil. So what if it meant just watching over an American tourist on a holiday to visit relatives. *Am I up to it?* He had doubts, of course, but he knew he must prevail. A man of action, intense action—it showed in everything he did from playing tennis or golf to sailing to his naval career. Settling behind a desk made him nervous. Yes, certainly he held a critical job ferreting out enemy commerce spies and protecting the seaborne lifeline, but a man of his nature could only do it for so long and stay sane. He stretched a hand out across the pale blue, floral print tablecloth. The two men shook hands with a firm, forceful grip. Of course he would take the assignment.

"Godfrey has sent us his administrative assistant to work out the details. You know him, I believe—Lieutenant-Commander Ian Fleming, RNVR."

"Yes, Fleming. Good chap. Reuters reporter before the war. Aspires to write spy novels, I understand."

INTREPID chuckled. "I suppose. At any rate, he will coordinate the operation from London. We'll meet him tomorrow to lay out the final details. You'll be sailing day after tomorrow on the *Zamzam*, an Egyptian ship, I believe, named for some holy well near Mecca. By the way, your operational code name will be ANTIMONY."

The second jolt. *ANTIMONY! How many years since he had heard that word.* ANTIMONY—his First World War code name at Naval Intelligence. Just as the element antimony, which, when blended with other metals, produces harder, more durable alloys, so too would this ANTIMONY harden the system to counter the Nazi threat. *ANTIMONY is resurrected!*

On the uneventful drive back to New York, the traffic seemed lighter than usual. Just as well though. ANTIMONY'S thoughts rolled along, so much so that he paid little attention to the road. He thought of Alice. He thought of his shipmates defending King and Country, many now in a watery grave. He thought of the old days when he would spend months in the field, always just a step or two ahead of the Kaiser's men. And he pondered. He wondered whether he could still handle the task. *What if the Nazis had more on their minds than merely observation? What if CHARLEMAGNE had not told them the entire story? What if he walked into a trap with no way out?* But despite a thousand ifs, a thousand reasons not to go, one overwhelming, overriding reason remained—ANTIMONY, nemesis of the Germans years before, back in action again, daring the Huns to send him their best shot. *By God—he is resurrected. ANTIMONY is resurrected!*

Street lights sparkled as he motored into Manhattan. *Pray God, these lights never go out. Never!*

CHAPTER 2
FOR TOMMY JOHNSTON

A two-rap knock on the cabin door—quick, but firm—interrupted the silence.

"Come," replied the short, ruddy-cheeked Scotsman not looking up from the deck log spread out in front of him on the doughty, gray metal desk. He kept writing as he exhaled another puff of smoke from his prized Meerschaum pipe. A gray-blue ring wafted towards the overhead and oblivion. The first officer silently entered the cabin.

"The pilot boat will be alongside in a few minutes, Captain," the first officer spoke in clipped, but excellent English.

Without looking up, the captain both acknowledged and dismissed the man. "Very good, Number One. I'll be up to the Pilot House in a moment or so."

"Aye, Aye, Sir."

The first officer exited as quickly and quietly as he had entered. Another smoke ring drifted up. Captain William Gray Smith, Master of the 8,300-ton Egyptian passenger liner SS *Zamzam*, rushed to finish the deck log before they pulled pier side in New York. He loved New York—the tingling, constant excitement of the place, and quite a contrast to darkened, cringing European ports. Almost the entire world at each other's throats, and yet, New York stood as vibrant and alive as ever in ecstatic obliviousness. He finished the deck log (polishing it up, really). As a legal document it demanded accuracy. He ran the rickety old scow as he would the *Queen Mary*. His command, his ship, he loved the old tub despite her decrepitude and questionable crew. Anyone who ever had command at sea knows the feeling. Smith picked up the handset of the telephone bolted to the desk, flipped the Bakelite switch one notch clockwise to Engine Room, and spun the crank twice. Two loud, metallic clangs echoed off the sweaty metal bulkheads below.

"Engine Room," answered Chief Engineer Burns, the only other Briton in a polyglot crew of Egyptians, Sudanese, Greeks, Turks, Yugoslavs, Czechs, and a Frenchman.

"Chief, the pilot boat is almost alongside. Stand by for maneuvering bells. I'll be in the Pilot House."

"Engine Room, Aye. Standing by."

Captain Smith heard the rhythmic beating of the old reciprocating engines in the background. He dropped the telephone back into the cradle and stood up tapping the bowl of his pipe—a good pipe, but it doesn't like to stay lit. He fumbled about in a jacket pocket and found a yellow and red box of Swan matches. A bright flash and acrid smoke erupted as the match scratched across the rough, phosphorus strip. Smith sucked in as the tobacco glowed orange-red in the nicotine stained, brown pipe bowl carved in the shape of an elephant's head. Yes, a very good pipe. He tossed the spent match into a metal ash tray and buttoned the salt-tarnished uniform buttons. As he reached the cabin door, he grabbed the gold coil embroidered hat.

In the Pilot House, the early spring freshness tingled his nose. Off the starboard bow still several miles away, stood the Statue of Liberty. Coming up on the port side, bouncing in the waves, a small but steady pilot boat, its bow raising and crashing down hard, crested each wave.

"Ahead Dead Slow."

"Ahead Dead Slow, Aye," responded the lee helmsman.

The Engine Order Telegraph bells clanged twice as the signal rang up. The Engine Room responded Ahead Dead Slow. *Zamzam* made bare steerageway as the boat bobbed alongside, the pilot gingerly making his way up the sea ladder. This competent seaman had shepherded *Zamzam* into New York harbor on many occasions. He would ease her into her proper berth with no problems. Lord knows, there were many ports where a ship's master stood in his Pilot House, mortally dreading that a harbor pilot would run his ship aground. Language difficulty often made this affair particularly thrilling. Why couldn't these buggers speak proper King's English, thought Smith on many, far too many occasions as he extended his hand in greeting to the well-known pilot.

"Ahead Slow," commanded the pilot with the ring of authority honed by decades of seamanship.

"Ahead Slow, Aye," responded the Turk manning the Lee Helm.

Smith nodded. The ship is in good hands. He allowed himself the rare luxury of daydreaming, of letting his thoughts drift off far away from the Pilot House. He stuffed his hands into the deep pockets of his blouse and brushed the edge of a piece of paper. Pulling out a yellowed, crumpled letter, a flash of anger came over him, then passed—old news, but still painful. Smith unfolded the paper and scanned it searching for the sentences he had read a dozen times before in the past six months.

"You may have heard by now that Tommy Johnston bought it last month. It was a small convoy from Halifax to Liverpool. A U-boat Admiralty said. His tanker just split in two and was gone," wrote a mutual friend, another ship's master.

A small tear welled up in the mariner's right eye—a small tear for Tommy Johnston. A Scot like himself, Johnston took him under his wing when Smith first sailed and became his "sea daddy," who brought the young officer along with compassion and professionalism. They remained close through the years and dozens of other ships, always corresponding and occasionally meeting somewhere for a pint and talk of home. When the war broke out, Johnston volunteered even though really too old. His tanker made a dozen trans-Atlantic runs without even seeing a German until a murderous night in August 1940.

Smith folded the letter, placed it back in the pocket and walked out onto the Bridge Wing. The silent lookout acknowledged his presence with a nod and, no doubt, returned to his own particular daydream. Flashes of silver reflecting sunlight off the curling waves caught his eye. Winter's recession yielded a bright, clear magnificent day. Smith gazed out at the Statue of Liberty. What a monument to the nobility of man. The letter burned in his pocket. What a monument to the cruelty of man. As William Gray Smith scanned the New York skyline, he came to a conclusion (more an acceptance of what he had known for some time). He must jump into the fray. Tommy Johnston knew this and had given his life. How could he carry on with his cushy little job on this insignificant passenger liner when his shipmates sacrificed everything to keep Britain alive. Smith smiled. For the first time in months, he truly felt at ease. He would make this last voyage as master of the *Zamzam* and then resign. Let some other soul have his ship. He would volunteer for a command on the bloody alley between the New and the Old World in a war at sea that would only become deadlier. The die, as Caesar had said, is cast. He placed both hands squarely on the weather-worn Bridge Wing rail and stretched, his back arching up. Simultaneously, he sucked in a huge quantity of air, fresh air—fresh sea air scented with the vaguely industrial aroma of a vibrant, free city. He felt good.

"Ahead Half," came the firm voice from inside the Pilot House.

Zamzam headed into New York to take on passengers and cargo bound for Baltimore, Trinidad, Recife (Brazil), Cape Town (South Africa), Mombasa (Kenya), and finally, home to Alexandria, the port city of Egypt. By mid-morning, *Zamzam* had berthed alongside a dingy concrete pier, rutted and pockmarked with oil-filmed puddles in Hoboken, across the Hudson River from Manhattan on the New Jersey side. Only the big, glamorous liners—*Normandie* or the *Queens, Mary* and *Elizabeth*—got the better berths near 48th Street in Manhattan, not a decrepit old Egyptian steamer. As the deck hands tightly secured the last line to a bollard, Smith relit his pipe and pulled in deeply. The pilot emerged from the Pilot House followed by the obsequious third officer and extended his hand. Smith grasped it firmly.

"Welcome to New York Captain, and best of luck on your voyage. Remember, the swamp is full of alligators." Both men grinned.

"Thank you, Jack. Once again, well done," responded Smith.

The pilot saluted, then floated effortlessly down the ladder to the main deck below. Ladders don't seem to matter much to old salts; they merely fly up and down them. Smith turned and stared at the Empire State Building. Smoke whirled about his head. New York!

Two knocks.

"Come."

The captain's steward stepped into the cabin. The elderly Egyptian bowed regally from the waist. "An officer to see you, Sir. He is waiting at the brow." The steward grinned a toothless smile.

"American?"

"No, Sir. Englishman for certain."

Smith's eyebrows raised in surprise. "Very well. Show the officer up. And serve up some tea."

"Right away, Captain."

The steward scurried away to carry out his assignment. Smith raised his finger and placed it on the top of his nose pensively. *A British officer. Very strange, indeed. Ah, well, it will be good to see him. Perhaps he has some recent news. No doubt bad, but news all the same.*

Two knocks. The cabin door opened. "Captain Smith, Sir." The steward bowed and retreated. The visitor stepped in extending his hand. Smith took it and shook firmly.

"Lieutenant David Halyburton, Royal Navy. Pleased to make your acquaintance, Sir."

"Do sit down, Lieutenant." Smith gestured towards the careworn but still comfortable sofa under a porthole. Halyburton turned, found a spot in the middle without stuffing showing through, and sat down lightly. The RN officer wore civilian clothes. He had that double-breasted blue blazer, old boy look of the public school type. Smith did not particularly resent this type of officer, but remained leery of them until they learned the ropes and proved their mettle. He could not help but notice the brass buckle-bound, very official looking brown leather, British government briefcase attached to the man's left wrist by a pair of Scotland Yard's best bracelets. *So this is not entirely a social call.* He tapped his pipe on the edge of the ash tray and cleared his throat.

"And what can I do for His Majesty's Navy today, young man?" The older mariner's gentile nature immediately put the visitor at ease.

"Actually, Sir, a great deal. First, let me show you my credentials." Halyburton fumbled about in his jacket pocket for a leather identity case. He stretched and handed it to Smith. The various papers identified Halyburton as the Assistant Naval Attaché to the British Consulate in New York.

Smith handed back the identity case. "Seen any action?" probed Smith seeking a common ground with which to break the ice.

The corners of Halyburton's mouth drooped, barely perceptibly, but just enough to be detected. His eyes seemed to grow darker—minute changes, but Smith had spent a career looking into the faces of sailors, prying out their thoughts and feelings. In this young, well-dressed, overly courteous officer's expression, he saw the anguish, the terror, the trauma of combat, and, he saw the dejection of a man who knew there would be much more carnage to come.

"Well, yes. I have, Sir. I served on HMS *Kelly* in the Med at the start of the punch up. Lord Mountbatten's ship. Then on to the . . ." The man's brow furrowed in subconsciously induced pain. "On the *Oedipus* for most of the past year on the North Atlantic runs."

Smith now knew the origin of the dark tone. HMS *Oedipus* had been torpedoed by a U-boat the previous November off Iceland. She sank slowly with few initial casualties. One hundred and sixty-three men went into the water. A passing Swedish ore ship had found the surviving sixteen the next morning.

"I've been in New York at the Consulate since January." The officer stared down at the shabby, frayed carpet covering the bare metal deck.

Smith shifted in his chair. "I understand." All men of the sea are brothers. All would understand. "I take it this is not a social call?"

The change of subject re-energized Halyburton. "Quite so. You must mean this rather attractive article of attire." He lifted the clunky briefcase from the floor. The chrome plated shackles clanked. "I'm closer to this thing than to my fiancé, I fear."

Both men chuckled. The tension broke.

"What I am going to present to you must remain in strictest confidence."

"Of course, Lieutenant."

The naval officer took in a deep breath and slowly exhaled. "I am going to ask you to violate the neutrality of your vessel."

Smith stared directly at Halyburton's eyes then to the deck below, then back to Halyburton. He rose, turned, and walked over to the salt-streaked porthole above his bed. *Zamzam* had not yet had a freshwater wash down. "Go on," he finally said, a slight edge to his voice.

"I am asking you to sail under Admiralty orders."

Smith had expected this hammer to fall eventually. It had to happen. Total war is total after all. Neutrals could stay uninvolved for only so long. "Contraband?" asked Smith as he turned to face the RN man, with his hands clasped behind his back in a very nautical, authoritative way.

Halyburton had him. There would be no resistance from this Scottish master of an Egyptian liner. He unclasped the two brass hasp locks and removed two documents. Out came a typed green paper and an Admiralty Signal Code Book for merchant vessels. Halyburton laid both on the edge of the desk. "We are asking you to do three things. One, to sail without running lights at night. Two, to show no national ensign during daylight. And three, to copy the Admiralty merchant broadcast and to carry out any directions given to you. Here is the code book currently in use." He lifted up the cover of the book on the table, then let it drop.

How cleverly sublime! The British Admiralty would make his ship a target—a target in the propaganda war. "You realize that this is inviting German attack?" Smith rocked slowly on the balls of his feet. He knew that many of the same class of ships as the *Zamzam*, while old, had been converted into armed merchant cruisers early in the war. To sail without running lights or a national ensign might cause a German captain to attack *Zamzam* not realizing her neutral status. Halyburton nodded. "And you also realize that many of my passengers on this voyage will be Americans?"

"Yes Sir. I do."

So there it is. Smith twitched the corners of his mouth and turned back to face the dirty porthole, mulling the immense implications. What if a shipload of Americans, sailing in a neutral vessel, got attacked by a German raider, U-boat, or aircraft? It had worked in 1915 with the *Lusitania*, why not again in 1941? American public sentiment, still largely isolationist and anti-interventionist, would probably give Roosevelt all the justification he needed to become more involved in the war if not outright engaged. Churchill would have his ally, in fact, as well as in spirit.

"I see." Smith turned back to Halyburton. "And what if I refuse to go along with this ruse? What then?"

"Well ... ah ... I suppose there is the matter of your owner's ... . Let's face reality, Captain. Just how neutral can an Egyptian shipping company be with the whole bloody state of Egypt under Axis siege and the Eighth Army billeted in their flower gardens, if you see my point."

"I take your point."

Of course he did. It would be a simple matter for the company to replace him with a more compliant master if he refused to violate neutrality. In fact, he had no intention of refusing at all. He would contribute to the war effort even in such an offhand manner. He simply wanted to test the officer's willingness to force the issue. A violation of neutrality in wartime carried grave implications. The Royal Navy clearly counted on that fact. *Zamzam* would become a target.

"Very well. This vessel is now in violation of international neutrality laws. You have won your point, Lieutenant Halyburton. What are the instructions?" Smith returned to his chair and sat down.

"You will have your wireless operator monitor the Admiralty merchant ship broadcast channels. The frequencies for this time period are listed on the green sheet. Actually, Sir, you are a totally passive player. You are not to respond to signals or to generate wireless traffic on any of these frequencies. Let me be quite clear on this point."

"Noted," responded Smith.

"Your signal and code book is here. Please keep it locked in your safe. Only yourself and your Chief Engineer—Burns, I believe—may decode traffic."

"What about my first officer? I believe him to be trustworthy." Smith shifted in the chair.

"No, I fear not. Only native Britons on this one, Sir."

Smith nodded in acknowledgment.

"I presume that you do not have a weighted bag, so I shall send one over. I'll address the parcel to your attention. Above all, Captain Smith, the code book and operational plan must not fall into German hands for any reason."

"Of course. And when do I begin my little deception? As soon as I am out to sea?"

"No, not at all. You will receive a broadcast signal addressed only to MEMPHIS instructing you to implement PLAN GREEN."

Both men's eyes turned towards the paper on top of the code book. Smith picked it up and scanned it. Labeled PLAN GREEN and addressed to MEMPHIS, it displayed no official Admiralty seal, letterhead, or signature, in short, nothing to relate the document back to any office of His Majesty's Government. PLAN GREEN, Halyburton explained, called for *Zamzam* to proceed precisely as he had outlined. Additional instructions dealt with security. A knock on the door interrupted the conference. Smith snatched up the two documents and quickly slid them into the middle desk drawer.

"Come."

The steward entered carrying a tarnished silver tray with a steaming pot of freshly brewed tea and a dish of biscuits. Wartime shortages being such, this represented quite a feast and the steward beamed, eager to please this very important visitor and his captain. He placed the tray on the coffee table in the center of the cabin.

"Thank you, Ahmed. That will be all."

"Yes, Sir." The Egyptian bowed and exited.

Smith poured tea and milk. Even in wartime there could still be some civility. He offered the biscuit dish to Halyburton. An hour later, the RN officer departed with his now empty briefcase. Safely ensconced in the sea cabin safe lay the codebook and the green paper. Smith went topside to observe the activity on deck. He stood on the Bridge Wing gazing at the barebacked crewmen below handling cargo under the first officer's crisp direction. On the pier, the first few passengers had arrived even though they would not sail for two days. Smith presumed that they had come to scope out their accommodations and bring luggage aboard. Then again, other passengers would arrive, huffing and puffing, porters in tow, just as the brow lifted. He chuckled to himself. He always got a strange assortment of passengers on this ship anyway. Little could Captain Smith have known, standing tall on the Bridge Wing, taking in the sights, sounds, and smells of New York on a fine March day, just what an unusual crowd he would receive for his final voyage on the *Zamzam*. *Well, Smith, you are in the war for certain now. A little sooner than expected, but nonetheless, in the war. God Save the King! For you Tommy.*

"Pan American's Yankee Clipper Flying Boat from Lisbon, via Bolama, Belem, Port of Spain and Bermuda is now arriving."

Pan American's New York Marine Air Terminal remained a gateway to the New World in 1941. The Boeing 314 Flying Boat brought evermore refugees—Jews, intellectuals, scientists, and all manner of people fleeing the Nazi onslaught. U.S. Customs and the Immigration and Naturalization Service agents stationed at all ports of entry to determine the right to enter the U.S. scanned passports, entry visas, and immigration papers. But, if a refugee seemed legitimate and had some sort of papers—well—if he or she had beaten the odds and gotten this far, who would turn them away. Certainly not the men and women who dealt daily in the flotsam of war, many of whose families had fled Europe only a generation back. Unfortunately, this human kindness had its dark side. The Lisbon flight represented a primary insertion vehicle for Axis agents seeking anonymous entry into the United States. J. Edgar Hoover's FBI closely watched the gaggle of Europeans coming through the arrival gates, but did not uncover all of the agents. Two passengers on this particular flight would have been of interest to the two G-Men surreptitiously watching. A tall, bearded Jewish musician wearing a gray Italian fedora hat clumsily manhandled his cello case through Customs, apologizing profusely for the commotion he caused. He proudly displayed his letter offering employment with the New York Philharmonic. The other man, whom the Customs men already knew as an always polite (in that Northern European sort of way) Dutch diamond buyer, had made the Lisbon to New York run several times over the past year. Both men passed through without a hitch. As the second of the two travelers passed the waiting, watching FBI men, the one drinking coffee by the snack vender shook his head. Oh well, no one interesting today, he thought. *Maybe tomorrow.*

CHAPTER 3
CANNELLONI AND DEATH

Two men, one tall with a striding, almost loping gait and the other, short with a purposeful air, walked briskly down the sidewalk away from Times Square and the Theater District—to the casual observer, simply two successful blue and gray pinstriped businessmen enjoying the unusually warm weather. They turned the corner and headed down West 47th Street towards the Hudson River. They came upon their target, an old building set close against the pavement. A flat black metal rail enclosed the steps leading to a landing below and a glossy green metal door with polished brass handle. The taller man looked about anxiously checking for uninvited observers. He saw none and whispered to the shorter man. The green door opened and both men disappeared into the darkness beyond. Seconds later, a third man wearing a Homburg hat pulled down low to the top of his dark sunglasses stepped from the shadow of a recessed doorway in the next building. He glanced left, then right. The only other person on the block stood at the corner tapping a Camel out of the pack. He crumpled the empty package and slipped it into a pocket. The third man casually strolled over and paused above the steps leading down to the green door. He nodded to the man on the corner and stepped down the several concrete steps to the landing below. The other man lit his cigarette, tossed the spent match into the gutter, looked both ways, then ambled across the street before disappearing into an alley on the other side. The third man opened the green door. The smell of the place struck him square in the face.

Mama Leone's! What a magnificent aroma, that delightful mixture of garlic and vinegar, tomato sauce, and aged cheeses. He stepped into the darkened, noisy den of culinary delight. The host greeted him after a few seconds. He indicated an isolated table in the corner of the main dining room—the

perfect observation post. As the man passed through the noisy, happy, bus-
tling dining room, he glanced over to his right at the equally isolated table in
the opposite corner. There sat the first two men—the tall one and the shorter
one—the objects of his observation. They did not see him as they quietly
engaged in animated conversation. *Good.*

"Isn't this place a wee bit too public?" asked the taller man anxiously.

"Certainly, Commander Fleming. Which is precisely why I like it. You
see, unlike London where Jerry has to keep his head low or have it shot off,
this is New York, strictly neutral New York." INTREPID gazed out across the
cavernous room at the multitude of diners. "Practically anyone in this room
could be an enemy. Or a friend."

"Isn't the office secure?" asked Fleming, looking up from the extensive
wine list.

"Probably," replied INTREPID. "However, we are guests here posing as
diplomatic functionaries. It would not serve our interests or that of our
hosts, to be so clandestine as to arouse the suspicions of, shall we say, other
interested parties."

"And of the isolationist anti-British faction?" added Fleming.

"Just so, Commander. Joe Kennedy has gotten them fairly riled up these
past few months. Good God, can you imagine the furor if those people suspected that British intelligence operations were being run out of Rockefeller
Center. There would be blood running in the streets. Roosevelt's unfortunately."

"Isn't he fairly secure after his reelection last November?" asked Fleming
turning the menu page trying to appear as a nonchalant diner.

"Certainly. But don't forget the little matter of impeachment. There is a
very strong isolationist faction in Congress, which might well fly off the handle. No, Commander, we must be very careful and very discreet. This place,
I might add is an additional benefit of that discretion."

Fleming glanced over at a table several feet away where an olive-skinned,
Mediterranean waiter placed a steaming dish of pasta in a meat sauce decorated with a thick layer of melted Parmesan cheese, in front of an obviously
delighted diner. "I see what you mean. It certainly beats bangers and mash
at the old Crown and Anchor." Both men chuckled. "What about security?"
mumbled Fleming, now intensely studying the pasta menu.

INTREPID signaled the waiter. "See that man at the corner table?" He nodded towards the watcher across the dining room, now minus the hat and sunglasses.

Fleming moved his eyes only, not wishing to appear like a total rube.

"One of Bill Donovan's men. There's another one across the street in an alley. They are my watchers and guardian angels. Not strictly legal, mind you, but you will find that Colonel Donovan has, shall I say, many unconventional resources. If that man were to come over and recommend the chicken cannelloni, for instance, it means he has spotted someone a bit too interested in us."

"I see," nodded Fleming, still engrossed in the bulky menu. "How is it, by the way?"

"How is it?"

"The chicken cannelloni. How is it?"

"Excellent," responded a smiling INTREPID.

The antipasto tray arrived featuring fresh red grapes from California, prosciutto ham sliced ever so thinly and wrapped around melon just arrived by refrigerated freight car from the hot fields of northern Mexico, and a huge chunk of wonderfully aromatic cheese surrounded by hard salami slices. The tangy, spicy aroma wafted up to Fleming's eager nostrils. Creamery butter and crusty Italian bread topped off the glorious repast. What a striking contrast to the dull drabness of wartime London. He couldn't remember the last time he had eaten fresh fruit. Mama Leone's exuded a festive, carnival atmosphere with red and green streamers and decorations everywhere. Glossy photographs of hundreds of celebrities who had dined at the famous eatery ornamented every wall. It did not matter that his nation was locked in mortal combat with this place's home country. This is New York, the melting pot. These are Americans.

"I gather you have some concerns about the Commodore?" said Fleming raising a steaming forkful of manicotti to his mouth.

"The same as you have, I suspect," responded INTREPID as the sharp knife slid through the tender veal, which almost didn't need a knife.

Fleming nodded in acknowledgement with a mouthful of the hot pasta and meat.

"Commodore Braithwaite is an excellent man, one of the best field agents ever, but ... "

"But is he too old?" interrupted Fleming.

"The unknown variable, I fear," answered INTREPID.

Fleming had not had such a dessert in months—a chocolate concoction with nuts and toffee topped by a mountain of whipped cream. *By God—fresh dairy cream! This is too decadent, but certainly worth the miserable, bumpy, cold ride across the Atlantic.* "Admiral Godfrey feels very strongly about this. I might add, so do I. Commodore Braithwaite is quite capable, but again, the question is one of stamina, of response to a crisis. This is where we get into a sticky situation."

"I agree," added INTREPID, sipping the hot, steamy cappuccino from the delicate cup. "But do we have a choice? Every one of my suitable men is either engaged in this Balkans business or is indispensable at Camp "X" and, I expect Hitler to strike Yugoslavia any day now. Even if I recalled someone, they couldn't arrive in time for the sailing."

He took another sip of the frothy liquid.

"Couldn't we arrange for the *Zamzam* to suffer a few day's delay?" offered Fleming, picking up a spoon for his assault on the dessert.

"Too risky. It might tip off Jerry that we are on to him."

"Quite right," replied Fleming, his mouth full of gooey chocolate. He swallowed. "But let me emphasize the point, Sir, and London is adamant on this." He waved the dessert spoon in the air to add emphasis to his statement. "We will only concur with the assignment of Commodore Braithwaite to this mission if you feel comfortable with him. You must be the final arbiter of his suitability. This is of course, beside the fact that you are the senior officer in all Western Hemisphere operations, therefore, this one will be under your direct supervision. Everyone in London, of course, will cooperate and assist as we are able. But, Sir, you must be confident, or we cannot support it. We have to feel that ultimately he is up to snuff."

"Yes, I understand. I have worked closely with the Commodore. Mentally and intellectually he is prepared for a field assignment."

"And physically?" Fleming added tentatively.

INTREPID took a sip of the heavy coffee and smiled. His calves and forearms still ached from the tennis match. Another man appeared at the host's podium. He spotted the two British intelligence men, waved and pointed to them. The host nodded as ANTIMONY strode over to the table.

"Lieutenant-Commander Ian Fleming, you know Commodore John Braithwaite."

"Indeed, Sir. I trust you have been well." Fleming extended a hand.

ANTIMONY smiled and grasped the handshake. "Quite well. Stephenson here is the perfect host." In a low, clandestine whisper, he added, "The man is a ruddy slave driver, you know."

All three men laughed as discreetly as possible.

"Lunch, John?" INTREPID offered as the attentive waiter hovered over his shoulder.

"No thanks. Just coffee. Black, please."

The waiter bowed and hurried away. He recognized a good tip table. The three men engaged in the usual trivial small talk for several minutes over coffee. After a while, Fleming began his brief—the how, why, and wherefore of the mission. By his description, it seemed like a "milk run," as the pilots would say. ANTIMONY had long ago learned never to take any mission lightly. Never underestimate the enemy. Be prepared for any event. Observe the trivial and make contingency plans. These cautions formed the heart of the extraordinary treatise on intelligence fieldwork he had written for the NID in the early 1920s. Any field agent who failed to plan or took the assignment lightly did so at grave risk to himself and the mission. *No, Mr. Fleming, this is not a "milk run."*

"What if the Germans plan on more than simply following Verdi? Have you considered the threat of kidnap or assassination?" asked ANTIMONY staring directly at Fleming over the top of a steaming cup.

The NID man shifted nervously in his chair and tapped his napkin with a fork. He cleared his throat. He no longer needed to sell Braithwaite on the mission. The time for candor had arrived. "We have, Sir. There is ... there is always that possibility. But London considers it unlikely until Verdi has led them to the special weapons plant. Why kill the golden goose before she lays the egg, if you see my point?"

A blue-orange flame shot out of INTREPID's lighter as he lifted it to the tip of a Cuban cigar presented to him by Churchill before he left London. The PM had excellent smoking tastes. A bluish cloud rose towards the beamed ceiling above. The cap of the chrome Zippo clicked shut. "By that time, John, the SOE boys will have relieved you in Cape Town. We only want you to take him that far," added INTREPID breaking the tension.

ANTIMONY stared at Fleming in a sort of "have you told me the whole story" gaze. He finally spoke. "Do you completely trust CHARLEMAGNE?"

Fleming glanced nervously at INTREPID. Very few people even among the intelligence community knew about the highly placed German source. NID jealously guarded knowledge of his existence. CHARLEMAGNE would only communicate one way with the British with no way to query him further or clarify some hazy issue. And, the German appeared to only trust navy men—probably, a mariner himself. INTREPID nodded.

Fleming took a deep breath. "We do, Sir. He's obviously a German patriot, loyal to the Fatherland, but not to Hitler and probably not a Nazi either. He only gives us enough information to thwart German operations, never enough for us to seriously damage them. I think he is hoping for a stalemate and a negotiated end to the war, the sort of thing that would allow us to survive and Germany to keep its European conquests. They can then deal with Hitler on their own terms."

ANTIMONY chuckled. "Churchill will never do that. This German walks a terribly thin tightrope, eh, Bill? Let's hope he's not selling us a bill of goods. Very well, then, I'm game. She sails tomorrow evening, I believe."

INTREPID reached into his suit pocket and pulled out a beige, stiff paper folder and slid it across the table to ANTIMONY. The Commodore opened the one-way ticket from New York to Cape Town, South Africa, aboard the MISR Lines steamer S.S. *Zamzam*, departing Hoboken at 1900 on the 20th of March, 1941.

"What name are you traveling under?" asked Fleming.

INTREPID reached into another jacket pocket and lifted out a leather wallet. He tossed it on the table in front of Fleming. The NID man put down his cappuccino and opened the wallet. "Edward B. Prince. Is this passport genuine?"

"As the Americans would say, it is the real McCoy. We have friends in very high places, Commander," responded INTREPID.

"Indeed you do," chimed in Fleming, closely examining the official document. "And what does the "B" stand for, Mr. Prince?"

"Black," came the nonchalant reply.

"Edward Black Prince," chuckled Fleming, amused at the clever reference to the 14th century English Prince of Wales, a military genius who died before he could inherit the crown. "Droll, very droll." He handed the wallet to ANTIMONY.

"This really seems like it should be an American operation. After all, Verdi is a Yank now. What about the FBI?" ANTIMONY directed his question to INTREPID, who leaned back in his chair and folded his hands on the tablecloth in front of him.

"Donovan tells me that Hoover intends to put two men aboard. I doubt they will be of any use to you. I advise you to avoid them. These chaps are good at their own domestic operations, but they have no expertise in foreign intelligence. I'm afraid the *Abwehr* man will spot them straight away." He leaned forward in his chair. "That may work to your advantage. They might draw off his attention and make your cover more secure. Jerry probably does not expect British intervention, but he will be on guard for the Americans. Use them if you need reinforcement, but be careful with them."

"Understood," responded ANTIMONY.

The previously adversarial relationship with J. Edgar Hoover's FBI had become far more cooperative since INTREPID began allowing Hoover to take the credit for the positive results of BSC operations in the U.S. It made INTREPID's operation less visible, and consequently more effective. The three men left the restaurant, fully satisfied as to two things—one, that the British taxpayer had just provided its civil servants with one of the most magnificent lunches still available in the Western world, and two, that all parties concurred in the choice of Commodore John David Fairchild Braithwaite, VC, DSO as His Majesty's representative onboard the liner *Zamzam*, bound for Cape Town and Alexandria, carrying one of the most precious cargoes in the world, an émigré Italian-American physicist by the name of Verdi.

Mama Leone's. Fleming would indeed remember this wonderful place. Next time, he would try the chicken cannelloni.

Two men, ill at ease, strode down the brow of the *Zamzam*, talking quietly. The late evening air, heavy with murky fog, had settled over the waterfront shrouding it with the promise of a chilly night. At the foot of the brow, the taller man stopped and offered a cigarette to the shorter man, who declined. They had just booked passage on the *Zamzam*, departing the next evening for Baltimore. Normally, bookings would be made with the company's agent downtown, but—well—last-minute instructions to audit the books of their company's South African subsidiary and, though irregular, could we book on board and by the way here is a $10 spot for your time and trouble. The purser gladly accepted his gratuity and, no, it's no bother at all—understand completely—see you tomorrow, etc., etc. He added two names to the ship's passenger manifest and assigned the two gentlemen, so anxious to book passage without prior arrangements, to First Class cabins. The men paid in advance, tipped nicely and appeared polite, so what could it hurt? The purser locked their cash payment in the ship's safe, closed his manifest log, switched off the overhead light, and with a brisk rattling of his keys, (more so to demonstrate his unchallenged authority among the stewards and mess boys), locked the office and ambled down below to his cabin to change clothes for a last night on the town and a chance to waste his new-found fortune.

The men hurried back up the deserted waterfront towards the main gate. They heard the traffic beyond the monolithic, dark warehouses lining the docks. The short man pulled up his jacket collar to hold out the chilling fog. The taller one, eyes darting back and forth, mumbled to the other, who nodded and picked up the pace. In a warehouse shadow, face hidden under the brim of a gray Italian fedora hat, stood another man dressed in black. His breath came in short, shallow, slow, deliberate inhales and exhales. He muffled his breath with a woolen scarf, which also prevented any telltale signs of condensation—a careful man. Scanning up and down the piers, he saw no one except the new passengers walking rapidly towards him. Seeing no topside activity onboard *Zamzam* or any nearby ships, the dark man darted over and knelt unseen beside several lube oil drums sitting on wooden pallets in a graveled loading area. Slowly reaching into the inside jacket pocket, he pulled out a sleek, silencer-equipped assassin's weapon and aimed between two oil drums. Twenty yards. Ten yards. The short man would come into view any second. *Hold it. Hold it.* His eyes blazed. *A shoe. A leg. Hold on. A torso.* A sharp pneumatic whiff. Aargh! The short man crumpled over as the round exited his back just an inch from the spinal column. He pitched forward onto the wet, oil-coated concrete. The assassin leapt up from behind his concealment, his weapon trained at the gaping mouth of the tall man. Years of training and drill kicked in. Instinct overtook momentary paralysis. As the assassin's trigger finger squeezed off a second shot, the tall man dove for the ground and rolled. The bullet whizzed past his shoulder.

Where is he? Where the hell is he? The assassin had lost the target. The barrel wavered in indecision. He stepped back. *The enemy must be below him—below the drums!* A powerful hand thrust out from his left. The assassin spun around, bringing down the gun. Spit! Spit! Two slugs crunched into the gravel. *Too high!* The man on the ground had outflanked him. A hand lunged at the shooter's throat, fingers outstretched. The assassin sidestepped to his right. The man in the fedora brought his right knee up hard into the man's groin as he flew by. A loud, throaty groan burst from his mouth. As he hit the gravel hard, half rolling onto his side, his foot lashed out and clipped the assassin's knee. The man in black lurched, unable to get off a good shot. The fallen enemy rolled away, grasping his groin in agony, struggling to rise. The assassin recovered. Despite the fog, he clearly saw the man's face for the first time—a soft, baby face cringing in pain, desperately struggling to regain his balance and go on the offensive. The enemy had done well, but not well enough. *Too long!* He waited too long. The man on the ground rolled away and into a crouch. In spite of his agony, he composed himself for one more lunge at his tormentor—but slowly, much too slowly. The man in black chopped him in the chest. A whoosh of air came as his lungs expelled their breath. The man staggered, hands flailing, vainly trying to latch onto the assailant. The attacker chopped him on the back of the neck as he went down. The body slumped forward, still alive, but barely conscious.

The assassin in the gray fedora quickly looked around—still no activity on the pier. No other eyes witnessed the desperate struggle beside the oil drums. He straddled the prostrate man below him. From a jacket pocket, he pulled out a hideous device with wooden handles joined together by a strand of thin wire. Making a large loop by flipping one handle over, he snapped the wire over the victim's head and jerked the handles taut causing a gurgling, hissing noise as wire sliced through the garroted man's neck.

No time to waste. The assassin dragged both bodies over to the Ford coupe parked just behind the next warehouse. As they rounded the building corner, a wallet fell from the garroted man's jacket and clinked on the concrete. The assassin picked up the wallet, glanced hurriedly at the metal piece that flashed momentarily in the lamplight, then stuffed the FBI badge back into the man's pocket. He bundled both bodies into the trunk and slammed it shut. He had planned carefully. A canvas hose connected to a salt water pump stood ready near the warehouse, always charged for firefighting. He lit off the pumps by pulling down a red handle. Within seconds, high pressure water erased the pools of dark blood glistening in the lamplight. Mixed with salt water, the evidence of the night's work drained down the pier and off the edge, into the dark water below.

CHAPTER 4
PANDORA'S BOX

"You're all set. Departure is scheduled for 2100 tonight."

"Excellent. I'll be leaving in an hour."

"Very good, Sir."

"Certainly. Good day." ANTIMONY hung up the phone slowly. *So it really would happen—bloody hell—going back into the field!* He turned, faced the floor mirror next to the dresser and gazed at the image, then turned sideways to observe the profile. *Not bloody bad.* He glanced at the bronze-cased clock on the mantle—just past noon. *Best hurry.* He wanted to arrive early to observe passengers coming aboard. Would he be able to recognize the *Abwehr* man? It depended. It depended on the enemy's skill. ANTIMONY had to be better. He strode over to the leather and brass bound suitcase lying open on the elaborately-carved four-poster bed. Was he not the author of the definitive treatise on covert fieldwork? Hadn't he lectured at all the Service Academies on fieldwork and enemy recognition techniques? Was he too rusty, too out of practice? Surely he could match his opponent toe to toe in a physical struggle. He proved that on the tennis court. He honed his small arms skills at regular range practice. No, the real test for this middle-aged, graying, retired naval officer would not be physical. The test would be mental. Could a man not used to the rigors of field duty maintain the required mental stamina, emotional endurance, and intellectual sharpness? His superiors believed he had all of the qualities based on past achievements. Had he softened with age? Was his advantage diluted? He tossed several pairs of socks into the open, yawning suitcase. *Damn it!* He drew in a deep breath and glared at the image in the mirror. *Self-doubt is the easiest path to failure, you old sod.*

ANTIMONY fumbled under the dust ruffle, his hand searching for a hard, square object. Grasping a protruding handle, he dragged it out of its hiding place. A lead wire sealed the steel box with double combination locks, one on each latch, which had been delivered from Camp "X" by courier the night before. The fastener, stamped with the letters CPX, showed that the box had not been tampered with. ANTIMONY had not left his elegant flat on East 72nd Street since it arrived, but always security conscious, he jiggled the seals out of habit, then dialed in the combinations. First the right latch then the left popped open. From a top drawer of the bureau amongst a gaggle of combs and brushes, he lifted out a wire cutter and clipped the seal. The resident inventor at Camp "X", who developed "aids" for agents and saboteurs, had put together this grab bag collection of useful items. ANTIMONY lifted out a pair of black shoes of superb workmanship, which he turned over and around inspecting the stitching and the smooth, wrinkle free turn of the top grain leather. A label proudly identified the seller as Richman Brothers Department Store of Albany, New York. The kit included a birth certificate and marriage license discreetly filed in the Albany county courthouse for Edward B. Prince the previous day.

He depressed a soft spot on the right heel. A twist to the right opened a latch and the entire heel came off in his hand. A dough-like substance molded into the hollow heel had the look and feel of moist clay (actually several ounces of a new type of plastic explosive particularly well adapted to field work). It came in thin sheets that could be folded and molded into any shape or design. He clicked off the other heel. The hollow cavern contained two sets of electrolyte detonators. When one broke the tiny glass vial, acid ate away the organic membrane that blocked the completion of an electrical circuit fired by a tiny, but powerful battery cell—just enough current to set off the detonator, which in turn set off the charge. *Very clever, but whatever happened to the old fuse and firecracker method? Well, old boy, time marches on.* When he first saw the shoes demonstrated, he commented about agents walking very softly lest they set off the detonator. The inventor laughed and said maybe they would run faster having explosive feet. No danger really. The shoes had been tested by pounding them on steel and concrete and even crushing. The metal and cork shielding kept the electrolyte vials firmly in place and besides, one had to manually attach the battery wires. This entire process took less than five seconds. ANTIMONY placed the shoes on the oval rug beside the bed. He would wear these shoes to break them in.

The sun danced off the crystal decanter on a table near the Palladian-style windows. The sherry glowed amber, then gold, then a deep rich mahogany as sunlight flitted about and through it. The lead glass sparkled bluish. AN-TIMONY paused for a moment to watch the extraordinary light show. The wonderful beauty of the sparkling glass and the warmth of the golden brown fruit of the earth starkly contrasted with the cold, hostile, ugly creation he pulled up from the box. He cradled the gun in his right hand. The steel gray metal of the Smith and Wesson Model 645 .45 felt ice cold to the touch. It would blow a man backwards at close range. Camp "X" sent five 8-round ammunition clips. In the leather suitcase, under a seemingly flush bottom, a pouch compartment had been designed for a mission where an agent's baggage might be searched. The gun and one clip fit snuggly inside. Nothing could rattle and when sealed back up, it would take a considerable talent to find the way into the pouch or to even realize it existed. He opened and closed the suitcase top several times. *I'll be damned if I can see it. Let's hope Jerry never gets the chance to try it.*

Other delights came out of the Pandora's Box of human destruction. The quite handsome chrome plated key ring from which dangled three keys, two brass and one chrome, went into his pocket. The Camp "X" inventor dubbed it the "key to the Gates of Hell." *Simple enough. Good description.* When one pulled hard on the chrome-plated key, a spring latch let go and out came a wire, custom made for garroting an unsuspecting enemy. The fountain pen stiletto blade seemed especially fun. ANTIMONY shook his head in amazement as he carefully stowed away his new tools. In the confines of a solitary small ship at sea, it would be insane for the German to attempt any overtly threatening action. Nonetheless, ANTIMONY would use his newly acquired weapons if need be.

He opened another suitcase identical to the first one and packed four suits, all perfectly appropriate to an American businessman traveling to South Africa—a double-breasted blue pinstripe, a more subdued gray her-ringbone, the mandatory blue blazer with gray trousers for more relaxed moments, and a white linen suit for tropical climates. Everything he needed went into the two suitcases. A rule of the trade—never travel with more than you can take in two hands. To complete the ruse, however, a steamer trunk loaded with clothing and clearly labeled as belonging to Mr. E.B. Prince of Albany, New York, had already been sent to the pier. After all, a few well-placed dollars might loosen up a steward and allow an enemy access to the baggage hold. His would be there loaded with typical, if unnecessary clothing. He wondered if the German would load his own deceptive luggage. ANTIMONY's trunk would soon be loaded aboard the ship seen by a pair of hidden, but keenly observant eyes shaded under a gray fedora hat. Extra shirts, undergarments, socks, and shoes rounded out the wardrobe. He shut the suitcase with a click of the solid lock.

ANTIMONY would miss this cheery apartment in a Victorian mansion surrounded by gardens on Manhattan's Upper East Side. The residential neighborhood, though quiet and secluded, had all manner of nearby shops and tradesmen. Despite his pitiful Navy pension, his private income had provided him with an excellent living. Well, had he not spent his life living in tiny, uncomfortable cabins in the service of King and Country? By God, he would enjoy the use of his money before he passed on. After a life of bare metal bulkheads and gray steel decks, grim surroundings broken only by the occasional porthole curtains and a few framed mementos, he fully intended to savor the present furnishings. He had no children to worry about, only himself, without Alice ... without Alice ... .

He pulled on a gray tweed jacket and, checking his appearance in the mirror one last time, took a tug on the red foulard tie. He tiptoed out into the darkened hallway with the innovative black shoes tightly laced up. In spite of Camp "X" assurances, he still treaded gently and carefully. In the front sitting room, open windows let a breeze pour in, causing the curtains to dance daintily. From a rolltop desk, he extracted a round leather pouch holding six gold coins—emergency money. Even if he lost his hundreds of paper dollars carefully distributed about his person and hidden in his belongings, these coins could buy an incredible array of goods and services anywhere in the world. He dropped the coin purse into a side pocket of the jacket.

Finally, he lifted out another weapon. Unlike the heavy, man-stopping S&W in the suitcase, this small, light, easily concealed piece would slow down an assailant long enough for an escape. He had had it for years. He cradled the Beretta .25 in his palm. Unlike the .45, the metal felt smooth and warm to the touch, no doubt due to the shaft of sunlight streaming in and striking the blue steel barrel. Dropping several extra clips into the deep outer pocket of his jacket, ANTIMONY turned the gun over and over before sliding it into a holster discretely sewn into the jacket pocket.

The desk's brass latch turned with a reassuring, heavy metallic click. He bent down to the floor and with an index finger, traced a faint scratch mark in the wood up to the edge of the wall bookshelf. A light press caused a wood piece to pop out of the wall revealing a wooden tray carved into the bottom of the bookcase, a secure hiding place for knickknacks such as desk keys. He dropped all of the keys he wouldn't need into the little box for safe keeping. The hidden tray slid back into place, invisible to the unknowing eye. He stood up and reached into his jacket, pulled out the Beretta and gave it a last check out.

A loud bang! *A shot! From the street! In the line of fire! The open window!* ANTIMONY dove for the floor, hand extended to break his fall. He hit the carpet and tucked his shoulder as he rolled towards the wall. He came upright, back to the wall, grateful for the bricks between himself and the assassin, forefinger laid astride the trigger guard, Beretta poised in midair awaiting action. Instinct alone caused him to dive and roll out of the line of fire. After twenty years he had not lost that. He gasped from the sudden, violent exertion. ANTIMONY closed his eyes, head hard up against the wainscoting. *Breathe deeply. That's it, catch your breath. Collect your thoughts. He must be across the street in the apartment building. What's the angle? No glass fragments on the floor. The bullet must have come in between the sill and the sash—only six inches. The man's a marksman.* He looked across the semi-dark room at the opposite wall scanning for the telltale wood splinters or crumbled plaster where a slug had slammed into the wall. Nothing, simply nothing. He scanned the entire wall, floor to ceiling—as pristine and undisturbed as new. Only then did he become aware of the growing hubbub below and the chorus of voices. ANTIMONY slid closer to the open window. He clearly made out two distinctly New York voices shouting at each other, gaining in volume with each insult. From the background came the murmuring of a gathering crowd—not the sound of anxious people startled by sudden gunfire, but the noise of anger and irritation—the sound of an auto accident!

Gingerly, he uncocked the Beretta's hammer and slowly laid it down on the floor beneath the window. Creeping up to the edge of the window frame, he slowly eased himself up and scanned back and forth across the windows opposite searching for any clues—a reflection off a rifle barrel, a shadow against a far wall—anything that would give away an assassin's position. *Nothing.* Here and there people leaned out of open windows wondering about the furor in the street below, many amused at the unfolding spectacle.

He raised his eyes up enough to see the incident below. Two cabbies argued as to who had caused the rear-end collision. One flailed his arms over his head screaming at the other for following too closely. A mounted policeman, attracted by the noisy din, trotted onto the scene and pointed to the curb with a threatening nightstick that seemed to say "get these cars out of the middle of the road and I will sort this mess out." Still shouting obscenities, each cabbie returned to his vehicle. A loud, sharp bang, then another blasted from the rear end of the first taxi as it limped towards the curb. ANTIMONY turned his head away from the window and collapsed back against the wall, knees in the air, forearms trembling, hands dangling in midair, fingers limp. His pounding heart calmed, the pressure of the blood racing past his temples subsided as the adrenalin charge faded away. For a full minute he sat immobile, eyes closed, breathing steadily and controlled until finally came the slow rhythmical in and out of a man calm and relaxed. The backfire of a stalled taxi had sounded like a gunshot. The second car had simply rammed into it. ANTIMONY had not heard the screech of brakes and the crunch of metal that occurred during his acrobatic roll to the floor. *So, it's only a stupid car accident on a lightly traveled residential side street.* But, it showed him two things—one, that his reflexes and instinctive reactions remained good, and two, that he had suddenly become a very nervous man.

The bored crowd dispersed. The policeman's mount aimlessly pawed the sidewalk while the rider wrote up a citation. ANTIMONY stood watching for several minutes. In the hallway, a grandfather clock chimed. *Must be moving along.* ANTIMONY reached down and picked up the gun, which disappeared back into its hiding place. Only now did the full impact of his new mission actually strike him. Lack of vigilance in this world meant failure or death. He must relearn the lessons of an earlier life. He would use everything at his command to confound the enemy. He had been the best. He would be again.

A tall, middle-aged man wearing a gray tweed suit and carrying two leather suitcases entered a taxi in front of Rockefeller Center.

"Circle the block twice, then stop where I tell you."

"Sure, Mister," responded the nonchalant cabbie refolding his sports section.

The taxi headed west then circled Rockefeller Center. After two slow revolutions, the fare with the distinct upstate accent spotted a tall figure dressed in a baggy suit in need of a press standing by a fire hydrant with a copy of the "New York Times" tightly rolled in his left hand and a bulky black briefcase in his right.

"Stop here," the gentleman in the back pointed to an empty space forty feet from the hydrant.

The taxi pulled over immediately as the cabbie reached for the meter handle to total up the fare.

"Wait."

"Okay, mister. It's your nickel."

The passenger sat back. After a couple of quiet minutes, the cabbie lit up a cigarette. Pungent smoke drifted about the cab. What an odd fare he thought. Most people on a gorgeous day like today liked to chat, but not this cold fish. The fare seemed to be brooding and watching in the half-light of the back seat and just didn't want to talk despite a couple of abortive attempts by the driver. *Well, no bother.* The truth is, he didn't care after a day of yakking about the weather and how pleasant it was for this early in the season and would it mean an exceptionally hot summer and how 'bout them Dodgers and blah, blah, blah. He would just sit quietly and enjoy his cigarette. Maybe ogle a few tight-waisted secretaries swaying by. *What the hell.*

A Ford sedan pulled up in front of the hydrant with two men in it, a broad shouldered, athletic-looking driver and an older man sitting in the back seat, his face hidden under a broad brimmed panama hat. The waiting man recognized the car and casually strolled over. He opened a door, stooped down and bounced in.

"Follow that gray Ford," said the fare, leaning forward in the seat.

Jesus H. Christ! Not one of these. "Yes, Sir."

The last time he did this for a fare, he wound up in the slammer overnight for careless and reckless. *Jesus H. Christ! Should have stayed in the rag trade with the old man.* The cab pulled out into the oncoming traffic four cars behind the Ford.

"Listen, mister. I don't make enough at this job to get arrested for speeding or nothin' like that. You know what I mean?" the cabbie pleaded, a hand raised in resignation so as to emphasize his point.

"Don't worry. You won't have a problem."

The driver shrugged and pressed the accelerator closing the distance to the Ford. *Jesus H. Christ and Mother Mary, full of Grace!*

The quiet man in the backseat turned and looked behind them. Two car lengths back in a black Plymouth, sat two more men wearing dark sunglasses. He turned back around and chuckled softly to himself. *Colonel Donovan's men would eventually learn not to be so obvious.* After crossing the bridge into New Jersey, the car ahead turned into an enclosed compound area in the Hoboken waterfront district and stopped in front of a shabby commercial warehouse. Both passengers got out and looked around as discretely as possible, turned and waved off the Ford. The driver nodded and pulled away, slowly rolling to a stop several yards down into an alley between two buildings blocking any escape or entry into the dock area except by the main gate and providing a good observation point. The tail in the Plymouth pulled in and stopped just inside the chain link fence. Both men got out scanning in all directions.

"Here, Sir?"

"This will do."

The cab pulled up to the pier entrance where the Ford had discharged its two passengers. Without a word, the man in the back seat handed the driver a ten dollar bill for a $1.75 fare. The cab driver reached into his change purse. The fare lifted his bags out of the back seat, sat them on the curb, and shut the door with a solid thunk.

"Thanks." The odd fare picked up his bags and walked towards the piers.

"Thank you, Sir!" replied the cabbie, his extended hand holding eight singles and a quarter. "Thank you, indeed, Sir," he laughed as he turned his cab back towards the street.

ANTIMONY strode across the dirty pavement towards the *Zamzam*, never speaking to or even acknowledging the presence of INTREPID, Fleming, the Ford driver or Donovan's two watchers in the Plymouth. Six pairs of keenly interested eyes watched as he handed his passport to the customs official, then made his way up the brow.

CHAPTER 5

COGNAC, A LADY, AND
FOUR AND TWENTY VIRGINS

D espite the night's fog and drizzle, the morning sun had dried out the wooden decks only to have a midafternoon shower give the ship an extra wash down removing the last traces of crusty salt. The old girl looked as good as she could thought Captain Smith as he strolled out onto the port Bridge Wing to observe cargo and passenger loading. Passengers straggled aboard in clusters. There would be no gala *bon voyage* party with streamers, confetti, and ship's orchestra blazing away on a Sousa march—not on this low cost, no-frills line. In actuality, most of the passengers would embark in Baltimore the next day. A group of Royal Air Force wives traveling to join their husbands in Egypt comprised the largest group scheduled to embark in New York. Most had left Britain by various neutral vessels. In the days before the war, they would simply have taken the P&O directly to Alexandria. Now, however, their circuitous route took them to New York, South Africa, and eventually on to Alex—a laborious journey complicated by the continuous threat of violence. Then came the Roman Catholic missionaries, mostly French Canadian priests headed for the tribal areas in Basutoland to do God's work. The rest of the passengers comprised a mixed bag of Europeans and Americans, largely business types, including several diamond trade businessmen (many of them Jewish refugees from Amsterdam and Antwerp). Not like the old days when he first sailed as a mate on the White Star lines before the first war mused Smith. The RAF wives stepped gingerly around and through the puddles on the pier as best they could. In the past, the elegant ladies would have been carried directly to the brow by a sort of rickshaw cart. There would be no dirty water soiling their shoes—indeed not in the old days! A seagull whizzed past his ear temporarily distracting him. Smith grumbled at the intruder into his reminiscent thoughts.

The wind fluttered the manifest sheets. He gripped the top of the pages, held them down firmly and noted that some passengers had been added by the purser. He made a mental note to send these names along with their payments to the company office. Movement over on the port side caught his eye where several deckhands had rushed over to the rail. The captain looked onto the pier to see what caused the commotion. He squinted in the late afternoon sunlight. *Yes, of course. That had to be it.* She stood on the brow giving her name to the purser. Tall and leggy, a well-sculpted brunette had appeared, not beautiful in the popular sense, but nonetheless striking in a classical way. Her dress immaculate, demeanor precise and confident, she stood erect in a haughty, arrogant way. Yes, this woman will attract a lot of attention he thought scanning the passenger list. *Ah yes, must be her. Mrs. Joan Avery, traveling alone. Booked in First Class cabin number 8S with private bath.* The elegant lady disappeared into the superstructure followed by three stewards loaded with expensive, new luggage, all eager to please and no doubt expecting rich tips from the obviously well-heeled passenger.

Smith shook his head. Every voyage seemed to have its characters. Within the small, closely quartered community of a ship, relationships intensified. He had even performed a marriage some months back on the Alex run. Wartime and strange environments do such things. He heard a girlish giggle from down below. Coming off the brow strutted three very proper young ladies barely out of their teens. *They must be part of the RAF wives contingent.* Many of them had been married only a few months—another product of war. No doubt, some married the day before their new flyboy husbands shipped out to North Africa. And, some of the newlyweds might be widows by the time *Zamzam* reached Alexandria. In Baltimore, they would embark a large group of Americans bound for North Africa to serve as volunteer ambulance drivers of the British-American Ambulance Corps for the Free French forces. This would be a vivacious group. Mixing young wives, who hadn't seen their husbands in months amongst a group of rowdy, randy young men for a period of weeks could cause a great deal of commotion— rather like mixing gunpowder and sparks.

On the pier, porters and longshoremen hustled about getting last-minute cargo and luggage aboard. Smith scanned the docks for the source of a new raucous noise. A longshoreman on a break had propped up a Motorola radio on a crate. Sitting with doughnut in hand and legs crossed, his feet wildly tapped to the rhythm of the "Hut-Sut Song," in ignorant bliss, totally impervious to the conflict tearing apart the world. Smith took a deep breath and shook his head. *Who knows. A year from now?* That's about what he suspected it would take the Americans to be in this punch-up—a year, perhaps. The tune changed to something about railways. "On the Atchison, Topeka and the Santa Fe" blared out of the tinny sounding radio as toes tapped. Captain Smith closed the passenger manifest, gazed once more across the skyline and went back down to his cabin just aft of the Pilot House. A couple of hours later, there came a knock at the door. He had been composing a letter to the company—his resignation.

"Come."

"Beg your pardon, Sir. We have all passengers onboard except for two gentlemen. The pilot is also aboard, Sir," The purser advised. The Egyptian bowed gracefully.

1850-ten minutes from scheduled departure time. Burns, the Chief Engineer, had been working on getting up steam for most of the afternoon and she was ready to get underway at last. "Very well, pass the word to the first officer to bring in the brow. We shan't wait for those two chaps. Please announce all ashore going ashore."

"Immediately, Sir." The purser bowed again as he backed out.

Smith ambled up to the Pilot House. On the fore deck, First Officer Feidel Stanko directed the line handlers. *A competent officer. Better than most. Underway watch properly set. Good.* Smith picked up the handset of the ubiquitous black bakelite phone on the aft bulkhead, so common aboard ships, and vigorously spun the crank twice. The phone responded with two loud, clanking bells.

"Engine Room, Aye," responded Burns.

"Are you ready to answer all bells, Chief?"

"Aye, Captain, that I am. As best as this old wreck can."

Smith grinned. He heard the chuckle on the line even over the thrum thrum thrum of the electrical generators. "That will do. Thank you, Chief." He replaced the handset. The old girl could only make thirteen knots top speed and struggled to maintain ten. Constant breakdowns seemed more the norm than the exception on this vessel, but then, a few screws, some bailing wire and adhesive tape worked wonders, figuratively speaking. He walked out onto the port side Bridge Wing. Below, line handlers secured mooring lines as the metal brow dangled in the air, hauled up from the ship's side by a steam crane. On deck, the first officer cupped his hands around his mouth and shouted.

"Ready to get underway, Captain."

Smith waved in acknowledgement. Stanko hurried the men on deck out of the way and on to their stations. The tugboat along the starboard side gave a single blast of a steam whistle. Inside the Pilot House, the mate shouted "Underway" and so began the next voyage of the *Zamzam*.

"Astern. Dead slow."

"Astern. Dead slow, aye," responded the lee helmsman.

"Starboard 15."

"Starboard 15, aye," answered the helmsman.

The mate made three blasts of the ship's whistle as *Zamzam* backed slowly into the Hudson River. When several hundred yards out from the pier, the tug let go the line and *Zamzam* sailed on her own again.

"Port 15, ahead slow."

Once the pilot had taken over, Smith allowed himself once more to sink into quiet contemplation observing the passing New Jersey shoreline, the towering monoliths of Manhattan, and the dark water foaming around the bow of his ship forming ripples gracefully radiating out and away. He felt the steady, rhythmic vibration of the engines under his feet and heard the "shew, shew, shew" sound of the single screw as it turned through the water churning up aqua and emerald green foam in its wake. Within a couple of hours, they had reached the open sea, southbound for Baltimore.

ANTIMONY leaned over the edge, held safely by the worn, wooden rail. He spotted a group of porpoises following alongside the ship, playfully arching out of the water, through the salty, foaming spray and just as effortlessly, plunging back into the waves below. He always marveled at their grace.

"Excuse, please, Mr. Prince. Mr. Prince. Sir." The steward beside him stood grinning, his white teeth made more vivid against his walnut brown skin. The starched white linen uniform had the stains of many spills still in evidence. *Well, it's not the Queen Mary for sure, but then, comfort and luxury are not a part of this mission.*

"Yes?"

"Mr. Prince, the captain requests the honor of your presence at his table in the Dining Saloon for dinner at eight sharp." The Egyptian grinned broadly.

"Very well then, eight sharp," ANTIMONY responded courteously.

The steward, his mission accomplished, bowed, spun on his heels and retreated into the superstructure. ANTIMONY turned back towards the sea and resumed his leaning against the rail. The porpoises leapt gleefully in and out of the ivory foam.

The Dining Saloon, a crowded, cramped assortment of tables, offered intimate twin seat tables up to large, round ten to twelve seaters. The captain's table featured a faded leather top and some old and careworn but still serviceable chairs, with a phone attached to a leg and hardwired to the Pilot House. The ill-lit Saloon, no doubt someone's idea of a romantic restaurant, had a very practical feature. Diners could not really tell what they had been served. *Zamzam's* chef (not exactly *cordon bleu*) usually had more of the cooking sherry in him than in the cuisine. The best way to describe the evening's repast might be a rack of elderly lamb, aged potatoes, last year's broccoli, day before yesterday's wine, army surplus rolls and for dessert, a flan with some sort of curdled custard. ANTIMONY hoped this would not to be the norm. He was wrong.

At the captain's table sat the third officer, a timid, uncomfortable little man, whose eyelids twitched, and, of course, Captain Smith (whom ANTIMONY immediately liked), a brusque diamond buyer from Chicago all too impressed with his self-importance, and the eldest of the RAF wives (her husband being a group captain). And there sat the elegant, if a bit standoffish Mrs. Avery, resplendent in a triple strand pearl necklace with matching drop earrings. She said little throughout dinner. ANTIMONY could not help but wonder why she would take this gem of a liner for passage, but, maybe she had a quiet liaison to keep. She had a husky voice, no doubt caused by the continuous chain of long, thin Turkish cigarettes she smoked through a carved ivory and silver cigarette holder. The ship's orchestra made an attempt at entertainment. Consisting of a little group of so-so musicians—a piano player, drummer, clarinetist, and base player—when not playing for dinner, they held other positions such as stoker or deckhand. The captain had done his best to assemble something resembling a proper ship's orchestra. Passable, if not inspiring, ANTIMONY liked their arrangement of Irving Berlin's "What'll I Do." It reminded him of Alice. At least they played quietly enough so as not to interfere with conversation.

"So, Mrs. Avery, are you going out to join your husband?" inquired the captain in an attempt to break the ice, noticing a diamond ring on her left hand and presuming it safe to mention the subject.

"No, my husband is dead."

Eyes lowered down into dinner plates.

"I'm sorry to hear that. My condolences, Madam."

"Oh no, not to worry. I appreciate your concern. I realize that a married woman traveling alone can be taken as, shall I say, potentially scandalous unless she is joining her husband." She smiled and took a long drag on her cigarette. "My husband was killed last autumn. He was a volunteer RAF pilot shot down over the Channel."

"We are all deeply moved by your husband's courage and sacrifice, Mrs. Avery. Had I been a few years younger myself, I might have volunteered, but here I am," added ANTIMONY, anxious to become known, not as an outsider, but as a gregarious, outgoing American businessman. He took a bite of the tough, stringy lamb.

"I am most grateful, Mr. Prince. Thank you. Actually Captain," she flitted into the next subject effortlessly, "I'm bound for Cape Town to visit my sister. You see she married a South African merchant some years back and I fear has left dear old Manhattan for good. I just received a letter from her inviting me over to visit in my time of need. It just came in the post day before yesterday. I'm oh so grateful that you had a cabin still available."

"Not at all, Mrs. Avery. I'm glad you could make the trip with us. We shall endeavor to make it a most interesting voyage indeed."

Mrs. Avery cocked her head at a slight angle and smiled sweetly, almost syrupy. "I'm sure it will be, Captain Smith."

Cutlery clattered on china. The man from Chicago looked up and grinned sheepishly. "I'm so sorry. Very clumsy, very clumsy." His face red with embarrassment, the poor man had been trying to manhandle an undercooked potato with knife and fork and had lost his balance. Smith merely grinned. He understood the man's frustration. After all, he had to eat the swill day in and day out, voyage after voyage. He signaled a steward, who brought a new plate for the befuddled man. It wasn't any better, unfortunately.

After dinner had been cleared, ANTIMONY lingered awhile in the Dining Saloon. The energy in him built like a dynamo. To be in the field on an assignment (albeit, not a glamorous one) after months of sedentary activity, both at the Admiralty and at BSC, felt wonderful. By God, it felt invigorating. He took a drag on the Havana and a long draw of his cognac. *Hennessey, 1938. A good year*. It tasted marvelous. At least the chef could not muck up the alcohol. All of the diners had departed to locations elsewhere. Only he and the cleaning crew remained. They quickly shoveled dishes off tables onto carts destined for the scullery and whipped white linen table clothes in the air scattering crumbs all over the deck.

Snifter and cigar in hand, ANTIMONY headed aft to the cramped little ship's bar. It would open in a few minutes and he wanted to see who showed up and what they ordered. He had long ago learned in the intelligence trade to observe minutia—eating habits, for example, or what a man ordered to drink or how he held a cigarette. Any one of these traits could give away national origin before a word is spoken. But, as ANTIMONY well knew, only a careless agent ever let this happen. In the high-stakes world of intelligence and counter-intelligence, the very best never let their guard down. Keenly aware of small indicators, good field agents researched and rehearsed their roles over and over again. No, if this *Abwehr* man is good, ANTIMONY would not flush him out that easily, but then, it's always worth a shot. Maybe, just maybe, this German might be a bit careless in his habits or mannerisms or a little too rehearsed. Then he would have him. ANTIMONY settled back into the pleasant comfortableness of an old leather sofa. No one else had entered the bar yet, but eventually, some would drift in. ANTIMONY would be there lying in wait for the prey. He took another drag of the excellent cigar and a long draw on the brandy.

Late in the afternoon, *Zamzam* tied up in Baltimore to embark more cargo and passengers. Boarding would begin the following morning. By 0700 the new crowd of *Zamzamers* had begun to congregate on the pier making last-minute checks of luggage, issuing instructions to family members, saying good-byes, and so on. ANTIMONY came on deck from the Dining Saloon. Breakfast had been another non-memorable event—cold sausages, runny scrambled eggs, and dry toast. *God save the Robertson's orange marmalade!* He craved a cup of tea, but resisted. The role of Edward B. Prince, commodities buyer from Albany, demanded that he not be too terribly British. Although many Americans enjoyed the wondrous, warm, dark brown liquid for breakfast, he would follow the more common American habit of coffee, black with plenty of sugar. As he exited the Saloon, he felt a belch coming on and quickly glanced about. *Take a note—avoid the sausages.*

The spring sun felt good on the back of his neck. He had felt a bit queasy when first underway. It's a strange thing about being at sea. Even for someone who never had seasickness, he still felt slightly lightheaded on the first day in a new ship. It just took a few hours of rocking and rolling to readjust his equilibrium—that's all. Generally, a trip topside to see the horizon or to get out of a confined space cured all. He felt good this morning. Strolling aft, he took up a position just forward of the stern jack. The Egyptian national ensign fluttered limply in the light, damp morning air. For just a brief moment, he felt a pair of eyes—demon's eyes—boring into his back. He whirled about—no one there. It's an odd feeling being the hunter and the prey at the same time. Turning again to gaze at the gathering throng below, he narrowed his eyes to tiny slits allowing in only enough light to see the objects and human shapes bobbing about below. Somewhere, somewhere stood his prey. ANTIMONY will find him and neutralize him.

The observations in the bar had been fruitless. No, not fruitless. He had eliminated several candidates—always useful, at least a good start. No, it's not the physician bombed out of his practice in Surrey and now headed for South Africa to start up a new practice. Not that one. Ditto the very proper, monocled, former head of the India Survey now in his sixties and retired but headed back to take up his old post. Fortunes of war, you see.

All of the younger scientists had gone into the Services, and war or no, the work must continue. Perhaps the Canadian agronomist headed to Nigeria to study some type of jungle fruit? Not likely. How about the Dutch diamond man, Van Eyck? The seemingly pleasant, innocuous man had shared a Dewar's with ANTIMONY in the bar. He appeared innocent enough, but ANTIMONY sensed something not quite right about this fair-haired, blue eyed Dutchman claiming to be a diamond buyer for an Amsterdam consortium, recently fled to Lisbon, but now reemployed in his old trade. No, nothing overtly wrong or seemingly out of place about the Dutchman. No, something else. He just didn't fit. Perhaps he went a wee bit too far in trying to justify his presence, the great importance placed on this particular buying trip, how he hoped the ship would arrive on time, *ad nauseam*. If he had in fact made the trip on many occasions, what made this one so extraordinarily important? Most frequent business travelers become nonchalant after a few trips. Bartender, fix me a drink, another damn run to Africa. No, this man is too eager. He just didn't fit. ANTIMONY would keep his eye on this one. Other than these four, nothing else had come of his playing barfly. *And yet ... and yet, the man is here.* ANTIMONY had felt a malevolence off and on ever since sailing. Thirty years of leading men had taught him a great deal about human behavior. He had learned to trust his intuitions about people. And this intuition fairly screamed at him. A demonic evil has boarded *Zamzam*, a presence that well might plunge him into the abyss. *He must constantly be alert.*

"Cigarette?"

ANTIMONY spun on his heels. His right hand reached for the Beretta hidden in a jacket pocket. He jerked his hand back before it found the opening to the pocket.

"Professor Carstairs! I'm sorry, you surprised me."

He eased his hand back onto the rail, away from the pocket.

"Didn't mean to startle you there, old boy." The Canadian offered a pack of Camels with the ends of two cigarettes protruding from the top.

"No thanks, really."

"Yes, I should give them up myself. I've developed a bit of a hacking cough. Fine day isn't it. Mind if I join you?"

"No, not at all. *Me casa es su casa*, or in this case, my rail is your rail."

They both laughed and leaned against the wooden rail.

Damn! Bloody stupid and careless, drifting off into a daydream like that. Damn bloody careless! Tighten up, old sod or you may be fish food. Too many years away from the action. Too much paper shuffling has dulled the senses. Don't let it happen again. The malevolent presence crept up again. It must be found out.

There! On the pier! There he is. Dr. Verdi, the man whose presence made ANTIMONY's mission on this squalid little vessel a necessity emerged into plain view. Verdi would be the most engulfing draw on his attention from now on, a focus aimed at a single goal—to safely see the physicist to South Africa. Something started down on the pier. A tall, lanky man, apparently a longshoreman, dashed towards Verdi running hard. ANTIMONY jammed his hand into his jacket pocket, fumbling, vainly trying to grasp the Beretta. *Bloody Hell! Too far for a clear shot. The man will be upon Verdi in seconds. A wild shot would probably hit a nearby passenger. No good. A shout. No! Too much noise.* He would never be heard above the din of human voices and the rumble of deck machinery. *A shot! A shot! A shot in the air.* Maybe the assassin would be scared off. *Just maybe.* His hand gripped the pistol. *No! Wait!* The man turned; he simply changed direction, veered off and passed Verdi by several yards. Then ANTIMONY saw the object of his dash. The running longshoreman fell into the arms of a girl at the opposite end of the pier. They embraced as lovers should. ANTIMONY's fingers relaxed. The Beretta fell silently back down into the deep pocket.

"Careful there, old boy. Are you still with us? You're as white as a sheet." The Canadian placed his hand on ANTIMONY's shoulder as if to steady him in case he collapsed.

"I'm okay. No problem. I think it's just the sea air or being on this big boat. I'm not at all used to this rolling."

"I know what you mean—affects me too. Probably has something to do with the quality of the cuisine or the lack thereof."

Both men laughed. It relieved the tension. Even so, all during the conversation, ANTIMONY had kept his eyes on the physicist, only sparing slight glances over at his rail companion. The rust showed. Years and years of being out of field work had removed the edge and made him easily panicked or distracted. This simply would not do. He must find the spark again. The razor sharp instincts and feline aggressiveness of action must be brought back if he hoped to carry out his mission.

On the pier, a group of missionaries (one hundred and twenty or so Protestants, mostly Southern Baptist, Methodist, or Lutheran) all bound for various backwaters of Africa had congregated near the brow. They had grouped together to sing a traditional hymn before boarding *Zamzam*. In truth, it might have been appropriately subtitled "God Save Us From Harm As We Commit Our Lives On The High Seas To This Very Shabby Derelict Excuse For An Ocean Liner, Amen." They actually sang "Lead Kindly Light."

A few yards away, under the leadership of one Frank Vicovari, stood two dozen volunteer ambulance drivers. Not to be outdone by the large group of missionaries, Vicovari gathered the ambulance drivers around him much like the quarterback of a college football team. When they broke the huddle, every man among them had a Cheshire cat grin on his face. Vicovari lined up his troops and raised his hands. They began their awful caterwauling on the downbeat. ANTIMONY laughed gently, mindful not to offend anyone watching. He knew the song from years ago as a wing three quarter playing the noble game of rugby for Balliol College, Oxford. He still remembered the words and silently sang along with the rugger ditty about some Scottish lassies:

> Four and twenty virgins came down from Inverness.
> And when they went back there were four and twenty less.
> Sing balls to your partner, bums against the wall.
> If you've never been shagged on Saturday night,
> You've never been shagged at all.

As the throaty chorus of young rowdies raised its raucous tune, the missionaries responded in ever-increasing decibels until they fairly shouted. The young men, not to be outdone, raised their volume up a few notches as well. And so it went on that pier in Baltimore.

On the Bridge Wing, Smith stood with Burns going over the engineering logs prior to sailing. He frowned as he observed the battle of wills below. Though not a particularly superstitious man by nature, like most seamen, Smith had a little streak of it. It comes with the uncertainty of life on the sea.

He turned to Burns and spoke grimly, "Mark my words, Chief. It's bad luck for a ship to have so many Bible punchers and sky pilots aboard. No good will come of this."

Burns merely nodded in agreement. On the stern, ANTIMONY felt the demon's eyes burning into his back.

"And when they went back there were four and twenty less."

CHAPTER 6
A HOPELESS SITUATION

"**D**r. Verdi, please let me introduce myself." ANTIMONY extended his hand in a friendly shake. "I'm Edward Prince. I'm so glad to meet you finally."

"Oh. Well, how do you do," the physicist answered tentatively, not quite knowing how to respond to this overly friendly greeting.

"I have read your latest book on molecular fission. It is amazing, Sir. Very impressive." Fleming had briefed ANTIMONY on the bare essentials of the subject.

"Oh?"

The scientist warmed up to the intruder. "And do you think it is possible, Mr. Prince?"

"Possible?"

"Yes, to derive useful energy from the fission of atoms?"

"Well ... uh ... yes, as a matter of fact, I do. I'm not a scientist—merely a, let's say, moderately successful businessman, but, by golly, your theories and those of Professor Einstein's really do make sense to me. I really think you can pull it off."

Well done, old boy. When in a muddle, agree and compliment, compliment and agree. Flatter this man's ego. Get him on your side. Both of your lives may depend on it.

Zamzam pulled out of Baltimore on the afternoon ebb tide and turned southeast for the open ocean and the Caribbean. ANTIMONY had noticed the physicist strolling on deck and decided to make his move. He had been scouting the new passengers but noticed no obvious telltale signs. The two men strolled down the port side as salt spray flew up and over them. The previously placid sea now whipped up frothy beads of white foam capping the rolling waves.

"So, Dr. Verdi, what brings you onboard this jewel of a ship?"

"Oh, I'm going to visit my brother in South Africa. We haven't seen each other since we left Italy. I came to the States and he opted to run a chromium mine in the outback." He knitted his eyebrows and mused for a moment. "No, no the outback is in Australia. The *veldt* is what they call it—an old *Afrikaaner* word."

"I see. I may have run across him. My company does a lot of business with mining outfits. I make this trip about once a year."

"Yes, you might have."

They reached the stern and stopped to watch the water churning up behind the propeller.

"Aldo. Aldo Verdi."

ANTIMONY scratched his left ear as if in deep thought then rubbed his chin with thumb and forefinger in a studious manner. Of course he knew of Aldo Verdi. He had read the FBI dossier the afternoon he boarded the ship.

"I don't believe I've met him. He's not one of my customers—worse luck. Perhaps you can arrange an introduction for me."

"Indeed I shall. It will be my pleasure."

A Middle Eastern voice came over the general announcing system. "Dinner is now being served in the Dining Saloon."

"Excellent! I am utterly famished. It must be the sea air. I always eat too much when I'm at sea."

ANTIMONY chuckled. *Not on this old scow you won't.* "I fear you may be disappointed. The food on this ship is, well, it's not exactly what you'd call *haute cuisine.*"

As the two men walked slowly back towards the fore part of the ship, ANTIMONY's eyes darted about in an unobtrusive manner searching for the telling look, the gaze that strays just too long, the suddenly averted eyes; he looked for anything out of place. And he found it—right there on the deck. As they came down the ladder from the stern deck, he noticed a black object just beneath the ladder. No one else might have noticed it, but then, no one else would be that keenly alert to his surroundings either. ANTIMONY leaned down and picked up a matchbox, a black, glossy enameled kind that better hotels give away as advertising tools. He turned the shiny box over and over.

"What did you find, Mr. Prince?" inquired a curious Dr. Verdi.

"Oh, just a matchbox someone dropped. Nothing of consequence."

Wrong! Printed in bright gold letters, ANTIMONY read the name—Hotel Atlantic, Hamburg. Hamburg, Germany. The *Abwehr* man had committed a potentially fatal error. He had not divested himself of all signs of home. Certainly another passenger might have dropped it, but his instinct told him that this item belonged to his man. Few passengers would have been to Germany lately, certainly not the British or Canadians. Most Americans avoided Germany except when on diplomatic missions these days. No, this little box belonged to his man. It also provided his first substantial clue. The *Abwehr* man is probably a smoker—a smoker with expensive tastes to have stayed at that hotel. ANTIMONY slipped the matchbook into his pocket. It landed with a thunk as it struck the Beretta. The enemy's armor had been pierced ever so slightly. Amongst this small group of *Zamzam*ers hid a careless man. *A good day for a fox hunt. Tally Ho!*

The sky settled down after an early morning squall with heavy rain showers. A few billowy clouds dotted the sky here and there, but all in all, it had turned into a magnificent day as the ship reached the Gulf Stream, that warm current of water that originates in the Gulf of Mexico, tracks up the southeast coast, and at Cape Hatteras off the North Carolina Outer Banks, strikes the southward moving, colder Labrador Current. It would be warmer for the remainder of the journey. Standing on deck enjoying the magnificent weather, ANTIMONY watched the gentle roll and swell of the waves not even breaking into white, foamy caps. He had spent much of his naval career in the turbulent, frigid North Atlantic and North Sea. His Mediterranean tours had always been a haven from the foul northern weather. He liked this sea and sky. It would help to relax some of the voyage's tension and anxiety.

The sea, however, had not been kind to other *Zamzam*ers. The pitching and rolling a few hours earlier in the midst of the squall had been just too much for the land lubbers, many only onboard since Baltimore—a rude eye-opener for those who had been promised a smooth voyage. Perhaps a huge ocean liner fulfilled that marketing promise, but certainly not on a rinky dink 8,000-tonner like *Zamzam*. ANTIMONY stood at the rail just outside the double doors leading into the Dining Saloon amused at the woe begotten humanity around him. Some really did look almost green. Every now and then, one of them, glassy-eyed and staring off into no particular space, would suddenly grasp their throat, race to the rail and, most unflatteringly do as the Australians say, "chunder in the deep blue sea." The Yanks had added a colorful expression to sea lore with the addition of proper toilet facilities to ocean going vessels. Here one might be said to, "pray to the great porcelain god Ralph." ANTIMONY chuckled to himself. Well, the squall had passed and the forecast called for sunny days, warm nights, calm seas, and clear skies all the way to Brazil, surely a cheering thought to all of the Ralph worshippers.

He strolled through the double doors into the Saloon. After meal hours, it turned into a large, casual lounge. Unlike the bar aft, the Saloon served no alcoholic drinks—just lemonade and other nonalcoholic beverages. The polarization of cliques took shape almost immediately. The ambulance men, businessmen, and the more adventurous souls gravitated towards the smoky bar for carousing, card playing, and other sins. The missionaries, both French Canadian Catholic and American Protestant, tended towards the Saloon along with the older, more sedate passengers and most of the RAF wives; there the tables offered cards, bridge, rummy, or whatever. Board games became very popular. For those who preferred to lounge in the sun, the deck space just outside the Saloon had several wooden deck chairs so commonly associated with ocean travel. The Sun Deck also offered table tennis. *Zamzam* carried cargo as well as passengers, therefore, the main deck, raised stern and forecastle decks, crowded with derricks, winches, booms, and similar cargo handling devices, left little spare deck room. Passengers made out as best they could. But, until he discovered the enemy, ANTIMONY must frequent all areas. Perhaps the matchbox mistake had been a single error. If so, the invisible German could be anyone.

As he entered the Saloon, ANTIMONY glimpsed the just printed announcement tacked onto the wooden notice board. He paused to read it along with several other passengers. It announced that a ship's lifeboat drill would be conducted this morning at 1100. All passengers should read and follow the directions carefully and should find their name listed beside the assigned lifeboat. Below the announcement, a diagram of the ship indicated the location of boats while a series of dotted lines showed the preferred route

to each boat from the several exits onto the decks. The stilted, formal instructions in English and French read:

> Immediately upon the passing of the word by
> the Mate on Watch, each passenger
> is politely requested to return to his own
> cabin or berth in order that he might
> retrieve his lifejacket. Passengers will be
> so kind as to note that their lifejacket will
> either be stowed under their berth or, as is
> the case for the First and Second Class passengers,
> conveniently stowed in the clothes closet. Please place the
> lifejacket over one's head and carefully adjust onto the
> shoulders. A web strap will encircle the small of the
> backbone and will attach to the buckle on the left front
> portion of the jacket. Once this is done, all passengers
> should hurry, without racing, to their assigned lifeboat.
> Please await further instructions from the designated ship's
> crewman.

Well, this always engendered a little bit of excitement. He scanned the passenger list and found his name on the roster for Boat No. 3, starboard side,
main deck. Verdi went to Boat No. 6 on the port side. Not to worry, however.
Should the occasion arise where they must man the boats for real, he would
simply show up at Boat No. 6 and attach himself to the scientist. In the case
of an actual sinking or even a precautionary abandonment, there is rarely
time to confirm a list of names. Everyone jumps into the nearest boat, and
when it's full, it's lowered away.

As he stood gazing at the notice board as if in a trance, he remembered an
afternoon in early November 1915—a beastly day, one best forgotten, except
to honor the dead. As a junior officer just promoted to lieutenant, he served
as Gunnery Officer of HMS *Halberd*, a new "K" class destroyer. Typical of
the destroyers of the day, the small, lightly armed vessel looked more like
a large patrol boat than a major fleet warship most unlike the sleek, fast,
graceful, powerful greyhounds of the kind he had commanded in the 1930s.
Why the captain had even contemplated that he could best the German *Bre-
slau*-class light cruiser with his outgunned destroyer, he would never know,
though ANTIMONY suspected the man's sense of duty demanded that he

defend the colliers hauling coal down the coast from Newcastle to London. For whatever reason, the doughty little ship charged into the fray unleashing a spread of its main battery of torpedoes and salvos from the three 4-inch guns. Even though a torpedo found the mark, the German's dozen 4.1-inch guns straddled the attacking destroyer, hitting the Bridge first. In the open air, covered only by a canvas canopy, metal shards flew everywhere killing or wounding everyone. The captain died in a puddle of his own blood from a gashed throat. Round after round pummeled the ship as it careened about, out of control. A shell entered the hull just below the waterline and exploded in the Engine Room. In spite of being brought dead in the water, *Halberd* fought on, pouring its own destruction onto the German, also dead in the water from the torpedo wounds. Her guns roared in defiance in their own version of David and Goliath. He had continued directing fire despite a painful wound in his right leg. Blazes broke out all over the wounded cruiser as British gunners found the mark. North Sea water, cold and murky, poured through the holed hull of *Halberd* as she settled by the stern. To the utter dismay of the destroyer crew, the enemy cruiser got up steam again, heading for Germany with a decided port list. The enemy had had enough of this feisty little British warship. As the German disappeared over the horizon, out of gun range, and as ranking surviving officer, he had ordered "Abandon Ship." Unfortunately for the crew, most of the lifeboats had been bashed to pieces or blown overboard leaving only one serviceable boat for over fifty surviving men. They strapped together pieces of wood debris as well as could be, constructing several makeshift rafts. As the night passed, men took turns in the water or in the boat and rafts. The ship disappeared within minutes after abandonment creating a gurgling, sucking noise. Of the fifty-three men who had gone into the water that cold November afternoon, only twelve remained the next morning when a fishing trawler finally rescued the survivors. This disaster had left on ANTIMONY a vivid, stark memory never very far from his consciousness. As a cruel compensation for the survivors, they learned that the crippled German cruiser had made only twenty miles towards home before she too had to be abandoned with a similar loss of life. The sea plays no favorites. The horrible night, the sound of wounded men screaming and drifting away in the numbing water ran through his mind in agonizingly vivid imagery as he stood immobile, staring at the innocuous, overly polite, matter-of-fact announcement of the ever so casual and routine lifeboat drill.

"I see we are in the same boat, Mr. Prince."

His hands jerked spastically as if grabbed by the nape of the neck. "What ... who," he blurted out, almost but not quite reverting to his regular accent—a very close call.

"I said, I see we are in the same lifeboat," repeated the tall, dark-haired woman standing beside him.

"Ah, yes. Mrs. Avery. I'm sorry, I didn't see you standing there. I'm afraid I was daydreaming."

"Yes, of course," she smiled sweetly.

"You are right." He moved his finger up the alphabetized list to the "As." "Here you are, Lifeboat No. 3, starboard side. Well, we shall certainly have a wonderful time riding out the waves in that boat."

"Indeed we shall, Mr. Prince."

Daydreaming had put him in a weak position. Had it been the enemy agent rather than Mrs. Avery, he might have been undone. Providence looked after him on this occasion, but, he must be more careful. A passage he had written in his treatise on field work passed through his mind: "The agent who is not fully conscious of his total environment at all times runs the very grave risk of compromising the mission or the ultimate penalty—death." He must remember his own words and avoid any future daydreaming. He had been fortunate thus far, but what about the inevitable time when his luck would turn. Then, his wits, stamina, training, and intelligence counted most. *Was he still up to the challenge? Was he ready? He needed to know.*

"Would you care to join me for breakfast, Mrs. Avery?"

"I certainly would, Mr. Prince. That would be most delightful."

Vowing to avoid the sausages, he instead opted for the bacon, eggs, toast. The bacon must have come from the same poor hog. This trip might just turn him into a vegetarian. At least the chicken had not yet failed him. How could you turn out a bad hard-boiled egg? *Zamzam*'s chef might yet manage to do just that.

Mrs. Joan Avery of New York fascinated him far more than the breakfast. In 1941, very few Americans traveled abroad. The separation from Europe and the Far East by two great oceans no doubt fueled the traditional American isolationist tendencies and made it damned infuriating even trying to lead the American public to the watering hole, much less make them drink. They would soon learn that the evil forces in the world affected everyone, but, in early 1941, the isolationist in them prevailed. Mrs. Avery spoke of her world travels in the 1930s demonstrating an impressive knowledge of world events, people, and places. A bit standoffish, she never seemed to mingle with other passengers, preferring instead the solitude of her cabin. Twice, he had seen her in the bar for a cocktail or sherry, but other than that, he had not seen much of the stately widow. Though tanned, she never appeared on deck to take in the sun as so many of the younger women did after the long winter stretch. But, he avoided her personal life and private habits as none of his concern. Still she did make for an odd and enchanting dining companion.

To put it kindly, the lifeboat drill came off amateurishly. When the mate passed the word over the general announcing system for all hands and passengers to standby to man their lifeboat stations, first in English, then in Arabic, most of the passengers had already prepared themselves. Several minutes later came the word for all passengers to please proceed to their assigned lifeboats.

After breakfast, he had located his life vest hanging in the cabin closet. Though old and grimy, he could make out the markings on the underside of the Kapok filled vest indicating it was the same design used and abandoned by the Royal Navy years earlier. The company had apparently bought the surplus stock—serviceable, if not the best. He pulled the bulky and uncomfortable vest over his jacket and snapped the strap around his waist. Comfort is not an issue when the only thing keeping your head above water is the heavy collar under your neck. He proceeded aft towards the door leading out onto the main deck. Somehow, he expected to see an efficiently run drill with sailors on station taking the muster as passengers arrived and boats swung out ready for orderly loading. Instead, sailors scrambled all over the ship. An engineer, filthy with oil and bilge water, almost knocked him down as he stepped away from the ladder onto the main deck. Utter chaos prevailed. Passengers, unable to find their correct boat, milled about aimlessly. Here and there, ship's officers shouted and cursed in all sorts of languages, doing their best to direct not only passengers but their own men. ANTIMONY suspected that the officers by and large comprised a competent lot, but the engineers and deck crew appeared pretty useless when it came to running a ship. The chaos on deck confirmed that initial impression.

"Excuse me, Mr. Prince. Do you know where Lifeboat No. 3 is? We're frightfully lost and none of these Egyptian chaps are of any help," pleaded an elderly man in a white linen suit with a straw Panama hat.

"They can barely speak any English, George," piped in his proper upper-middle class English wife, frustration showing on her face.

"Certainly, just follow me. I think I have the picture. Follow me."

He really wanted to say that they weren't bloody likely to get any proper assistance either, but he held his fire. Once they reached Cape Town and Verdi came under the protection of the SOE men, he would not travel any further on the good ship *Zamzam*, or any other like her. The notion of a quick set of hops back to New York on the new Boeing 314 flying boats equipped with the latest in conditioned air and prompt, polite stewards and lovely young stewardesses seemed most appealing as he dodged bodies all running amok on the deck. "Lifeboat No. 3, starboard side," he announced.

The scene that greeted them at Lifeboat No. 3 did not surprise him. The assigned boat officer had gone to restore some order to Boat No. 4 across the deck, which normally would have been the second officer's assignment. This left a very flustered able seaman in charge. He could not read the names on the muster list despite being in Arabic and English and had passed the clipboard around. In barely recognizable speech, he asked everyone to raise their hand if they saw their name on the list. A gaggle of passengers, all jostling and bumping, tried to get a look at the clipboard. The poor seaman threw his hands up in exasperation.

Enough of this foolishness! His frustration now came to the fore, causing him to violate a cardinal tenet of field work—never make yourself too obvious, and if you must, never give away to a spying enemy anything about your personal strengths, weaknesses, or characteristics. In now so doing, he signaled to all present his skill as an organizer and a leader, potentially a dangerous mistake. Surely, the same thing happened at other spots about the deck. Perhaps the *Abwehr* man did the same thing at his boat for the same reason. He stepped up out of the crowd, raised his hand boldly and nodded to the hapless sailor. The man understood immediately and, welcoming the assistance, smiled, nodded, and turned to help two shipmates, who grunted and struggled with a stuck davit winch. He noticed that Mrs. Avery now had the clipboard. "Mrs. Avery," he extended his hand. "Please."

She handed over the clipboard. The crowd around her pulled back, grateful for someone in charge.

"Okay folks, I'm going to call off your names. Please raise your hand after I have called your name. Does everyone understand?" He paused for a moment while a priest whispered in French to the two other clerics huddled around him.

"Fine. Just raise your hand, please. Father Auberjohnois." He checked off the priest's name at the top of the list. "Mr. Autry. Thanks, good, Mrs. Avery ... ."

Of the thirty names, six came up missing, but presumably they had gone to the wrong boat. The three sailors finally loosened the davit and lowered the lifeboat to the rail where it would be a simple matter to clamber over the rail and into the boat. That is, unless the ship listed at any significant angle or was heavily down by the stern or bow. ANTIMONY shook his head at the thought of abandoning this ship and lowering boats under those conditions. By the time he finished reading off the list, the first officer arrived on the scene. Calmly, clearly, and logically, he explained all of the steps necessary to get into the boat safely—how to load, where to sit, who should load first, how to properly wear the Kapok vest and so forth. After nearly an hour of this chaos, the captain mercifully concluded the drill. ANTIMONY could only imagine that an abandon ship for real on this vessel would likely result in an utterly hopeless situation. As he reached his cabin and unbuckled the Kapok straps, a foreboding thought came over ANTIMONY. *Had he been too forward, too revealing for safety? Had the German taken note? Had he compromised his cover? He could not be as careless a man as the foe had been. Damn it all! Bloody rusty!*

ANTIMONY made it a point to mingle with every passenger, especially the gaggle of missionaries. What better cover for an *Abwehr* agent than as a soft-spoken, mild-mannered French Canadian priest. The Protestant missionaries, mostly from the South, constituted a different story altogether. Only a brilliant actor could hide for long among them. No, the man had to be either Canadian or European. That is where he would concentrate, and, as "Big Bill" Donovan might say, "glad hand every son of a bitch until someone's palm starts to sweat." He had narrowed the hunt down to just three primary suspects, including the Dutch diamond merchant Van Eyck and the British veterinarian who seemed, well, simply too standoffish as if hiding from or hiding behind something. A new candidate had appeared recently—Father Villeneuve. Not known by the other priests, he claimed to have just arrived in Montreal as a refugee from Occupied France and had immediately volunteered his services as a missionary to Africa, an offer the bishop readily accepted—certainly plausible, but the element of doubt warranted a watchful eye.

He grew especially close to Verdi. Not the shy, introverted type that one often associates with scientists of his stature, Verdi appeared to be an outgoing, conversant man who spoke flawless English. ANTIMONY spent many hours walking the decks or sharing a drink in the bar with this man. If he had to "nanny" the physicist to protect him, he must know his habits and he must be able to anticipate his reactions. As each day went by, his confidence grew. He felt more at ease with his capabilities and with his mission. It looked increasingly as if the mission might be uneventful—"a milk run." No—experience and skill prevented that thinking from slipping in. If the mission went easily enough, then all the better, but he knew to always expect the unexpected. Vigilance, vigilance, and more vigilance.

Two days out of Recife, Brazil and the wind, up from the south-southeast at ten knots, pushed away the heavy, stifling humid afternoon air. The bar opened at seven and ANTIMONY had agreed to meet several new acquaintances for after-dinner brandy and cigars. God knows the brandy helped to digest dinner. He had dined again at the captain's table. A seemingly pleasant and competent man, ANTIMONY hoped he could rely on this Scotsman in a pinch. Strolling along the stern deck absorbing the day's final sunshine, he became faintly aware of a presence behind him.

"Braithwaite!"

He froze. In a fraction of a second the world came apart like an overripe fruit falling from a tree and splitting on the hard ground below. The blazing sun suddenly felt like razors reaching out to slash and slice him to shreds. *Don't panic.* He kept walking slowly, ignoring the single spoken word behind him, hand already in his pocket. It tightened around the Beretta's grip. *What to do? No malice—By God—there was no malice in the voice. If anything, friendly. Confusion.* He kept walking.

"John Braithwaite?"

Again, a nonthreatening, questioning tone of voice. In his peripheral vision, he saw no one else on the deck. *Good.* He could confront his accuser without interference or danger to an innocent. ANTIMONY turned around slowly, the sun directly behind his head. The man squinted, placing his palm to his brow to shield his eyes.

"It is you! Son of a bitch! Braithwaite, John Braithwaite isn't it?" The man extended a hand. *The enemy extending his hand!* ANTIMONY had turned, fully ready for action with hand on the pistol grip. But, if necessary, he would leap across the deck into the enemy. Surely, the German would not expect an older man to react in such a way. Surprise would be his ally. A swift hand at the throat would be his weapon. But now he stood facing a man perhaps older than himself, a nonthreatening man who extended his hand in a gesture of friendship. His hand relaxed on the pistol grip. He felt the threat ebb away. The tension in his muscles eased. He would still be noncommittal.

"I beg your pardon?"

The man smiled and withdrew his hand. The interloper had a vaguely familiar look about him, a face from a long time ago. *This could not be an enemy. Not at all. A friend? An ally?* The last bit of tension drained out. "Sorry to startle you."

ANTIMONY said nothing. He stared blankly at the man awaiting the next move.

"You are John Braithwaite, though. I'm sure of that. Royal Navy, Intelligence Division. I've been wondering why you looked so familiar ever since we came aboard in Baltimore, but it didn't click until just now. Son of a bitch! John By God and Damn the Torpedoes Braithwaite!"

The man looked more familiar now, but ANTIMONY still could not quite place him.

"I'm Colonel Fred Hobgood, United States Army Signals Intelligence, retired. You must remember me—the Bahama U-boat project. Back in, oh, early 1918."

There it is. Bloody hell! Of course. Fred Hobgood, U.S. Army Signal Corps, Signals Intelligence Division. ANTIMONY extended his right hand. "Colonel Hobgood, of course! You startled me. How have you been all these years?"

Compromised, cover blown! ANTIMONY envisioned only disaster coming from this chance meeting of an old comrade in arms. Hobgood shook heartily. He lowered his voice, moved in closer, and motioned ANTIMONY over to the rail with a nod of the head. Both intelligence officers, by habit, checked the area for prying ears. They leaned over the wooden rail, staring at the dark water below.

"It's obviously still ANTIMONY, isn't it, Mr. Prince."

Could this be the man the Americans had sent on this mission? Had they sent in an over-the-hill desk warrior to do a young man's field work like his own government had done? No, probably not. The FBI men had, simply put, missed the boat. G-Men had a certain button-down formality about them that made them easily recognizable in a crowd, especially this crowd. *So who could this man be. Sheer coincidence? It must be.* "Pinned to the bulkhead, I fear," ANTIMONY responded.

Hobgood chuckled. "You Navy types," he smirked shaking his head. "Once a squid, always a squid." The army man would get in his thrusts before any damned navy man could parry.

"I'm retired now, these past three years," pleaded ANTIMONY.

"Apparently not too retired, ANTIMONY. Cut the bullshit, John. You're safe with me."

He had worked night and day with this man for three months. *Safe? Yes, safe.* Hobgood would be discreet and cooperative. "Well Sir, I am obviously on a mission. You, being the consummate professional that you are, have as we say, blown my cover. What will it cost me?"

Hobgood pursed his lips and grinned. "A bourbon and water and twenty years of gossip."

"Fair deal," replied ANTIMONY, visibly relieved. He looked at his watch. Not quite seven. The ambulance drivers would not be in for a few minutes and the rest of the tobacco men would drift in about half past eight so it would be safe for a while yet. He had noticed the beefy man amongst the six North Carolinians, but until now, had not recognized him.

"I'm a buyer with the American Tobacco Company out of Durham now," he confided as the two old warriors settled into a comfortable stall in the aft section of the bar. "I made bird colonel in '34, but Jeez, army pay is pretty poor. Retirement pay is even worse, so, when I retired in '39, my old room-mate from Chapel Hill got me a job with American Tobacco. Good to get back home. My family's from Siler City, you know." Hobgood laughed at the blank expression on ANTIMONY's face. "Oh, yeah. Siler City. Three stop-lights and eight thousand farmers. It's a little tobacco town about forty miles southwest of Raleigh."

ANTIMONY nodded. He had been to Raleigh.

"It's good pay with good benefits. I can't complain. I'm not wild about the travel. Lord knows I did too much of that for Uncle Sam, but I had a good career. I'll tell you, though, don't count me out. I figure a year, two at most, we'll be in this war against the Nazis. Roosevelt wants it in a bad way. He just has to have a provocation." He took a long sip of his Jack Daniels. Within a few minutes, the bar filled up with rowdy young men. Fortunately, they made so much noise that it drowned out the hushed conversation of the two older men. They spent two hours talking about the decades since the previous war. While good to find an old and reliable confidant, ANTIMONY did not tell him about the current mission. Hobgood didn't ask. Both men understood the ground rules. By nine, they had talked themselves out. Hob-good yawned. "Listen sport. Call on me if you need to. I'm not sure just how neutral I can be when the back's up against it. I'm here in a pinch, under-stand? And I speak German fluently. I've spent most of the last six months in Berlin trying to sell tobacco to those square-headed bastards. Call me when you need me, okay?"

"Done, shipmate." ANTIMONY stood up and extended his hand. Hob-good responded with a warm, firm grip. He could count on Colonel Fred-erick Hobgood, US Army retired, but he hoped to God he wouldn't have to. After the army man departed, ANTIMONY sat alone smoking a Dominican cigar presented by Hobgood. The steward came by; he ordered a brandy. His innate sense of events caused him to suspect that the next few days would be critical in his hunt for the *Abwehr* man. But now, he felt more confident as a smoke ring rose and drifted halfway across the bar. *Zamzam* sailed on through the Caribbean night.

CHAPTER 7
PENNSYLVANIA 6-5000

"I'll take three." Three red-backed playing cards flew across the table face down. The requestor grimaced as he picked them up and slid them into his hand. "Alright gang, I'll bet a nickel. Throw it in boys."

The next man looked to his left, then to his right, then dropped his cards on the table shaking his head. "I'm in. I'll see your five and raise you a couple." Two pennies clinked on the pile of coins.

The next player smiled. "I'll take that action," he said as he dropped seven cents onto the pile.

The fourth man, still disappointed in his new cards, reached into his pocket and took out an ornate, beaten silver cigarette lighter. He flipped open the top and punched down on the roller with his thumb. Metal whirred as the flame shot up. He made a gesture as if to light the useless poker hand. Everyone laughed heartily. He had been losing badly all evening and the humor seemed perfectly appropriate.

"I take it, Clyde, that you have folded," sniggered the gloating dealer, who had started the present round of betting. "Play 'em and lay 'em." His full house easily whipped the three of a kind and 8s and 9s. The dealer raked the pile of coins onto his side of the table. He had done well that night.

"What's cooking, shipmates?" quizzed Frank Vicovari, who had come back from the bar with a tall glass in hand.

"Clyde here just lost the family summer house in Maine, Frank. Bar Harbor, isn't it?"

"Gee, guys, make me feel good, how 'bout it. I haven't even inherited the place and I've already lost it in a poker game."

Good-natured laughter erupted as the winner slid a quarter across the table. "Here you go, Clyde. Put a down payment on the repurchase before Grand Mama finds out."

Another round of raucous laughter erupted from the ambulance drivers. They clearly enjoyed the *Zamzam* cruise in spite of the drab food, poor service, and generally run-down state of the ship. Determined to make it an adventure, they succeeded stunningly well, much to the general annoyance of the more staid passengers. The two dozen young men—these ambulance drivers in their jaunty khaki uniforms—carried on the American tradition of volunteer foreign service, such as the pilots who flew for France in the First World War (*Lafayette Escadrille*), the volunteers to the International Brigade in Spain, and the American RAF Eagle Squadron in the Battle of Britain. These young pups enjoying their wonderful adventure, had never known the brutal reality of a world at war. They soon would thought ANTIMONY as he sat at a corner table observing the shenanigans of the drunk and definitely disorderly poker players.

Six young women ranging from remarkably attractive to somewhat plain entered the bar—the wolves' lair. Brave young girls. Catcalls and whistles came immediately from the tables occupied by men slouched in an advanced state of drunken dishevelment. The RAF wives pretended to ignore the harangue, though, truth be told, they knew full well what would happen once they entered the bar. Were they available? Some of the drivers seemed damned determined to find out. In the stresses and strains of war, the bonds of marital fidelity are often loosened, especially given the continuous threat of immediate, violent death. Yes, some of these women had to be susceptible to the charms of these educated, well-off, American adventurers. The ship itself lent an air of daring to the whole scene—a battered, derelict Egyptian liner chugging across the dangerous ocean with an exotic assortment of passengers all bound for some sort of African adventure. No Hollywood screenwriter could have dreamed up a more perfect scenario. In another corner of the bar sat four middle-aged tobaccomen. With the women's appearance, they all glanced up for just a brief moment, then went back to more important issues over smokes and bourbon, to wit, would Coach Wallace Wade's powerful Duke University Blue Devils football team, candidates for an undefeated season, be invited to the Rose Bowl this season. Ned "Uncle Ned" Laughinghouse led the group of buyers representing several tobacco interests, who had been contracted by the British government to convince Rhodesian growers to sell in the American market. The Crown welcomed any source of foreign capital to maintain the Empire's economic viability. A friendly enough lot, they stuck to themselves, usually in their customary place in the bar, where they plotted out a successful Duke season. ANTIMONY had not yet ruled out the possibility of one of these men as his target. But, the Southerner, so striking and regional not only in accent, but in mannerisms, would make the German immediately suspect unless he had lived and worked in the South for many years. Besides, these men seemed to all know each other. No, the man couldn't be one of them.

As the bar filled with thirsty or bored *Zamzam*ers, several ambulance drivers stood hovering over their mates swapping lies about each other's exploits while on the playing field or in the fraternity house. One table had given up their seats to the RAF wives, who now sat quietly chatting and enjoying sherries. Other people drifted in and out of the crowded, hot, smoky bar.

"Hey Frank, what are you drinking there?" shouted a tipsy ambulance driver.

"I'm not sure." Vicovari turned towards the bill of fare, hand-painted, hanging at a slight angle above the bar window. He pointed at the sign. "It's called a Zamzam. I don't know what's in this thing. I don't want to know either. Try it, you'll love it," he slurred as he staggered ever so slightly, pointing up at the sign reading the "Zamzam, an original drink at only one dollar American."

From deep within the ship came a whirring noise. The lights in the bar flickered as the power surged and fluctuated, then dimmed to total darkness.

"Damn!"

"I beg your pardon."

"Sorry, Ma'am."

"Frank, get off my foot."

"Sorry, old sport."

"What next?"

"We may never get to Africa."

The rhythmical, mesmerizing chug of the engines had ceased. It is a sound one becomes accustomed to at sea, so much so that it isn't really noticed until it's no longer there. The bar grew quiet and still with only the faraway sound of the waves splashing up against the hull. From a distance came the muffled voice of a mate shouting to a crewman somewhere below on deck, and a reply in broken English. The gentle roll of the ship, now more pronounced without forward momentum, felt relaxing to ANTIMONY. He noticed the myriad of clashing scents in the bar. In the light, his eyes and his ears had been his chief sensory detectors, observing and listening for the enemy's telltale *faux pas*. Now, deprived of sight, his nose became even more alert. Amongst the acrid tobacco smoke wafted the faint, sweetly pleasant scent of perfume, both feminine and enticing. Hanging above all of this drifted the smell of hard alcohol and stale beer. Mingling here and there, he detected the odor of people of Middle Eastern origin.

"Maybe we ought to move out on deck," remarked an ambulance driver.

"Hear, hear," came a formal English voice in reply.

The barman managed to light a lantern. He knew to expect this sort of thing. The light sparkled as beams shot out and bounced off the metal bulkhead. Heads and bodies appeared grotesque and distorted in the flickering yellow light. "Please, please excuse, please," pleaded the Egyptian as he made his way, stumbling into and around bodies, forward to the doorway leading out onto the main deck. "Please, ladies and gentlemen. This way to the main deck, please."

The lamp lit the doorway exit. One by one, bar patrons moved out, many nervous and fidgety. Total darkness in an enclosed space unnerves many. The RAF wives went first followed by the tobacco men, then the ambulance drivers, half supporting, half carrying several of their less steady comrades. ANTIMONY brought up the rear followed by the barman carrying the lantern.

"Oops! I'm so sorry. I do beg your pardon," the woman gasped as she ran into the man.

"Quite all right, Madame. I am very clumsy," replied the blond haired man with a heavy continental accent.

"Oh no, my fault entirely. I'm ever so clumsy in the dark." The pretty Englishwoman blushed with embarrassment, but one could not tell this on the darkened deck.

"Well then, would you care to share the rail with me? I have a lovely spot here that is much more than my share," offered the man.

"Oh, thank you, Sir. You are most kind." She wedged into the space next to him.

He turned back towards the sea below. Their chance encounter had not been accidental. The stranger had had his wandering eyes on the woman, the prettiest of the lot, from the moment she had come aboard *Zamzam* with the other RAF wives. He had been on deck before the power loss and had watched her going into the bar with the other RAF wives earlier, but had remained on deck. When the lights went out, he saw everything with his night vision and intentionally stepped in front of her as she made her way aft along the narrow walkway outside the bar. "I'm Charles Van Eyck. I am very pleased to meet you."

"And I'm Abigail Ashton, but most people call me Abby. I'm pleased to make your acquaintance Mr. Van Eyck. You're Dutch aren't you? I'm just awfully lost when it comes to continental surnames. Please do forgive me," the woman rambled on.

"Yes, Dutch. From Rotterdam, but I now live in Lisbon. I am a diamond buyer. You're English? Is your husband in the Service, then?"

She beamed. *How did he know so much about her? So awfully embarrassing.* Then again, this is a quite attractive gentleman even though she could only see him partially in the dark. "Oh, yes. In the RAF. He's ever so dashing. A pilot you know. Pilot Officer Nigel Ashton. He flies a Spitfire. I'm going out to Egypt to be with him. It's oh so exciting don't you think?" she babbled.

This poor woman is still a schoolgirl thought Van Eyck. She should be an easy mark for his amorous advances and yet another sexual conquest for the totally ruthless, amoral Dutchman. "You must be so proud of your husband. Out there fighting the enemy. I only wish I could do more for the cause against the Nazis but," he shrugged his shoulders, "my country has been overrun, defeated. What can one do?"

"Exactly what you are doing Mr. Van Eyck. You are keeping the engines of commerce alive and running so that when we free Europe from the Nazi tyranny, we will still have a strong economic foundation to build upon."

Did she dream that one up or did she read it somewhere in some British propaganda rag? Well, it sounds stirring in any case. Let her feel that way. I'm just earning a living. "Just so, Mrs. Ashton. Just so. Still, I am constantly looking for a way to aid the war effort." *Yes, like servicing the physical needs of attractive wives whose husbands are away fighting.*

"Are you traveling alone or is your wife along for the trip, Mr. Van Eyck?"

She's probing. This one's an easy mark. "My lovely wife is home in Lisbon with our children. She prefers not to travel. I fear I only see her for a few months of the year."

He felt a soft warm hand on his as it lay on the rail. *She is an aggressive little vixen.* He could pick them, the ones with the wandering eye, that is.

"Not to worry. I'm sure you will be home with your family in no time at all."

"No, not if this ship keeps breaking down. We're terribly behind our published schedule as it is, Mrs. Ashton."

She laughed. "Oh, please, call me Abby."

"Indeed, yes, please call me Charles."

They both turned and stared out across the ocean below. The moon had emerged from behind the storm clouds casting a silvery glow to the ship and the people on deck. The introductory small talk phase ended. Van Eyck had broken the ice much easier than he had expected. *This just might be a most pleasurable voyage.* They stood in silence leaning over the rail, the moon reflecting off the water below and dancing across the handsome faces of these two wanderers caught up in the exotic surreal existence of a crazy little ship on a gently rolling sea. The wind picked up, but the sea remained calm and the night quiet. The storm of a few hours earlier had passed and there would be clear sailing all the way to Brazil. One by one or in little groups, *Zamzamer*s felt their way back to their cabins. ANTIMONY finished his cigar and flicked the butt over the side. He watched the glowing red coal tumble and spin as it fell towards the sea, then a small hiss of steam where it hit the water. He stared at the cigar as it drifted slowly away.

The ship's engineers worked all through the night to repair the leak in the main fuel line. By midnight, they had an emergency generator back on line. By 0400, the ship made eight knots steaming southeasterly along the South American coast.

"Ladies and gentlemen! Please to advise you that this evening, the Cabaret El Zamzam will present a night of good old Yankee swing band music and close dancing in the main Saloon. Please to put on your dancing slippers to while the night away. Thank you very much," the excited purser announced to the passengers gathered for dinner.

A friendly, affable sort, and one of the few crewmen actually liked by the *Zamzamer*s, he puffed with pride at the announcement of the dance. A fair musician in his own right, he played the tenor saxophone. Every time the ship pulled into a port where an American swing or jazz band performed, he would go to hear them. Tonight, though, he could shine.

"I think I heard this band in a whorehouse in Marseille," chuckled Hobgood. In spite of his severe Southern Baptist upbringing, the good Colonel had also "seen" much of the world. Everyone at the table chuckled along with him.

"Well, I am most willing to give the chaps a chance. It can't be any worse than playing cards and shuffleboard all day," interjected Dr. Starling, who had become a regular dining companion.

"Here, here," added Mrs. Starling, who struggled with a tough piece of beef.

ANTIMONY had given up and placed his knife and fork down on the plate parallel to each other and perpendicular to the edge of the table. A rush of panic struck him. His eyes darted around the table and over to the next, then towards the entrance. *How could he be so bloody stupid?* He picked up the fork again and speared a piece of fatty, gristly meat. He popped it into his mouth hurriedly, not quite chewing before swallowing the piece whole. This time he replaced the fork on the plate except that the tines crossed the blade of the knife. Such a small thing, really, but such mistakes get you killed in his line of work. In Europe, people routinely placed the knife and fork parallel on the plate after one is finished eating. This action is universally accepted by the host or waiter as a sign that one is finished dining and will not be embarrassed by having the plate removed. In America, however, this convention is not generally practiced. *Damn, how could he be so stupid.* He had worked so hard to master the American habit of cutting, then laying down the knife, transferring the fork to the right hand and so forth. He had broken the British habit of keeping the fork in the left hand, tines down, with a far more vigorous use of the knife beyond simply for cutting. Wasn't this just what he looked for to betray the German—the little mistakes? No one had apparently noticed his error as they engaged in several conversations ranging from the weather to the sad state of modern music, etc., etc.

Hobgood noticed him chewing on the gristly meat. "Good stuff, eh? We ate better in the trenches during the first war."

"Your trouble, Mr. Hobgood, is that you have become pampered and spoiled on good North Carolina barbecue. To these Egyptians, this is no doubt a feast of the first order," ANTIMONY added snidely as Hobgood snorted.

"No doubt, Mr. Prince, no doubt, but I'd give a month's pay right now for a good plate of barbecue with hush puppies and coleslaw and some Brunswick stew. Maybe some fried chicken and potatoes boiled in butter and a big slab of pecan pie and ... ."

"Enough, Colonel Hobgood! We take your point," blurted out Dr. Starling. Hobgood smirked and winked at ANTIMONY, then took another bite of an indeterminate boiled vegetable.

The notice board posted at the main entrance to the Dining Saloon proudly announced the evening's bill of fare as roast filet of beef with new potatoes, fresh green spinach in white sauce, dinner rolls, biscuits, cheeses, and assorted sweets. ANTIMONY noticed as he entered that someone had added their own editorial comments. The newly revised menu read: "roast filet of shoe leather with shriveled potatoes, dried up green grass in motor oil, World War I surplus hard tack rolls, moldy cheeses, and assorted fat pills." No doubt it had been one of the ambulance drivers, but really not too far off the mark.

ANTIMONY recovered from his *faux pas*. His heart rate returned to normal. *God that meat was bad! Maybe a double dose of a sweet, gooey pastry would help wash it down. That and a stiff drink in the bar afterwards. Well, at least maybe the alcohol would kill off some of the bacteria.*

At another table, a priest became animated and excited. He loved jazz and played a pretty mean trombone. So what if the bishop, still conveniently back in Quebec, thought that jazz and swing music had to be works of the Devil. He had the germ of a plan and excused himself from the table. "Pardon, *Monsieur*. May I have a word?"

"Yes, indeed, Father. How might I be of service to you this fine evening?" replied the purser, all smiles.

"I am a great admirer of American big band music. I have my trombone here as well as many, many musical arrangements. I would consider it a great honor to play with you and the ship's orchestra at the dance tonight. I might add, *Monsieur*, that I know of three other passengers—a fellow trombonist, a trumpeter, and a bassist—who might be similarly interested."

The Egyptian's smile turned to a bright sunbeam. *Of course!* He had dreamed of playing in a big band and here might be at least a chance to try it out. "Yes indeed. Of course, Father. We would be most honored indeed. Let us say at eight bells, here in the Saloon."

The priest extended his hand and warmly gripped the purser's consummating the deal. *By Mary and Jesus, they would have fine music this night. Amen!* As the Canadian priest jubilantly bounced back to his table to join his more somber and staid fellow missionaries, he could not possibly foresee that tonight's concert would be the first of many in the weeks to come. Most would be for a far different reason than simple frivolous entertainment.

By nine that evening, the party ramped up into full swing. The boring days at sea interrupted only briefly by moments of excitement such as power failures, had made many passengers stir crazy. ANTIMONY, used to long arduous days at sea, felt relaxed and refreshed. There had been moments of anxiety certainly, like the cutlery incident, but, by and large, he felt good. He had not yet identified the enemy, but, neither had the man made any overt move towards Verdi. Perhaps the trip would be as Fleming and INTREPID described—an observation mission only for the German with no real threat. The feeling of evil had abated in recent days as they made their way towards Brazil and his confidence increased. Never far from his sight, ANTIMONY stayed close to Verdi, observed him, and kept a keen watch for any overly interested passengers. Verdi could not become annoyed and subsequently suspicious or antagonistic. At the same time, ANTIMONY could not give himself away to the unknown *Abwehr* man who, no doubt, searched for the foe as ardently as did himself. Despite his calming notion of control of the situation, the nagging question came back to him time after time. *Where were the FBI men? What had happened to them?* The question would not go away.

"Damn good music!" exclaimed Hobgood, his foot tapping out the intoxicating rhythm. "I heard Glenn Miller do this one last year in Atlanta. Great tune! These guys aren't too bad, you know."

The addition of the four musicians to the ship's orchestra added a wonderfully rich sound. The lead trombonist, standing tall in front with subdued light glinting off the brass and the slide of his instrument angled high in the air, doowopped through Glenn Miller's "In the Mood." The stark clerical collar over somber black suit seemed a most unusual feature. Well, *Zamzam* is a strange little ship with an odd assortment of passengers, so what the hell. The trumpet player, a heavy equipment salesman from Chicago, ran nimble fingers over the valves reaching out for the highest note, crescendoing into the climax—"dat diddle dit dit dit, dat diddle dit dit dit, dat diddle dit dit dit daaah, wah wah wah wah waaaaah! Whuum!" Wow!

Passengers jumped to their feet clapping. Stupendous! On the dance floor, couples breathing heavily after the exhausting jitterbug, applauded lustily. The priest beamed, bowing and beaming some more. He looked over at the Monsignor. Even the elder churchman clapped. The Egyptian sax player counted off—one, two, three, and…. The melodious, soothing sound of "Moonlight Serenade" wafted through the room. Most of the dancers, still winded, had taken their seats to slug down a refreshing drink of whatever they had be it gin and tonic or lemonade. A few dancers remained on the dance floor, mainly husbands and wives. Here and there, a slightly bolder couple embraced and twirled slowly, rhythmically, mostly the ambulancemen and more daring RAF wives. Many simply swayed to the relaxing, soothing melody.

In the Pilot House, Captain Smith completed his nightly navigational calculations. Back on course, they should make Recife by day after tomorrow barring any more damned engineering casualties. Already several days behind schedule, this cost the company not only money, but credibility. He popped open the brass speaking tube.

"Engine Room, Pilot House."

"Engine Room, Aye," responded Burns.

"Chief, can you give me any more turns without endangering the plant?"

"Aye, Captain, maybe a few, but this plant needs an overhaul. I'll get you to Alex, but she needs laying up. The old girl is tired."

"Very well, Chief. Do what you can. We need to make up some time."

"Engine Room, Aye."

The captain flipped the lid back over the voice pipe. He felt a slow rumbling (more of a vibration) under his feet. It subsided shortly. He looked at the RPM gage over the lee helm. The chief engineer had squeezed ten more turns out of the antique engines. It would have to do. It meant another knot or two at least. He walked out onto the Bridge Wing. The breeze across the deck created by the ship's forward movement helped to cut down the discomfort of the heavy, humid evening air. The water below glowed as it washed over the bow and down the length of the hull. It sparkled silvery white as the phosphorous in the sea life shone in the tropical night, one of the more stunning sights at sea—this eerie glow from the agitated water.

From below he heard the music as it drifted up. One of his favorites he mused. The mate rang the ship's bell—two distinct gongs—two bells, 10 p.m. The captain stepped back onto the darkened Pilot House, lit only by the low glow of red lighting over gauges and instruments. He picked up the day's navigational calculations and disappeared into his cabin. He would finish up his log entries and go below to join in with the revelers and relax for a couple of hours.

"Mrs. Ashton, might I have this dance?" asked the immaculately attired and groomed Dutchman.

A girlish giggle came from across the table followed by a quick hand to mouth to stifle it.

"Oh go ahead, dear. Enjoy yourself." Mrs. Blythe, the RAF group captain's wife, had assumed command based upon her husband's seniority. She kept her ladies safe from harm and cohesive as a group. Having their husbands in imminent daily danger and traveling country to country in a circuitous route to Alexandria could be unnerving to these mostly very young women. Thank goodness for the strong hand of Mrs. Blythe. "Go ahead Abby. It will relax you."

"Well, certainly. Yes, Mr. Van Eyck. You are most kind." The smiling woman bounced out of the chair and onto the dance floor with the dapper Dutchman.

"It's times like these that I most miss my late wife." Verdi leaned over the table and spoke directly to ANTIMONY.

"Yes, I do know what you mean, Dr. Verdi. Sometimes it's a bit difficult to deal with." He thought of Alice—sweet, remarkable Alice. He recognized the pain in the physicist's voice. Like himself, the scientist had thrown himself entirely, body and soul, into his work to overcome the pain, the anguish, the bitter memories, and thousands of what ifs. The physicist leaned back in his seat and swayed, his head slightly left, then right to the tune's hypnotic flow. Let it rest, thought ANTIMONY. *Enjoy the moment, enjoy the music, treasure the memories. There is work to be done, but not now.* He let his mind simply drift away.

Like a dagger thrust between the shoulder blades of the unsuspecting sentry, the intruder thrust upon the scene. ANTIMONY'S eyes shot open. He had been half asleep dreamily following the rhythm. He bolted up in his chair as if an electric shock had passed through his body, eyes searching the Saloon. *What is different? Anyone who had not been there before?* His eyes bounced from table to table, from couple to couple. No one new appeared in the crowd—only the gently swaying dancers on the floor and the relaxed patrons at each table—everyone all smiles and laughs as it had been before. The feeling of danger grew stronger like the storm surge racing over the unprotected beach in a savage assault. ANTIMONY had not felt the sense of danger like this in days. He stood up, a little too quickly, perhaps. The jaunty Tommy Dorsey tune continued on. The feeling became directional. He felt the malignant presence elsewhere—not in the Saloon, but elsewhere. He scanned the room again. *Who is missing? Who has left?* His hands trembled. *Damn it!* He had been sloppy. He had let his mind drift off, mesmerized by the music. He had escaped the *Zamzam* for only a few minutes and it had cost him. He had squandered an advantage. He had let the enemy through the observation net and that enemy now took some action somewhere else on the ship. *Where is Van Eyck? Where is Villenueve?* Both had temporarily taken a break from the revelry while he daydreamed. *Damn it to Bloody Hell! Move! Now! Regain the advantage! Assess the situation! Make a plan! Move! Now!* "If you gentlemen will excuse me, I need to take a little breather." *Follow the lead. Follow the intuition.* He exited the Saloon onto deck. *No, not here—only the couple by the rail in deep conversation. Inside the ship. Cabins!* Of course, the enemy lurked in the cabins looking for the half hidden or careless clue. *Must get to the cabins!* ANTIMONY headed topside up the ladder to the First Class cabins. As he reached the dimly lit passageway, he heard a click, a distant metallic click—the sound of a cabin door shutting. He froze. *Do not surprise an intruder.* ANTIMONY lightly stepped to the bulkhead and squeezed up against the cold, flat metal. His right hand inched down towards the jacket pocket, careful not to make a telltale sound. Fingers closed around the Beretta. It slowly came up out of the pocket. He brought the gun up to a poised position ready for any action.

Every instinct told him that his man stood only a few feet away and vulnerable to discovery. ANTIMONY'S heart pounded. Blood surged through his temples, his mouth as dry as chalk. Ever so slowly, he edged towards the angle in the bulkhead, inch by inch. He heard the faint noises of the man in the passageway. It seemed like hours, but only a matter of a few seconds passed between the time he heard the click of the door latch closing shut and the time that his left eye emerged from beyond the edge of the bulkhead. Though only a fraction of a second, his brain registered everything before his head popped back out of sight. He had seen the man's head turning in his direction, no doubt to ensure a clear passageway for his escape. ANTIMONY inched closer to the bulkhead edge, Beretta poised, ready for action. His breathing came shallow with open mouth slowly taking in and exhaling air to prevent any noises from the nose. He heard footsteps going down the passageway towards the opposite end away from him. *Should he follow? No.* He didn't want to alert the enemy that he had been seen, and the man might well be lying in ambush somewhere along the corridor. It is ever so easy to make the sound of shoes receding away, then creep back on tiptoe to wait in ambush. *No, he had seen enough for one evening.* With his own cabin directly across the passageway from Verdi's where the intruder had been, it would be best to play the game and stroll down the passageway to his own room.

ANTIMONY stepped out into the passageway. The pistol safely back in his jacket pocket. His eyes strained to see the other end of the dimly lit corridor. He saw no one. He whistled the first tune that came to mind—"When Johnny Comes Marching Home Again." As he approached his own cabin, he reached into a trouser pocket and jangled keys, perhaps louder than called for. Looking both ways, he inserted the key into the lock, which snapped open with a loud metallic click. Stepping in and stopping the whistling, he strode over to the wash basin, turned on the water, then positioned himself behind the door, ready to pounce on the intruder should he come through the unlocked door. ANTIMONY waited for several moments. Apparently the man had not been aware of his presence after all. He turned off the running water. As an old sailor, used to times when freshwater usage had been limited, it galled him to have wasted several gallons of the precious stuff, but it had been for a higher purpose.

He stepped back out into the passageway, pulled the door shut and waited for a moment. Hearing only the low humming of the electrical generators, he turned and walked in the direction of the intruder's retreat several minutes earlier. The passageway exited onto the deck. The intruder had disappeared. He returned to the passageway where he now became the intruder, the interloper. He fumbled in his pocket. Out came what appeared to be a nail file, very thin, very delicate, but in reality, no such thing. Looking both ways to ensure privacy, he stepped up to Verdi's cabin door, inserted the pick and in less than five seconds, the lock surrendered to the burglar's tool.

Signs of a search appeared, but only to the trained observer looking for the slightly out of place item. The man had been thorough, but even the best can leave a visible clue. In the clothes closet, a pair of shoes had been moved. A little saliva on the thumb pressed to the deck showed the area of dust and no dust where a pair of shoes had just been. In his haste, the intruder had failed to mentally mark where the shoes should have been replaced. *So our man is not at all invincible.* ANTIMONY already suspected this, but it reassured him to see the evidence. Until this point, the enemy had been very good and extremely efficient save only the matchbox error. ANTIMONY presumed that the man had merely searched for information about his mark hoping to find documents or other clues as to the real mission of Dr. Enrico Verdi. At any rate, ANTIMONY concluded the man had found nothing since no evidence or documentation existed. The chase would continue.

As he exited the cabin, his eyes fell on a photograph on the bureau. He felt as if a knife went through his heart. *Had the German seen this? If he had, had its significance registered?* The silver frame on the bureau held a photograph of a young, exceptionally attractive smiling young woman with Northern Italian features. The inscription at the bottom of the photograph read in a very crisp but feminine handwriting: "To Papa, from your loving daughter Angela, Milan, Christmas, 1940."—Verdi's daughter, at least three months earlier and most likely still squarely in the middle of Fascist Europe. *Could she now be a prisoner in Milan? Probably not. Political prisoners generally did not send photographs to their families abroad, so most likely still at school, perhaps at the University.* He now faced an unforeseen complication. It now became doubly imperative that the German be identified and intercepted quickly upon docking in Cape Town. Perhaps the men back in London had built an elaborate scheme to fool the man into believing he had actually seen the mythical weapons facility. Then again, maybe they would simply make him disappear. Chances are he might be a candidate for DOUBLE CROSS to serve as a double agent. ANTIMONY doubted this. His senses, his intuition, his observations told him that this man should not be toyed with. No, the way to deal with this German seemed clear-cut—take him out of the game permanently.

He turned off the overhead light and put his ear to the door. Hearing no movement in the corridor, he carefully opened the door a crack and listened again. Still nothing. In a moment, he slipped out into the passageway and made his way back to the Saloon. He glanced down at his watch. Gone only ten minutes, a quick head call would be his reasonable excuse. ANTIMONY had retaken the high ground. He had seen his quarry, but had not been seen. Though only a flash, the memory had branded into his senses—that of a man dressed in black something like a priest's garb, but without a clerical collar. ANTIMONY had not seen the face but he had observed the hat pulled well down over the man's head to conceal his face in shadows—a gray hat, a gray Italian fedora.

"Charles, you foolish man. I can't! You know I can't. It's ... it's positively immoral. I'm a married woman. You know that," she protested.

"And I'm a married man," he retorted.

She pursed up her lips in protest.

"Tell me, Mrs. Ashton, when was the last time you saw your husband? No. No, slept with your husband?"

"Six months ago. But what has that to do with anything?" she protested.

"It has everything to do with it. I too have not seen my wife in weeks ... months. The point here is that we are two adults thrust together by this dreadful German war in the middle of the ocean on this filthy, little ship. We have needs, Abby, basic human needs. Who knows, we may never see our spouses again."

Her resistance crumbled in the well-oiled, soothing words of the charming Dutchman. Married for only three months when the RAF snatched up her husband and sent him off to North Africa, it simply could not be more unfair. *Why should she have to suffer so and the moon is ever so lovely tonight.* The first wall breached, Van Eyck placed his hand on her flat, smooth abdomen. No resistance. He slowly ran his hand up her stomach to her chest and cupped a breast hidden behind layers of cotton cloth. She shivered, but he would not let go of the breast. He squeezed softly at first, then harder and harder, almost to the point of pain. Abby sighed. A glassy look came into her eyes. The second wall tumbled down. The Dutchman had broken through. His smooth speech had broken down her defenses. It had not been difficult. Of all the RAF wives onboard, this one proved the most susceptible to his smarmy charm. In spite of their best efforts, the rowdy ambulancemen had gotten nowhere in their attempts to entice and seduce the wives. By sheer, blind luck, Van Eyck had latched on to the one most likely to succumb. "Shall we take a nightcap in my cabin, Abby?"

"Yes. Oh, yes, yes, let's do." She felt the strong arm on her tiny waist and trembled at the thought of going to this man's cabin. The final wall collapsed, her defenses shattered. Tossing all discretion aside, she gripped the man's hand and squeezed. It felt good. Abby Ashton needed a lot of affection and this charming man gave it to her. They walked aft hand in hand up the ladder to the next deck into the area of First Class cabins.

ANTIMONY entered the double doors leading back into the Saloon where "Woodchoppers Ball" blared. Exhausted but excited and animated jitterbuggers crowded the dance floor in and amongst the tables and chairs, swaying and bouncing in the candlelit, smoky air. As ANTIMONY passed through the doors, a smiling woman grabbed him by the wrist. She pulled him onto the dance floor and bounced wildly arching her back in a deep dip and twirling under his arm. *Why the hell not.* He swung the young lady out to the furthest reach, then curled her back in. Across the room, "Twinkle Toes" Hobgood pranced away with Mrs. Blythe to the Glenn Miller tune "Pennsylvania 6-5000." Even the normally staid Verdi cut a rug with one of the ladies whose exhausted husband had collapsed in a chair, but still had enough energy to applaud his wife's dancing. Even some of the more daring churchmen (with the exception of the Southern Baptists, who had stayed in their cabins) attempted to dance. Unbeknownst to ANTIMONY as he reentered the Saloon, lurking in the shadows of an air intake on deck, stood a lone, quiet figure, who riveted his attention on the couple jostling up the steps and disappearing into the passageway of the starboard side First Class area. The figure wore a black suit with a gray fedora pulled down over his eyes.

CHAPTER 8
A CARELESS MAN

With the next morning, the tropical sun washed into the cabin through the uncovered porthole. Even though still early spring in the Northern Hemisphere, near the Equator, hot and humid weather prevailed. ANTIMONY had sweated all night soaking the sheets with perspiration. He stood up and opened the thick glass porthole covered in crystalline salt particles caked around the rubber gasket separating metal from glass. Corrosion showed through the flaked paint. He had taken great pride in the brightly polished, spic and span appearance of the destroyers in his flotilla. Many of them now lay rusting at the bottom of the Mediterranean, the North Atlantic, or the North Sea. All had given a good account of themselves, though. The commodore had trained them well, and, even though retired before the war, the drilling and pride he had instilled in his men had carried on.

The party had kept him out way past his usual bedtime, dancing and drinking the night away following his encounter with the enemy. His head throbbed and eyes ached, but a deep breath of the fresh sea air pouring through the open porthole smelled wonderful and had an instant curative effect. *Much better. Missed breakfast. No matter. Needed the sleep.* Lunch would be served in a couple of hours—enough time to wash up and take a head clearing, hangover-curing stroll on deck.

In the Dining Saloon, he made certain to sit with Van Eyck and Father Villenueve. Having long since ruled out the veterinarian, it now came down to these two suspects. He studied their every habit, every move, every word, waiting for a telltale error that would give it away. At the same time, he had to be exceedingly cautious. If he observed, so too did the German. His best asset might actually be his age. Who would expect the British Intelligence

Service to send a man of fifty out on a field assignment. His age might be an Achilles heel if a physical confrontation occurred. On the other hand, it represented an *aegis*, his protecting shield that might well forestall detection.

In addition to the priest and the Dutchman, Mrs. Avery sat at the table along with Mrs. Ashton and Dr. and Mrs. Starling. ANTIMONY had noticed something going on between Abby Ashton and Van Eyck—more than simple courtesy. It showed in the way they danced in the Saloon and the inordinate number of hours spent on deck together in the past couple of days. This is what the captain meant when he contemplated the gunpowder and match effect of some twenty-odd young, rowdy ambulance driver volunteers mixed with an equal number of RAF wives, many of whom had not seen their husbands in as much as a year. Explosive? Definitely! Other RAF wives, though, had begun to shun Mrs. Ashton for her indiscretion.

ANTIMONY ordered the veal. A rumor had flown around that while in Baltimore, the chef had gone ashore and bought out the day's production of a local shoe factory, ergo, veal for lunch—really not that bad, just not that good either.

"I think the diamond business must be oh so fascinating," cooed Abby, staring into Van Eyck's eyes.

"Why, yes. Yes it is, Mrs. Ashton. I find it most splendid. I enjoy the travel, especially meeting such fine people."

"What is it, precisely, that you do Mr. Van Eyck?" quizzed Mrs. Avery in an almost threatening, interrogating way.

Van Eyck stumbled. The tone of the questioning threw him. He blushed for only a second—not long—but just enough for ANTIMONY to detect his discomfort with the question. Van Eyck quickly recovered his composure, raised his cup to his lips, blew some steam off and took a sip. ANTIMONY knew this trick—a stall to allow for a brief moment to create a plausible answer to an awkward question. Every person could and would do it every now and again, but why would a man who had supposedly traded in diamonds for several years be thrown by such a straightforward question regardless of the manner of its asking.

"Well, Ma'am," he stammered, "I ... uh ... uh ... go to various diamond mines with which my company has contracts and I select what seem to be the most appropriate stones. We don't purchase anything just because it comes up out of the ground." Van Eyck hit his stride now, fully recovered. If only a cover story, he now remembered his lines. "We have a very specific market in engagement rings and jewelry such as necklaces and earrings, you see, so I am looking only for stones that could be cut nicely for those purposes. When I find what I need, I sign the contract, record the precise measurements, weights, carats, clarity, and so forth and arrange for shipment and payment."

"Oh? Why do you have to record anything, Mr. Van Eyck?" quizzed Abby.

"So that the buggers won't cheat them and send a different stone, my dear," chuckled Dr. Starling, who subsequently received a swift jab in the ribs from Mrs. Starling.

"Just so, Dr. Starling. People can be very greedy, you know."

Several people nodded their heads in agreement.

"Have you been going to South Africa for many years?" inquired Mrs. Avery.

"Well, yes, since 1932. My company is headquartered in Amsterdam, but I work primarily out of Lisbon and New York. The war has had a—how shall I say it—debilitating effect on our business, but the North American market is still very strong."

"The Nazis need diamonds too, *Monsieur*," bitterly interjected the previously silent French priest.

The table became very quiet—no clank of cutlery, no rattle of china. After a few moments, Van Eyck responded. "That is quite true, Father. Business is business in spite of the war."

ANTIMONY buttered a biscuit, placed a small slice of cheddar on top and took a full bite, never taking his eyes off the diamond man. "So, Mr. Van Eyck, have you ever dealt with the Van Guere Company?" A setup! No such company traded in diamonds. ANTIMONY invented the name off the top of his head. He continued crunching on the biscuit. Van Eyck blanched again. ANTIMONY sensed a kill.

"No, I have not. I don't believe I recognize the name. Are you sure that it is a mining company?" Van Eyck had done some homework.

"Actually, no. It's a mineral commodities company. I have occasionally bought some chromium from them. I thought you might have heard of them since they do deal with the mines."

"Mr. Prince, my only concern is the quality and usability of the stones, and, I might add, it has been exceedingly profitable."

"Oh. Just thought I'd ask."

Van Eyck had an "I just beat you" expression—a classic Cheshire cat sort of grin. *Well, he is good if he isn't who he says he is, but he's still the number one candidate* mused ANTIMONY. He pondered how to ask the next question without tipping his hand, but the priest did it for him.

"Have you been selling in Germany, *Monsieur* Van Eyck?" He spat it out with the same invective as before, determined to cast the man at best as a cooperative businessman and at worst, a Nazi collaborator.

"Actually, Father, no, I haven't been to Germany since, oh, 1930 or thereabouts. And no, I personally do not deal with the Germans." Again, the smug expression followed.

The conversation drifted on inanely for several minutes particularly between Van Eyck and Mrs. Avery. ANTIMONY finished lunch and leaned back in his chair to simply observe and listen. All the while, his eyes kept drifting over to Verdi two tables over and involved in an animated discussion with some ambulance drivers. ANTIMONY looked for eyes spending an inordinate amount of time fixed on the physicist. He felt the presence of the demon in the Saloon, but could not tell from which direction. And then, like a gift of manna from heaven, Van Eyck made his fatal error. The smooth-talking Dutch diamond buyer committed a gross error. It all started rather innocuously. Mrs. Avery took out her holder and inserted a cigarette.

"Does anyone mind if I smoke?"

"No, not at all, think I will myself, etc.," came the chorus from around the table.

She stared straight at Van Eyck. ANTIMONY picked up the signals immediately. The sexual tension between Mrs. Avery and Van Eyck had been building despite the giddy presence of Abby Ashton. It almost smoldered as the sensual widow stared down the length of the holder.

"Allow me," Van Eyck volunteered. Reaching into a jacket pocket, he pulled out a fine antique beaten silver lighter probably kept for sentimental rather than functional purposes. It flashed but didn't light. ANTIMONY expected the sparks flying between these two to ignite the cigarette on its own. After several tries, Van Eyck conceded and put the lighter back in his pocket. "I've got some matches somewhere." Mrs. Avery waited patiently while he again fumbled about in his pockets. He pulled out a black enameled matchbox, extracted a match, struck it and held it to the end of the cigarette. As he did so, he held the black enameled box in his right hand. The matchbox with the raised gold lettering read The Hotel Atlantic, Hamburg—very odd for a man who had not been to Germany in several years. ANTIMONY sat motionless in his moment of triumph. *I have you, you bloody Nazi bastard!* Van Eyck had finally made the fatal mistake. ANTIMONY now knew the enemy. He now had the upper hand. In his moment of triumph, ANTIMONY did not notice that other eyes at the table observed the telltale matchbox so carelessly brought aboard by the *Abwehr* man. The ship would berth at Recife the next day. A cable would be sent to New York to a minor British diplomatic office at 6553 Rockefeller Center.

Barely visible beneath a port side boat davit, a figure stood in the shadows of the main deck. Despite the moon and stars in the clean, clear night sky, the dark recesses of the superstructure concealed the figure. Further aft on the deck above, a door opened then closed with a harsh metallic clank. Amber light flooded out onto the deck below. The figure in the shadows thrust itself back against the bulkhead. A steward ambled aft and below, entering into the skin of the ship impervious to the dark presence a few feet forward. The figure slowly moved out from under the boat davit and leaned over the rail. The warm South Atlantic below roiled and foamed around the hull, slicing through the otherwise calm water. The figure looked up and down the length of the ship. From the Saloon, he heard the tinny sound of the ship's orchestra and the rumble of happy conversation intertwined with the music. Aft, all seemed quiet except for a rowdy party in the ship's bar. Satisfied that he had not been seen or heard, the figure silently crept aft to the doorway from where the interloper had just exited. *No, too much light, may be seen.* He gently removed his black-gloved hand from the handle and looked about. *There it is.* Ten feet further aft, almost at the ladder leading down to the main deck below, a service door opened into an unlit corridor and emptied into the passageway he needed. He had scoped out this route earlier in the day. Crouching down low, he moved aft, now within the rear sightline of the lookout on the Bridge Wing. Though the swine probably slept at his post, prudence said do not take the chance of being seen. Reaching the doorway, he placed his hand on the lever and with eyes and ears trained in the art of detection and surveillance, he paused to look and listen. Hearing neither sounds of human movement nor motion of persons strolling about, he pulled down gently on the lever until the doorway gave way and swung open. Inside the corridor, he pressed against the bulkhead.

Slowly, he parted the blackout curtain covering the main passageway. The reddish corridor lighting glowed dimly. He opened the curtains wider and looked up and down the corridor. Like a jaguar after a helpless prey, the figure shot out of the corridor and down the main passageway. On cat's paws, he rapidly made his way to his objective—cabin 10C, portside. The lock easily gave way. Out came a pen light from his jacket pocket. A soft, reddish glow shot out across the room, too faint to be seen from under the door. The search began. In the far corner sat a leather strap bound canvas suitcase. A key padlock threaded between the buckles secured the suitcase from unwanted or casual inspection. The intruder laughed softly. After a visual inspection of the lock—German-made and stamped 1940—he removed a slender, hooked metal tool. *Another careless error, you fool!* He inserted the tool into the keyhole and jiggled. After pausing a moment to listen for unwanted intruders in the passageway, he carefully unbuckled the straps and ran his hand along the suitcase's outer edge feeling for signs of a booby trap. *No hard place, no metallic device, no wires. So far, so good.* He gently pressured the top, feeling for the hard spot that should not be there. *Again, clear.* Pointing the red light at the zipper and lock area, the intruder carefully examined every facet of the hardware. *Nothing.* Apparently the owner felt that the lock represented sufficient protection or that even if rifled, an intruder would find nothing. Not so. The man in black carefully lifted the top of the suitcase and ran his hand in around the edges. A noise. He froze. *Someone in the passageway.* He tensed, ready to spring out at anyone disturbing his burglary. The interloper passed by the door—staggered really—to a cabin further aft. First came the noise of a key being inserted in the lock followed by an alcoholic belch as the cabin door swung open. The intruder smiled. *Dead drunk, not a threat.* The hand ran around the edge of the violated suitcase. He first felt the grip, cold and rough against his finger. Under a folded shirt, he closed his fingers around the cold, hard grip of a pistol and pulled it out. The intruder shook his head. *Walther service pistol, latest model, standard Wehrmacht issue.*

"You are very careless, Mr. Van Eyck. It will be the death of you yet," the intruder hissed softly under his breath. He popped out a fully-loaded clip, then shoved it back in and replaced the weapon under the neatly pressed shirt. With nothing else of interest in the suitcase, he realigned the clothes, locked and buckled it, leaving no sign of the intrusion. A fifteen-minute search of the space revealed nothing of interest. It would appear to be the cabin of a Dutch businessman traveling to South Africa until he got to the small bureau up against the rear bulkhead. There, in a pewter frame displayed in the middle of the bureau with a Belgian lace doily underneath, sat a photograph of a nice, clean, neat middle class family with the well-dressed, well-appointed happy Dutch wife in a crisp summer dress and two smiling, blond-haired children—a boy about ten and an adorable six-year-old heartbreaker of a little girl dressed in a sailor suit. Towering over all of this domestic bliss stood Van Eyck smiling broadly. In the background, the Eiffel Tower loomed over their heads. At the bottom of the photograph, the legend read in Dutch, "Paris, Summer 1939." What had drawn his attention to this pleasant family holiday photo displayed rather too obviously atop the lace and in the middle of the bureau as if meant to attract attention? He examined the photo carefully, running the red light up and down. *Something else here. Something not quite right. What is it? Yes, there it is.* In the background, among a group of vehicles behind a Paris taxi cab, sat a truck—a military truck, a German military truck. The intruder shook his head in amazement. The *Abwehr* man should find new employment, perhaps a tour of duty in northern Norway would help. He replaced the faulty photograph on the bureau and tiptoed over to the door where he ran his light up and around the frame and across the door jam. As careless as this German had proven, the intruder could not take any chances that the door had been rigged to indicate unwanted entry. As he suspected, he found nothing. Apparently, Van Eyck felt that his cover would be sufficient.

A noise came from the passageway—a female voice, low and throaty. The intruder froze. Moments later came a lower pitched man's voice, slurring with alcoholic stupor. *Van Eyck!* The intruder sprang backwards. He looked to his left. *The closet!* He reached it just as the key rattled in the lock.

"Shhh, you'll let everyone know what we're about. Shhh!"

"Yes, madam," came the syrupy response.

The intruder quickly, but quietly, pulled the louvered door shut. Light spilled over from the passageway as the cabin door opened, then closed. Though aware of movement in the room, he could not yet see the couple, but heard a shuffle of shoes and the rustle of a starched cotton dress rubbing up against some piece of furniture. The white light pouring into the room temporarily disrupted his night vision. A lamp next to the bed clicked on. The ship rolled only slightly, but in his drunken stupor, Van Eyck pitched forward into the arms of the woman—partly accidental, mostly contrived.

"You are a bad boy, Charles," she whispered seductively.

The intruder's hand inched slowly into his jacket pocket and grasped a long, narrow object, cold and hard. He lifted it out, aimed one end at the deck, and with his thumb, depressed a grooved rise. The six-inch stiletto blade shot out towards the deck with a barely perceptible whoosh followed by a metallic click as the spring-loaded blade locked into place. The intruder stood frozen, motionless, his breathing slow and deliberate, waiting for discovery and the carnage to follow. Van Eyck, the indiscreet German agent and Mrs. Abby Ashton, the adulterous British wife stood locked in a passionate embrace, lips together.

"Oh, Charles, you feel so good."

He only grunted, still reasonably alert in spite of the alcohol. With hands wrapped around her waist, he unbuttoned the carved bone buttons running up the back of her dress. She moaned softly as his fingers ran up and down her spine. She massaged his shoulders. Van Eyck pulled the cloth just off her shoulders, exposing bare flesh. He nibbled and kissed her, starting at the shoulder and working his way up to her ear. Abby wriggled. She inserted her hands in the armholes of his jacket and pushed it off his back, while he continued nibbling at her ear. The jacket fell to the deck below. She pulled the ends of his already askew tie. With her right knee thrust between his legs, she rubbed gently up and down his thigh. Their breathing came heavier now. The air filled with a warm, moist, passionate aroma. He placed his hands on her bare shoulders and gently pushed the remaining cloth over and down her long, slender arms. The dress fell to the deck in a crumple around her feet revealing a black lace camisole, lace garter, and panties with sheer silk hose recently purchased in New York. He leaned back as Abby stepped forward out of the pile of cloth and out of her pumps. He reached up under the camisole and popped the snap of her brassiere. Abby cooed softly as the bra dropped off her shoulders onto the deck. As he ran his hands up the sides of the lingerie, large hands cupped each breast, gingerly massaging her. The nipples grew harder with each pulsating wave of passion flashing through her young, supple body.

From the closet, the intruder saw all of this through the cracks in the louvers. Her young body had not yet felt the ravages of age or childbirth. Abby had firm breasts, a small, muscular waist and full, rounded hips. She reached up and pulled out the hair barrette. Her long, dark brown mane cascaded down her back as she shook her head. She unbuttoned his shirt. He shuddered and ran his hands up and down her back as she swayed to and fro with his motion. When the final shirt button came undone, Van Eyck grabbed her briskly by the arms and pulled her into his chest violently. Her taut nipples pressed into his bare, muscled chest, separated only by the thin, sheer black silk. She gasped as he caressed her neck with his tongue—mad, hot, passionate lust.

The intruder stared at this scene playing out in the soft glow of the table lamp. He gripped the stiletto tighter, knuckles turning white as the blood flowed out under the tension. Finally, he relaxed his grip. As the couple rolled and groaned on the bed, sweat dripping from their naked bodies, the intruder stood, impassionate, feeling only hatred. He hated the German for his carelessness and he hated the woman for her lack of decency. While her husband fought in a life and death struggle in the North African desert, the little trollope rolled in the hay with the handsome, fair-haired "Dutch" diamond merchant. She will get her due soon enough, he thought almost aloud. With the stiletto in his hand, he could be on them in an instant and snuff out their useless lives. *No. Two missing passengers would arouse much too much interest.* Instead, he gingerly released the catch on the weapon. The blade zipped back into the handle with only a slight hiss. *Another day. Another day.*

When the adulterous couple finished their torrid mating dance, and, intoxicated and exhausted, had fallen asleep in each other's arms, the intruder gently pushed open the louver doors and slipped out of the cabin. He encountered no one on the way back to his cabin. He had found what he had set out to find. He had seen more than he cared to see. His course of action now become clear.

CHAPTER 9
DANGEROUS TANGO

Ah, Recife, gateway to Africa. This port city on the easternmost extension of Brazil made for a convenient stepping-off point for vessels headed for Africa. Ships would take on all manner of fuel, supplies, water, food, cargo, and even an occasional extra deckhand (if one is not too particular about the man's background or recent history). And, other attractions beckoned the seafarer facing the long trek across the South Atlantic; sex and entertainment ranged from the casual to the exotic to the bizarre. Girls from all over the world, many of them refugees from the growing German empire in Europe, crowded into the red-light district providing their particular form of entertainment to the lonely seafarers who jammed the filthy streets, ill lit cafés, and bars. Recife also offered quality entertainment. After all, this was South America, the continent of dark, beautiful women, and the tango! Couples from Brazil, Uruguay, and Argentina danced the night away to the seductive, rhythmic, highly stylized, passionate beat of the dance clubs. But Recife had another side considerably less glamorous or seductive. As a hotbed for espionage, Axis agents abounded. Always outnumbered, the British could only afford a token presence. ANTIMONY had now entered unfriendly territory.

As the ship pulled into the crowded harbor, which reeked of fuel oil and human refuse, the last SOE man in the city had just been pulled out and reassigned to Buenos Aires. ANTIMONY stood alone against the enemy juggernaut. He would have to be nimble. The problem lay not only with the Germans and Italians. Many South Americans openly expressed sympathy with the fascist regimes, which provided a fertile recruiting ground for Axis intelligence services. These locals served as the eyes and ears of the *Abwehr*, seeking any information on shipping movements to and from North America. This intelligence went directly to the U-boat Command Center at Lórient in Occupied France where Admiral Karl Doenitz directed the undersea onslaught against the life-sustaining convoys from the New World to the Old. They reported to the German Naval Attaché at the Consulate. Though not professional agents, these casual Brazilian spies could be called upon to provide temporary manpower services to their German employers. Late by a week, the *Zamzam* had been due to arrive on the 1st of April. Even by the 8th, INTREPID still had no relief to send to ANTIMONY. He would be on his own to Cape Town.

As the ship chugged into the harbor and made pier side, a near revolt erupted among many passengers. The poor state of the ship, the bad food, and the surliness of the crew aggravated the passengers, many of whom expressed a keen desire to depart the ship and wait for better transport. Captain Smith pointed out that they might have to wait a month or more for another liner, which could be even worse. *Worse than the Zamzam? Not possible*! Faced with the option of staying aboard or waiting for weeks in the steamy port, most opted to stay aboard. With only ten or twelve day's sailing time to Cape Town, surely they could make that. As the ship tied up, several irate passengers lined the rail, anxious to get off the tub if only for a decent meal ashore. Some of the more frustrated shouted obscenities and jabs at the slowness of the innocent dockworkers.

As two journalists headed for assignments in Africa for *Life* Magazine stood on the pier waiting to board, one of the American passengers shouted: "If you two intend to come aboard this wreck, don't ever say we didn't warn you about what you're in for. The food's lousy, the crew's lousier." He pointed up at the single stack amidships and laughed. Clearly showing through in spite of the layers of rust and caked salt, the letters of the steamship line—MISR—could be seen. "They even call her the Misery Ship!"

Several passengers standing within earshot bellowed in hearty laughter at their joint bonds of discomfort. Not all laughed. ANTIMONY's eyes scanned the dozens of people on the pier, mostly longshoremen shouting in Portuguese with an occasional Spanish speaker shouting back just as rudely. He searched for any sign of recognition or of too much interest. He must know the territory; he must identify friend or foe. He saw neither. He became aware of Hobgood standing behind him doing the same. No words passed between them, only the recognition of professionals on the same side. No one on the pier seemed out of place. No fair-skinned European stood back among the shadows. Not even a darker-skinned Brazilian's eyes strayed a little too much from his immediate task. At the same time relieved and concerned, the acid boiled and tumbled in the pit of his stomach as he stood alone on the enemy's turf. Hobgood leaned over and whispered as he brushed by ANTIMONY. "Looks like the cavalry didn't ride over the hill, buddy. Then again, I don't see any Indians, either. Good luck, squid."

Typical of South and Central America, islands of extravagant wealth, hidden behind stone and brick stockades with decorative and difficult to scale wrought iron grillwork with lawns and gardens immaculately manicured by the sweat of thousands of poor laborers just grateful for a chance to work, dotted the city of Recife. Surrounding each graceful oasis of privilege and influence lived the rest of the population often existing in one-room hovels with tin roofs and cardboard walls. Running water consisted of a communal tap or pump, often hundreds of yards away. In the midst of this contradictory economy sat the New York Club, a favorite watering hole for passing seafarers and passengers weary of shipboard life seeking a change of pace. The legendary New York Club had the best acts in town. Entertainers from all over the continent came to Recife just to headline and make a name for themselves. All types of humanity from the hard-looking, bleary eyed deckhand up to the elegantly tuxedoed and gowned fashionable folk made up the audience. The tango—"The Dance"—ruled the New York Club.

Verdi had tired of the dull routine of *Zamzam* life. So, when a steward told him about the New York Club, he decided to spend the evening off the ship at the club. At dinner, he proposed an adventure ashore. The two Presbyterian missionaries instantly rejected the offer. Uncle Ned Laughinghouse belly laughed and warned him against the perils of such a sinful place. He winked at Verdi. Actually, he bowed out due to a previously scheduled poker game in the bar with some uppity, flabby-mouthed Yankee ambulance drivers. Dr. Starling claimed indigestion and a nervous stomach. Verdi stared down into his soup, shook his head and sympathized completely with the poor man. Even Mr. Prince seemed reluctant. Verdi detected a bit of tension in his voice. *Odd. Well, maybe he's had a bad experience in a nightclub. No matter.* As a young man in Milan, Verdi had often taken in the nightlife. He loved the excitement, the tension, the pure animalistic sexuality of a good dive. Ever since his wife had died of cancer, though, he had lived like a monk in a cloister. The lab and home had defined the boundaries of his existence for the past few years. *Damn it all, he would go to the place even if by himself and damn the naysayers and damn the beggars and damn the thieves and damn the world!* Enrico Verdi had no inkling of just how thrilling his evening at the New York Club would be.

Verdi strolled down the narrow, rough pavement towards the club still damp with puddles from the late afternoon squall. Under his feet, broken and crumbled asphalt crunched. In the shadows of the decaying old buildings lining the street, formless, loose shapes skittered away as he approached and passed by. These people of the night, the refuse of the port of Recife, represented no threat. An attack on a tourist by a street person meant instant retribution from the authorities, and, most likely a savage death while "attempting to escape." The port made a great deal of money from the transiting ships with their passengers and crews; police and municipal authorities shared in this bounty. They would not tolerate attacks on visitors. No, Verdi felt safe as the shadows flitted away.

He turned down a side street, following the steward's instructions. As soon as he did, he heard, or rather sensed, movement ahead—more a rhythmic motion in the air that drew him forward. The dim yellow street lamp threw an oily, yellowish light over the damp pavement. The moist night air made him feel clammy and uncomfortable. As he walked on, he followed the rhythm in the murky, humid air. The ancient gray building, just as the sailor had described it, had a sign dangling from a rusty iron rod—a weathered mahogany slab painted with the image of New York skyscrapers. He recognized the Chrysler building, but everything else represented the artist's conception. He knocked twice and waited. As he did so, an elderly sailor with crusty, gray-streaked beard, and an old slouch cap pulled low over one eye, slipped in between him and the door, nudging him out of the way.

"*Perdona me, Señor,*" blurted out the Spaniard as if a pardon would set right his rudeness.

The door opened. Not worth a row with the old seaman, who scooted into the club fairly pushing the doorman aside as he wobbled in and scurried towards the bar, Verdi stepped back. "A most unpleasant fellow," responded Verdi, shaking his head.

The doorman answered in passable English, "Many pardons, *Señhor.* We cannot always control the quality of our clientele ... but...." He shrugged his shoulders. As Verdi removed his hat and stepped into the doorway, he did not see the one shape that had not flitted away. This shadow stepped out into the street under the pale lamplight and quietly walked away. The shadow wore a black leather jacket and a dark gray fedora.

Inside the club, the air choked with acrid smoke and the sweetness of heavy perfume, Verdi waited by the hatcheck stand while his eyes adjusted to the place. The nightclub with seating for two hundred or so patrons, belied the shabby exterior. Through the haze, he saw the stage below in the shape of a half moon with a parquet mahogany dance floor. Behind the stage, with bright scarlet curtains on either side for the performers to emerge from and exit to, stood the bandstand. A black trumpet player, beads of sweat welling up on his crinkled brow, belted out his "ride" of the Tommy Dorsey tune. The rest of the house band, mostly black Americans, swayed gently as they punched out the light, dancing rhythm of the swing tune. *Good to hear this.* These expatriate American musicians played their hearts out in this smoky Brazilian nightclub. Glad he had come, he passed his hat to the bright-eyed teenager manning the hat check booth. After a few moments, just as the trumpeter finished his solo to the vocal applause of his fellow musicians, the hostess approached. Pretty, with an air of casual sensuality about her, she appeared to be of mixed blood, probably from the islands. She smiled and nodded. In Portuguese, she must have said, "This way, please." At any rate, Verdi followed her and took his seat at a small table next to the dance floor. The band flowed to the steady rhythm of a *Bossa Nova*.

Outside in the street, two men, both larger than the usual Brazilian and rough looking, emerged from behind the building into which the gray fedora had disappeared. Their shoulders sloped down and both held their heads low as if they did not wish to be recognized. They whispered to each other in low, guttural Portuguese. They approached the door of the club. As one knocked, the other looked left, then right, noting that no one saw them enter. They stepped into the club leaving the dark street empty. The orchestra finished the Latin number. The master of ceremonies, flamboyant with a fleshy grin too large for his face, announced the next act—a tango by the club's headliners for that week. The two men sat down at a table several feet from Verdi's. Having a whale of a good time, he did not notice them.

"Ladies and Gentlemen, now appearing for the first time in any club in Recife, from Buenos Aires, the Prince and Princess of the Tango—Manuel and Carmen!"

The audience burst into a rabid applause. Many had come just to see the couple perform. Many had come several times. The local press described the act as devastatingly great. A bolt of light stabbed out of the darkness overhead. The tight beam of amber light caught two heads together, expressions frozen, jaws locked in defiance. Carmen's head tossed back, chin in the air creating a stone cold expression of arrogance. Manuel stared at her icily, light flashing off his oiled, coal black hair. They burned red hot with passion and anger as if thunderbolts would flash from those eyes at any second. Savage, machismo—the tango!

The piano player counted off the downbeat. With a jerk of her shoulders, Carmen whipped about, facing her partner. The sexual energy between them crackled. Manuel whirled her around and thrust his arm forward carrying hers with him. She jerked her head around and their eyes met, those blazing, passionate eyes. The spotlight opened wide to capture their entire forms. Feet moved in precise, practiced patterns. The light had gone from amber to hot white. The audience froze, entranced by the dynamic energy moving rhythmically across the half-moon stage. Verdi's eyes never left her face. Manuel flung her violently. She extended to her full body length, head thrown back, her dark hair just touching the floor. And then just as violently, but gracefully, he pulled her back in with a spin, locked into his muscular arms—a dance of domination and lust. The light changed to scarlet red. Long, thin fingers clutched his waist as they side-stepped downstage, pivoted and changed direction, teeth clenched in ecstatic animal sexuality. The rhythm pounded to the point that Verdi could sense no other sound— driving, moving, embracing, entrancing. His eyes moved away from her face and down the long graceful curve of her back, past her taut, slim hips to her slender, muscular legs. Manuel twirled Carmen again as they began a series of precisely timed, intricate steps. And too soon, it ended. Carmen's arm lolled over gracefully, her back arched, Manuel's arm around her waist and eyes locked together. A cheer erupted from the audience as patrons leapt to their feet clapping and whistling. Verdi shot out of his seat joining in the tumultuous applause. The couple, after holding their finale pose for several seconds, twirled about, and, facing the audience, hand in hand, took a long low bow. Verdi noticed that both smiled for the first time. It had been a wonderful performance and they knew it. The audience roared on and on and on. Verdi finally sat down.

"Dr. Verdi? Dr. Verdi?"

He looked up and over his shoulder away from the dance floor and into the faces of the two rough-looking Brazilians.

"Dr. Verdi? Dr. Enrico Verdi from Chicago, USA?"

Verdi nodded in acknowledgement. These men with no smiles did not impart a good feeling to the scientist.

"Dr. Verdi," The first man fumbled in his coat pocket and extracted a worn leather case, "I am Inspector Cabrillo of the Recife Police." He flipped open the leather case revealing a tarnished silver badge and yellowed cardboard identity card. "We regret to disturb your entertainment, but there is an emergency, *Señhor.*"

What could possibly be the emergency and what could have sent these two policemen looking for him? "What kind of emergency, Inspector?"

The two men hovered over him menacingly as if to say come with us and do not argue. The second man remained silent with no expression. "I do not know, *Señhor.* The captain of your ship—the *Zamzam*—rang us up and requested that we escort you back to the ship. It is some emergency. He did not say what it is, but he is very concerned. Please, *Señhor,* our car is just outside." The Inspector stepped aside so as to allow Verdi to slide his chair out.

What kind of emergency could possibly require his immediate presence unless the captain had received a telegram? Yes, perhaps a wire from Chicago. Something must be very wrong. He slid his chair back. "Yes, of course, Inspector. Let's go immediately."

He slid his chair back under the table. The orchestra had struck up another swing tune. As he stood by the hatcheck stand while the young lady searched for his brown homburg, the second man, clearly nervous, looked from side to side, eyes darting about the floor of the nightclub. Verdi thanked the girl and dropped a quarter into her tip plate. She grinned and thanked him. He nodded as he placed the hat on his head and turned towards the door. Out in the dimly lit, murky street, the policeman pointed towards an alleyway. This is very odd, thought Verdi. *Why wouldn't the police simply park in front of the club? Why park in an alley? This is very strange.* He walked across the street and entered the alley, sandwiched between the overtly polite Inspector and the nervous companion. A few yards inside the alley, just visible in the streetlight sat a Daimler sedan. They approached the front right door. Cabrillo opened the door for Verdi as the second man hurriedly moved towards the rear of the vehicle, his right hand inside his jacket.

This is just not right thought Verdi. *Just not right.* He hesitated. "Excuse me. May I see your badge again Inspector and the other policeman's as well?"

The man's face went blank—totally expressionless. After a moment, his mouth moved, but before he could say a word, the nervous man jumped to the door and jerked out a pistol, waving it in the air. "Please, *Señhor.* You should do as you are told. Sit in the car." His bravado, even combined with the waving of the gun, could not mask the tension in his voice and the anticipation of an attack at any moment. He did well to worry.

The lunging figure's shoulder caught the Inspector in the solar plexus. With a violent explosion of air from his lungs as he fell backwards against the car, the Inspector crumpled to the pavement. His hands flew up grasping his windless chest, face puckered in pain, eyeballs bulging. The gunman attempted to bring his weapon to bear on the charging assailant. Too late! The man pushed the arm with the gun into the car's roof as hand and weapon flailed inches above the passenger's seat. The assailant's left hand shot out and into the throat of the gunman, fingers clawing into the soft flesh. The policeman gagged. As he tried to bring the weapon down for another try at a shot, the attacker reached out with his left hand and grasped the door handle. He slammed the door hard against the gunman's forearm. The man screamed in agony as the force of the door snapped his arm. Fingers shot out as they flexed while the pistol fell to the seat, bounced, and tumbled onto the floorboard. The attacker, hunched low to achieve maximum leverage, yanked the door open a few inches and with all his weight behind him, slammed the door again, hard against the disarmed man's broken arm, who screamed in fearful pain and clutched his left shoulder with his free right hand.

Verdi had stepped back away from the car in shocked disbelief. *What is happening here?* He did not understand. He wanted to run and get as far away from these crazy people as possible, but something froze him where he stood. Something screamed in his subconscious mind—*stay put. This attacker is your friend. Do not run. There is danger in flight.*

The Inspector recovered enough to stand though still out of breath. He staggered forward. The assailant, enjoying the fruits of his surprise, lunged out with his left foot, but slowly, as if he were an older man. Not the movements of youth, thought Verdi. Perfectly on target, the leather boot toe caught the Brazilian square in the crotch. Trying to howl in pain, he opened his mouth, eyes jammed shut in agony, but no sound came out. He had no air to race, screaming across the vocal cords into the night mist—only deep, excruciating pain from his ravaged testicles. With nothing else to do, he fell forward, hands clutching his crotch. As the Inspector pitched forward, the attacker struck him across the back of the neck, a hard, merciless martial arts blow. The prostrate man collapsed into a heap onto the wet pavement. Not dead, only unconscious, and by the time he awoke, his unbearable pain would have passed. He would feel the results for days. The attacker now visibly slowed. His breath came hard and heaving with exertion. The gunman sobbed with the agony of his shattered forearm. He managed to pry the door open, away from his ravaged arm. The assailant's right hand jabbed out catching the man in the abdomen. He lurched forward and fell prostrate across the body of his companion. The attacker stretched his arms across the roof of the car for support, gasping for breath from the exertion. After a few breaths, he turned and looked square into Verdi's face. *It's him! The Spanish sailor. The rude Spanish sailor from the New York Club. What is happening here?* The bearded man reached into the car and across the front seat. He grasped the car keys and yanked them out. With his right hand, he fumbled around on the passenger side floorboard until he felt the hard, cold metal of the gun. He raised up, slid the gun into his belt and dropped the keys into his duffel coat pocket.

"Who the hell are you?" Verdi demanded.

"A friend, Sir," replied the bearded sailor in an undisguised, very King's English accent. "Shall we be off?" He pointed back down the alley towards the pier area and the *Zamzam*.

A mile away, at a different pier, a small motor launch bobbed gently at the quay. Its shabby appearance belied the finely tuned engine plant below. Designed for speed, the decrepit appearance merely served as camouflage. The man in the gray fedora paced anxiously on the stone quay wall alternately looking at his watch and at the road leading on to the docks. Several miles off the coast in international waters, loitered the Swedish oceanographic research vessel, the *Printz Alexander*. Though she flew the yellow cross on sky blue neutral flag of Sweden, her crew consisted of German *Kriegsmarine* sailors. Posing as an oceanographic research vessel, she plied the coast of South America collecting data on British shipping movements in the South Atlantic. She also had a darker side. At night, out of the sight of passing vessels, sleek, black-hulled U-boats would surface near her and tie alongside. Going to and from the neutral ship would be all sorts of agents operating in Latin America. These invisible men would either be smuggled ashore during one of the rare port visits or brought in by one of the fast boats like the one presently bobbing at the quay with its nervous driver and impatient passenger. The *Printz Alexander* had received a wireless message from the German Naval Attaché in Recife to proceed to the usual rendezvous point, some fifteen nautical miles southeast of the port, off the normal shipping lines. The captain had complied and now nervously circled slowly around the rendezvous area. He had been ordered to expect two passengers for transfer to a U-boat. No small boat appeared. He would remain on station for only another two hours. Interestingly, the orders came not from the Naval Staff or the *Abwehr*, rather from *SS* Headquarters.

"*Señhor*, I do not like this. Something has happened. I feel it here." He jabbed his thumb into his belly. "Your men are in trouble. We should leave now."

The lightning bolt stare from the tall man in the gray fedora froze the Brazilian boat driver to the deck of the speedboat. Without a word, the man drew out a Luger from his waistband and aimed it directly between the eyes of the nervous sailor. The man in the boat slowly raised his arms—no sudden motions.

"*Herr* da Gama, the *Führer's* government pays you a premium price for your services. I should not want you to lose your contract and your business, through some, shall we say, accident."

The Brazilian swallowed hard. *Jesus, this crazy Nazi is insane! Play along with him. Dear God don't let him shoot. Hail Mary, full of Grace ... .* "No,

Señhor. I should not wish for that. We shall stay as long as you desire. I am always grateful for the business of the great and grand Third *Reich*."

The man in the fedora lowered the gun and placed it back in the small of his back. He looked again at his watch. The sniveling Brazilian could be right, though. Something had indeed gone wrong. He would wait another ten minutes, then go back to the Club. Perhaps they had not yet made their move. He had used the two most reliable men available. Then again, perhaps as he suspected, an Englishman on board whom he had not yet identified, had successfully scotched the kidnapping.

The two men darted between buildings, zigzagging their way down to the piers. As they made their way, street by street, cautious of ambush or chase, Verdi sensed a recognition. He knew, or at least recognized a certain familiarity about this old sailor, who had prevented his kidnapping. The bearded man carried the captured gun in his right hand as he carefully checked and double-checked each corner before allowing the scientist to proceed. After several minutes of this game, they rounded the final building. There, in the distance, under the glare of the port lights, sat the *Zamzam* swaying in a slight swell. The man placed his hand on Verdi's chest and pushed him back into an alcove formed by several pallets. Verdi crouched down. The man emerged from the alcove and carefully checked all of the sight lines leading to and from the ship and their position. After a couple of minutes, he returned to the back of the cargo area, placed the gun on the cobblestone and removed the dirty smock. Amazingly, underneath, he wore a clean, crisply starched white shirt, only slightly wrinkled from the violent encounter in the alleyway minutes earlier. He even wore a blue silk foulard necktie. Very odd thought Verdi. He removed the floppy Basque cap to reveal a full head of light brown hair flecked with gray around the temples. With a pull and a tearing sound, the streaked brown beard tore away from his face, glycerin still hanging in patches from his smoothly shaved face. Verdi stared straight into the man's face.

"Mr. Prince? What the devil is going on here and who the hell were those two?"

ANTIMONY returned to his flat, unaccented American voice. "I fear, Dr. Verdi, that there are forces at work here beyond what I had anticipated. Let me assure you that I am your friend and protector. That is all you need to know for now. But we must be exceedingly cautious from here on. They have failed this time. They will be relentless."

"Germans," he spat out in a low whisper.

ANTIMONY nodded. "And you must know why they are interested in you. Though I must admit, I suspected for observation only. It would appear to be for a far more sinister reason."

"I believe you Mr. Prince. But, if that is their intent, would it not be more prudent to leave the ship and fly back to the States? What if they have an agent on board?"

"It isn't and they do."

The scientist looked puzzled. ANTIMONY held up his hand for silence. They heard the noisy singing of a pair of drunken ambulance drivers weaving their way back to the ship. Once out of earshot, ANTIMONY lowered his hand.

"I considered that, but the next flight doesn't leave until day after tomorrow. This is the German's turf. They have agents and hired guns everywhere. I doubt we would even be allowed on a plane given their failure this evening. No, the safest place for us is on that disgrace of a ship far out to sea. As for an agent, there is one onboard. Not to worry. I know who he is. I don't think he knows me, however. Diligence is our watchword."

Verdi nodded in acknowledgement.

"Go first. We must not be seen together. Report the incident to the officer of the watch, but say only that a local man, who left immediately after, disrupted the kidnap attempt and that you fled back to the ship straightaway. Say no more about the incident and go immediately to your cabin. I shall knock six times, three sets of twos. Do not let anyone else in. Do you understand?"

"Yes."

"Right, then. Off with you."

Verdi had been gone by almost an hour and made his report to the second mate. The minutes dragged on endlessly as ANTIMONY waited in the shadows on the pier. *Discipline. Must be disciplined. Give the ruse its due. Give him the hour.*

ANTIMONY staggered up the brow appearing tipsy. The sailor on watch jumped to attention, a metal clipboard in his hand. ANTIMONY leered at him drunkenly, although completely sober. The man's white hat with the MISR Line cap badge sat askew, almost falling off his head. *You sod. Had this been my ship I would have had your pay stopped and you would have been brought to Captain's Mast for bloody dereliction of duty.* Obviously, the man had been asleep on watch awakened only by the clanging of heavy footfalls on the metal steps of the accommodation ladder. Then, he reconsidered. Captain Smith had to work with the men the company sent him. *This is not a smart Royal Navy warship with top flight, proud, professional sailors.* No, he couldn't be too harsh. Just getting the thing underway and sailing from port to port had to be a struggle.

"Your name, please, Sir?"

"Mr. Prince of New York, son." He slurred the words "New York."

"Very good, Sir. I am most pleased to see you have had a wonderful night on the town. Please be careful in going to your cabin. Goodnight, Sir," replied the overly polite, but slovenly sailor.

"Damned right. I had a great time," mumbled ANTIMONY as he staggered away towards First Class. After fumbling for a few seconds, he pulled the room key from his pocket. In fact, he listened for any sign of pursuit or intrusion. The delay with the keys allowed time for reconnaissance without giving away his true intention. After a few seconds and satisfied that no one followed or watched, he hurried over to Verdi's cabin and knocked using the prearranged code. The door swung open.

"And just who in the name of Mary, Joseph and the Saints are you?" demanded Verdi.

The shock of the last two hours had abated. He had blindly followed the man's orders. Confused and disoriented, but now lucid again, a fiery Italian anger burned in his deep set, dark eyes. Brow flush, his Latin temper boiled over the rough treatment. ANTIMONY, his savior, became the target of his wrath. About to speak again, his mouth opened.

"Please sit down, Dr. Verdi," demanded ANTIMONY in a tone more an order than a request, as he motioned to the writing table by the porthole. The scientist shut his gaping mouth and plopped down in the chair. ANTIMONY looked him directly in the eyes, the glare of the lamp flashing across his hard set eyes.

"You are in grave danger, Sir."

"I say it again. Who are you?" the physicist asked in a more sedate tone.

"I am a friend. Your guardian angel if you will."

The scientist mulled the response pensively. Several seconds passed. Both men, one sitting on the edge of the chair, the other hovering over him, stared at each other, studying the other's face.

"I should have suspected something like this. Are you FBI or are you British Intelligence, Mr. Prince?"

"That's not important, Dr. Verdi. I am a friend, and I'm going to get you safely to Cape Town."

"I see," replied the scientist curtly.

Another long pause set in. *Damn it all, the man needed to know at least something. If he was going into danger, at least let him know why. A genius and a noted scholar as well as research scientist, his agile mind could grasp the intricacies of the previous few days' events. And, he would appreciate what he could not be told.* It may be a mistake, but at this moment it seemed to be the right thing to do. ANTIMONY sat down on the edge of the bed after first putting an ear to the door to check for eavesdroppers.

"Dr. Verdi, I am going to tell you as much as I think prudent. You have a right to know at least some of the details since your life is at risk. Let me first state that the original threat assessment was that the Germans were only interested in following you. My mission is to watch over you and ensure your safety. I see by tonight's actions that the threat scenario has changed and not in our favor."

"You'd best fill me in, Mr. Prince."

For the next few minutes, in a voice barely above a whisper, ANTIMONY told the scientist as much as he should prudently know. He told him about the German *Abwehr* agent, about the bogus research facility and so forth. He didn't reveal the more sensitive aspects of the case. Should Verdi be interrogated, he must not be able to compromise anything of value.

"Who is this German, Mr. Prince? Do you know?"

"Yes. It's Charles Van Eyck."

"The Dutch diamond buyer? I'd never have guessed it. Are you certain of this? When did you find out?"

"Quite certain. I have suspected him for some time. He confirmed it himself yesterday with a box of matches."

The scientist looked puzzled.

"Not to worry. I'll explain it someday. He is the man. Stay away from him. And never, ever, leave the ship again until I give you the word. Never go out on deck at night. Stay in your cabin with the door locked at all times except when you can be in a crowd of people. Any questions?"

"No, it's all perfectly clear."

ANTIMONY reached into his pocket and pulled out the Beretta. He held it up. The lamplight glinted off the steel metal. Verdi cringed.

"Do you know how to use one of these?"

"I had hoped to have left that behind in Italy."

"I fear not, Doctor. It's a cruel world. You have to accept that," he admonished as he handed the gun over.

"Yes, Mr. Prince. I know how to use one. I spent two years on the Austrian Front in the last madness. I am prepared to use it."

"Excellent. Keep it hidden, but with you at all times. That is important. By the way," he asked as he stood, "do you have a daughter in Milan?"

"How did you know that? Oh yes. It is your business to know that. Yes, I do. Little Angela. Well, not so little, now. She's twenty-two, but you probably already knew that. Yes, she is in Milan at the University finishing a postgraduate degree in Art History. She will be home to Chicago in June about the time I am scheduled to return."

"Cable her in the morning before we sail. She may not be safe. Have her get to the States immediately, do you understand?"

"She won't like that."

"It can't be helped. It may already be too late."

His face, formerly flushed with anger, now blanched white with fear—fear not for his own safety, but for his daughter's, his innocent, only child. "I shall."

ANTIMONY stood for a moment scanning the brilliant physicist, the reason for his being here and for his current dilemma. *He will hold up. He will make it. The enemy is known.*

"I should get back to my cabin. In the morning, I want you to make a full report to the captain, but say you were assaulted but unharmed and do not wish to press the issue with the local authorities."

"Won't Van Eyck try again?"

"Quite likely. That can't be helped now. But he will stay underground. He knows you didn't actually see him and that he is still not found out. Let's play him along a bit further." ANTIMONY put a hand on the door knob, paused, then turned.

"If he is a known threat, then why not—how do you put it—dispose of him or have him arrested?"

"Because to do so, Doctor, runs the risk of compromising our sources. And, besides, we have big plans for Mr. Van Eyck. Very big plans."

The scientist nodded as ANTIMONY opened the door and departed.

ANTIMONY collapsed on his bed. He had passed the first crisis. He had won a battle. He must be stronger yet. More battles would come—many, many more. He closed his eyes.

CHAPTER 10
BULL'S EYE

Zamzam ran at eight knots. The mild vibration in the upper superstructure didn't concern Smith as he sat in his chair in the Pilot House. Sipping a lukewarm cup of tea, he savored the warm, aromatic brew, flavored with dark, sticky brown sugar obtained on a port visit to Haiti months earlier—excellent sugar but the last of it, worse luck. Granted, not the normal British habit of white sugar and milk with his tea, but he had acquired a taste for the dark brown kind in the islands. The Boatswain's Mate rang the ship's bell six times. Smith always felt a sense of well-being on hearing that reassuring metal sound. He looked at his watch. *Right on time.* He would stay in the Pilot House until 1845 then have a late dinner with several missionaries. He took another sip of tea and settled back in his chair. The South Atlantic sun dropped beneath the horizon casting an orange-red glow—his favorite time at sea. The serenity relaxed him, but this being wartime, the ship's High Frequency antenna hummed.

Down in the Wireless Room, Senior Wireless Operator Anwar copied the merchant broadcast channels. His receiver spat out a rapid series of electric dots and dashes with an irritating interference-induced, noisy background hum. He had been ordered to listen on this particular frequency by the captain every evening from 2200 to 2230 Greenwich Mean Time, in port or out. A damned nuisance, but with his cushy job as Senior Wireless Operator, he really couldn't complain. Anwar tuned his receiver. *Ah, there it is.* Though not supposed to know about this channel, he wasn't stupid. He had listened to it before, this back-channel used by the Royal Navy for "special maritime operations receive only channel;" no one responded. The RN operators transmitted "in the blind," hoping that the designated station would pick it up. The dits and dahs reverberated off of the bare metal bulkheads of the tiny

Wireless Room, mostly unintelligible coded drivel, he thought, but then, he only had to listen for his call sign, night after boring night.

Zamzam rolled gently in the South Atlantic swells as Anwar daydreamed, remembering the sweet little Brazilian girl from the night before. He always enjoyed Recife. He laughed, thinking about the steward he had to roust out of a bordello that morning so the ship could sail. *God how the captain exploded. Bad enough to be already a week delayed, but to have a late sailing because a steward couldn't get himself . . . . What was that?*

The channel had been hot for fifteen minutes when the signal arrived. Anwar bolted upright in his chair. *Again. There it is!* He grabbed the message pad and a pencil. It came again amongst the gobbledygook of meaningless characters continually keyed in the same sequence to confuse the inevitable German listeners. After the fifth time, there followed a series of characters. To the wireless operator, they meant nothing. To the captain, they meant everything. First came the four letters—A ... W ... S ... T—repeated five times with an interval then repeated three more times followed by a series of numbers and then repeated three additional times. This redundancy ensured that a whole message had a chance of receipt even in the worst of electromagnetic conditions. He carefully jotted down each character and then checked and double-checked his notes. *Reception loud and clear tonight. No need to repeat it, mates.* He clutched the telephone, already set for the Pilot House, and whirled the crank around twice. The sudden double blast of bells startled everyone as the mate picked up the handset.

"Pilot House, Aye." After a moment or so, he replaced the handset and turned to the old man. "Captain, the wireless operator requests your presence in the Wireless Room. He says it is most urgent that you come down now."

Smith nodded and slid out of his chair. The china cup rattled as he handed it to the mate. His heart raced. He expected this urgent signal. As he entered the Wireless Room, Anwar bolted up from his chair almost knocking it over in his excitement.

"Captain, a most urgent message has come in just as you instructed me," Anwar gushed.

"Good work. I'll be in my cabin. Stay on that circuit in case there is more." He took the message sheet from the eagerly thrust forward hand, spun on his heels and exited. Just outside the Wireless Room, he stopped and folded the message, placing it into his uniform shirt pocket before hurrying to his cabin, careful not to go too fast so as to arouse concern. No one passed him as he made his way. Once inside, he closed the teakwood door, slid home the deadbolt lock, and closed the porthole curtains. Suddenly very dark in the cabin, he clicked on the desk lamp, sat down, and removed the folded paper. In hastily scratched writing there appeared the four letters "A ... W ... S ... T" followed by a series of random characters. Read by themselves, they meant nothing. Translated using the proper codebook, the meaning would soon be very clear. He walked over to the safe hidden behind a heavy blue curtain, hands trembling with nervous anticipation. He fumbled with the combination lock. He had opened this safe a thousand times, but still he fumbled. Finally, on the third try he heard the familiar sound of the last tumbler falling into place and grasped the tarnished brass handle. The bolts pulled away with a metallic thump and the metal door swung open. Smith spotted the object of his search, a brown, tightly sealed envelope. Printed in bold red letters on both sides read the threatening warning—TO BE OPENED BY CAPTAIN ONLY.

Carrying the packet gingerly to the desk, Smith delicately slit the flap sealing the envelope and pulled out the contents—a very official looking paperbound book, not very thick, entitled ADMIRALTY SIGNAL BOOK FOR MERCHANT NAVY VESSELS. He scanned the cover. In smaller letters near the bottom, it read SOUTH ATLANTIC-EFFECTIVE DATES 1 MAR 41 to 31 JUL 41. Out came the second item, a green sheet of paper labeled at top and bottom MOST SECRET. He opened the signal book and decoded the characters. It took only a couple of minutes. He rechecked his work. *Yes, correct.* Captain Smith held his message pad under the lamp and read aloud to no one but himself.

ADMIRALTY TO MEMPHIS
EXECUTE PLAN GREEN. REPEAT. EXECUTE PLAN GREEN.

Those few words represented the most powerful message he had ever received as a ship's master with immense implications for himself and the neutral liner plowing across the South Atlantic. He held the green piece of paper to the light and read it silently. The code word for the *Zamzam*—MEMPHIS—referred to the ancient Egyptian city of kings.

IMMEDIATELY UPON EXECUTION OF PLAN GREEN, YOU WILL EXTINGUISH ALL RUNNING LIGHTS. BY DAY, YOU WILL

FLY NO NATIONAL ENSIGN, BUT WILL HAVE ONE STANDING BY. YOU WILL TRAVEL AT COMPLETE DARKEN SHIP, TAKING SPECIAL CARE TO MASK ALL PORTHOLES, DECK HOUSE ENTRANCES AND OTHER SOURCES OF LIGHT LEAK. YOU WILL AVOID ALL SHIPPING TRAFFIC OF A SUSPICIOUS NATURE. REPORT TO NAVAL AUTHORITY UPON DESTINATION ARRIVAL.

The ship had been issued blackout curtains just after the war had broken out and a diligent watch would ensure that the passengers kept their porthole light curtains secured at night. He would comply with PLAN GREEN. He glanced at the desk chronometer. *Ah, nearly time for dinner.* He slid the code book, green paper, and message back into the envelope, stapled the flap shut, replaced it in the safe and locked it tight, spinning the dial several times just to be sure. Returning to the desk, he lifted the telephone handset and spun the handle twice.

"Pilot House, Aye."

"This is the captain. Locate the first officer and have him report to my cabin straightaway."

"Very good, Sir."

Though alarmed, the first officer understood the implications of the actions. He would, however, comply with the captain's instructions and implement a roving watch to ensure a complete blackout. As he exited the captain's cabin, Fiedel paused for a moment, and began a series of Praise Allahs as he went into the Pilot House. It would be a very bad voyage.

In the Dining Saloon, the captain rose from his seat. As he tapped a spoon on his water glass, the room suddenly became hushed. Even the two tables of ambulancemen quieted down. Smith cleared his throat. "Ladies and Gentlemen. As you are all aware, we are now entering waters that have become, shall we say, dangerous to merchant shipping in the past few months. We must take special precautions to ensure that we do not run into ... errr ... trouble." He paused and took a deep breath. "Accordingly, from this point on until we reach Egypt, we shall be running at darken ship. What this means to you is that at all periods of darkness you must keep your porthole blackout curtains tightly pulled shut. When you exit onto deck, kindly be careful with the blackout curtains which you will find installed so as to prevent errant light. Should you have any questions, please refer them to the first officer. Thank you for your kind cooperation and attention. Please continue your dinner."

At his customary table in the far corner of the Saloon, ANTIMONY slowly tapped his napkin with a dessert spoon. Verdi, with great concern showing in his face, leaned over towards him and whispered. "Mr. Prince. Would not traveling without lights make us more of a target for the Germans rather than less?"

ANTIMONY ceased his tapping and looked into the physicist's eyes. "Indeed, Dr. Verdi. It will indeed."

The Packard pulled to the curb slowly and deliberately. It sat like a regal chariot awaiting its master, cylinders humming with power and efficiency. The driver sat immobile and impassive in the front seat, eyes darting back and forth scanning the street and sidewalk for anything out of the ordinary or for anyone too interested. INTREPID stepped out of the shadows of a bus shelter and hurried over to the car, fast enough to be prompt, but not to draw attention to himself. The door clicked shut. Without any word of command, the driver signaled and pulled out into the jostling stream of traffic. Heavy, tinted windows dampened the normal traffic noises.

"We have problems," said the man seated next to INTREPID in a low, slow drawl.

"When do we not," responded the Canadian.

"Quite right. Only this is a special problem."

"I'm not at all certain I want to hear this," replied INTREPID hesitantly.

When the usually enthusiastic, even effervescent Bill Donovan spoke so despairingly, it represented cause for great concern. "The FBI men are not aboard *Zamzam*. Their bodies were discovered last night."

INTREPID drew in a heavy breath. In his mind's eye, he visualized his agent, his friend, ANTIMONY, alone, onboard the liner, facing the enemy without hope of reinforcement. "How did it happen?"

"We don't know," replied Donovan, staring aimlessly out the window at the movement in the street and into the crowd of pedestrians. He continued, "They were found up in Yonkers by the local police stuffed in the trunk of their car. Good God, Stephenson, they were in a residential neighborhood just parked along the street. They had been there for days!"

INTREPID visualized a nondescript automobile sitting serenely along the side of a quiet, residential street shaded by huge elm trees with children playing hopscotch on the sidewalk and star-struck lovers strolling by. *Christ Almighty!*

"I'll tell you, this killer is a real hard case. One was shot in the head and one had been garroted. Damn, it was ugly."

"How were they discovered?"

"Well, the homeowners returned from a vacation trip to Florida. There was the car parked in front of their house. No one had reported it. Hell's bells, I guess everyone just assumed it was theirs. Anyway, then they went to check it out and there was a very peculiar odor coming from it. You can visualize the rest of the story."

"Yes, I can," INTREPID grimaced. He tapped the armrest. His nature told him to take some decisive action. He also knew nothing could be done. "How did you find out?"

"It wasn't too difficult. Their orders, direct from Hoover I might add, were to book passage onboard the ship the night before she sailed. We already knew from a contact at the company's agency that you can do that and that there were cabins available—several in fact."

"Why didn't they simply book with the agent? Why book onboard?"

"Simple. If anyone wanted to, he could check with the downtown company agent for last-minute bookings. Your man was already on the list. If we had two more, someone might figure out what was up and rabbit. If Fritz did have a man aboard as we suspected, we wanted the guy. Or, rather wanted ... no ... want your SOE men to pick him up in South Africa. Now, Braithwaite's cable from Recife confirmed that suspicion. We have had our eyes on the Dutchman for some time, but damn it all, the boys at the Marine Air Terminal failed to follow him when he arrived from Lisbon on the Clipper."

"I see."

They came to a light. Across the street from the intersection stood that mammoth monument to the Industrial Revolution, the Empire State building.

He rolled down the window. To INTREPID, it had always had a dual meaning. On the one hand, here towered industrial technology at its best. On the other hand, what had the world done in terms of the destruction of old values and standards of decency and behavior? He had been one of the last chivalrous knights, the fighter pilots of the previous war and an ace in air combat to boot, who had practiced a code of honor long held to by the fighting man of the civilized world. And now, a generation later, these airmen of the same nations bombed cities devastating civilian populations. In the name of civilization, men murdered other men and left their bodies to rot in the trunk of a car. He gazed up at the spire atop the building, then rolled the window back up. With the steeple on top, it seemed like a cathedral wherein man worshipped a new god, a different god, an unfeeling, immutable god made of nothing more than steel, concrete, and electricity.

"They were not to report in until the ship reached Brazil."

"Which they obviously did not."

"Right. So when we confirmed through the Consulate in Recife that the old tub had sailed and that they hadn't seen hide nor hair of the two, then we started checking. The first place was the local police cases of unknown person homicides."

"And?"

"And you guessed it. Bingo! Yonkers police had a double John Doe homicide on their hands. They did manage to get a couple of prints which they had sent to D.C. to the Bureau, but that's still in the mail somewhere."

"Who made the I.D.?"

"Johnstone was their control. He went up to the county morgue last night. Christ, it must have been awful for him. Those men were his friends, Bill. We sent those two on a real simple mission just to babysit some scientist for Christ's sake! Now this. This is getting out of hand and I'm scared to death, I'll tell you."

"Have you told the President?"

"No, and I intend to sit on this for a while. The American scientific community can get pretty hysterical about things like this, especially the isolationists. If we go up the line, some of them will hear about it, and you know what they say about loose lips."

"Yes, and we could easily compromise sources. I agree. Let's sit on it as far as higher authority goes. There's no way we can warn ANTIMONY. Let's hope the mission is as anticipated, and Jerry simply wants to follow Dr. Verdi and no more. If that's the case, then he should be all right until they reach Cape Town. At that point, Gubbins' SOE boys can pick him up."

"Sounds good," responded Donovan. He reached forward across the seat and tapped the silent driver on the shoulder. Without turning or speaking, the driver nodded and signaled a right turn. "All else being equal, I've got to admit, I don't like the smell of this one, Bill. I really don't. It stinks like a week-old red herring to me. If the Huns only wanted to follow him, then why tip us off by taking out the FBI tail. That doesn't make a bit of sense to me. The killer had to know we would find the bodies eventually. I doubt this was an untimely random event. And, truth be told, those FBI guys look like G-men—not hard to spot and keep clear of at all. This doesn't sound like a typical *Abwehr modus operendi*. It sounds more like an *SS* pattern. Then again, the source said nothing about that level of interest. I damn sure hope your man ANTIMONY knows what he's doing."

"He does. I'll advise Admiral Godfrey and Lieutenant-Commander Fleming as soon as I get back to the office. If London has any brilliant flashes, I'll advise you straightaway."

"Thanks. Yeah, keep me in the loop. Hoover's madder'n hell this morning. He's blaming me and you, so keep your head low."

"Right. I shall."

The Packard pulled up to the curb at the identical spot from where it had left only a few minutes earlier. With only a brief nod as if to say goodbye, good luck, and I'll see you soon, the two intelligence chiefs parted. INTREPID closed the car door with a solid thunk. He stood there while it pulled away from the curb back into traffic. He put his hands in his coat pockets. The weather had turned cool again, just like his disposition. *Somehow, he must get word to ANTIMONY. But how? He would work on this one. Perhaps a telegram sent by way of the steamship line, but what kind of code to use? They hadn't had time to devise one. What if the Germans figured it out? No, too damned risky.* INTREPID walked back towards the office as the cold wind whipped up the back of his collar.

Anwar propped his bare feet up on the steel table that served as a desk in the Wireless Room. There had not been much going on that afternoon—just static on the international commercial bands. Very little wireless traffic went out these days. Belligerent vessels avoided giving away their position for fear of discovery, identification, location, and attack. Even neutral vessels kept their silence. What an eerie feeling just listening to the crackle and occasional static pop on the receiver. Nonetheless, international law and the company required him to monitor the hailing channels along with the captain's "special watch," so he did, routinely, daily, and laboriously. As senior operator, he had only the best hours, always the 0800 to 1600 watch. He shifted his feet to improve circulation. Normally, ship's wireless operators didn't stand watch barefoot, but no passengers came into the Wireless Room and the old man never came down unless called. Who did he have to impress? He had grown up in the Cairo slums, barefooted and hungry, vowing to lift himself out of misery and poverty. He had done so thanks to a British shipping line willing to take him on and train a promising young Egyptian in the science of wireless communications at sea. He had become comfortable with the gear, but not with shoes. The fan behind him whirred its regular, metallic, low-pitched hum. The simple ordinary seaman or stoker toiled in the broiling tropical sun on deck or down in the engineering spaces where they sweated and cursed, but the senior wireless operator lived in relative luxury, cooled by the whirring bulkhead fan, shoes shoved under the work desk, leaning back in his chair reading a western by the American novelist Zane Grey. *What a life! Just past 1500—relief will be along in about half an hour. Easy day today, praise Allah!*

"QQQ pause QQQ pause QQQ."

His brown feet flew in the air. The novel fell in a crumpled heap on the metal deck. Anwar almost fell out of the leaning chair with the sudden intrusion into his silent, dimly lit space. The sender transmitted fast and furiously with maximum power out. The signal, a strong ground wave, nearly overpowered *Zamzam*'s receiver.

"Allah be praised, he is close," whispered the man to himself as he adjusted the receiver sensitivity to a less than eardrum shattering blast. The signal continued, repeated over and over in groups of three QQQs—the standard warning for a suspicious ship sighting. Anwar scrambled for the phone. The circuit went silent.

"Pilot House, Aye."

"Wireless Room. Most urgent! Is the captain there?" he blurted out nervously. A ship obviously in fear had transmitted an anguished signal. His breathing came quick and shallow.

"Wait," came a muffled sound on the other end, then the clear voice of the mate. "The captain will be down in a moment."

The line went dead. He put the phone back into the metal holder on the bulkhead and turned back towards the wireless table. He looked down at his bare toes. He had completely forgotten. In an instant, he pulled on his socks and the black leather shoes, turned on the overhead light and stowed the novel in the bench drawer. When the captain entered not quite a minute later, he sat alert at the wireless table, one earpiece on, the other just off the ear. In front of him on the Morse message pad, he recorded the signal with the translation "suspicious ship" scribbled underneath.

"What do you have Anwar?"

"Most disturbing signal, Captain." He handed the message pad to the captain. "From the signal strength, she is very, very close to us. Should I send a response?"

"No." Smith thought of the Plan Green deception. He may be a target in the Admiralty's eyes, but why court danger. "We'll listen for a while."

Anwar nodded and turned back towards his receiver, pencil hovering over the blank message pad. It came within a few minutes, tense and unmistakably clear—a text signal preceded by a series of "Rs." Smith stood impassive, immobile, leaning over the operator's chair. The intense Egyptian hunched over the table furiously recording the ominous message. The captain did not require a translation. He had heard the signal before. He knew what it meant. The series of "Rs" meant "Raider"—another ship in trouble in the South Atlantic. A plaintext signal followed.

"Being chased by German raider. Course 000. Fourteen knots. Posit 2230S1610W."

Her international call sign followed. The captain yanked the international call sign book from the metal shelf above the receiver set and furiously searched for the call sign.

"She's the *Tai-Yin*, Norwegian registry."

The endangered ship's frantic message repeated over and over.

"Stay on this," the captain ordered tersely as he pulled the decoded signal off the message pad. I'll be in the Chart House."

"Yes, Captain. I shall ring you up straightaway." *So much for a peaceful afternoon. This thing could go on all night.* Nothing more, however, would be heard of the *TAI-YIN.*

The captain, clutching the urgent signal, returned to the Pilot House. The noon position had been taken and plotted three hours before. On the South Atlantic chart, the mate had marked the symbol for the noon position and a pencil line extending away from it, marked hour by hour along the dead reckoning (DR) track. *Zamzam* had held her course and speed throughout the period—110 at eight knots. Set and drift caused by current in these waters appeared negligible, so, he could be fairly certain of a good position. The first officer joined him, hovering over the chart as he plotted the Norwegian's position barely twenty miles to the southeast of *Zamzam*, just below the horizon. No wonder the signal had been so intense. The ship had stumbled right into the middle of the war. The captain and first officer raced across the Pilot House to the starboard wing. Both scanned the horizon with binoculars, but saw only the gently rolling waves and a hazy blue sky. No ship appeared nor could they hear the sound of distant naval gunnery. Returning to the chart table, Smith placed a straightedge on the dot representing the Norwegian and drew a line out for several inches due north, 000 true, her reported course. Both men peered at the DR line.

"180 degrees due south?" asked the captain, expecting some input from the first officer.

"Aye, aye, Sir. Opposite angle to their course should open the distance most rapidly."

"Good." Smith stuck his head out the doorway of the Chart House into the Pilot House. "Steer 180. Maximum speed."

"Aye, aye, Sir. 180, maximum speed," responded the mate.

Down in the Engine Room, the engineer on watch cursed as he opened the valve wheel controlling the flow of fuel oil to the engine. The ship could barely make thirteen knots and even then, the shake, rattle, and roll proved very uncomfortable, not to mention noisy. At that speed, they likely would blow some part of the engine or suffer a breakdown, which always made their lives miserable. The engineer on watch roundly cursed the Pilot House.

In the Saloon, a foursome played cards. Only two of the men felt the roll of the turn to starboard and the subsequent increase in the noise from the engine spaces. ANTIMONY peered over the top

of his cards. He knew what had happened. Hobgood sensed it as well, but, after looking up and around at the other players, he decided to ignore it and went back to his hand.

"Two clubs."

"Two spades."

"Three hearts."

Silence at the table. No one looked up from their cards at first, then one by one, every eye turned to ANTIMONY, his cards in his hand, his mind on the Pilot House and the ship's unexpected movements.

"Mr. Prince. It's your bid?" chimed Verdi.

"Oh, sorry. Let me see." Not really interested, he made a show of examining his hand. "Pass."

Across the table, Verdi seemed crestfallen. His partner had not supported him on the bid. It only took a few hands for Hobgood and another tobacco-man to thoroughly thrash Verdi and Prince, who had totally lost interest in the game.

"Please see my banker in New York for payment, gents," chuckled ANTI-MONY as he slid his chair back under the table. He quickly excused himself and headed out on deck. Hobgood, sensing something afoot, followed a minute later, but kept a discreet distance. Based on the sun's position, ANTI-MONY estimated their course as roughly due south, not easterly to Africa. He leaned over the side and looked astern. As he suspected, the rolling, bobbing, white foamy wake indicated that the once leisurely pace had increased to a sprint. *She must be making top speed judging from the creaks, groans, and vibrations.* He glanced at his watch—1535. It had been barely ten minutes since he first had noticed the course change. Two hairy, burly arms appeared on the rail, startling him. He had been in his own world, the realm of sun and horizon, course, and speed. The stranger intruded upon his concentration.

"Something up old man? Care to let an old Signal Corps guy in on it," asked Hobgood, lighting up a cigarette and tossing the match into the sea.

ANTIMONY followed the bobbing piece of wood as it rolled over and over in the bow wash until it disappeared aft. He turned, and leaned back over the rail, gazing up at the black, oily smoke pouring out of the single stack amidships. "We've changed course and speed. We're now headed south as fast as this tub can go."

No immediate response came from the Colonel. He took in another draw on his Lucky Strike. After several seconds, he spoke. "So what does it mean?" he quizzed in a low, concerned voice.

"I don't know just yet, but I don't like the feel of it." *Trust your intuition.* He had said this many a time in his treatise. Instincts, intuition, gut feeling, whatever one cared to call it. Very often in the field, instinct kept one alive. He had honed it over the years, both in the intelligence game and as a naval officer. It had rarely failed him. Just now, it screamed danger, danger, danger. This recent turn of events could not be good.

"Anyway we can find out what's up?"

"Yes, I think so, but it will take some time. I'll let you know."

"Fair enough." Hobgood took a draw and stared off at the horizon.

The Third Mate seemed a particularly amiable, talkative young man. AN-TIMONY sensed this early on and had cultivated a friendship. It would be useful to have an information source. As much as he might have liked to confide in the captain about his mission, he dared not. It would be a gross violation of operational security. On the other hand, a pliable mate with a talkative nature could prove quite useful. This young man had the 1600 to 2000 watch and always followed the same routine after his watch. He would exit the Pilot House, come down the ladder and back along the main deck starboard side towards his cabin. ANTIMONY had made a point of tracking his pattern. It now proved useful. He waited in ambush.

At 1800, the ship's course changed again, this time to 210—to the southwest. Right on schedule, the mate appeared. "Good evening, Mr. Prince. Enjoying the fine night air?"

"Yes indeed, and you look like a man who could use a drink."

"Well, it has been a very tense watch and I am off duty until the morning. Yes, very much I would like a drink. You are most kind."

It's amazing what three gin and tonics will do to loosen lips. Fortunately, this man did not subscribe to the Islamic prohibition on alcohol, no doubt the influence of the "decadent" West. The gregarious sailor would have babbled his entire life story had ANTIMONY allowed it, but only one facet of recent history interested him. The message from the *TAI-YIN*, the radical course changes to open the distance, the nervous captain pacing the Pilot House all during his watch—all came babbling out. ANTIMONY got what he wanted. This unexpected and potentially disastrous turn of events confirmed his intuition. At 2200, the ship steered 180, due south and still at maximum speed. By morning, she had returned to a southeasterly heading for Cape Town with no sign of the Norwegian freighter or of the reported German raider. By dawn, the captain, satisfied that the danger lay behind him, slowed her down to a more sustainable speed. In his cabin, ANTIMONY sensed the slowing, but in his gut, he knew the danger had not subsided; it had only just begun.

The amplified rapid fire series of dots and dashed rattled the wall speaker. The amplification helped the chief petty officer, lead telegrapher at this HF/DF station located at a lonely site in rural Cornwall close to Land's End and the roaring North Atlantic, to copy the German transmission. Radio direction finding (HF/DF) had been perfected during the last war. When ships at sea needed to communicate back to their home bases, they used High Frequency (HF) wireless. Unfortunately, HF requires a lot of radiated power, which transmits out in all directions from the source. In short, anyone listening in on that particular frequency can determine a line of bearing (LOB) on the signal source. Though the technique cannot determine exact range, a good HF/DF operator can, if he knew the general power out used by certain navies as standard operating procedure combined with the signal strength, make a good, educated guess as to approximate distance from the receiving station. The key to effective HF/DF, however, is triangulation. If two or more HF/DF stations receive the signal, then each has a separate LOB to the source. By simply plotting those lines of bearing on a chart, one can place the source with a high degree of accuracy. When three stations find the signal, the three lines form a very small triangle on the chart, placing the source somewhere within that triangle. The Royal Navy used HF/DF (Huff Duff) to localize and track German U-boats and commerce raiders and alert or safely reroute convoys.

The short burst transmission, only thirty-eight characters and most likely either a position or contact report, proved enough for a fix. The chief skillfully tuned his HF receiver and direction finder. He recognized the signal after only ten character symbols. A good HF/DF operator learns to pick up the characteristics of various wireless operators. He knew this one. Perhaps it's the speed or the rhythm or the length one allows for each dash, but every operator develops a unique telegraphic signature much like an individual's fingerprints. By the twenty-eighth character, he had localized the signal. The code did not concern him. Let the cryptoanalysts sort that out. He would figure out the bastard's location. And tonight, he had him by the balls.

"Bearing 197 degrees."

"Right, 197," responded the watch officer, an RNVR sub-lieutenant.

"Signal strength weak, but readable."

The watch officer drew his LOB from the station through the open ocean down to Antarctica.

"Time of transmission," the chief glanced at the clock as the last character clicked off, "1832 Zulu."

The watch officer jotted down 1832 Zulu, bearing 197. He put his hands on his hips and stared down at the chart, grinning like the cat that swallowed the canary.

"I believe we may have the bugger this time."

"Aye, Sir. We may well have. It's Atlantis all right. I'll bet my stripes on it. And she's operating in the South Atlantic between Brazil and Africa."

"Concur," answered the sub-lieutenant. "I'll call this one in. Let's hope someone else got it as well as we did."

The chief continued a manual scan of the most common German naval frequencies. He had done a good day's work here. The watch officer called in the intercept. In the Operations Intelligence Center beneath the Admiralty under twenty feet of steel and concrete, a crowd of WRNS, alert young women who had joined the women's division of the Royal Navy, meticulously tracked all sightings and reports. They moved markers across the huge, horizontal map of the Atlantic using a wooden stick much like a croupier's. On the board, markers represented ships at sea, known friendlies and hostiles. A WRN placed a marker labeled "Hostile" on the board. The thirty-eight

character transmission had been heard by five Huff Duff stations and identified as Atlantis, the notorious "Raider 16," the most deadly and successful of
all the enemy surface commerce raiders. Unfortunately, no RN warships operated near enough to intercept the German this evening. The triangulation
placed Atlantis square in the middle of the South Atlantic some 1200 miles
east southeast of Recife, Brazil.

CHAPTER 11
ADULTERY CAN BE DEADLY

The lion roared. Gray shadows flickered across the cavernous room. Around the lion's head appeared the Latin words *Ars Gratia Artis* (Art for Art's Sake), motto of the Metro-Goldwyn-Mayer studio. In the Saloon, passengers had gathered for the evening movie, *After The Thin Man*, starring Myrna Loy and Dick Powell as the urbane and ever so sophisticated Nick and Nora Charles—an old film, but no one minded. In the good old days, before the war that is, the fine liners that plied the Atlantic routes always showed first run pictures freshly issued by Hollywood studios or their British counterparts. Then again, the good old pre-war days had passed and the *Zamzam* would never be mistaken for a fine greyhound of the sea. So, they did the best they could, and, after all, a fine film is always timely.

ANTIMONY sat in the last row. Chairs had been placed row upon row and the tables moved off to the side after the evening meal. Outside on the Sun Deck, the last strains of an old hymn had just finished. The missionary trombonist regularly joined in playing for the evening Vespers service, which added an air of solemnity to the ship's orchestra. The crewman manning the projector flipped the start switch as soon as he had heard the last strain of "Ave Maria." The missionaries liked to end with that one, so he knew when to start. The light flickered on the white screen as all settled back.

Halfway through the film, ANTIMONY noticed Van Eyck leave the Saloon. Though tempted to follow, he sat still. Only a moment or two later, Abby Ashton also left ever so stealthily. *So—a liaison is in order. That should keep him out of trouble.* Verdi sat three rows up and thus out of immediate danger. ANTIMONY barely made out the flickering images on the too small screen from the back row, but he had long ago learned the value of observation from a distance. Besides, no one could watch him without being

127

overly obvious. He scanned the audience. It appeared safe. True to form, Nick Charles uncovered the murderer played by James Stewart. While somewhat disconcerting to see Stewart play the villain (he had built a film career playing the hero) every actor must break out of the mold occasionally. Isn't that what he did just now—play a different role? After the film, ANTIMONY strolled out onto the Sun Deck. Despite the still humid, oppressive air from the passing storm front, the stars indicated a general clearing.

"He's oh so like Nick Charles, isn't he Father?" gushed the woman behind him.

ANTIMONY spun around, startled by the intrusion. There stood Mrs. Blythe, Mother Superior of the RAF flock, and the Canadian priest—the one with striking blond, wavy hair and sky-blue eyes and the object of ANTIMONY's original suspicions. Most unlike the usually shorter and darker French Canadians ANTIMONY observed.

"Yes, Madam, very much like the gentlemen. You wouldn't happen to be a detective or some sort of secret agent would you, Mr. Prince?" queried the priest.

Blood rushed to his head. *Van Eyck is his man. Could this be a trap? Why did he ask that particular question? What of this tall Germanic-looking priest with the funny half-English, half-French accent?* ANTIMONY held his fire, studying the man's eyes. He saw nothing but innocence. *Could there be more he did not see? He must play out the scene. He had put himself on this stage—play out the game.* "I beg your pardon?" he replied to buy some precious seconds.

"Oh. So terribly sorry, Mr. Prince," beamed the effervescent Mrs. Blythe. "Father Villenueve and I were just remarking at how much you resemble Mr. Powell. Or I should I say, Detective Nick Charles. You would be ever so wonderful in that role. You're not an actor on the side are you?"

"No, indeed not, Mrs. Blythe. I'm merely a simple businessman trying to make a living in a harsh world."

"Pity," responded an embarrassed Villenueve. "You would make a smashing detective, *Monsieur*. Well, we'd best be getting along, Mrs. Blythe. We've disturbed Mr. Prince quite enough this evening."

"Yes, do forgive us, Mr. Prince."

The couple disappeared back into the Saloon where the mess stewards set out refreshments. A loud noise welled up from the bar area aft. Having a good old time, the ambulancemen had started reveling early and missed the film. ANTIMONY leaned against the rail observing the comings and goings of the passengers and keeping a sharp eye on Verdi. Van Eyck exited from the ladder up to the First Class cabins and headed straight for the bar, face flushed as if he had recently engaged in heavy physical activity. A minute or two later, Abby Ashton also appeared at the head of the ladder. Appearing flush but more animated and excited than Van Eyck, she paused at the top of the ladder to look in all directions. She could not see ANTIMONY standing in the dark, but he could clearly make her out in the moonlight despite the darkened ship. Satisfied that she had not been observed, she glided down the ladder, a light spring to her step, and proceeded back into the doorway leading down to the RAF wives' cabins. ANTIMONY chuckled and shook his head. This *Abwehr* agent may be good at some things, but in concealment and discretion, he is decidedly lacking. His fling with the young bride certainly provided fodder for gossip and rumor. This German violated a cardinal rule of the business—never call attention to yourself. The SOE men in Cape Town will have an easy job steering this man where they want him to go, and making him see what they want him to see.

A clanking noise came from aft. By instinct, ANTIMONY crouched low with feet spread well apart for balance and hands in the air, poised for action. The clanking continued. His breathing slowed to a normal pace. *False alarm.* He slowly straightened up and looked around. No one had observed his warlike stance and his spring to a defensive posture. *Damn! Must not do that again. Must not give up my cover through an unnecessary reaction.* The noise had come from a portside lifeboat. A breeze gusting up from the northeast rocked the boat, which had not been securely tied down. The ship's boats had been swung out the night they left Recife, the same night that the blackout started. ANTIMONY knew the significance of this act—most of the passengers hardly noticed. From what he had seen of the crew, Smith acted prudently. ANTIMONY had no wish to go to lifeboat stations with this sad lot. At least the boats now stood ready for loading—a small consolation. Up on the Bridge Wing, the mate shouted in Arabic. Apparently, a crewman had been sent off to secure the errant lifeboat. Shortly afterward, the clanging ceased. The decibel level from the bar increased, however.

He observed Mrs. Avery come down the ladder, head aft and enter the bar. *Hmmm. Somewhat unusual. She generally kept to her cabin and rarely went to the bar or the Saloon after meal hours. Oh well, maybe the mysterious*

widow is lonely tonight. ANTIMONY decided to seek the friendly silliness of
the bar himself. It might do him good, and, he could keep a watchful eye on
the indiscreet German.

"Mr. Van Eyck, you are a very attractive man," the tall brunette smiled
suggestively. The cigarette tip at the end of the holder glowed orange red as
she slowly, seductively drew in another breath. She exhaled, nose turned up
in a manner like that of the great Hollywood sirens. Van Eyck could take no
more. He had to possess this woman. He now regarded the affair with Abby
as, well, dull. A conventional British middle class girl suddenly thrown into
the arms of an exotic continental by the fate of war, she had been seduced by
the newness of it all, the fantasy of a voyage in dangerous waters, and the thrill
of a dangerous liaison. But exotic? About as exotic as a tin of evaporated milk
and as conventional in lovemaking as any frumpy Victorian wife. During
sex, she remained completely passive lying on the bed like a sack of potatoes.
In short—boring. This American woman though—the tall widowed Mrs.
Avery—now there is something altogether different. Most American women
he had encountered turned out just as frumpy as his English *hausfrae.* This
radically different woman had a sort of Old World flair about her, no doubt
due to wealth and travel. She exuded sensuality. Her every movement, sty-
listic and graceful to a fault, had attracted the attention of nearly every man
on the ship. Many of the ambulance drivers had tried; all failed to woo her.
She never took part in the social activities. Although she dined with different
parties, she had joined none. No wonder she attracted Van Eyck. And now,
she made her move. His face flushed. Excitement rushed through his veins.
His groin stirred. He had the feeling it would be a most adventurous evening. The amorous Dutchman looked away from her ice blue eyes and across
the small bar towards the exit onto the main deck.

"Would you care for a stroll on deck Mrs. Avery? The moon is up and you
can see for miles?"

"I would be delighted, Mr. Van Eyck," she replied in a husky voice as she
picked up the silver beaded purse from the table, long, red fingernails tapping on the wooden table as she did so.

Van Eyck could almost feel those long fingernails digging into his back as she writhed in pleasure under him. He took a deep breath and pulled the chair out from under her. Her slender hips gracefully lifted from the seat. The sequined evening gown rustled as she rose. He let her take the lead and followed a step behind. From a corner table, a half-crocked ambulance driver let out a whistle. Another let go a rude catcall. Van Eyck turned and smiled wryly at the table as if to say, "Who's the cat, and who has the canary."

Frank Vicovari raised a glass with a double shot of Kentucky bourbon. In one motion he downed the bronze liquid and then shook his head violently, his tongue flailing side to side. No intelligible sound came out—only a sort of "blah-la-la-la" noise. Everyone knew what it meant as all laughed. Another driver motioned towards the Egyptian barman, pointed to Frank and shook his head. The barman nodded and grabbed the bourbon bottle.

What the hell! I'll be drunk as a skunk in the morning, but who cares. At least it won't hurt so bad that someone else is getting some other than me. "Fill'em up boys," Vicovari pronounced gleefully.

On deck, the moon hung seductively in the clear night sky. Joan Avery leaned over the rail staring out at the rolling waves. She removed the cigarette from the holder and flicked it into the sea below then stood upright, opened the beaded purse and dropped in the holder. After several moments, she spoke. "Do you miss your wife, Mr. Van Eyck?" her blue eyes piercing into his skull.

"Why, yes. I mean to say, in an emotional sense I do." She had completely thrown him with the unexpectedly straightforward question. *Must recover! Must be on top of it!* "However, I must say, Mrs. Avery, that ... "

"Please. Call me Joan."

"Yes, Joan, I do a great deal of business travel often for months at a time. You can imagine what a strain that puts on one's physical relationship with one's wife." *Nice recovery.*

"Yes, I do see. A man like you must require some, shall I say, physical outlet," she responded.

Her eyes blazed in the oddest way he had ever seen. He saw passion but, more—some indefinite quality to her eyes. *Rage perhaps?* He did not know and did not care. *He must have this woman.* His hands trembled. She noticed. *Damn it all, she noticed.* She placed her hand on top of his as he squeezed the rail. "Yes, you might say that. Joan, my English is not so good. Physical outlet is an excellent description."

She tightened her grip on his hand. Her words came smoothly, like a cat's purring or perhaps a lioness about to pounce. His desire boiled white hot. *Now strike, while it is your moment!* She cut him off as she made the first move. "Why don't we go to my cabin for a night cap? I should be most honored, Mr. Van Eyck." As she uttered his name, her voice had an upward lilt.

What a most forward woman. Not at all what he expected from an American widow. They hurried quickly forward along the main deck towards the First Class cabins. She went ahead. In the dark void between the blackout curtains, her hand reached out and thrust into his chest—clearly a woman of physical power and great strength. Mrs. Avery proceeded on through the parted curtains while he waited. Satisfied that no one loitered in the passageway, her hand shot through the curtain, grasped his wrist and pulled him through. *By God, she must be anxious.*

The pair tiptoed down the empty passageway towards her cabin. The red glow of the nightlights added to the eroticism of the moment as shadows danced about her high cheekbones and cascading brown hair. They reached the door without encountering anyone. She pulled the key from her purse and with minimal motion, unlocked the door. Both stepped in quickly. *What a tigress!* No sooner than the door shut, she kissed him passionately all over his face, his eyes, his nose, cheeks and lips. Her hand reached down to his groin and rubbed slowly. Wild with passion, his fingers fumbled behind her back as they embraced and groped in an exotic mating ritual.

Her right hand opened the bureau drawer ever so slowly. Van Eyck never noticed. He undid the hooks and eyes of her gown. Finally, all came undone. The dress slipped off her shoulders. Van Eyck ran his hands up and down her smooth back. Reaching up, he grasped a handful of the lovely dark brown hair and gave it a tug—not a tear, just a gentle love tug. The dark brown wig pulled away from her head. His hand jerked up in surprise as the wig tumbled to the deck behind her.

Van Eyck leapt away—a huge step backward. His mouth hung open, eyes wide in astonishment, hands flailing at his side. He stood frozen in space, dangling in the air as if hanging from a gallows. He tried to gasp for air. None came. His tongue lolled from side to side aimlessly. He stood immobilized by his own incredulousness, a pistol only inches from his forehead. Mrs. Joan Avery's mouth turned up in the most malevolent grin he had ever seen. The odd fire returned to her eyes—rage and hatred.

"You are a traitor to the Fatherland, *Herr* Van Eyck!"

"What . . . I . . . who are you? I don't understand, I ... "

She removed the rest of the gown with her left hand as he stared, frozen in shock and utter amazement. The red sequined gown and black brassier fell to the floor revealing a smooth, muscular chest. Well-placed pads had given the appearance of small, but pert breasts.

"Who the devil are you?" he sputtered.

"*SS Sturmbannführer* Karl von Donop. I am also your executioner."

"But, but, do you not know who I am, *Herr Sturmbannführer*? I am *Hauptmann....*"

"I know your real name, you lecherous disgrace, *Herr Hauptmann* Limken. You are Admiral Canaris's fool. Do you think I am ignorant?" The *SS* officer's voice became shrill and strident, made even more bizarre by the short cropped blonde hair tightly pulled down by a silk hair net and the heavy facial makeup highlighted by ruby red lipstick. It is a horror scene from hell Limken thought. *It must be only a nightmare.* "Then, we are on the same side, *Herr Sturmbannführer*. Why do you raise a pistol to my head?"

"Because you are a traitorous swine!"

"No, it is not true. I am here on a mission to follow the Italian scientist—to follow him to the British heavy water plant in South Africa. You must know this *Mein Herr*. You must know this," Limken pleaded to the *SS* man, his arms flailing. "How can you possibly say I am a traitor to the Fatherland?"

"You have been carrying on with your little English whore, haven't you, Limken. Von Donop cocked the pistol, now aimed between Limken's eyes.

"No, *Herr Sturmbannführer*, I. . . "

"Please, *Hauptmann*. Don't bother to deny it. I saw you, the two of you. I was in your cabin that night before this piss ant little ship pulled into Recife. I saw you in your lust cavorting with an enemy of the *Reich*."

Limken's jaw went slack, his mouth fully agape. He tried to speak, but only gasps of air came out. Finally, he sputtered out some words through his panic. "But . . . that . . . was only sex. I mean, you cannot possibly think that I have been a traitor to the *Reich*. I have no feelings for the English bitch, *Herr Sturmbannführer*. It was only lust, I can . . ."

"Stop! You are a pathetic excuse for a field agent. I don't know why that fool Canaris keeps you around. Worse yet, you are careless and exceedingly sloppy." Von Donop reached into the same drawer from which he had earlier taken the gun, grasped a small, hard object and flung it across the room. Bouncing off Limken's chest, it clattered to the deck. The frightened German agent clambered down on his hands and knees and in the semi-darkness of the red-lighted cabin, he found the object, cradled it in his palm, and gasped—a black enameled match box with bright gold lettering that read the Hotel Atlantic, Hamburg. His head dropped. Von Donop again reached into the drawer and removed a long, slender object. He took a step towards the crestfallen *Abwehr* man, the object in his right hand. He lay the gun down on the edge of the bed. Limken looked up, hope in his eyes, seeing the gun pointed away from his head benignly lying on the top of the coverlet.

"In spite of your stupidity and carelessness, I still may be able to use you. You do have some talent to have made it this far, haven't you. Stand up fool and cease your sniveling." There came a slight metallic click as Limken stood up, his shoulders still drooping in shame. Von Donop stepped closer. "Then again," Von Donop muttered as his left hand shot across the short distance between them and, like a shark's jaw, clamped around the victim's throat, "You may jeopardize my mission. I simply cannot take such a risk. You can understand that, can't you, *Herr Hauptmann* Limken?"

Limken's eyes bulged. The swift attack caused him to stumble backwards, carried by the attacker's incredibly strong hand. The long, red fingernails, held fast by strong nail cement, dug into Limken's throat as tiny ringlets of blood oozed out and dribbled down his neck into the shirt collar. He gagged for air. The force and speed of the blow shut off his windpipe. Von Donop's palm pressed his Adam's apple back into his throat, further closing off the air passage. The ferocious and swift attack paralyzed him. His arms hung limp. His body did not respond. The *SS* man squeezed harder. A flash of polished steel shot across from behind him and up into the victim's chest. The thin blade drove up all the way into Limken's heart in one stroke, the only sound a sort of dull thump. Limken's eyes rolled up into his head.

Von Donop pulled the stiletto blade out with a sucking noise. It had done its work. Very little blood appeared outside, but inside, the ruptured heart poured blood out into the dying man's chest. The assailant released his grip on the dead man's bruised throat. Limken's body slumped then slid to the deck, eyes still bulging, tongue lolling, head slumped over his right shoulder. The *SS* man reached across the nightstand and pulled out the towel hanging over the wash basin. He wiped the blade clean and clicked it back into its handle. Then, straddling the dead man, von Donop opened up his jacket and pressed the folded towel against the rapidly growing brownish red spot on the man's white, starched shirt. It just would not do for a steward to be cleaning the very proper American lady's cabin and find dried blood on the deck, especially when the very charming Dutch businessman would go missing, presumed fallen overboard in a drunken stupor. *No, it wouldn't do at all.*

With the easy part over, the more difficult one remained—how to get the corpse onto the deck and overboard without any witnesses. Von Donop glanced at the table clock—only 2045. He would wait until after midnight. By then, most of the passengers would be asleep or too drunk to notice. The crew would not be a factor save those on watch. By then, he figured, those taking the midnight watch would be in place and those relieved would be gratefully in their own bunks. He sat down on the bed and waited for midnight. At 2300, he changed clothes. Even if seen, the witness would observe a tall, blonde man hauling the lifeless body, not the elegant Mrs. Avery.

The clock chimed once at thirty minutes past midnight. The *SS* man put an ear to the door. *Nothing.* Ever so gently, he twisted the doorknob and peeked out. *Good. No one in the passageway.* He shut the door and quickly walked over to the louvered alcove beside the body now wrapped in a sheet. Reaching in, he pulled out a gray fedora, popped it on his head and pulled the brim down low over his eyes. He hurried back to the door and cracked it open. Red light spilled into the cabin. Von Donop slid out into the passageway towards the exit. The British businessman in the next cabin snored loudly. Suppressing a gleeful laugh, he reached the exit. The earlier moon hid behind a bank of clouds. *Excellent!* He looked forward and up. The starboard lookout scanned the horizon forward; he would not look aft. The engine noise would mask the splash of the body hitting the water. No one would hear, not even the stern lookout.

Returning to the cabin, Von Donop reached over the form on the deck and placed both arms under the limp corpse. *Rigor mortis* had not yet set in, but the man would be heavy and awkward. He eased the door open with his foot and swung out into the passageway. A dead hand dangled from the sheet and flapped against his knee with every step. Reaching the exit door, he paused, listening for the sound of any movement. None. He pushed through the blackout curtain and onto deck. Von Donop stepped to the rail looking left and right. The lookout still scanned forward. He took a deep breath and with a grunt, hoisted the corpse up over the rail and pushed it forward. The body rolled over and over, bounced twice off the hull and hit the water with a heavy whump. Von Donop glanced up at the lookout. No reaction. He leaned back over the rail and watched the white object rapidly receding into the wake until completely out of sight. Satisfied with his successful mission, he returned to his cabin and threw himself onto the rumpled bed without even removing the fedora. He fell asleep almost before his head hit the pillow.

In the Pilot House, the mate thought he saw something just on the horizon—a dark low shape. He put his glasses to his eyes and scanned. *No. Nothing there. Full speed ahead.*

CHAPTER 12
THE CHEESE IN THE TRAP

t Bletchley Park, the ULTRA watch received a new batch of decoded German signals including a most interesting one intercepted off an SS high command circuit out of Paris direct into *Reichmarshal* Himmler's Berlin headquarters. The watch officer picked up the flimsy paper and squinted. "Right. On to it," she whispered.

Following the preamble heading came the address group: "*Personal Heydrich to Himmler.*" *This is exciting. So the Reichmarshal's number one lackey is in Paris. I hope he gets dysentery from a bad bottle of wine.* She read it aloud.

ARMAGEDDON ONBOARD ZAMZAM. REPORTS FBI PRESENCE NULLIFIED BEFORE SAILING NYC. SUSPECT BRITISH PRESENCE NOT YET IDENTIFIED. ABWEHR MAN VERY CARELESS.

ARMAGEDDON WILL ATTEND TO ITALIAN UNILATERALLY. HE REQUESTS SUPPORT ONCE REACH CAPE TOWN FOR TRANSPORTATION OF ITALIAN. ALL IS WELL. REPORTED FROM RECIFE. HEIL HITLER.

Within a half hour, a motorcycle courier carrying a sealed pouch roared down the road to London, a little more than an hour's drive. He neither knew what the double sealed envelope contained nor did he care; he only had to deliver it safely. Just past 0700 the cyclist pulled up to the doorway leading into Admiralty. At the entrance, he picked up the phone and announced himself. Moments later, an armed guard appeared and escorted the driver down the long corridor to Room 39. At the entrance sat another guard—a rigid, dour Royal Marine sergeant. Without a word, the marine inspected the driver's credentials, nodded and opened the door leading into the cavernous Room 39, liar of Rear-Admiral John Godfrey's Naval Intelligence Division. Moments later the courier stood before the desk of the RNVR officer. Lieutenant-Commander Ian Fleming took the envelope, signed the receipt in the appropriate places, handed it back to the man and thanked him. The motorcyclist snapped to attention, nodded, placed the folded receipt back in his leather pouch, turned on his heels, and strode out.

Fleming opened the ULTRA intercept straightaway as he always did in preparation for the Admiral's morning brief. As if a hand grenade had exploded beneath his chair, he bolted straight up, face blanched white. He shouted to the startled Dick Merritt sitting across from him. "Dick! Quick now! Ring up General Gubbins. Tell him we have an emergency situation. I'll contact the Admiral then I'm off to find Menzies," he shouted as he raced past the Admiral's Aide, blouse and service cap in hand. "And hurry!"

"Foot in the stirrup, Sir. Right. That's good. Now up and over you go. Very good. You'll be riding in the Derby before you know it, Sir. Best change first, though."

"I beg your pardon?" asked a puzzled Fleming. Then he understood. One does not normally wear a naval uniform while riding. "Yes. I see what you mean."

He noticed that the man had three fingers missing from his left hand. The groom saw Fleming staring and thrust up the deformed hand, the glove hanging limp where fingers ought to have been.

"Battle of the River Plate, Sir, back in '39 when we buggered the *Graf Spee*. 'ell of a punchup, that was. Me and me mates gave that Jerry a right good kick in the arse, we did. I've got to say though, those lads may be bleedin' Nazis, but they gave a good account of themselves."

The beige mare snorted and gave a shake of her long neck and head. Fleming reined in, heels clamped in on the flanks of the animal, squeezing hard. The horse understood and lowered her head in submission, tail swishing.

"What ship?"

"*Ajax*, Sir. The bleedin' stinkin' marvelous *HMS Ajax*. A right fine ship she was too. I was a Gunner's Mate in X turret. We took a hit. Four of us made it alive out of that turret, all of us wounded in some way. I was lucky. Just some extra fingers I don't need. Well, it put me out of the Service, it did. Worse luck. Been in for ten years before the war."

"You did your part. Let the rest of us take it from here." Instantly embarrassed at his patronizing of the disabled veteran, who, after all, had faced the Germans in a very real and deadly sense, Fleming stared down at the reins in his hands—hands with all ten good fingers. The old cruiser sailor, though, didn't seem to notice. Fleming faced the enemy daily in a war of a different nature, but one far more important to the nation's survival. He extended his right hand to the groom, who, beaming, thrust his back. They shook in an iron grip, shipmate to shipmate.

"You'll probably find the general about 'alfway down the path, Sir. He doesn't ride fast. More steady like."

"Thank you." Fleming pulled the reins over to the right. The disciplined horse responded as Fleming gently nudged her with his heels. The mare started off at a walk, then broke into a steady trot. As he picked up speed, he heard the groom behind him shout.

"Give the bloody bastards what for, Sir!"

He dug his heels in. The horse jolted into a canter down the long row of well-groomed trees of Rotten Row. Not a bad rider, the tall, lanky Scot had not ridden since the war started. But, like learning to walk or to ride a bicycle, once learned, one never forgets how. As tree by tree passed, he became more and more at ease. The leather reins felt natural in his hands. His hips swayed up and down, in and out of the saddle, each movement following the rise and fall as the mare's strong legs galloped steadily on. Up ahead, he saw a lone rider on a black stallion, barely at a trot, obviously enjoying the soothing scenery, the fresh, crisp air, and the momentary respite from the stress of the daily struggle. Brigadier-General Sir Stewart Menzies, Director-General of the Secret Intelligence Service (SIS, also known as MI-6), and known simply as "C." Fleming had always envisioned him as the model for the "M" character in his yet to be written spy novels. On most early mornings, if one wished to speak to the general, one must go riding in Rotten Row, the centuries old trail in the heart of London where one could hire a mount and relax for an hour or a day even in wartime. *Even in wartime! How sanguine we British are. In the death struggle of a world war, a fight to the finish to determine if people will be free from totalitarian tyranny, with German bombs falling daily all about their ears, with the City of London lit up like a Guy Fawkes Day bonfire on more nights than not, with Britain and the Commonwealth standing as the only bulwark against the hegemonic aspirations of the Nazi Empire, two Scots went out riding in the park. Good God! What a funny lot we are.* Then again, nothing delights the British quite like the prospect of an utterly hopeless situation. "Sir Stewart! General Menzies!" Fleming reined in. The mare pawed the loose, wet turf. The SIS Chief had already turned at the rapid approach of another rider obviously in great haste.

"Ah, yes. Young Fleming. How goes it over at Admiralty?"

"Better, I should hope. We are grabbing the Hun by the nose and pulling hard, though."

Both men turned their horses back down the path and began a slow walk. Menzies, dressed in tweed jacket with proper jodhpurs and boots topped with a floppy Irish Donegal hat, had not failed to notice Fleming's uniform. The gold coil embroidery of the Royal Navy cap badge occasionally caught the sun. It shimmered in the morning light.

"You didn't come down here simply to ride, did you Fleming?"

"Indeed not, Sir. We have a, shall I say, sticky situation, brewing down at NID. Some intelligence came in from ULTRA on the *Zamzam* affair."

"Indeed," nodded "C," noting Fleming's edginess. "What is the source?"

"Himmler to Heydrich on the SS High Command Net. ARMAGEDDON is aboard *Zamzam*."

Menzies jerked on the reins. The horse started and whinnied. Menzies knew the codename's meaning. He silently stared off into the ancient oaks lining the path. Like Britain herself, the oaks had stood for ages. "I see. Our SS chappie. What are we about then?"

"The Director wants yourself and General Gubbins in on the inner circle of this *Zamzam* thing." "C" knew the rough details of the operation already but for the next few minutes, Fleming retold the entire story as they made their way back to the stables.

Menzies and Fleming took their seats at the polished oak conference table. Admiral Godfrey and General Gubbins, head of SOE, had been seated for some time. Menzies leaned forward, fingers interlocked, hands stretched forward, awaiting the grim details. Godfrey nodded to Fleming who flipped open the highly classified personnel dossier.

"ARMAGEDDON. Code name for Karl Heinz Wilhelm von Donop, *Sturmbannführer SS*. The man works directly for Heydrich. He is so secret that his own military intelligence people don't know who or what he is."

"How did we find out about him?" queried the SOE Chief.

"One of our first ULTRA intercepts. It seems Herr Heydrich couldn't resist bragging to Himmler about the exploits of his man ARMAGEDDON." Fleming paused and looked down at the paper before him. "Heydrich fancies this name ARMAGEDDON. Our boy von Donop is capable of wreaking great destruction on our intelligence apparatus—enemies of God and the Third *Reich*. His words."

"I see." Menzies unlocked his fingers and stretched his arms to their full length. He placed his hands palm down on the table and let out a deep sigh.

Fleming continued. "There is no current photo of von Donop, but once we matched the name, the backroom boys pieced together a personnel history. It's sketchy, but useable." Fleming handed a black and white glossy photograph to the SIS Chief. The caption on the reverse side read "von Donop taken 1934 as a cabaret performer in Berlin." The tall man in the photo appeared elegant, well-built, and handsome, if slightly effeminate. Menzies passed the photo across the conference table to Gubbins. "He was a cabaret performer in the early thirties before joining the *SS* as an intelligence officer in 1935."

"What type of performer?" mused Gubbins, not looking up from the smirking face in the photograph.

Fleming cleared his throat. "He was a female impersonator, Sir."

Gubbins squinted as he stared at the face in the picture and shook his head. "Yes, quite right. I can see that. Bit of a ponce, is he?"

"Not necessarily. It seems there was a rather notorious episode with a countess in '32. Wife of an Austrian diplomat, I believe. There are other such incidents. Don't underestimate this man. In spite of his rather unusual former profession, we are certain that he is the most dangerous field agent the Nazis have. He is a killer, Sir—a cold, heartless, ruthless, totally amoral killer.

And, he is quite clever and resourceful. The last evidence we have of him or rather suspect, is Paris last January, and ... "

"And?" questioned Admiral Godfrey, looking up at Fleming.

Gubbins broke in. "We lost four SOE men that month in Paris. Four very good men."

A profound depression settled over the room made more ominous by the darkening sky. The coal fire in the grate sputtered as it faded into ash leaving a cold, damp chill. It promised to be another dreary, rainy London spring day. No one spoke for some time. Only the hissing of the occasional flame in the fireplace, the splat of heavy rain drops pelting the glass, and the rubbing of polished shoes across the stately Persian carpet broke the mausoleum-like quiet.

Menzies sardonically broke the silence. "So, Godfrey, the only thing we have between this bloody Nazi and our errant American scientist is Commodore Braithwaite, who thinks he is on a busman's holiday?"

Godfrey stood and placed his hands firmly in the pockets of his uniform blouse, thumbs pointed down in the traditional naval fashion. "Not exactly, Stewart. Our man ANTIMONY is most resourceful. He has been in dicey situations before."

"Nonetheless, he is facing the Hun's best man if young Fleming's dossier is to be believed. And this man is much younger and apparently much fitter. What does ANTIMONY do if this von Donop or ARMAGEDDON, did you say, decides to get physical? What if the Jerrys decide they want to kidnap Verdi or worse. How will ANTIMONY react? Will he be able to overcome this Nazi? I have grave doubts, gentlemen."

The air grew stuffy and oppressive as the darkened clouds choked off the sunlight. Fleming spun around. He had been standing by the waning fire deep in thought. "We must warn him of the threat even at the risk of some security compromise," he spoke slowly but sternly.

"Concur! But how do we do that? *Zamzam* is a neutral. Do we just broadcast to the world? Dear John, watch out for the big, bad Nazi dressed as a tart. No Commander, we have a real problem here. I think our only hope is to intercept the lot of them once they reach Cape Town and pray God the German hasn't acted yet."

"Precisely, Stewart. Some sort of passport foul-up and then we can take all of them into custody until we sort it out." replied Godfrey.

"That is," the older men jerked their heads around, eyes boring into Fleming's, "unless he in fact does act before they make port."

"I think it's time to brief the PM, Godfrey," grunted Gubbins.

"I concur, Colin," responded the DNI looking over at Fleming still by the fireplace.

"I'll see to it straightaway, Sir."

"And Ian," Fleming froze in midstride, "I think it best that you fly to New York tonight and personally brief INTREPID. This is too sensitive for normal traffic. He will want to pose questions, I suppose, and we had bloody well better have the answers."

Fleming hustled out of the depressing room and back to his desk. He realized that he still had the von Donop file and laid it face down on his already cluttered desk. He lifted the phone and dialed the very private number.

"The old boy won't like this, Ian. He was up all night wrestling with this Greek business," cautioned the voice on the line.

"It's important. It truly is. Thanks for the favor. I'll send round a bottle of Glenfiddich courtesy of the DNI when this bloody business is ended."

"Right then, 0900 hours sharp," responded the Prime Minister's Private Secretary.

Fleming rang off and dialed the next number—the manifest office for the Atlantic Ferry Organization. As the phone rang, he shook his head. God how he hated those night flights to Canada jammed into the cold and damp space of a Short S.33 Sunderland Flying Boat.

"Manifest."

"Cubby, you old sod. Ian here. What do you say to a rubber of bridge tonight?" (their code for a request for a lift on the nightly shuttle to Halifax).

"Well, let me check my busy social calendar. Yes. I think I can make it tonight, say eightish, my place?"

"Consider it booked."

"Right. Yet another chance to take away some of that undeserved Navy pay."

Fleming chuckled softly as he replaced the telephone. He slumped down in his chair and rubbed his eyes with the upturned palms. An already long day already promised to get even longer. As he sat, tired eyes shut, he realized that he smelled of horse sweat and tack. *Well, can't be bothered with that just now.* He had to pack anyway. A quick shower and a change of uniform could be arranged between the meeting with the PM and his flight time. His breathing became more rhythmical and he drifted off as the adrenaline surge dissipated into exhaustion. Seconds passed, perhaps minutes. He started up, eyes bolted open. In his trance, he saw the early spring flowers just outside the Admiralty windows as they always appeared this time of year. But then they vanished, seared away into nothing. A gray, dead ash covered the ground. Not a living creature stood on the cold, burned earth, only the charred stump of a knarled oak remained of the heart, the soul of the city. The British Uranium Committee's brief from a few days back on the potential destructive capability of an atomic weapon seared his imagination as had nothing else before. ANTIMONY must be warned. Verdi must be protected. He would happily make the miserable airplane ride.

Winston Leonard Spenser Churchill, Prime Minister of the beleaguered British nation, sat impassively at the head of the inelegant, but functional table in a chilly, ventilated room several yards beneath the dangerous streets of London. The War Room underneath Whitehall had practically become his wartime office. He looked exhausted but alert sitting in his blue coveralls, an outfit he frequently wore while working in the underground command center. He held in his stubby but strong fingers, the perennial Cuban cigar, its grayish smoke wafting up towards the heavily reinforced concrete ceiling. Though at times he appeared disinterested and distant, Churchill actually digested every word, every phrase, every nuance. He heard and pondered. Fleming concluded his brief and sat down. All heads turned towards the PM, who closed his heavy-lidded eyes and took another long draw on the pungent cigar.

"So, gentlemen. You feel it is … umm … imperative that our man ANTIMONY be assisted in some manner." His eyes shot open.

"Indeed, Prime Minister. The consequences of the capture of Dr. Verdi are potentially disastrous. They already have Nihls Bohr, the Danish atomic physicist. We really aren't certain how far along their atomic weapon development program is, but with Verdi under their control working for them . . . . Sir, the risk is simply too great," responded Godfrey.

"And you are certain that this *SS* man . . . umm . . . ARMAGEDDON isn't there just to assist the *Abwehr* agent in following the good doctor."

"No, Sir. Not at all," shot in Fleming.

"And why, pray Commander, do you say that?" Churchill pursed his lips.

All heads swiveled onto Fleming. The Navy man straightened his back, his tall frame dominating the table in front of him as his confidence sharpened. "Because, Sir, if he were, I feel certain that our *Abwehr* source would have alerted us. I don't think they are even aware of his presence. It's simply not in his history. Von Donop is Heydrich's frontline man. We know that Heydrich aspires to replace Canaris to be the actual if not *de facto* head of the entire Nazi military intelligence apparatus. Based on the types of missions ARMAGEDDON has been sent on and the antipathy between the *SS* and the *Abwehr* people, I just don't believe that they are working together. Therefore, Sir, the only conclusion I can draw is that the *SS* intends to do something further. It simply must be either to kill or kidnap Verdi. Either way, it would be a tremendous coup for Himmler and Heydrich if they pulled this off. Why else use an agent of von Donop's caliber?"

Churchill nodded and looked over at Admiral Godfrey. "And does the DNI concur, Admiral?"

"Yes, Prime Minister. I concur precisely with Commander Fleming's assessment."

Churchill leaned forward, hands outstretched over the table.

"MI-6 concurs as well, Prime Minister," responded "C".

"Very well, then. In spite of the very real naval resource problems I am wrestling with, I am going to authorize Admiral Somerville to detach two ships from Gibraltar to intercept *Zamzam* and remove this gentleman, Dr. Verdi."

From a dark corner of the room came a shuffling noise. "Sir, I must protest this action," came a deep voice from the shadows. "Such an overt act might well let on to Jerry that we are reading his wireless traffic. We cannot, I repeat, cannot risk compromising ULTRA."

Churchill leaned forward and stared the dark man straight in the eyes, cocking his left eyebrow. "Meaning?"

The colonel arched his back bringing his chiseled but haggard face into the glare of an overhead, uncovered lamp. "Meaning, Sir, it would be better that the Germans murder the scientist than to allow ULTRA to be compromised."

War is a heartless bastard. Fleming shot up like a spring—an instinctive reaction. All crumbled. He must save it. His mind whirred. *An idea!* "If I may, Prime Minister, Colonel, let me offer a compromise. What if the warships merely escorted the *Zamzam* to Cape Town? Perhaps they could signal her that, say, due to the threat of German raiders operating in the area, they were, oh, going to provide an escort. Might not this intimidate ARMAGEDDON into postponing any adverse action until they debark. Then, of course, the SOE men will be able to protect our bird and eliminate the Nazi once for all. Perhaps we could protect Verdi, maintain ANTIMONY's cover, and negate the Germans in one stroke." Fleming relaxed. *There! He might have just saved them all.* Churchill glared at the staff officer in an odd manner as the other men at the table smiled.

"Thank you, Commander." Churchill rose. Wooden chair legs scraped over the hard, uncovered linoleum as everyone scrambled to rise to attention. "Gentlemen, will you all please step outside for a moment while the Colonel and I discuss the matter?"

The PM's question really represented a command. The visitors to the inner sanctum scrambled as gracefully as possible for the door and exited into the passageway.

"Good show, Ian," beamed Godfrey as the door clicked shut.

After several agonizing minutes, the door opened. The General Staff officer showed them in. Churchill had departed by a side exit. The supplicants stood in an anxious huddle.

"The old man is going to authorize it. Mind you, it's against my better judgment, but if young Fleming is right, we all win."

Godfrey smiled and extended a friendly handshake to the colonel. "Right then! We'd best be arranging for a telegram from the New York shipping agent to ANTIMONY as soon as possible. INTREPID can code it so as to alert our man to the danger without compromising his identity. See to that first off when you arrive in New York tomorrow morning will you Ian."

Almost in a whisper, the General Staff officer spoke, slow and painfully. "There is another way to warn your man ANTIMONY before the destroyers can catch them up."

All eyes shot towards him, surprised by the totally unexpected new element.

"*Zamzam* is sailing under Admiralty orders."

Only the whirring of the overhead fan disrupted the silence caused by momentary disbelief.

"What? She is a neutral vessel," retorted Godfrey, amazed at the revelation.

"Not so strictly neutral, Admiral. She is operating under Plan Green, Sir."

"And what the devil, Colonel, is Plan Green?" blurted out a testy Menzies, piqued at not knowing the full story behind what obviously represented a high-level special operation.

The officer took a long, deep breath and slowly exhaled. "Bait."

"I beg your pardon?"

"Bait, General. The *Zamzam* is bait for the Germans. She is meant to be found and attacked."

The ceiling seemed to crash down on Fleming as he collapsed back into his chair. *Incredible!*

"Let's all sit down, shall we. And you had best explain what you mean, Colonel," responded a visibly angry Godfrey.

The officers took their places around the conference table.

"Indeed, Sir. The *Zamzam* was formerly the *Leicestershire*, built originally for the Bibby Line in 1909. Many of her class, including the *Zamzam,* were used during the first war as troop transports. The MISR Line purchased her in 1933 to transport passengers, mainly Muslim pilgrims. But, many of these same class of vessels are now used again as armed cruisers. In short, she looks like one of ours."

"And how do we get Jerry to just attack this seemingly belligerent vessel?"

The Colonel winced. "She is sailing without running lights or national ensign, General Menzies."

"And why should we want the Germans to attack this particular vessel, Colonel?" asked Godfrey, already suspecting the reply.

"Because, Sir. The *Zamzam* is carrying over a hundred Americans, especially several missionaries bound for Africa.

"An ally into the fray," whispered Fleming aloud, paraphrasing a popular Churchill expression.

"What was that, Commander?"

"Nothing, Sir. It's just the *Lusitania* affair again, only this time, we are creating the crisis ourselves by enticing Jerry."

"Just so! Whose bloody ridiculous idea was this, might I ask?" exploded Godfrey.

"Does it really matter, Sir?"

Godfrey leaned back in his chair, glaring at the embarrassed staff officer's ashen face. "No. I suppose not. So what do you propose?"

"I propose that we send a signal to the Master of the *Zamzam* to warn him and ANTIMONY of the threat. And, we cancel Plan Green for this voyage. Captain Smith is the only one who has access to the Merchant Code we issued to them, and we believe him to be a reliable sort."

Godfrey leaned forward, assuming a stern headmaster's demeanor. "Concur. Hopefully, they can protect the American. You just may have cost us a great deal, Colonel. I must say, I resent the secrecy with which some of your operations are conducted. Where it may impact us, it would be polite to inform the Service agencies of your plans. And I might add it's a damned immoral, barbaric thing for us to put innocent civilians in harm's way, regardless of the consequences for the free world should we lose this punch-up. Good God! What have we become!"

The murmuring about the table expressed the sentiment.

"I'll see to the appropriate signal, Sir," responded the chastened officer as he rose and backed out of the room with a short, but polite dip of the head. Silence followed for several moments.

"Well gentlemen, I feel the need for a pint at the Bell and Clapper. Care to join me?" chipped in the Admiral as he slowly rose.

As the intelligence men walked down the passageway towards the exit lift, Godfrey turned back to Fleming, who trailed behind in deep contemplation. "When you brief INTREPID on this ghastly muck, impress on him the urgency of having the SOE men fully briefed as to who they are facing in Cape Town."

"Let's pray the damned ship makes it to Cape Town," added General Gubbins as he strode through the parted doors. 0920 in London—0620 in the South Atlantic.

PART II
WALTZ OF THE DRESDEN

CHAPTER 13
RED SKY AT DAWN

O543—too early in the morning for most passengers except those irritatingly energetic early morning types. A knock at the door caused Smith's eyes to jerk open. Even though he had been half-awake for several minutes, the harsh sound settled the issue—time to take the morning navigational star sights before sunrise obscured the twinkling points of light. The first officer stood outside in the passageway, impatient to get on to his breakfast after an uneventful watch.

"Come."

The door opened quickly, but silently. "It's time to shoot stars, captain."

"Thank you, number one. I'll be up in a moment."

"Very good, Sir."

Smith's bare feet hit the cold metal deck. He yawned and rubbed the bridge of his nose between thumb and forefinger. His middle-aged body rebelled against the rigors of sea life. He needed a regular schedule, a normal cycle of sleep and waking. *Just getting too bloody old for sea duty. Maybe I'll retire soon. Maybe after a few convoy runs. Maybe.* He flicked on the red glowing lamp that preserved night vision but provided enough light to see by. Mariners train themselves to operate in the half-dark, half-light surreal landscape of red-lighted ship spaces. The rising steam from the wash basin felt good against his stubble-bearded face. Scooping up a handful of water, he splashed it across his jowls, reached out for a towel hanging on a foldout rod and patted his cheeks dry. 0547. Reaching for the medicine chest handle, a funny sort of thought came over him from nowhere in particular—a sudden jolt of fear passed quickly as he located his shaving brush and Barbasol can. 0548.

A frantic knock startled him. Dropping the shaving brush into the basin, Smith whirled about on his heels. "Come!" The door flew open. In the dim glow stood the first officer, tension spread over his taut face—the worried look of a fearful man not quite certain precisely what he needed to do. Out of breath from his race in from the port Bridge Wing, he sputtered. "Captain! A ship is overtaking us on the port quarter at high speed!"

Without a word, Smith lunged for the door, the first officer already two steps ahead of him. The RRR signal from the *Yai-Tin* clanged in his head. His worst, most dangerous concern since leaving Recife now seemed to have occurred. They sailed without running lights or national ensign under Admiralty orders into the enemy's lair. *God save them all!* Dressed only in pajamas, he reached the Bridge Wing in a few bounds. Binoculars firmly pressed to eyes, both men scanned back and forth over the low, menacing form astern of them. "How far out do you make her?"

"About 10,000 yards. Very close," replied the first officer, his eyepieces fogging up from the damp perspiration and early morning humidity.

"I agree. She is running on a parallel course overtaking at high speed. She'll be directly on our beam in a few minutes. Run aft. Break out the largest Egyptian ensign we have. Run it up the jigger. Go man! As fast as you can!" the captain shouted in the half dark of the new dawn.

"At once, Captain!"

The intruder showed no running lights, sat low in the water, but appeared to be a merchantman. Just as he ordered the mate to signal a greeting to the unknown vessel, she suddenly turned to port giving a full broadside aspect, the correct angle to unmask main batteries. The first salvo fell sixty yards short on a direct line with *Zamzam*'s Pilot House. Great spouts of water rose high in the air, glittering in the waning moonlight and crashing down hard back into the dark sea below sending out ripples of disturbed water in all directions.

"The bloody bastards are going to sink us without a trace!" he shouted in terror and rage. Smith leaned over the rail and looked astern. The green Egyptian flag fluttered in the morning breeze. He could barely make it out even from his close vantage point. All thoughts of the Admiralty's covert plan evaporated. He had to save his ship! "Damn! The bastards won't be able to see that. Damn!" Turning and racing into the Pilot House where the mate pleaded frantically for directions. Smith shouted orders. "Left 15. Order all stop."

The helmsman spun the wheel over 15 degrees. *Zamzam's* bow swung left. In the Engine Room, the watch officer felt the thud of the shells plummeting into the water just yards away, but tons of seawater muffled the explosion. He thought they had struck some object, perhaps a small vessel or a whale. Bells clanged frantically as the handle swung around to Full Ahead, then all the way to Full Astern, then back to All Stop. *Emergency Bells!* "Allah protect us," he whispered as he leapt over to the throttle wheel. With four quick turns of his muscular arms, he shut off the fuel flow. The clattering, noisy engines ceased their motion. For a moment, the Engine Room became deathly still except for the low humming of the electrical generator and the whishing of the screw slowing to a halt. Another whumping sound came from the starboard side.

In the Pilot House, Smith heard the whistle of shells passing overhead, landing very close on the starboard side. Showers of salt spray plummeted down on the starboard decks. Shrapnel from expended shells arched up out of the water and rained down on the metal housing and wooden decks with a clatter. Smith knew what came next. The Germans had just finished what they called "locating the finger between." The Americans called it "bracket and halving"—fire short then long, observe the fall of shot, then calculate a firing solution to the target. The next volley would come crashing down on *Zamzam* carrying hellish fire and destruction. *He must stop it.* Smith gripped the Bridge Wing rail so hard that his knuckles turned white. *He must signal the beast. They must know the tragic error.* The EOT answered All Stop.

"*Herr Kapitan.* She is coming about, target angle now 220 degrees," shouted the officer from the starboard Bridge Wing of the German commerce raider *Atlantis*.

"Very good," he acknowledged turning to the first officer. "No doubt to unmask her batteries. Why has she not responded with counter-battery? Surely she must be at Action Stations by now."

"I cannot say, *Herr Kapitan.* She is most unlike any armed cruiser I have ever seen," he responded, shaking his head.

"She has hoisted colors, Sir," came the voice from the Signal Bridge.

"The white ensign?"

"I cannot tell, *Herr Kapitan*. The light is too bad."

"Very well." Pausing only a moment, he spoke into a telephone on the Bridge Wing. "Do you have a solution?"

"*Jawohl, Herr Kapitan*," came the voice from Fire Control.

"Fire the next salvo." On a visit to England in 1937 for the coronation of King George VI, the German captain's Royal Navy escort had pointed out several ships of this same class and had commented on their use as troop transports in the first war. Surely, *Tamesis* had just ambushed such a ship. But, a hint of doubt now crept into the captain's mind.

Smith saw the reddish-orange muzzle flash from the demon ship, stark and wonderfully colorful in the gray half-light of dawn. Huge clouds of billowing, burning gases exploded, hurling metal objects out at incredible speed. A horrible wrenching noise welled up from amidships followed by a muffled boom. A shell hit on deck had penetrated two layers of wood and steel and exploded in a food locker. Within a second, two ear-wrenching bursts boomed above and behind the captain. Shell fragments rained down on the deck below, but none close to him. One exploded high up in the rigging causing little structural damage. The other plowed into Lifeboat Number 4, blowing it in half, spraying wood splinters over the deck and into the water below. The two halves of the boat dangled limply from their davit lines, swaying to and fro like men hanging from a gallows.

"I must signal them. I must stop them!" Smith shouted as he raced back into the Pilot House. *The Morse Blinker on the mast!* He tapped out the international signal for "I am the *Zamzam*, Egyptian, cease fire, cease fire." Over and over and over he jabbed at the keypad.

The first officer rushed into the Pilot House. "Not working! The line to the Morse, it is cut . . . dangling loose . . . cut!" he heaved out of breath.

"Damn it! Wireless!" He screamed into the brass voice pipe to no reply. "Wireless! Are you there, man?"

The wireless operator had been there but not anymore. The first salvo startled him. Violating orders, he lifted the heavy port side blackout curtain and saw the low slung, dark raider and the flash of the second salvo. The man panicked, deserted his post, and raced out of the space, arms flailing, tongue hanging limp in utter terror. He raced aft, then forward, then finally down below to warn his shipmates. The captain's voice from the metal tube shouted to an empty space.

"He must have been hit, Sir," volunteered the first officer.

An Egyptian merchant officer cadet—a tall young man in training to be a deckmate—appeared in the Pilot House out of breath from the race up the four decks from his berthing compartment. Smith motioned over. The youth hovered over him.

"Find a torch, Abdul. There are several in the Boatswain's Locker up forward. Bring it here as fast as you can. Run, lad!"

"Yes, Sir. I'm flying, Sir!" The cadet raced down the ladder towards the bow. Another boom came from the port side. The German fired a fourth salvo at the helpless ship.

"She is slowing, *Herr Kapitan*. I think she must be at All Stop."

"What!" Captain Rogge strode out onto the Bridge Wing and snapped the binoculars to his eyes. The junior officer pointed to the *Zamzam's* wake, now barely a ripple. She had fallen abaft the beam of the raider by several yards.

"All Stop," he shouted back into the Pilot House.

"All Stop," responded the lee helmsman.

"Why has she not returned fire, First Officer? Is she trying to lure us into a trap?"

"Do we continue firing, *Herr Kapitan*?"

"Yes. Continue firing." The German captain raised the binoculars again, scanning for the hidden guns of this most peculiar British armed cruiser. *They had to be there. Why did he not return fire?*

In the Engine Room, a metallic clunk, a grating sound of metal on metal deadened by surrounding seawater, vibrated through the space. A fraction of a second passed before the flash of bright light and ear-splitting crash sent debris and metal shards in all directions, but apparently hitting no one. The armor piercing shell struck the Engine Room below the waterline behind an electrical generator, which absorbed the impact and most of the shell fragments. As the machinery toppled forward, sparks flashed with the popping and crackling of rampant electricity. In a second, everyone in the space heard the low, obscene gurgling noise as the holed hull pulled in seawater at the rate of hundreds of gallons a minute. Already the air in the space felt heavy and oppressive as sparks danced off metal bulkheads and support struts. The heavy air pressed in on the men in the dark as the roar of incoming water grew louder. Emergency lanterns first failed, then seconds later, activated with a whimpering sputter, illuminating the Engine Room in an eerie, pale glow. Shadows of men and wounded machinery flickered and danced off the terracotta bulkheads as the splash of water and the hysterical shouts of panicked men mixed with the crackle and pop of electricity. No hope thought Burns. The first salvo had awakened him. He had clambered down the ladder only moments before the shell struck the hull scant feet from him. He dove out of the path of the falling electrical generator. "Right! Everyone out. Move!"

The Egyptian assistant engineer echoed the order in Arabic—a damned useless order at that. The terrified crewmen had already begun their scramble out of the Engine Room. Burns looked over at the engineer who had kept at his post on the throttle through the entire episode. He motioned to him. "Go, son. We can't do anything here. Wait for me at the hatch."

"Yes, Chief. I shall await you." The Egyptian scrambled up a ladder through a drenching shower of salt spray coming through the gash in the ship's side. Already, two feet of oily, filthy water rose up from the bilges to engulf any who challenged it.

"Pilot House." No response. "Pilot House!" Burns shouted into the voice pipe.

"Pilot House," responded the first officer.

"We've taken a shell hit here below the waterline. Number 1 electrical generator blown out. Rapid flooding. There's nothing more I can do here. I'm abandoning Engine Room. No casualties that I can see."

After a pause, in a voice filled with anguish, but calm, the first officer responded. "Very good, Engine Room. Secure the space. We've lost all ship's power but the emergency lights are on. Good luck."

"Same to you. Engine Room out." Burns and the Egyptian stood over the bulky metal Engine Room hatch, breathing heavily. Slowly, they lowered it down into place and with a quick turn of the hand wheel, dogged it in place. With luck, watertight integrity would hold. *Zamzam* would not sink with the Engine Room flooded but should water spread to other below deck spaces, the crippled ship would go down fast. Burns glanced over at the engineer. The man shivered, his lower lip hung limp and flapped in the demonic red glow of the emergency lamps. He rocked back and forth. Burns sprang up and dropped the dogging wrench to the deck with a loud metallic clang. He placed his hands on the man's shoulders to calm him, thinking it only fear, and felt a warm, moist stickiness as he lifted his hand from the shoulder. A trickle of blood, bluish-purple in the surreal light, ran down his palm into his shirt cuff. The chief engineer winced. He liked the young intelligent, motivated, and dedicated engineer. As the panicky crewmen scrambled for safety, this man stood to his post with a piece of shrapnel lodged in his shoulder. Burns turned the man around. The dark blood dripped on the metal deck through the torn linen shirt. He slowly turned him around again.

"Rasheed, we're going topside to find Dr. Rufail. Do you hear me? Do you understand? Dr. Rufail!"

The Egyptian slowly, painfully shook his head. The adrenalin rush had kept him going thus far. It now failed. Rasheed's head dropped onto his chest, saliva drooling down onto his chin. Burns slid his shoulder up under the wounded man's arm pit and guided him slowly forward and up the narrow metal ladders, up two decks and out onto the main deck, away from the gushing, gurgling of the flooded Engine Room below. In the east, the sun lay just on the horizon in the red sky dawn.

Smith watched the cadet disappear into the dark passageway aft of the Pilot House as the senior wireless operator appeared in the doorway. He had been in the crew's mess drinking coffee when the first rounds came over.

"Anwar! Over here, quick lad!" shouted the captain, motioning to the chart table. Both men converged on the metal table at the back of the Pilot House. Smith grabbed a piece of notepaper and a pencil and scribbled as he talked. His jowly cheeks, normally ruddy, had turned pale and wan. "I can't raise the Wireless Room. It must have been hit. If the gear is still operable, send out this signal as fast as you can. Keep repeating it as long as you are able. Here then. Good luck." Smith shoved the paper into the man's out-stretched hands, who turned and raced out of the Pilot House, scurrying towards the Wireless Room one deck below. As he leaped onto the ladder, he paused a moment on the top rung to scan the paper.

"SOS SOS SOS. RRR RRR RRR. Under attack by unknown raider. Dead in the water. Many hits. I am the Egyptian liner *Zamzam*. Position 25 degrees South 006 degrees East."

Anwar turned the corner and bolted through the open Wireless Room door. *No one here and no damage. The blackguard has run.* Anwar cursed the coward as he flipped toggle switches to power up the transmitter. He would send out the message on the standard international distress frequencies. Every ship in the area should be listening, including the German. Maybe that would stop the shelling. *No! There's something wrong.* He flipped the toggle switch up and down. The needle in the glass window did not move.

He reached for the other transmitter. The needle read zero voltage. *Damn! No power going to the antenna.* Anwar could not see the dangling long wire antenna hanging limp from its mounts on the mast, severed by a 150mm shell only moments before. He pounded on the table top. *Call the Pilot House, tell the old man. Nothing else to do.*

Senior Wireless Operator Anwar didn't hear the screeching of the shell as it careened into the side of the ship one deck above, a direct hit in the captain's cabin. The overhead collapsed throwing him to the deck. His head struck the metal desk. Anwar faded into oblivion. He didn't see the debris falling down on top of the radio sets crushing them. Hot glass vacuum tubes exploded as electric sparks shot out of shattered radios. Papers and clothing from the captain's foot locker rained down. Prostrate on the deck, Anwar felt nothing, not even the pain from the gash in his abdomen or the sharp edged, ugly metal sliver jutting from his side.

The force of the explosion pushed in the bulkhead dividing Smith's cabin from the Pilot House. Steel slivers sprayed the Pilot House ripping and cutting as they struck objects, blowing out glass windows, and in a gruesome scene, impaling the leather captain's chair. Amazingly, none hit any of the four men in the Pilot House. The force of the explosion threw all of them to the deck causing contusions and bruises, but no wounds. A gray hazy smoke reeking of sulfur poured into the Pilot House from the shattered cabin.

Just aft of the amidships watertight door port side, another shell smashed through the hull into the cabins just at the waterline. Frank Vicovari and Dr. Starling, awakened by the explosions, had both thrown on the first clothes available and come out into the passageway when the round careened into the ship shooting tiny pieces of hot metal into their legs and abdomens. Vicovari crumpled as the pain shot up through his side from his maimed legs. His mouth opened to scream. Nothing came except a pitiful rasping sound. He staggered into the bulkhead gasping for breath in the suddenly stifling, oppressive passageway. Clutching his torn, open flesh, the ambulance man collapsed to the bloody steel deck. The impact flung Starling against the bulkhead. His body slid down to the deck ending up a heap of blood and torn clothing next to the unconscious Vicovari. Mrs. Starling had been in the cabin and not hit. She thrust her head out into the nightmarish scene, screamed and rushed to her bloodied husband, cradling his head in her lap. She moaned for a few moments, then, as composed as she could be, called for help.

Further forward, the ship's surgeon, Dr. Rufail, raced about the deck screaming, a metal splinter lodged in his eye. He yelled frantically for someone to pull it out so he could treat the wounded. Cries of panic, pain, and fear rumbled up and down the dark passageway.

Ned Laughinghouse had been hit also. He had raced up the amidships ladder portside when the shells started to find the target. As the shell struck Lifeboat No. 4, he jerked around instinctively when a hot shard drove through his skull and lodged in his brain. He collapsed, sprawled on the amidships hatch. "Must stop the bleeding! Must stop it now!" he shouted, surprisingly still conscious and lucid. He pulled a handkerchief from his back pocket and pressed it against the wound. In intense agony, streaks of pain, terrible and intense, shot out from the wound. Blood poured down into his eyes as he fought to remain conscious. Two ambulancemen ran up the ladder after him. They gently lifted him off the hatch and carried the limp man to the starboard side, away from the evil monster draining the life from the helpless ship. There would be much work for the half-blinded doctor this morning.

The cadet, his previously starched white uniform streaked with oil and grease from the grimy Boatswain's Locker, arrived back in the Pilot House. In the dark space he had found a spare signaling lamp amongst barrels of lubricating oil and extra anchor chain. Dodging the splash of yet another shell, he reached the Pilot House heaving in fear and exhaustion and thrust the lamp into the waiting hands of the captain. As he did, he stood immobile, awed by the destruction. The EOT bent over several inches; the ship's wheel leaned at on odd cant as if praying to Mecca, metal splinters sticking out of the wooden wheel. The glass from the blown-out windows lay on the Sun Deck below. The bulkhead chronometer, its glass shattered, registered the time of impact—0601.

Smith and the first officer raced out to the Bridge Wing. "She's starting to list, captain! A couple of degrees to port, I think."

"Yes. The Engine Room. Let's hope the watertight hatch holds." The captain hoisted the heavy light up to the rail. It clicked on with a reassuring dull whump. The bright, white light shot out across the black water, aimed at the attacker's Bridge.

"Bloody bastards," he shouted as his forefinger touched the yellow button, ready to flash to the Germans. The first officer waved his arms to attract attention. Smith clicked in International Morse Code repeating over and over the desperate signal as he sighted down the black rubber lamp handle.

CEASE FIRE. ZAMZAM. EGYPTIAN LINER. CEASE FIRE.

Overhead, more shells screamed in. Aft of them, they heard a dull clank as the final round in the salvo struck home. A moment later came a dull, muffled explosion as the round exploded deep inside the hull near the crew's mess. Up above on deck, shrapnel and loose metal sprayed up and holed two more lifeboats.

"Bridge," came the voice from the Signal Bridge above.

"*Ya*. Go ahead."

"Signal from the enemy ship, Sir. I read CEASE FIRE ZAMZAM EGYP-
TIAN LINER CEASE FIRE. She is repeating the signal."

The German officer blanched white. His lips trembled. *Good God, what
kind of savages have we become! A neutral passenger liner!* "Very well, acknowledge the signal."

"Aye, aye."

"*Herr Kapitan*!" The watch officer hustled out to the Bridge Wing towards
the commanding officer, his face flush with rage.

"*Herr Kapitan*," shouted the quartermaster of the watch who had been
staring incredulously through his binoculars at the target as the raider closed
in the gathering light, "there are people milling about on deck. They look like
civilians. Passengers!"

The watch officer reached the Bridge Wing frantically waving his arms
and shouting. "She is the *Zamzam*. A passenger liner!"

"Are you certain? Are you sure?" thundered *Kapitan zur See* Bernhard
Rogge over the boom of the nearest 150mm loosing its deadly load just below them.

"She is signaling! There!" He pointed to the dim blinking light. Rogge had
not yet seen it. He had been concentrating on the fall of shot onto *Zamzam's* stern, quietly cursing his crew's somewhat surprising number of misses
against a dead in the water target.

"Cease fire!" he roared as he spun and bolted into the Bridge to the telephone on the rear bulkhead. He twirled the crank. "Cease fire. Cease fire,
now!"

"*Jawohl, Herr Kapitan*," answered the startled gunnery officer in Fire
Control.

Puffs of gray smoke drifted up from the gun muzzles. The heavy morning
air reeked of acrid cordite. In spite of the ceasefire order, the gun crews continued to train their weapons on the target, awaiting the order to send her to
the bottom. Tension built in the gun tubs. *What if she opens up and returns
fire. Why ceasefire now?* In Gun Plot, no one spoke. They simply stared at
their range and bearing calculators or nervously fingered their controls.

On the *Zamzam*, a sucking, gurgling noise welled up from the massive, jagged wound below the waterline. The ceasefire quieted the screams of the crew and passengers cowering on the open decks. Smith slumped on the rail and dropped the signal lamp to the wooden deck grating. His hands went limp and dangled over the rail. Smudges of black, smoky grime turned moist on his cheeks as tears welled up. The first officer did not notice. He nervously eyed the increasing port list now fully five degrees. Objects on deck, loosened by the blast or carelessly left about, slid over the side or collected in wet heaps against the railing. Number 4 Lifeboat dangled, swaying from its davits in the freshening wind. Up above in the rigging, a loose piece of metal held up only by a strand of wire rhythmically bumped into a mast. It sounded like a hammer steadily thumping on a metal pipe. A crunching, creaking sound welled up from the keel as the old ship died.

"She won't last long, Captain." The first officer jolted Smith out of his trance—time for action.

"Yes. You're right. Let's get it organized."

The two men went back into the destroyed Pilot House. Smith depressed the talk button on the ship's general announcing system. Nothing—all power lost, even the emergency backup. An abandon ship would be bad enough. Without ship's power, it would be ghastly. He turned to the first officer.

"Go down to the main deck. Do what you can from there. I'll organize things here."

"Yes, Sir!" As he reached the doorway, he glanced back and paused a moment. "Should you change, Sir?"

In the fury of the past few minutes, Smith hadn't noticed that he wore only his pajamas and slippers. He grinned. "It wouldn't do for the ladies to see the old man in his night shirt, would it?" he smirked, recovering some semblance of humor.

"Indeed not, Captain. Indeed not."

"Very well, then. Let me see to a few things here and I'll catch you up on deck."

The first officer nodded, turned and headed down towards the carnage below. The mate and the helmsman had both stood by quietly in a corner of the Pilot House. The captain noticed them cowering. "You two! Get to your lifeboat stations. It's going to be bad. Keep order as best you can. Understand?"

"Yes, Captain. Very much!" The two terrified men followed the first officer out of the Pilot House.

For a moment, Smith stood alone among the carnage of his ship—not much of a ship, but his nonetheless. Now she had fallen victim to this bloody awful war. *How many of his passengers and crew had perished? How many would die in the days to come? What would the Germans do to them?* He wiped his sweaty, grimy brow with his pajama sleeve. *No time to think about that now. There are more immediate matters to attend to.* He reached into the still intact cabinet under the chart table and pulled out the battery-powered loudhailer. The squawk of feedback noise told him it remained operable. Out on the Bridge Wing, he lifted up the loudhailer to speak the saddest orders of his maritime career. "All hands make preparations to abandon ship. All hands and passengers to your lifeboat stations."

An echo bounced off the water, more a murmur really, as if the souls of those lost at sea mourned another seafarer lost, another ship going down. He moved to the starboard side and did the same. Below decks, here and there, little clusters of passengers and crew gathered and aimlessly shuffled towards their stations. Panic subsided. The lifeboat drill had helped. Smith went back into the Pilot House and pulled out a canvas bag from beneath the chart table. They would need some essentials should the Germans abandon them. Into the bag he tossed the ship's deck log (there would be time for final entries later), pencils, navigational instruments and books, binoculars, charts, a magnetic compass, ship's registry papers, the heavy duty signal lamp, and finally his old brass sextant, which he had sailed with for over thirty years—the pitiful history of a pitiful ship all tossed roughly into a dirty canvas bag. He sat the bag in the middle of the debris-strewn deck.

In his cabin, shattered bulkheads hung like heavy shroud curtains. He gingerly climbed over the jagged metal. The safe—the first priority—remained intact. Tumblers clicked into place. Out came the contents—a Webley revolver, an extra box of shells, a Very pistol with three flares, and more official documents stuffed in a brown manila folder. Finally, out came the truly critical objects—the papers and codebooks that clearly identified the *Zamzam* as sailing under British Admiralty orders. If the Germans boarded the ship before she sank and recovered this material, the merciless assault would be justified. He looked back over towards the rear bulkhead where a heavy leather sofa sat only minutes before. The blast had lifted it up and flung it across the cabin, scorching the leather and landing it on top of his bunk. The real object of his gaze still lay on the deck—a heavy canvas bag with leather draw strings and a twenty pound block of concrete in the base, still where he had stowed it the day the RN officer brought it aboard in New York. Smith dumped the classified material into the bag, looked about the space for more material, saw none, and yanked the straps tight. A double turn of the drawstrings secured the bag. Small holes in the cloth allowed water in quickly. As Smith heaved the dangerous material overboard, a sense of relief washed over him. With a quick gurgle, the bag disappeared. Perhaps simply due to the destruction in the cabin or just in the anxiety of the moment, he failed to notice the Admiralty message confirming his orders to sail without running lights or national ensign received the evening before. In a rush, he had failed to lock it in the safe with the rest of the decoded signals. *No bother. Just slide it under the desk blotter to deal with in the morning.* The devastating evidence still lay under the blotter half hidden by a fallen blackout curtain. Smith had completely forgotten it.

He needed clothes. Despite the destruction, he found the closet intact once he pulled down the sagging louvered doors. Out came his best uniform. From below on deck, he heard the creaking of winches and davits mixed with the chorus of shouting, cursing, braying voices. Confusion mounted. *No time to completely change. Throw on the uniform over the pajamas. No one will care.* He hustled over to the desk to retrieve his personal items including a wallet and several bank notes. He still did not remember the paper under the blotter. Slamming the desk drawer shut, Smith strode hurriedly out of the cabin and retrieved the loudhailer. The chaos from the port side grew in intensity. He would station himself there. The ship had put on another degree of list. It wouldn't be long now. The death watch proceeded degree by degree.

ANTIMONY dreamed of a picnic on a craggy Welsh mountain. Alice, fair-haired, young, and pretty in a plain, home and hearth sort of fashion appeared to be as natural as the surroundings. The snowcapped mountains of late spring thrust themselves into the blue sky above. Multicolored wild flowers added a pristine cleanliness to the high mountain meadow. What a marvelous anniversary celebration picnic, all fluffy with fresh fruits, Cornish pasty, cheese and biscuits, and a fine wine. Suddenly, without warning, from over the top of the distant mountain came a screech. The shadow of an evil, malignant bird of prey, its dark spiked wings spreading over the valley below blotted out the sun. The wind whipped up tumbling the linen cloth and the picnic over into a heap. Flapping wings produced a terrible high-pitched scream. Tall grass bent down cowering before the monster. The bird opened its pale, translucent, hooked beak and screeched again—not an earthly noise, but more a short, explosive rush of wind followed by several others in rapid succession. He clutched his bride close to his chest as they crouched in the tall grass hoping not to be seen.

His eyes shot open. In the dark cabin, he heard the bird of prey hovering above, wings beating the rushing air. Silence. Then it came again. He saw only the darkness of the room yet there came again the screaming whine of the wings. *No! Not the wings. Not the . . . !* Crash! From the beak came a roar, an explosion of noise and dread and hatred. *The beast! Where is it? Where is Alice? Where . . . .*

And then he awakened completely. Thirty years in the Fleet made him recognize the sounds of naval gunfire striking home. He jerked up. *Light! Must see!* He flipped the switch. Nothing. One hand felt for the door knob while the other unbolted it. He yanked it open and stuck his head out. In the passageway, a few passengers huddled in terror. *Move, man. Now is the time of grave danger! Move!* He raced to the closet door and practically ripped the dressing gown from the clothes hook. Without any shoes or slippers, he charged back out his cabin door and across the passageway now red-lit by the emergency lanterns, and pounded furiously on Verdi's door. Within seconds, the physicist whisked open the door and stood ashen-faced, but calm. ANTIMONY pushed in practically knocking Verdi down and at the same time, shoving the door shut.

"Mr. Prince, what's happening? It sounds like artillery shells landing." Many months on the Isonzo River Front in the First World War had taught him to recognize and fear the sound of incoming shells.

"It is. We're under attack. Probably a German raider."

"Then that might explain the unusual course changes yesterday."

"No doubt. There's no time for idle chatter. Get dressed quickly. I'll be right back. We must get up on deck. This superstructure gives no protection. At least on deck, we can gauge where and when the shells will land."

"I see. Spot the muzzle flash and track the fall of shot pattern and all that." The Italian Army veteran understood completely. Without a word, ANTI-MONY nodded and bolted out of the cabin and back across the passageway. He dressed quickly, wearing his most durable trousers, the tweed jacket and the explosive shoes, which might come in handy. Hidden in the jacket lining, the gold coins felt heavy. He slipped the stiletto pen in his shirt pocket and the key ring in the trouser watch pocket where least likely to fall out in the water. Rushing to the clothes closet, he dumped a pair of dress shoes out of their velvet shoe bag, dropped the Smith & Wesson and the pistol taken from the Recife kidnapper into the bag, double wrapped the cord and dropped it into a side pocket. Finally, his wallet and American passport slipped into an inside pocket, which fortunately buttoned down for added security. *Right then. Ready for action.* Back in Verdi's room, the physicist had similarly dressed.

"The gun?"

"Pardon?"

"The Beretta. I need the gun back. We might well need them, but if we are rescued by the Huns, I'll have to dispose of them all," he whispered as he held open the velvet shoe bag.

"Here it is." Verdi had already put it in a pocket. As ANTIMONY retied the bag containing all three weapons, Verdi slipped the picture of Angela out of the silver frame and tucked it in his jacket inside pocket. ANTIMONY understood completely.

"Ready?

"Let's face the music, Mr. Prince."

"Right. Stick close to me. Wherever I go, you follow. If anything happens to me, stay away from Van Eyck—he's the enemy. Don't get anywhere near him, understand?"

"Completely. What about the boats? We are assigned to different ones."

"Go where I go. Even if this crew can get the boats properly loaded, which I doubt, they will not care who is where. Any questions?"

The scientist shook his head affirmatively and with confidence. *This man will be all right.* He stretched out his hand in a shake for good luck. Verdi grasped it firmly and confidently. "Right then, here we go."

Out in the eerily lit passageway, Dr. Rufail cradled a passenger, trying to calm and sooth her despite the blood flowing from his own wound. "There,

there, Madame. Everything will be fine. Please trust me. All will be well, but I must tend to the wounded," he whispered, handing her back to her shaken husband.

ANTIMONY felt the glow of admiration for the Egyptian physician. All over the ship, similar acts of individual courage occurred. ANTIMONY and Verdi made their way over and around the huddled and cringing passengers through the passageway leading out onto the main deck. Once there, he motioned Verdi to sit with his back to the bulkhead, then sat down beside him to pause and consider their next move. The raider, nowhere in sight, had to be on the ship's opposite beam. *Good. This will provide some cover on this side.* They would remain there and await events.

The shelling ceased. Panicky noises replaced the screech of shells and tearing of metal. ANTIMONY stood up. From around the corner came grunting and cursing. Two ambulance drivers held the ankles and shoulders of a blood-soaked, unconscious man, whose arms dangled limp, occasionally dragging along the deck. They carefully lowered him to the deck. The blood, once pouring from the wound in Ned Laughinghouse's head, had checked temporarily. Though unconscious now, he shivered from shock. The two men lifted his head up and propped it up against an upturned deck chair. Hobgood carefully lay a blanket over the prostrate man. As he did so, he looked up and saw ANTIMONY a few feet forward. He looked back at the shivering man, then back at ANTIMONY, shaking his head dejectedly. ANTIMONY looked down at the wet deck below in resignation, staring at his highly polished shoes. *Welcome to the war, Yanks.* From behind and above came the blare of the loud hailer. Captain Smith ordered abandon ship. ANTIMONY well knew what the captain felt. It had to be the most utterly dejected feeling in the world for a commanding officer to order the abandonment of his ship, the ultimate failure in a sense. Even though it could not be helped, it still wrenched at the guts. No captain who ever faced it really gets over it entirely.

"Well, now the real fun begins," he whispered under his breath.

Verdi stood up and dusted off the back of his trousers. "What do we do now, Mr. Prince?"

"Just as we rehearsed it, only you stay with me. Don't go to your own boat. Believe me, they won't be taking any kind of muster. This will be an every scoundrel for himself proposition."

Within a few moments, passengers huddled by the boats, most wild-eyed, but relatively calm. The *Zamzam* crew appeared tense and nervous. Ship's officers, sensing their fear, shouted orders in English and Arabic. As a result, the boat loading began with an unexpected sense of order. As the ship settled deeper in the water, though, ANTIMONY knew that the calm would turn to panic. Around the corner came more injured waiting to embark. Two more husky ambulance drivers, each cradling one shoulder, carried Vicovari, whose fractured right ankle caused him to grimace with searing pain on each movement. From his left thigh, shredded trousers hung limp and sticky with blood. He had been lucky though. The metal shard had not severed any major blood vessels. They laid him down on the deck just out of the rising sun's rays, next to the unconscious Laughinghouse. Further down, on the port side, two men carried Dr. Starling out onto deck to No. 9 lifeboat. Though it swung out, due to the increasing list of the ship, the distance from rail to boat meant a precarious leap. Mrs. Starling applied a compress to his forehead. The bleeding from his right thigh had stopped, revealing an ugly mass of torn muscle and white pale skin. Clumps of clotted, dried blood stuck to his mangled pajama leg.

"Let go the winch," shouted the boat officer.

The crusty metal winch, in need of a good dose of grease, nevertheless gave way, and the boat lowered into the water, bobbing and rubbing up against the hull. A crewman above lowered the portside accommodation ladder down to just where the bow of the boat rhythmically banged against the hull. Until this point, the *Zamzam* crew had behaved well and competently. Until now. But then, hordes of crewman coming up from below, many only half-dressed, rushed the ladder, shoving and shouldering out passengers standing ready to go down. The second mate shouted and bellowed, but to no avail. The riot started. Crewman leapt over each other in pell mell haste to get into the boat and pull away. They knocked Mrs. Starling to the deck along with several other passengers. One of the rafts from the stern, already in the water carrying ambulancemen and RAF wives, passed a few yards away. They laid to the oars to pull away from the ship. Seeing the growing scene of panic, the men stopped rowing.

"Hey, you lot, passengers first!" shouted an irate ambulance man, standing up in the raft.

It did no good. Shouting, bellowing crewmen waved away passengers trying to come down the ladder. Mrs. Starling, seeing the boat attempting to pull away, raced down the ladder to hold it. It did no good. Three men brought her husband to the rail when they realized the boat had moved. She reached out, but a wild-eyed, screaming steward batted her hand away. Off balance and exhausted, she pitched over into the sea and drifted back towards the stern, held up only by her Kapok life jacket and weak paddling.

"Damn!" shouted the enraged ambulance driver. "Let's get her!"

The raft reached her just as she rounded the stern. Two pairs of strong arms pulled her exhausted, heaving body into the already overloaded boat. Elsewhere, the same horrendous scene played out. Once the boats hit the water, the crew attempted to pull away, many only half full, frantically waving away the frightened passengers. On deck, ambulance drivers rounded up the women and children and herded them into the remaining boats, shoving aside the panicky crewmen. Where ship's officers remained in control, things went fairly well. Here and there, little groups of passengers took charge showing individual acts of courage. At one starboard side position, a passenger lowered a rope ladder to the waiting boat below. A woman with her feet crushed by a falling cabin ceiling lay on deck, semiconscious and in tremendous pain, still clutching her two small children. One of the tobacco buyers leaned over and lifted her off the deck and over the rail. Her feet dangled uselessly over the side of the ship as he carefully lowered her down the ladder, one rung at a time. Around the ship, other such incidents occurred, some even humorous. The ship's nurse had rescued a dachshund and carried him into a boat. A magazine editor traveling on assignment to Africa commented, "Well, at least we'll have fresh meat"—the sort of dark humor that the *Zamzam*ers would soon need.

The senior wireless operator had remained at his post even after being wounded. Though delirious and with pain shooting up his side from the gash in his stomach, he crawled back to the wireless table. In his half-crazed, half-conscious state, he tapped out the SOS on the Morse key still screwed down to the table top, but the wires leading to the transmitter dangled loose, severed by the explosion. The first officer found him this way several minutes later as he patrolled the area searching for wounded or lost passengers.

"Come along now, Anwar. You've sent your signal," he whispered as he gently pulled at the man's shoulders.

"No, Sir. Must send signal. Must send signal. Get help," wheezed the delirious operator. Tears welled up in the first officer's eyes. He wiped them away on his grimy, smoky sleeve.

"Come. They've received your signal. Help is on the way."

Only with this assurance did the Egyptian leave his wireless set, his useless, destroyed wireless set. They proceeded aft portside and into a waiting boat. Not until the boat pulled away did anyone realize that shrapnel had holed the boat in several places. Water seeped in. Men and women went over the side into the warm South Atlantic, their heads bobbing up and down. Many shouted for help. Some floundered. Some screamed, some merely cried. Another lifeboat, crammed full with mostly crewmen and RAF wives struggled several yards away. In the water, conscious, but weak with blood loss, Anwar's head rolled back and forth. His arms flashed as he drifted past.

"Swim for it! We're just here, come on now, lad. Swim! Here!" Mrs. Blythe could not get his attention. Anwar drifted past about twenty yards away.

"It's no good, Mrs. Blythe. I'll get him," a young woman shouted as she took off her shoes and threw them into the bottom of the boat.

"Are you sure, Kathleen?"

She made no response, but dove into the rolling sea and swam strongly towards Anwar. She put an arm across the man's chest. He sputtered with seawater in his open mouth. With a strong kick, she propelled them back to the boat now forty yards away. Many sets of hands reached out over the gunwale and pulled the pair into the boat—the heroic swimmer and the courageous wireless operator. Seated in the stern, Abby Ashton sobbed uncontrollably, her shoulders heaving as wet tears rolled down her cheeks. Mrs. Blythe picked her way over and around legs and bodies to the stern.

"Abby, stop that." Mrs. Blythe admonished. "Abbey, dear, everything is going to be fine." It did no good; the woman only sobbed louder. Mrs. Blythe's flat hand cracked into the woman's face. Abbey sucked in air, startled at the violence, but ceased her wailing. "Abby, I said get control of yourself. You must get control, do you hear?"

The crewmen laid to the oars, pulling the boat away from the ship and towards the German coming around the *Zamzam*'s stern. In the bow, the courageous swimmer, exhausted and sickened from her effort and the oily film of fuel oil on the water, leaned over the bow of the boat and vomited, retching, coughing, and gagging. No one cared at the loss of grace. Four oars caught the water and the boat glided through the wake.

Back aboard, at another station, several crewmen made a charge for a boat. Big and hulking, Hobgood stepped in front of the first crewman blocking his path. "Wait your turn, Sonny. Wounded first."

The crewman shouted, cursed, and screamed at Hobgood in guttural French. The retired Army colonel pursed his lips, simply nodded, reached over and grabbed the insolent Frenchman by the shoulder and under the crotch and tossed the man overboard, some thirty feet to the waterline. The surly crew got the message.

And so went the abandonment of the *Zamzam*. One lifeboat never left its davits. Another got stranded on the Sun Deck. The comedy of errors demonstrated a curious mixture of cowardice and panic from some of the crew and heroic acts of individual crewmen and passengers. Amazingly, no one died in the water as other *Zamzam* boats and rafts or German boats plucked out waterlogged people from the sea. The ship, after its early flooding, stabilized. The watertight Engine Room hatch held sturdy in spite of the incredible pressure pushing up on it. She steadied out with a ten degree port list. In the confusion, two dozen passengers along with the captain and the first officer, had been left behind, including several ambulance drivers and Dr. Starling. Many ambulance drivers voluntarily stayed aboard to help passengers into the boats even at the risk of their own lives. In this tragedy on the high seas, sacrifice and integrity mingled with darker sides of humanity—selfishness, cruelty, panic, and despair.

As the crewmen lay to the oars pulling towards the German ship now only yards away, ANTIMONY reached into his pocket and pulled out the cloth bag, heavy with its lethal cargo. He gently lowered it to the water and let go. Without so much as a gurgle, the heavy bag sank. No one noticed. No one would even care had they noticed. He turned and looked back on the pitiful vessel that had been his home, his focus, his mission for these few weeks. In the day-to-day dance of point-counterpoint, move and countermove, check and mate with the enemy, he had been winning the game. And now, another player, who stumbled into the game by accident of war, had turned the odds heavily against him—the challenge greatly increased, the odds far worse. He had been up to the first innings. Could he stay up for the rest of the match. He must. The simple little visit to a long-lost relative had suddenly, violently, turned into a potential disaster of earth-shattering importance. And, he might be the only bulwark between Verdi and the Nazi regime eager to have his knowledge and skill. ANTIMONY stared back at the *Zamzam* and let out a long low whistle of air. 0630—barely a half hour after the first shell landed.

CHAPTER 14

THE MASTER IS INDISCREET

The raider edged around *Zamzam*'s stern, moving cautiously, still fearing a trap. In spite of overwhelming evidence of the victim's impotence and of its identity as simply a neutral passenger liner, Captain Rogge refused to take chances. On the raider's rails stood sailors armed with machine pistols and rifles, ready to rain gunfire down on the ragtag flotilla of boats and rafts at the slightest provocation. Indeed, some in the boats wondered whether they intended to do so anyway to cover up the inescapable evidence of the international *faus pax*. In a way, ANTIMONY wished he hadn't disposed of the pistols. If a shooting spree broke out, at least he might take out a couple of the bastards, small retribution for the murder of hundreds of innocents, but an act of defiance nonetheless. He sighed in relief as the first boats reached the raider and sailors tossed over lines. Another comic and disheartening scene in this human drama occurred. As the rescue lines dangled down from the rails, instead of securing them to the bobbing boats so that they could be pulled to the ladders, *Zamzam* crewmen attempted to scramble up the lines. This most unprofessional display of bad seamanship and lack of good sense made ANTIMONY wonder just how the old tub had ever managed to get underway. Sailors above shouted and cursed in German. An officer, clearly in charge of the boat evacuation, pulled a pistol from his holster and held it high in the air with obvious intent. He shouted a quick order to his men, who jerked the lines back up throwing off the crewmen who clung to them. They hit the water, frantically splashing and flapping. The lines came over again.

"You there. Make those lines fast to your boats. Do it quickly!" came the angry command from above in clear English. The men in the water ignored the order and grabbed and clawed for lines pushing each other aside or under the surface. The officer turned to the sailors manning the rail. Rifle bolts pulled out, then snapped back in. *They are going to shoot them off the lines! They are going to shoot them!* ANTIMONY stood up to shout. As he did so, a *Zamzam* mate in another boat bellowed in Arabic to the splashing men in the water. The message got through. One by one, the panicked crewmen let go of the lines and swam away from the side of the ship. From around the stern of the raider came two motor launches from the opposite side. The two boats throttled down to pick up men in the water. ANTIMONY sat down. A potential disaster had been averted.

"Come alongside, please. We are taking you aboard," came a voice through a megaphone in clear, crisp, concise English. The calm but firm command eased jittery nerves. The *Zamzam's* flotilla of boats and rafts lay strung out for a quarter of a mile. The steadier crewmen still manning the oars managed to put them in some semblance of order in spite of a swell. In the bow of his boat, an elderly woman fainted. ANTIMONY stood up and, stepping over feet and legs, moved up to her. Of several people near her, no one moved to help. Less than an hour before, these people—businessmen and their wives, the occasional tourist, people just transiting from one point to another— had been peacefully asleep, rocked by the gentle swaying of the ship. And now, they drifted in the ocean. Their home for the past several weeks lolled crumpled and wrecked. Men with guns, destructive men with rifles pointed down at them, ordered them to come into the lair of the monster itself. They had only the clothes they managed to throw on in the confusion. Families had been separated, children from parents, husband from wife. Some loved ones might still be back on board. And above this all, no one bobbing on the warm sea that April sunrise could say for sure what fate lay ahead in the next few weeks, days, or even minutes. It is a shock, not in the classic medical sense; it is an emotional, intellectual shock. It is pervasive and debilitating. Sudden disaster at sea robs one of initiative, then of energy, then drive and finally, if it goes on long enough, of the will to survive. If the conditions are right, usually weather and sea state, the entire process can occur in only a few hours. ANTIMONY had seen that phenomenon before. He had seen robust, strong, healthy, young men give up and slip beneath the water in only a few hours on a frigid November night in 1915. All of these thoughts passed through his mind as he pushed and shoved forward over the slack-jawed, sunken-eyed, ashen-faced passengers. Very well, then, it will be up to those who do not suffer as much to help those who do. There can be no retribution or acrimony, only survival and support. It is the way of the sea.

"Here you! Help me lay her out in the bilges. Quickly, now," he shouted to the nearest man. The commodore took charge. The middle-aged businessman responded to the voice of command—clear, concise, authoritative, and determined. The man lifted the woman's feet up and slid them over the tops of several ankles while ANTIMONY held and guided her shoulders until positioned down in the bottom of the boat away from the sun. He dipped his handkerchief in the water and applied it as a compress to her head. A woman, one of the RAF wives, had been jolted out of her stupor.

"Let me help, Sir. I've done some nurses' aid work—last year, during the Blitz."

"Thank you, Ma'am."

She took a silk handkerchief out of her purse, which she had managed to retrieve, and patted the woman's face gently. The elderly woman soon recovered, her eyes opened wide. "Here now, you stay down where you are at. We'll be aboard the ship in just a few minutes. You're going to be fine."

She mumbled a thank you as ANTIMONY made his way aft back to his seat next to Verdi.

"What's going to happen to us, Mr. Prince?" asked the physicist with concern, but not panic, in his voice.

As he observed earlier, Verdi would come through this ordeal. He would not fold. He need only be guided properly. "I wish to God I knew. I suppose we have just become hostages of some sort. At least, they aren't going to massacre us."

ANTIMONY scanned the attacker memorizing every detail. He remembered his treatise—observe every minutia, every detail no matter how seemingly insignificant or trivial. Observe and remember. It could well turn out to be the difference between mission accomplished and mission failed, or, indeed, between life and death in the field.

The flat black hull absorbed rather than reflected light, especially effective at night when approaching a target. Her gray deck housings and superstructure, the best camouflage color at sea, shrouded the fuzzy line between sea and sky. She looked to be about 8,000 tons and appeared to be a large merchantman. As they came round her stern, he noticed the name printed on the hull—a point of irony—*Tamesis* of Norwegian registry, home port

Tonsberg, Norway. In English, *Tamesis* means Thames, the river of London. He saw a gun on the stern—a 150mm from the bore size. All of the other deck guns had gone out of sight carefully disguised behind false deck houses or lowered below deck on elevators. She had a single, large stack amidships just aft of the multilevel deck house. Several cargo handling cranes located fore and aft on deck seemed mainly for show, though they would be used to handle the underway replenishment of stores and ammunition.

As each boat pulled alongside the vertical ladder, the officer at the rail, when satisfied that the boat had been secured, ordered the refugees to come up. German sailors came down into each boat and helped the women, children and older people up the treacherous, precarious rope ladder. From above, they lowered stretchers and carried the wounded up by heavy attached lines and hauled up the small children in rope baskets, many of them bawling and screaming. The no-nonsense but polite demeanor of the Germans calmed the terrified refugees. Here and there, many chatted softly while being careful to stay out of earshot of the wary Germans. The boat unloading went quickly without further incident.

As ANTIMONY climbed up the ladder onto the deck, he scanned the scene memorizing every detail of the *Tamesis*. An officer, speaking in broken English, directed the *Zamzam*ers over to a companionway leading up to the amidships area. ANTIMONY looked out at the *Zamzam* lying like a beached whale just a few hundred yards away. Two motor launches loaded with sailors sped towards the crippled ship. The first boat pulled alongside the accommodation ladder now at a perilous angle to the water. An officer leapt onto the small, circular landing and grabbing the rail tightly, pulled out his pistol. Holding it high in the air as a warning to any would-be assailant, he leapt up the ladder two steps at a time. At the top rung, he crouched down low in anticipation of an ambush. When nothing happened, he motioned to the waiting sailors below. One by one, the Germans sprang onto the landing and up the accommodation ladder. The officer, however, did not wait for the troops to mass. He scouted out the upper deck then sprang to the exterior ladder and in four bounds arrived, pistol thrust out ahead of him.

During the previous several minutes, Smith surveyed *Tamesis* through binoculars paying particular attention to the two menacing motor boats circling the hulk like prowling sharks. The first officer, with filthy, oily stains from the boat davits covering his white uniform, had a grim expression as if a dear friend had been lost.

"The Germans will be here soon. How many left aboard?"

"I count ten other than us, Sir. I have ordered them to muster on the Sun Deck. We have one raft left plus one fouled on deck. They are mostly the American ambulance drivers. I think we can rely on them to remain calm," he replied.

"Good. You look a mess. Why don't you go below and change into a fresh uniform. We mustn't give the Huns a bad impression, must we?"

"Indeed not, Sir," replied the first officer noticing the captain's stiffly starched, bright white uniform with the blue and white pajama cuff showing from the sleeve.

Moments later, Smith heard the thumping sailors coming up the accommodation ladder. He looked down at his canvas bag. Most of the items he no longer needed, but, he wouldn't part with his personal items—treasures really—accumulated over his seafaring career. *The bloody squareheads will have to shoot him to pry them away. Well, they might do that anyway.* He put the glasses down on his chair. *Perhaps, one final look through the demolished cabin just in case he missed anything.* The smoke had fairly well cleared and he could see *Tamesis* through the shell hole on the port side. *What a bloody mess they made, these Germans. There will be hell to pay for attacking an unarmed merchant.* He had left behind nothing that he could see and turned to exit the cabin. *No! what's that! On the desk? Holy Jesus, no!* The brown, curled message paper stuck up out of the desk almost completely covered by the blackout curtain. *How could he be so careless? How could he have left it there? How did he miss it before?* No excuse, really—a careless blunder. He raced over to the desk, arms grasping out for the paper, tripping over an upturned swivel chair. He snatched up the message. *What to do with it? The weighted bag is long gone.* He couldn't stuff it in a pocket—he might be searched. He could tear it up, but this might cause some suspicion if they found shredded message paper. *The captain's head!* He would tear it up and flush it down the water closet. There had to be sufficient water pressure left for one flush. The shredded bits of incriminating paper would empty into the ship's waste holding tanks and go down with the ship. He started toward the toilet. *No. It's no good.* He heard the clank of heavy boots on the metal ladder outside. *No time!* The enemy had arrived. *One last hope. One last chance.* He flipped up the leather blotter on the desk and scooted the paper back under it. He hoped they might miss it, not expecting a compromising message to be there. He hoped. *The Pilot House—must get out into the Pilot House. If they find me here, they might be suspicious.* Smith stepped out onto the *Zamzam's* demolished Pilot House just as the German officer rounded the doorway leading in from the Bridge Wing. With a weapon leveled menacingly at his chest, Smith slowly raised his arms in the universal sign of surrender.

"Take it slowly, young man. I am not armed. No one on board is. You and your men are quite safe."

The German paused, pondered, then shook his head. "Very well, *Kaptain.* I take you at your word." He slid the pistol back into the brown leather holster.

"I fear you have me at a disadvantage, Sir. I am Captain Smith, Master of the MISR liner *Zamzam* of Egyptian registry."

The officer smiled sheepishly. *The old fool. You have me at the disadvantage. We have just attacked an unarmed, neutral passenger liner. How is that going to look to the world? No, Sir, the advantage is all yours.* "*Leutnant* Mohr of the *Reich Kriegsmarine.* My pleasure, Sir. We are here to secure your vessel. You may lower your hands now."

"Yes, quite. I am at your disposal, Lieutenant."

Three husky sailors arrived in the Pilot House taking up posts behind their officer. While Mohr seemed calm, the three men behind him appeared decidedly nervous and edgy. Smith hoped they would not also be trigger happy, thinking of the passengers and crew still aboard the ship.

"May I look at your papers," Mohr asked politely, already knowing the answer.

"Go ahead," answered Smith.

Mohr smiled. "You won't object to my men searching the Chart Room and your personal quarters, would you?"

Smith thought of the hidden message. *Jesus Christ, I object you stupid Nazi. You can go to hell in a hand basket, you barbarian Hun!* "Not at all, Lieutenant. As you like," replied Smith, disguising his mounting panic.

Mohr turned to the boarding party and spoke in a whisper. "Search the Pilot House, the Chart House and the captain's quarters thoroughly. Turn over everything. Find anything you can. I am especially interested in why this vessel was not flying its ensign when we attacked and why she ran with no lights. Perhaps this British captain, in his haste, forgot something. Is everything clear?"

"*Jawohl, Herr Leutnant,*" answered the senior sailor. The men raced around the officer and over to the Chart House where charts, navigational instruments and the LORAN navigational set lay smashed and strewn about. They clanked and banged like men searching for something, but not really knowing what. Mohr pulled a notebook from his breast pocket and a pen from another. He opened the book. So, Captain Smith, where were you bound for?"

"Am I obliged to tell you that?"

"I think not. You are not a warship nor are you a prisoner-of-war," replied the officer with stiffness in his voice that replaced the relaxed tone of a moment before.

Smith had touched a live wire. The Germans had committed a gross error in attacking a neutral. It represented a card Smith could play to ensure proper treatment for his passengers and crew especially those of British or Canadian nationality, who stood most at risk. "I understand," he replied.

"On the other hand, since you are not an enemy or a POW, there is no reason for you not to cooperate as we try to resolve this, shall I say, delicate diplomatic matter, Captain Smith," said the officer, his suntanned face wrinkling up in a forced smile.

Wicket down! I have him. I'll play this for all it's worth. A crashing noise came from his cabin. He winced. *So, this is what the Admiralty hoped for— an unprovoked attack on the high seas. Well, it worked you calculating bastards. You sank my ship.* "Certainly, Lieutenant. I have nothing to conceal. We originated in New York on the 22nd of March where we embarked passengers and cargo, then on to Baltimore for the same. We put into Trinidad, then Recife for stores and more passengers. We are bound for Cape Town and then back to Alexandria, our home port. As your men in the cargo hold are no doubt finding out, we are carrying no contraband or war material of any sort."

"No doubt," replied Mohr, rapidly taking notes. He shifted his weight back and forth. "And, Sir. Your passengers? Who are they?" *Ah, yes, the passengers, the big prize in this little charade. Indeed.* "They are mostly Americans, some Canadian missionaries and an assortment of Europeans."

The mention of Americans made the German clearly uncomfortable. In spite of the *Führer's* bombast about the inconsequence of American entry into the war, any German military man could see the disaster inherent in her involvement. This *Zamzam* affair muddied the waters considerably. "How many Americans, Sir?"

"138, Lieutenant," an impish grin broke over Smith's hitherto stone face. The German took a deep, short breath—a bad situation all around.

"Herr Leutnant!"

Tamesis's damage control officer had just concluded his tour of the ship to ascertain her seaworthiness. In spite of the port list, she had stabilized with no danger of immediately sinking. As the Engine Room filled, the list actually decreased to only a few degrees.

"Excuse me, *Kaptain*." The officer curtly nodded his head and backed out onto the Bridge Wing, notebook still in hand. *"Ja,* how does it look?"

"She is sound. The Engine Room is completely flooded, but is holding water tight integrity. None of the other below deck spaces are flooded. There is considerable shell damage, mainly port side amidships, but nothing threatening. We shall have to scuttle her with explosives."

"Ja, I concur. How many passengers and crew have you found?"

"The captain and first officer, one child, one wounded passenger and eight American passengers."

"How badly is the man wounded?"

"Quite so. He will require the surgeon."

"Very well. See to it."

"Jawohl, Herr Leutnant." The man pivoted formally and clanked down the rusty metal ladder, shouting orders to the men gathered below. Mohr finished making notes in his book and had just stepped back into the Pilot House when a sailor raced out of the cabin clutching a beige piece of paper. Smith's heart thumped. He had just forfeited his neutral, noncombatant status. *God help the passengers.* Sweat broke out on the back of his neck. Outwardly, he appeared calm and rational, very much in charge. Inwardly, he churned.

The petty officer thrust the crumpled paper into Mohr's hands. A broad grin spread rapidly across his face. His blond eyebrows, bleached almost to invisibility from the months at sea, came together in an expression of cherubic glee. *Saved!* He read the Admiralty signal to *Zamzam.* The series of letters and numbers across the page in pencil had been translated by Smith—a message clearly not meant for any but *Zamzam* and one directed to a ship undeniably sailing under Admiralty orders—the smoking gun. The German carefully folded the message paper and put it into his pocket, making certain to button the flap. He eyed Smith, standing stiffly with no expression on his face at all. "So, Captain Smith. You are not quite all that you would seem. Sailing under British Admiralty orders is not the normal thing for a neutral vessel, now is it, *Herr Kapitan*?" gloated the German officer.

Smith's wicket fell without enough runs. The Germans had won. "I have no comment, Sir."

"As you wish." Mohr turned to the third man who had come into the Pilot House. "Signal *Tamesis*."

"*Jawohl, Herr Leutnant*."

The man jumped forward to attention, semaphore flags in hand. Mohr scribbled a message on a blank piece of paper, ripped it out of the notebook and handed it to him.

"*Herr Kapitan*. Signal from *Leutnant* Mohr just received."

"*Ya, danka*," he acknowledged as he took the message. Rogge read it with a broad smile.

> MOHR TO TAMESIS. HAVE DISCOVERED BRITISH ADMIRALTY CODED MESSAGE HIDDEN IN CAPTAIN'S CABIN.
> NO OTHER MATERIALS FOUND. SHIP STABILIZED. REQUIRES EXPLOSIVE FOR SINKING. TWELVE ON BOARD, ONE BADLY WOUNDED. NO CONTRABAND FOUND. REQUEST INSTRUCTIONS.

"Signals!"

"*Jawohl, Herr Kapitan!*"

"Take this down. Send it to *Leutnant* Mohr."

> BRING ALL SURVIVORS BACK. AM SENDING DEMOLITION CREW. STAY ON BOARD WITH ALL BUT ESCORTS FOR PASSENGERS. CONTINUE SEARCH. WE WILL BRING BACK ALL
> CREW AND PASSENGER LUGGAGE THAT CAN BE SALVAGED. STAND BY
> FOR FURTHER INSTRUCTIONS.

"Do you have that?"

"*Jawohl, Herr Kapitan.*"

Within a few minutes, the demolitions officer received his orders to embark a team on board the crippled vessel, set timed explosives, and sink the evidence of their mistake. On the deck of *Tamesis*, ANTIMONY read the semaphore signal from *Zamzam*'s Bridge Wing. He squinted and craned his neck as much as possible without attracting attention. The sun, now well up on the horizon, sparkled off the swells making his vision that much worse. He had kept up his visual signaling expertise. It would help him now so long as he pretended to be ignorant. Just a little too much interest in the ship's operations or an overheard conversation could be disastrous to his cover. He could only see the signal from *Zamzam*, not the reply from the Signal Bridge above. Even so, it told him enough of the captain's response. He tugged at Verdi's jacket sleeve.

The scientist had been absorbed in his own thoughts, paying little attention to the events going on around him. The determined tug at the elbow shook him out of his daydream. ANTIMONY motioned ever so slightly with his head towards a bulkhead ten feet away, shaded by the upper deck. Their sudden movement startled a guard. He leveled his Mauser at ANTIMONY's chest. The man, a boy really, spooked at the sudden movement, could quite easily shoot them both. Slowly, ANTIMONY and Verdi raised their arms. Their careful motion calmed the man. With one finger pointing out at the sun and the other hand indicating the shaded area, ANTIMONY indicated to the guard that they simply wanted in the shade. The sailor grunted, slung his rifle and turned away. ANTIMONY closed his eyes and slowly let out the huge volume of air, which he had sucked in when the Mauser's muzzle pointed straight at his heart. This would be a game of cat and mouse from here on out. He no longer had the luxury of unfettered movement. The difficulty of his job had multiplied a thousand fold in just those few moments of gunfire. They reached the safety of the shaded bulkhead. He leaned over to whisper.

"They found an Admiralty signal. *Zamzam* sailed under Admiralty orders."

"That might explain why we couldn't show lights, wouldn't it?" Verdi concluded.

"Precisely. I'm afraid it complicates our status considerably," said an obviously worried ANTIMONY.

"How so?"

"We are no longer from a neutral ship mistakenly attacked by a German raider. They have attacked a vessel sailing under Admiralty orders without national ensign or lights. The attack is now completely justified—at least strictly legally, if not morally."

Verdi's forehead wrinkled up in an expression of fear and doubt, visibly shaken by this revelation and the implication. "So what does this mean for us? Are we now prisoners of war?"

ANTIMONY looked out over the deck. Everywhere groups of passengers huddled. Some cried, some stared, some comforted others, all frightened and dazed to one degree or another. He turned back to Verdi. "I am not a lawyer, but I'll venture to say that our status remains the same. We are," he chuckled, "Americans and therefore neutrals, regardless of the particular state of the ship we were on. The law of the high seas in wartime might allow them to attack the ship, but they still must treat us as neutrals and repatriate us. That's how I see it. With hope, these Huns have a legalistic bent."

Verdi nodded, his anxiety partially assuaged. He would feel better once they put ashore—anywhere.

"One other thing—I think they are going to scuttle the *Zamzam* with charges. The old girl seems to have settled out."

"Is there a chance they will release us and let us proceed on the *Zamzam*?" his voice grew faster and higher pitched, showing the flicker of hope behind it.

"No. They will destroy the carcass of this latest kill. They will sink it."

Down below in Sick Bay, a ship's doctor quickly prepared the most badly wounded passengers for surgery—all accomplished briskly and efficiently. The other casualties—Anwar and others with minor injuries—also received the necessary treatment. The German medical staff appeared sympathetic, which calmed the raw nerves of the wounded. Up on deck, a small table and chair had been set up under a canvas awning. An imperious looking officer sat down flanked by sailors. Another officer addressed the crowd.

"Ladies and gentlemen. I realize that in the confusion, you might have left your documents on board. Please be assured that we will try to recover these for you. In the meantime, please step to the table and present to the officer whatever documents you may have. If you have your passport, please show that. If you have even a simple driving license, that will be excellent. Please now, one at a time, please step up. The officer will instruct you where to go next. Thank you for your attention."

"Name?"

"Edward B. Prince."

The German printed the name in bold letters in the ledger. "Nationality?"

"United States."

"Place and date of birth?"

"Albany, New York. Twenty-eighth of August, 1890."

"Occupation?"

"Mining equipment sales representative. I sell to the diamond mines, you see, and ... ."

"Thank you, Mr. Prince. Do you have a passport, Sir?" The German cut off his rambling, which had been intentional. ANTIMONY needed to create the image of a garrulous, middle-aged American businessman, part of the game of disguise and deception being played out here. "Yes, I do." He reached into the jacket pocket. His fingers brushed the metal pen—the one with the deadly stiletto within. Please don't make me have to use this one, he thought as he pulled out the passport. As the German flipped through the pages noting the various South American and African customs and immigration stamps, ANTIMONY noticed an oddity about the ledger. One column, labeled "Race," had been struck out with no entries. ANTIMONY could not know that the officer had written in the heading as a matter of course. Captain Rogge ordered him to remove it, saying: "We are sailors here, dealing with refugees at sea. We do not care what a person's race or religion is. This is not Berlin or Paris." The officer made a mental note. This lack of concern about the fundamental issue of race and religion would most certainly be reported up the chain of command. "Thank you, Mr. Prince," said the inquisitor dryly as he handed back the passport. "Please step to the right and wait for further instructions."

ANTIMONY replaced the passport and stepped over to the right, but still within earshot. Verdi stepped up to the table. *Would he give away the ruse?* ANTIMONY gripped the rail. *Please, Doctor, remember your lines. Don't ad lib.*

"Milan, Italy."

The officer gave Verdi a quizzical look. *Oh, well, so many of those wops went to America anyway, good riddance to them. They're not decent Fascists anyway.*

"I teach physics and mathematics at the University of Chicago."

ANTIMONY let out the breath he had held. Verdi passed the first test. ANTIMONY looked back at the hulk of the *Zamzam*. She looked strangely calm and serene, almost tranquil, with blue-green water gently frolicking and dancing against her sides.

For the next five hours, boats shuttled back and forth from the *Zamzam*. In an odd sort of way, it was piracy on the high seas, plain and simple. German sailors shot away the lock on the bar and walked into the lair of the ambulancemen seeking treasure worth far more to them in a practical sense than any Spanish doubloon—*Zamzam*'s liquor stores. They hauled away crate after crate of brandy, liqueurs, whisky—quite a haul. As the third boatload of the pirated alcohol came aboard *Tamesis* and a little too quickly hauled below by a gang of mess stewards, Hobgood remarked to the effect that maybe the bastards will drink themselves silly tonight, leap overboard, and the *Zamzam*ers would commandeer the ship. What a prize this one would be. One or two people chuckled at the droll remark; most just ignored it. Oh, well, it will be funnier with the passage of time, he speculated.

In a storeroom, the sailors found hundreds of cartons of cigarettes, cargo originating in the fields of North Carolina, made in the factories of Durham and Richmond, loaded at Baltimore, and destined for tobacconist shops in Cape Town and Johannesburg. The most precious commodity had to be the food stocks. The German Navy's usual stores for long sea voyages consisted of hams, smoked bacon, sausages, black bread and canned vegetables and fruits—not a bad bill of fare for the first few weeks at sea. For a raider, though, after months at sea receiving provisions only occasionally from a surreptitious rendezvous with a supply ship, the diet soon became bland and unappetizing. A large ship had a bakery where the cooks prepared fresh bread and pastries, cakes and strudels, but they really needed fresh meat, vegetables and fruit. From the reefers, two decks below the main deck, the Germans took fresh beef—huge, full carcasses of it, loaded at Recife, straight from the Argentine pampas. They found citrus fruit—oranges, lemons, limes, grapefruit—all from the groves of eastern Brazil, and they found fresh vegetables. At least the Germans will eat well for a while, thought ANTIMONY. He chuckled silently at the irony of it all as he observed the beef being hoisted up onto the deck where the scrambling stewards quickly wrapped wet towels around them. How could such good raw food as this be turned into such bad swill at the table. Then again, he considered the disaster of a head chef, French only by illegitimate birth, certainly not by culinary talent, passed out drunk more often than not. Maybe the efficient Germans will do something more inspiring with the booty now coming aboard.

The Germans searched every cabin and berthing compartment stuffing everything they could find into suitcases, steamer trunks, duffel bags and canvas sacks. Every now and then, an expression of delight came from one of the passengers as their belongings, thought lost when the ship had been unceremoniously abandoned, came up on deck. Radios, phonographs, suitcases, toiletries, even a child's tricycle came aboard. Rogge, however, keenly aware of the potential problems from the attack, seemed determined to soften the blow, and, perhaps mitigate the consequences. It worked. Passengers, previously rancorous and hostile towards the Germans, now became openly friendly and communicative. It is a strange quirk of human nature, one that aggressors and conquerors for centuries successfully used—deprive someone of their liberty, their freedom, their country, their way of life or whatever, then give them back something of value and, lo and behold, people tend to forget what had been done to deprive them in the first place. They actually become grateful and sympathetic to the depriver.

As ANTIMONY watched the German sailors sweating and huffing to hoist trunks and luggage up on deck and the smile when a passenger thanked them for doing so, he could not deny the fact that these young men, all in their teens and twenties, seemed hardly different from the young men he had commanded for thirty years. Instead of hailing from London or Bristol or *x* city upon *y* river, they came from Bremen or Bonn or Berlin. The Nazis must be stopped, put away for good, not only for the conquered masses, but also for the sweating, smiling young Germans of the raider ship *Tamesis*. In an odd sort of way, his resolve to accomplish this mission steadied that morning. It took on an even graver importance thanks to a few trunks and suitcases.

The *Zamzam*'s crew, separated from the passengers, would be handled differently to follow the line that the *Zamzam* represented a legal target. Only the captain and the most senior officers could communicate with the passengers. Smith, carrying his canvas bag, had been brought aboard, marvelous in crisp, freshly starched whites and escorted up to the Bridge by two dour sailors. His attitude and his actions would be the key to the treatment, even survival, of the *Zamzam*ers in the ordeal to come. He understood this fact and would act accordingly. Years at sea and in command had prepared him for this most important undertaking.

About noon, the Germans asked for volunteers to go below to the galley to bring up lunch for the passengers. Verdi, about to raise his hand, felt a firm grasp on his wrist holding it down. He turned, surprised to see ANTI-MONY behind him, hand firmly holding his wrist. Several other passengers trooped below in single file. Once the volunteers had gone, Verdi, clearly irritated, turned to ANTIMONY and whispered. "What was that all about, Mr. Prince?"

"It was about keeping anonymous. Don't volunteer for anything," retorted an annoyed ANTIMONY.

"I don't understand, Sir. Surely carrying food for us is not a problem," replied a perplexed Verdi.

"Quite right, but volunteers are quickly singled out. You will become known to them. You will become friendly and may say or do something compromising to yourself or to me. Remember that. You must be the invisible man here, Doctor. You must be as unnoticed as a bulkhead."

"I see. I'll be more careful," replied a dejected, but cooperative Verdi.

The treatise could not have been plainer on this issue. Never call attention to yourself. Never create a situation

where you are paid any attention beyond a casual acknowledgment of your existence. An untrained Verdi might well slip out his true nature or the identity and mission of the New York businessman, Edward B. Prince.

As the volunteers brought up and passed out metal bowls filled with a thick, hearty black bean soup with lime juice, something odd struck AN-TIMONY. He should have thought of it earlier. He had not seen Van Eyck since the night before. Surely he now stood in the captain's cabin spilling his guts and compromising his mission. Surely he would be better than that. A worried ANTIMONY would keep a sharp eye. With a spoonful of the hot broth halfway between the bowl and his mouth, he felt it again—evil permeating the air. He turned and looked up at the superstructure behind him. The feeling passed quickly, but it had been there as strongly as that first day in New York weeks before. *The cancer remained among them, but where? What of his plan? Did he know?* The lack of information ate at ANTIMONY's insides, and with his mobility curtailed, all the worse. The battleground had changed, but the fight raged on.

At just before 1400, the last boat pulled away from *Zamzam*. She had started listing more to port inducing further loss of watertight integrity below decks. Most likely, the tremendous upward pressure on the Engine Room hatch had broken the seal causing spillover. Or perhaps water had leaked into other below deck spaces through severed steam and ship's services lines. Then again, the water pressure might well have broken the seals around the propeller shaft causing flooding of the shaft alleys deep in the bottom of the ship—a moot point at any rate. Several pounds of high explosive timed fuse charges had been set by the demolitions officer. One way or another, the *Zamzam* would go down. From a deck above, the interpreter, speaking through a megaphone, addressed the crowd below, almost in the manner of a coach exhorting a team before the big game. What an incredible spectacle in treating the destruction of their home for the past weeks like a sporting event.

"Ladies and gentlemen. The ship is just about to be sunk. If you would like to step to the port side railing, you will be able to observe this," he announced.

In a bizarre turn, he even showed the *LIFE* magazine photographer precisely where to stand to get the best shots of the action. ANTIMONY peered across the opening distance between the two ships. Even at this range, he could make out the stern area of the *Zamzam*. The last contingent of German sailors to leave the ship hauled down the Egyptian flag. The ostensible reason, ANTIMONY learned from the first officer later that afternoon, had been to present it to Captain Smith as a memento. In reality, one could not miss the implications of the American photographer on deck above snapping away at the sinking vessel, the flag of a neutral nation no longer in evidence. The photographs documented the event.

A bright flash lit up *Zamzam's* starboard side just above the waterline. The boom came rolling across the water a few seconds later. The stricken ship, her keel broken and seawater rushing into her holed hull, groaned and strained. Water cascaded over steam lines and cabling snapping them like so many matchsticks. Non-watertight doors buckled under the crash of water, some ripped off their hinges. The nearly empty cargo holds became deep lakes filling with black water. Wooden pallets floated to the surface, bumping into each other and against the inner hull. The overpressure caused watertight hatches to spring. Fuel oil from severed lines mixed with black, heavy lubricating oils and the grease and sludge from the bilges to produce a thick, ugly rind of black, sticky oil on the surface. Up from the Engine Room bobbed an engineer's white hat, streaked and smudged, left behind in the helter skelter haste to evacuate the space earlier in the morning. In the ship's Infirmary, water crashed into the instrument cases throwing slivers of glass all over the surgery. Most of the medicines, drugs, and tools had been taken, but here and there, a syringe or box of gauze flew about the space. Swirling water enveloped the Galley. Huge cooking kettles broke free of their mounts and rolled pell mell down the deck crashing into the port side hull, crushing work tables and empty wooden crates in their path. Cutlery, freed from the confines of smashed drawers, bounced off the wet deck, caught in the swirling foamy water and piled up against the hull like so much wooden kindling swept away in a flood.

The ship rolled onto its port side going down by the stern. The stack, holed in the attack, lazily toppled over towards the water below. The ship reached a sixty degree roll, lying almost flat on its side. Water gurgled and bubbled up around her sides as she slowly sank deeper and deeper. And then silence. The top of the stack slipped under the water. *Zamzam* disappeared. No cheering, no talking aloud, no shouts, merely a few whispers came from the crowd of passengers. On the raider's Bridge, Smith gloomily watched her go down—his command, his ship, his mistress, as bad as she had been. Only one who had had a command at sea could know the anguish of the man at that point. A ship had died. The photographer lowered his camera and stared at the deck below. The German interpreter spoke the graceful epitaph of the *Zamzam* in a soft, almost whisper.

"Sometimes they die quite gracefully and always they are different."

Smith turned to the chief engineer and said, "She took it quite well, didn't she?"

No reply. The stack, broken away where the shell had hit, bobbed to the surface for only a moment, then sank again. Here and there floated bits and pieces of debris, mainly wooden deck chairs, parts of the rail blasted loose by the explosion and other floatable items not held prisoner within the fast sinking hull. This flotsam and jetsam would find its way to some beach somewhere, picked up by souvenir hunters, perhaps burned in a beach bon- fire or maybe drift for years on the ocean until the water and sun rotted it away—the fate of a ship lost at sea. It is a sad thing thought ANTIMONY as he watched the ship go down in silence. He had faced this before, he may face it again. Like the death of a loved one, it never gets easier.

CHAPTER 15
A SHARK IN THE NET

Within minutes of the sinking, *Tamesis* got underway steering south. The Germans knew that no SOS had gone out. The ship's wireless operators had zeroed in on the international distress frequencies listening for such a signal. Nevertheless, it never paid to loiter in the area lest an enemy warship had heard the gunfire and explosions or chanced upon telltale floating debris. Captain Rogge suspected that the British knew of his presence in the area. The *Tai-Yin's* distress signal had assured that. Speed is the best defense—clear the area as fast as possible.

Guards herded the passengers under the Bridge Wing and onto the forward part of the main deck. As he passed under the ship's bell suspended below the Bridge, ANTIMONY noticed the ship's engraved name—*Tirana* 1938, a new ship in great trim in spite of her long time at sea, with sparkling bright work and immaculate teak decks, the result of many laborious hours of "holystoning" the wood by scouring with pumice stone. He also observed signs of struggle. Gouged and shattered metal, filed down and painted over, clearly indicated shell hits. None of the vitals—machinery, propulsion, navigational spaces or guns—had suffered. As he scanned the deck observing while avoiding being observed, he took mental notes and surmised that this must be *Atlantis*, the fabled Raider 16, which in seventeen months at sea had devastated the Norwegian Antarctic fishing and whaling fleet and had generally terrorized the South Atlantic. She had tangled with several armed British vessels.

That evening, all of the passengers moved into an empty space three decks below the main deck and just below the crew's berthing. Dinner came— soup, black bread and tea. Though stowed forward in a cargo hold, no one could retrieve their goods, which upset many passengers, especially after the euphoria of seeing it brought aboard earlier in the morning.

In Sick Bay, Vicovari and Starling regained consciousness though in much pain. A delirious Laughinghouse writhed with the jabbing, shooting pain from his ravaged brain as he lay in the same blood soaked dressing gown in which he had come aboard. Morphine helped, but not enough. In the empty hold, ANTIMONY sat down on a wooden crate. As he did so, he noticed the stenciled lettering—Sydney, Australia, the booty of yet another *Atlantis* victim. In another crate he found a fine collection of books from the British Seafarer's Educational Library. Passengers milled about aimlessly, bored, uncertain, and frightened.

At about 2000, the first officer came through the space. He spoke quickly and quietly with everyone, then made a check mark in the chief steward's passenger manifest saved from the *Zamzam.* Smith had obtained permission from Captain Rogge to conduct a muster to see who might be missing. It took about an hour.

"Ah, yes, Mr. Prince and Dr. Verdi. Are we all getting along well? No problems here?"

"No, fine," responded ANTIMONY as Verdi nodded.

"No wounds or cuts?"

"No."

"Good. Well, get as comfortable as you can." He moved on to the next group. Smith appeared in the hold with the deck log and sat at a makeshift desk of crates and cable spools to chronicle the day's events. A ship's log is a legal document, valid in any admiralty court in the world. No doubt the ship's owners would press a claim against the German government. Cargo alone amounted to £3,000,000. Smith scratched out the final few entries.

ANTIMONY nudged close to the captain. Perhaps he could learn something useful by being unobtrusively within earshot.

"Muster complete, Captain."

"Good. What do we have?"

"Two passengers missing. Mr. Charles Van Eyck and Mrs. Joan Avery. No one remembers seeing either at all today."

"Very good." The captain took in a deep breath and let it out crinkling his upper lip. "We shall call them missing, presumed dead. Thank you, Number One." He reached out and took the manifest. His pen hovered above the log, poised in mid-air. *Time. Time for the final log entry.* He wrote with a flourish, then put the cap back on the pen, placed it down on the crate and slowly closed the book.

Conducted muster of crew and passengers. Two missing, Mr. Charles Van Eyck, Dutch and Mrs. Joan Avery, American, missing, presumed dead. All others accounted for. Log of the MISR lines *S.S. Zamzam*, home port Alexandria, Egypt, closed, 2125 hours, 17 April 1941. William Gray Smith, Master.

As the refugees ate their simple dinner, no one knew of the events taking place just a few decks above, events that would control their destinies for some time to come. ANTIMONY, glumly surveying their prison between mouthfuls of the pork and vegetable soup, would have been especially eager to have been a witness.

Just after 1600, *Tamesis* steamed at flank speed south to clear the area. The captain had been working on a signal for the Naval Staff in Berlin detailing the particulars of the incident, stressing the lack of running lights and the compromising Admiralty message. *Let the propaganda boys in Berlin handle this one. I am a warrior—a mariner—not a damned Nazi propaganda stooge! Let them handle it, the prancing boys in their black uniforms with overblown silver insignias.* A knock on the door interrupted his thoughts. "Come," he shouted, not even looking up from his paper.

"*Herr Kapitan*, there is someone here you should speak with, from off the *Zamzam*," announced the first officer.

"A passenger?"

The first officer screwed his face in an odd, contorted expression of confusion. "Honestly, I don't know. He was sent down below with the ship's crew, not the passengers, but he is definitely not one of those foreign mongrels. I don't know what to think of him, really."

"Well, send him in. Let's have a look at your odd passenger."

"You there, the captain will see you now." The first officer motioned a tall man with high cheekbones and crystal blue eyes into the cabin. His short blond hair fluffed up from want of recent combing. He had long but strong, almost effeminate fingers—the perfect model of Hitler's Aryan thought Captain Rogge as the young man snapped to a stiff attention in front of his desk and raised his right arm, rigidly pointing up and out in the Nazi Party salute.

"*Heil* Hitler," the man shouted, the words reverberating off the metal bulkhead.

"Indeed," responded the captain. Rogge looked beyond the tall man at the first officer standing just over his shoulder. His look said, "What the devil is this, first officer," who took the hint.

"Well, *Herr Kapitan*, it seems that this man claims to be an SS Officer. He spoke with a guard seeing to the crewmen. The poor fellow was so startled that he notified his officer, who brought this gentleman to me. This man just doesn't fit the crew, even though he told the investigating officer that he was a Polish ship's engineer. The *Zamzam*'s crew seemed to ignore him as if they weren't certain who he was, so I thought it best that I bring him to you since he demanded it."

The blond man smiled menacingly and came to a proper clicking parade rest.

"I see," responded the captain, now curious about the man dressed in white summer deck shorts and a crewman's uniform top.

"*Herr Kapitan*, I am *SS Sturmbannführer* Karl Von Donop, attached to *SS Reichsführer* Himmler's personal staff."

The captain raised one eyebrow as he stared at the man, still smiling that malodorous grin. He had seen it before, these Nazi thugs and their air of arrogant superiority. "Sit down." He motioned to the settee perpendicular to the desk and nodded to the first officer, who closed the door to avoid unauthorized ears, and then sat in another settee opposite von Donop. "Well, *Herr* von Donop. You had best tell me your story then," he said, leaning forward and clasping his hands in front of him.

"I have been aboard the wretched ship *Zamzam* for several weeks on a mission of the highest importance to the *Reich*. I am on this mission at the personal direction of the *Reichsführer*. You will appreciate that I cannot give you further details."

"I see. Then our little episode this morning has handicapped your mission."

Von Donop leaned back in the comfortable settee, but remained stiff and formal. "Actually, no. It has made my mission much easier, *Herr Kapitan*."

Rogge raised his eyebrows again and leaned back in his chair. "And what, *Herr Sturmbannführer*, am I supposed to do with you. I don't even know for certain who you are, do I?"

"A cautious, careful man, Captain Rogge. There is an easy way to find out. I see that you have not yet transmitted your after action report."

Rogge realized that the signal pad in front of him lay uncovered. He snatched it up so no one could read it and smiled. "You are most observant, *Herr Sturmbannführer.*"

"It is my trade, *Kapitan.* Might I have a signal pad and pen? I think I can solve your dilemma quite easily."

Rogge tore off a blank sheet from the signal pad and handed it to von Donop.

"I presume you have the *SS* High Command cipher codes aboard."

Rogge said nothing. No part of his body moved.

"Yes. You are a careful and cautious man. I appreciate that. There are too many others who are not. No matter. I know that you do. If you will send this signal, I think this could be cleared up to our mutual satisfaction." He scribbled on the pad.

> PASS TO SS HEADQUARTERS BERLIN, IMMEDIATE, EYES ONLY FOR REICHSFÜHRER HIMMLER AND HEYDRICH. REQUEST IMMEDIATE REPLY. HAVE ON BOARD ARMAGEDDON REPEAT ARMAGEDDON. REQUEST VERIFY PHYSICAL DESCRIPTION AND ADVISE ORDERS. CAPTAIN ROGGE SENDS.

He handed back the signal pad and pen.

"ARMAGEDDON. Very Biblical."

"It has its purpose, *Herr Kapitan.* Advise me when you have received a reply." The *SS* man, cocksure and arrogant, rose and turned to leave without the common shipboard protocol of being dismissed by the senior officer. Rogge's blood pressure rose.

"*Herr Sturmbannführer.*"

"*Ja, Herr Kapitan?*"

"You may well be who you say you are. But, this is my ship. I shall expect the correct courtesies and protocol regardless of who you may work for in Berlin. Is that clear?"

"It is very clear, *Herr Kapitan,*" he replied as he sprang to rigid attention, the party salute once again thrusting forward.

Rogge raised his right hand in response. "That will be all, *Herr Sturmbannführer.* Hans, put him in my galley and see that he gets a decent meal. I'll call when we receive a reply to his signal."

"*Jawohl, Herr Kapitan,*" the first officer responded clicking heels. "This way, *Herr Sturmbannführer.*"

Rogge stared down at the signal pad paper. *ARMAGEDDON. ARMAGEDDON.* He thought of the evil grin on the obnoxious man's face. He scratched out the last few words of his report and request for orders. He called the radio watch supervisor, who personally came up to his cabin, picked up the signals and transmitted them to Naval Headquarters, South Atlantic. Once it reached the receive site, operators passed it on the circuit to Berlin on the dedicated *SS* channel. Bletchley Park listened as did a score of HUFF DUFF operators around the world. The airwaves became very hot this evening.

"Bugger on the run!" shouted the chief petty officer using his own code word for a hot intercept. He tuned his HUFF DUFF receive gear to the frequency. He knew it well—one used frequently by the German raiders operating south of the equator. They generally sent out a strong signal given the space and power available on a large surface ship. Submarines gave the most trouble since they couldn't radiate out a lot of power. They just didn't have the juice. The raiders, though, would just blast out, covering the entire frequency, upper side band, lower side band, you name it, they would blast it out. Maybe they felt that because of the distance, this guaranteed reception in Occupied France. Well, good for the bastards. It made his job that much easier. Blast away, boys. It didn't take him long to get a line of bearing to the transmitter in the South Atlantic, a few hundred miles north northwest of Cape Town. Too bad the RN never kept many warships down there. He recognized *Atlantis* all right. Probably just some poor son-of-a-bitch wireless operator like himself caught up in the war.

"Watch Supervisor, I have a hot contact," he said into the voice box on the desk.

"Right. I'll be in straightaway."

The incredible occurred that early morning. The transmission kept going and going and going, not the usual few characters. No, *Atlantis* broadcast continuously for a full twenty minutes. She sure feels safe, he thought. *Well, old boy, we'll see if we can give you a torpedo up the old arse this time.* Reports from other stations in the HUFF DUFF net started to come in. They all had her, loud and clear—a good fix just past midnight on the new day, 18 April 1941.

The Bletchley Park ULTRA decoding watch officer had been on duty for over two hours without a single good intercept. A couple looked to be interesting, but the cipher boys and girls down the hall had not yet broken the new naval code. It generally took a few days of eye-glazing, bone-wearying, around-the-clock grunt work to fully decipher a new code, and then, damn it all, the rotters would go and change it again. The price of freedom is constant vigilance. She filed the undecoded messages in a special box for the wizards.

Hello! What's this! Here's one I know—SS Headquarters. The geniuses of Bletchley Park had cracked this one several days back and the *SS* had not changed it yet. Good thing. She lifted the thin paper up to the light. It would not take long to tap out on the *ENIGMA* cipher machine. 0210. *ARMAGEDDON ... ARMAGEDDON. Interesting code name.* She reached over to the series of clipboards hanging dutifully on the far wall. She rolled her chair over to the one in the middle, labeled Watch Instructions, lifted it off the hook and flipped through the crinkled pages in the pale yellow light of the desk lamp. *ARMAGEDDON. Ah, yes, here it is labeled MOST SECRET. Naval Intelligence Division, Attention Code 17F to be notified immediately upon receipt of any transmission referencing Verdi, atomic weapon or energy, SS Zamzam or ARMAGEDDON. Lieutenant-Commander Fleming. He will enjoy a wake-up call in the middle of the night.* She picked up the telephone on the desk and dialed the number for the ULTRA watch supervisor.

At just past midnight local time, *Atlantis* received the first of several incoming messages of that morning. The remainder would come directly from Naval Headquarters in Berlin. This first one came from *SS* Headquarters. It had a rather strange, almost threatening tone to it. The junior rating who delivered it to the captain could not read the PERSONAL FOR message from *SS* Headquarters in Berlin. He would not disobey his orders and dutifully handed it to Rogge.

ARMAGEDDON IS SS STURMBANNFÜHRER KARL VON DONOP.
APPROX 1.9 METRES TALL, BLOND HAIR, BLUE EYES, SMALL
MOLE ON BACK ABOVE RIGHT SHOULDER BLADE, SCAR FROM
BULLET WOUND TO ABDOMEN RUNNING FROM LOWEST RIB TO
WAIST, RIGHT SIDE OF BODY. HAS ONLY 3 TOES ON RIGHT FOOT
FROM WOUND IN ACTION. YOU ARE TO FULLY COOPERATE WITH
HIM AND PROVIDE ANYTHING HE REQUESTS. AUTHORITY IS RE-
ICHSFÜHRER SS HIMMLER. UNDER NO CIRCUMSTANCES REPEAT
NO CIRCUMSTANCE DIVULGE HIS COVER OR COMPROMISE HIS
MISSION.
HEYDRICH SENDS.

The ship's doctor could easily locate the scars, the mole and the missing toes. If this arrogant man is who he says he is, he must be treated accordingly. The sooner he's gotten rid of the better, mused the captain.

"Very good," he nodded to the radioman, who came to attention, pivoted on his heels and exited. Rogge handed the message to the first officer. "Better get von Donop up here. We have some work to do."

"Aye, Aye, *Herr Kapitan.*"

In less than five minutes, the three men sat in the captain's sea cabin enjoying a good American bourbon, part of the *Zamzam* booty. ARMAGEDDON laughed evilly as he described the damage done to the ship that had succored him for so long. It made the captain and first officer queasy and added to their dislike for the man. It's one thing to sink an enemy, even to rob him of his goods. It is quite another to revel and gloat in the consequences of your destruction.

"So, *Herr Sturmbannführer,* how can we assist you in your mission? By the way, might I ask what that is?"

"You may not *Herr Kapitan,*" hissed the blond man, his manner as violent and temporal as a wild summer storm. His eyes became tiny slits and his lips quivered as he spoke like a certifiable lunatic—the perfect one to work for Heydrich and Himmler. "It is of the utmost importance to the *Reich.* You will appreciate that secrecy is imperative, *Herr Kapitan,*" he said, calming down after his rancorous outburst.

"I understand," replied the captain as he topped off his glass. It would be a long night waiting for orders from Berlin and a little liquid fortification never hurt. It even made this buffoon more tolerable. "How may we assist, then?"

"By ignoring me, *Herr Kapitan*."

This is a novel twist. A Nazi who wants to be ignored.

"I shall dine in your mess and stay in my cabin. Should we transfer to another ship, these arrangements go with me. You will inform the crew that there is a special passenger brought aboard from the *Zamzam* and nothing—I repeat—nothing is to be said of him or even his presence to or in front of any of the *Zamzam* passengers. Failure to follow these instructions will have the most severe consequences. Am I perfectly clear on this?" He emphasized by pointing a finger directly at Rogge.

"Quite clear. The first officer will put out the word at morning divisional quarters."

The first officer nodded his understanding.

"Good. I will be then, your very own invisible man. There may be times when I'll need to observe the people you just brought aboard. I will have free rein to do so. Once we reach landfall, I can complete my mission."

Rogge glared at the strange man in front of him. *God knows what kind of mission this maniac is on that required him to be aboard an Egyptian liner bound for South Africa, a mission so important as to require a personal signal from Himmler. Such is the nature of war. What is it . . . ours is not to reason why, ours is but to do and die. English poem. Tennyson, I think.*

"Well, then, Kapitan. I shall retire. I'll advise you if I require anything." He snapped to attention. "Heil Hitler!"

Both Rogge and first officer responded with a spirited salute. This man had high connections and mustn't be trifled with. Von Donop understood his sudden power over these two professional naval officers and he relished it. As he exited the cabin, he had that impish, malevolent grin on his face. The two officers sat down in silence for almost a full minute. "Why is it that I feel like the fisherman who has just snagged a live shark in his net?"

"Because, Sir, that is precisely what you have done."

The captain smiled and drained his whiskey. *God that is good, but no more tonight. There is lots to do and a clear head is needed.* "Instruct the men that nothing about this man is to be said to anyone even among the crew. Let's scotch the rumors before they start. Begin with the radiomen who have seen this signal." He waved the flimsy yellow paper in the air.

"Ya. Herr Kapitan. I'll see to it straightaway." He stood up, bowed slightly from the shoulders and exited.

Already too late. Within minutes, the mess deck rumor mill buzzed about the very strange *SS* Officer aboard their ship and his secretive mission on the *Zamzam*. As every captain knows, there is no better communication source aboard ship and more power to the man who can control it.

Others read this same message that night. Deep in the rabbit warrens of Bletchley Park, cryptologists decoded the Heydrich intercept. Within hours, the decoded messages from *Atlantis* and back from Heydrich had been delivered into the hands of Ian Fleming in Admiralty Room 39.

0200. The phone rang twice. Rogge picked it up drowsily. "*Ya. Kapitan*"

"Wireless, Sir. We are receiving a reply from Naval HQ to your message of last evening."

"Good. I'll be right down. Notify the first officer immediately. Have him meet me in Wireless." *So, the giants are awake back in cheery old Berlin.* Perhaps they would relieve him of his burden. Perhaps the propaganda wizards would make his attack legitimate so he could go back to the job at hand of sinking enemy shipping. Perhaps. He slipped on his white tunic, buttoning the brass buttons as he passed the darkened cabin turned over to the strange, frightening man with the ominous code name—ARMAGEDDON.

No one below decks slept well. The only ventilation came from forced air blowers designed for inanimate cargo, not humans. Everyone lay on the hard metal deck in various states of restless discomfort even though some fortunate few had blankets and sheets volunteered by the *Atlantis* crew. Earlier in the evening when tempers heated up, Smith and a committee of passengers met with Captain Rogge. He had said to them, "I am sorry this had to happen. I can only tell you that we shall do everything in our power to put you safely ashore, but you must remember that this is war and in traveling on the ocean, you have assumed many risks."

Rogge took pains to emphasize the Admiralty orders, the sailing without running lights and the lack of a national ensign, almost as if rehearsing his own press conference. ANTIMONY had been asked to be a member of the committee, but had graciously declined. *Do not attract attention to oneself.*

Some passengers still in a state of shock at the day's events moaned or sobbed. Children cried, sniffled, or howled all night depending on their particular degree of fright and misery. One toilet served hundreds of refugees, including some 200 from previous victims, who had been aboard for weeks. A constant queue formed, snaking about itself as people awaited their turn, trying to ignore the overpowering stench of stale urine and excrement. The constant throbbing of the ship's diesel engines added to some passenger's distraction. To ANTIMONY, it seemed a melodic soothing hum and he nodded off around midnight, leaning against the metal hull, grateful for the release from reality that sleep brought. It proved short-lived. The ringing bells in his mind throbbed in and out, overpowering. Objects from the sky fell about him—limbs, human arms and legs, feet and hands. The whole world caved in on top of him. All the while, the bells, the bells, shrieked at him now, metal on metal, bursting his eardrums. The bells!

ANTIMONY's eyelids jerked open. His hands shot up from his side as they often do when one is suddenly awakened from a deep, tranquil sleep. The bells. They still rang, but only as a muffled clanging in the decks above them.

"I think something is happening," whispered a worried Verdi, clutching ANTIMONY's sweat soaked shirt.

ANTIMONY struggled to stand up. His legs, wobbly and uncertain and head still groggy from interrupted sleep, made him brace his back up against the hull. Gradually, sober wakefulness returned. The bells stopped. Instead, they heard the sound of heavy leather boots racing along the metal decks up above in the crew's berthing area.

"They are going to Action Stations," he whispered as he slid back down the hull to a sitting position, knees up in the air.

"What does it mean?" asked Verdi.

ANTIMONY looked around. In the dim light of an emergency lantern mounted in the overhead, he saw people putting on their life preservers, morbid souvenirs of the dead ship *Zamzam*. "It could mean just about anything out here. It might even be a drill, but I doubt that. They probably have just spotted another ship. It may be nothing. Let's hope so at any rate."

Verdi released his grip on the shirt and clutched his greasy, oily Kapok jacket instead. Little good that will do you if there is a riot, thought ANTIMONY. He visualized 500 panicky people trying to claw over each other to get out of the death trap hold while the ship sank. It became a moot point as the guard slammed the hatch and dogged it down from the outside. A loud murmuring came from the passengers. The old refugees ignored it all and went back to sleep. They had seen it happen a hundred or more times depending on their longevity, most recently early the previous day. If they drowned, they drowned, a sad fact of captivity at sea. ANTIMONY knew that the guard had secured the hatch to preserve watertight integrity—standard operating procedure for Action Stations. He strained to hear gunfire and put his ear to the hull listening for the telltale grinding of motors lifting guns to the deck or ammunition on hoists from deep within the ship. Instead, he heard only the steady drone of the diesels and the swishing noise as propellers whirled in the water.

"It must not be a fight," he said.

"What is it, then?" asked Verdi.

ANTIMONY could guess this as well. "Probably a rendezvous with a supply ship or another raider he answered as he put his ear back to the damp hull.

They had their answer in only a few minutes. The same guard, who spoke passable English, reopened the hatch. The air had grown noticeably fouler in just the few minutes and a gust of fresh, night air rolled over the hold, refreshing and cool in the stifling, dank refugees' prison. Sensing the fear and tension in the hold, the German sailor struck his head inside and shouted.

"It is nothing. We have met the other ship and you will be transferred in the morning. Good night." A universal sigh of relief erupted from the worried multitude sounding like steam being vented from a boiler. The Germans had obviously reacted quickly to the tactical situation. Perhaps they would be put ashore somewhere soon, but where? In whose territory? Would the Germans discover the secret of this mild, quiet scientist? Did they already know it? These questions troubled him far more than physical wear and tear, bad food or poor quarters.

350 miles SSW of Gibraltar. 1015 hours, 18 April 1941. On the Bridge of HMS *Devonshire*, the captain had come up to observe. He made it a habit to be on the Bridge at least once a watch for several minutes just to encourage the young officers and ratings and to show command presence. God knows he spent enough time up there chasing German submarines and shooting at

Italian aircraft. He scanned the horizon. The sun overhead shimmered off the sea surface, calm and beautiful with only a slight roll and no white caps. Only HMS *Dorsetshire*, 16,000 yards on the port beam, gracefully making fifteen knots, interrupted the tranquil view.

"Captain."

He turned, letting his binoculars drop to his chest. "Yes."

"Signal from Gibraltar, Sir."

"Very good," he replied, taking the clipboard to read the decoded message.

HUFF DUFF POSITIVELY IDENTIFIES RAIDER ATLANTIS AT 25 DEGREES SOUTH 006 DEGREES EAST AT 0100 GMT TODAY. INTERCEPT AT FULL SPEED, BUT ONLY AFTER CONDUCTING PRIMARY MISSION TO INTERCEPT S.S. ZAMZAM.

COMMANDER, FORCE H SENDS

Well, well, well. So this wild goose chase may turn to something after all. He initialed the message and handed the board back to the seaman, who walked over to the watch officer for the same ritual. An RNR lieutenant plotted the position on the chart behind the wheel. Hmmm—a long way off, but, still, the bastard had shown himself. We may be able to get her.

"Signal to *Dorsetshire* to close up and come to twenty knots."

"Very good, Sir."

"We may have some hunting to do," he chuckled as he put the glasses back up to his eyes, scanning the blue, pristine sea and sharp horizon in the distance. Vice-Admiral Somerville, commanding FORCE H out of Gibraltar, had been livid when he received the order to detach two cruisers for this hunt for a damned Egyptian liner. What bloody twit in Whitehall decided this one, he had raged. *Well, now perhaps they could bring the Admiral back a trophy in addition to the chaps off the liner. That would make this foray all the more valuable.*

Early the next morning, the passengers came up on deck. The sun and rolling ocean and the chance to breathe in the crisp, salty fresh air proved delightful after a night of terror and confinement in the hold. Their soon to be prison ship rode a cable astern of *Atlantis*—a freighter, somewhat the same size as the raider, but not as well maintained. ANTIMONY went to the rail to study her. She rode high in the water as if she had no cargo. Her hull below the waterline appeared badly fouled with sea life, mainly barnacles, indicating that she had been at sea for many months without a proper dry-dock overhaul. On deck, he clearly made out the outline of a gun, most likely a four-incher, thus making her an armed merchant. This gun shortly afterward disappeared back into its recess in the superstructure. The refugees remained on deck all morning. Many tried to recover their belongings, but the German sailors, polite but firm, shooed them away. Finally, an officer appeared and through a megaphone advised them not to worry; all belongings would be transferred to the new ship. A chicken soup with not much meat and the usual black bread and tea passed for lunch. Extra lime juice, sour and tart, helped clear away the foul taste in the mouth from the night before.

ANTIMONY could see why the new ship rode high in the water. A large diameter black hose snaked over the bow into the water and up onto the stern deck of *Atlantis*. Though lashed down to a deck fitting, it wobbled and surged. Most passengers did not even acknowledge it. ANTIMONY recognized right away the bow to stern underway refueling rig. The *Atlantis* received a good drink of fuel oil from the newcomer. Underway replenishment at sea is always a ticklish proposition, but these German sailors, practiced in many months of sea duty, seemed skilled and efficient. *Damn it all, these Huns are good in just about everything they do, especially killing people.* A revelation struck him at this moment of observation as the sailors carried out their tasks. *Here is a weapon! The Germans have not yet had the acrimonious feeling of defeat. A weapon indeed! The arrogant, overweening pride could be turned against them.* As he leaned against the rail gazing across the water at the fueling rig, he turned over and over in his mind that notion. Again from his treatise on field operations, he recalled an imperative—find a weakness in the enemy. It may be anything however large or small. It may be greed or even sexual attraction. *Find it. Use it. Exploit it. Turn it against him. It is your leverage, especially in an apparently hopeless situation. This is the weapon. Use it. Very well, then, this could well be that weakness—the arrogance born of overwhelming national pride and a lack of the leveling effect of defeat and humiliation that could lead to carelessness, lack of attentiveness, or worse—the underestimation of an apparently weak opponent. This is the anvil.*

His hammer would be experience, intellect, resourcefulness, and proven skill as a field agent. The opportunity will come to exploit it. Look for it. It will come.

After lunch, the Germans transferred the passengers, crew, and their belongings by motor launch to the new ship. The three badly wounded men—Starling, Laughinghouse, and Vicovari—remained on board *Atlantis.* An officer pointed out that the new ship did not have the hospital capability to properly see to them. He assured a concerned Captain Smith that they would be well taken care of and put ashore at an appropriate place once they healed. Several passengers, particularly the tobacco buyers and the ambulancemen, went down to see their mates before debarkation. Uncle Ned, still delirious, couldn't speak. Mrs. Starling at first refused to leave her husband, but after a tearful goodbye, Dr. Starling convinced her to go with the rest of the passengers. The other wounded transferred without difficulty. Ten sailors came aboard as guards. Knowing that the new ship was headed for home, Captain Rogge selected those most in need of leave or longest aboard. It must have been an emotional scene down in the berthing compartments as long-time friends and comrades in arms parted, perhaps for the final time. It is always an emotional time, but it is a ritual that has lasted as long as men have gone down to the sea in ships. It will always be so. Whatever tears, both inward and outward resulted from the parting, none but somber young men stood at the accommodation ladder carrying his sea bag, waiting his turn to embark. A tenth man stood in the queue. He looked a bit older than the others. Yet, he wore only a lower rated man's uniform with no ostensible rank. Very odd thought ANTIMONY as he stared at the man. Well, this is war, and after all, he had come back into it after retirement so perhaps this man did the same. Perhaps just a former sailor bored with a clerkship at some bank and thrilled by the chance to go back to sea. And yet, different. His countenance, his posture, his entire demeanor did not say lowly enlisted ex-bank clerk. Haughty and arrogant, almost aristocratic in the old world sense, he displayed a demeanor bred of centuries of being top of the heap in a very layered, class-driven society. No, this man seemed different than the other nine sailors, sons of foresters, farmers, fishermen, and shopkeepers—the sturdy yeoman as the British called them. This man bore watching.

Just as the odd man stepped onto the platform, he turned and looked at ANTIMONY. For only a moment—the flash of a second—ANTIMONY felt again that burning feeling of fear and danger. He had not felt it in some time. Instinctively, his head jerked up. *Had the man seen it?* He didn't know. *Where did it come from? Had it come from the sailor now loping down the metal ladder?* A sense of foreboding washed over him. The odd man's eyes appeared ablaze with fire and passion. In only a microsecond, those volcanic eyes seared into ANTIMONY's conscious mind—the eyes of a maniac. *Why had the feeling of dread and of evil come over him again and so strongly? Van Eyck is dead. Why did this man awaken that dread? What is it about him?* Maybe he resembled a similar man from some twenty-five years earlier in a different mission, in a different war. That man had had that same look of maniacal hot embers and that same haughty demeanor. Perhaps the unusual man reminded him of that long gone foe. Perhaps.

To avoid the fueling rig, each boat took a wide swing around and came up under the stern to the starboard side accommodation ladder. ANTIMONY read the painted-over raised letters—*Dresden*. Captain Smith, in the same launch, recognized the name.

"She is a *NordDeutcher* Lloyd ship. I've never seen her before, but I know she has always plied the South American west coast trade. She's a new ship, built, oh, '37 or thereabouts," he said with the admiration of a professional seaman.

"She is a bit the worse for wear, I should think," added another passenger.

In wartime, shipyard availability is a luxury. One fixes things as needed in whatever fashion one can. The neutral shipyards of South America, especially those of Brazil, Uruguay, and Argentina, welcomed the German ships. The availability of good yards and services did not pose the problem. When a German ship pulled into a neutral port, the British spy network came alive reporting daily on the vessel's status. Likely, on putting out to sea, the Germans would run right into the waiting arms of a Royal Navy cruiser or destroyer of the South Atlantic squadron. The *Graf Spee* episode, still fresh in the minds of German mariners, meant that yard availabilities would have to wait. Ships slipped into port at night, left at night, and made repairs when they could, as they could, and usually at sea. So, the *Dresden*, new and beautiful in 1937, looked old before her time and in good need of a complete paint job. Bales of cotton, neatly bound and stacked as high as prudent, crowded the deck, bound for the spinning mills of Germany.

"I wonder where this came from?" mused Verdi.

"Mississippi, probably," added another passenger. ANTIMONY wondered what those Southern cotton farmers would think if they knew that the good old boy cotton buyer down in Mobile actually acted as a German purchasing agent, not for the Brazilian government as he claimed. *Well, those farmers have families to feed. Perhaps they would rather not know. Their country will be in it soon enough, and then this silliness will cease. America will need all of her raw materials for herself and in spades.*

Looking back at *Atlantis*, he noticed four square ports just forward of the beam below the main deck line, cut out in the hull. He tapped Captain Smith's shoulder and pointed.

"Eh?"

"There in the hull, Captain. Aren't those torpedo ports?" he asked.

Smith squinted and peered using the back of his hand to shade the bright, midday sun. "You're right, Mr. Prince. They would indeed appear to be torpedo ports," he answered. His voice lowered almost to a whisper. "Good thing the Hun bastards didn't use them on us. We wouldn't have survived that sort of attack."

"True, Captain Smith." ANTIMONY turned back towards the *Dresden*. Torpedoes would only be used against an armed warship, not a wallowing, unarmed passenger liner, which could be subdued with gunfire. Why waste a precious asset on an easy victim. As they boarded the *Dresden*, the captain waited on deck to greet Smith and extend the professional courtesies called for by his rank and position. Captain Jager, master of the *Dresden*, knew just how easily the tables could have been turned and how easily it could be him coming aboard a British ship, his own sinking to the depths below. Thus, with a great deal of sincerity, he warmly greeted the British captain.

Jager, a short, barrel-chested, bow-legged man in his mid-40s, had the powerful frame and deeply tanned look of a man of the sea, accentuated by the white, starched uniform of the North German Lloyd Line. Not a warrior as Captain Rogge, this merchant master's demeanor contrasted with that of the men of the *Kriegsmarine* left behind on the *Atlantis*. As each boatload of passengers arrived, women and children moved to the passenger decks while the men and *Zamzam* crew went forward. A ship's officer addressed each group and instructed passengers to queue up at Hatch Number Two and the *Zamzam* crew at Hatch Number Three. A crude plywood partition had been erected separating the two. Once each group lined up properly, members of the *Dresden's* crew went down each line and passed out large cotton sacks. The officer instructed them to fill the sacks with cotton from the bales on deck. Boatswain's mates, wielding long, ugly looking knives, slashed open several bales. The action helped to calm some very real fears among the refugees about the German's intentions. The *Dresden* sailors harbored no malignant intentions towards the *Zamzam*ers; Germany had stumbled into a pile of diplomatic manure and thus far, had treaded most delicately.

In late afternoon, a command from the Bridge ordered everyone to move below and to drop the partially filled cotton mattresses on deck. A murmur came from the crowd, now suddenly thrown back into that state of confusion that they had lived in for two days. A missionary waved his Bible in the air and shouted fire and brimstone at the *Atlantis* sailors who had come aboard.

As they reached the hatch to go below, ANTIMONY placed a hand on the man's shoulder and spoke softly, but firmly. "It's all right, Padre. They are not going to hurt us. Okay? They are God-fearing men just like us, but they have their job to do, so let's just let them do it without upsetting them."

The man ran his fingers through his closely cropped hair and winced. "Yes. Yes. You are right, Sir. It's so evil what they have done to us. They will answer for it, you know. I shall pray for them, not harangue them."

"Quite right. Pray for all of us, Padre." The potentially explosive situation had been defused.

As they went down the hatch, ANTIMONY noticed that the Bible looked frayed and warped as if it had been dunked in water. Stacks of Bibles bound for the African missions had been stored on *Zamzam*'s lower decks. What a ludicrous scene it had been as one group of men set explosive charges while another spread dripping Bibles over the upper decks to dry. The salvage crew had returned most of the Bibles to the missionaries, who had been happy to get them back regardless of condition. War is an odd creature, evoking the best and the worst in humans.

In the hot, stuffy, and humid holds, only two light bulbs in the overhead swayed as the ship gently rolled, casting shadows and eerie shapes off the hull. One of the wittier ambulancemen relieved some of the tension when he remarked, "I paid for a First Class cabin. I'd sure hate to see Steerage Class." Nervous chuckles erupted throughout the dark, dank, ill-lit hold. The refugees could hear the grinding of motors and gears and the noise of metal fittings sliding and clanking across the deck.

"They're unhooking us from *Tamesis*," whispered ANTIMONY to his little group in one corner of the hold, which consisted of Verdi, a couple of the tobacco men and some ambulance drivers.

Already, the division into cliques that had been so apparent from the first day on the *Zamzam*, had reemerged. In one area, the Canadian priests, animated as if discussing their plan of action, spoke vehemently in French. American Protestant missionaries, many kneeling or standing in prayer, asked Providence for guidance or just for aid in the crisis. Many read their tattered, water-crinkled Bibles. In another area stood the businessmen and other passengers, mainly European. The Britons and Canadians knew that, unlike the Americans who would likely be repatriated soon, that as hostiles, their future remained uncertain. The American businessmen, among them Verdi and ANTIMONY, acted confident and defiant in that sort of brash American way—a sort of "how dare those Nazi idiots do this. I'm an American, by God, and you will answer to Uncle Sam for this, you pack of goose-stepping Krauts!" Don't lose that piss and vinegar, ANTIMONY thought as he listened to the heated discussion and veiled threats of reprisal. In a side corner of his group, the ambulancemen had decided that the burden of "policemen" and organizers seemed to fall on the young, strong backs of the drivers. Most of them came from the American aristocracy, recent graduates of places such as Harvard, Yale, Princeton, Penn, Virginia, Duke and North Carolina, the training grounds of the elite. Bred for leadership, their volunteering to assist the Free French represented on the one hand a sense of passionate, youthful adventurousness, but it also came from the sort of *"noblesse oblige"* these men had been trained for. In spite of their boorish behavior aboard *Zamzam*, this could all be chalked up to youthful exuberance—sort of a running fraternity party. With the chips down though, these men could be counted on. Already, they had formed *ad hoc* committees to see to crowd control, sanitary and living arrangements, care for the sick and infirm and other duties. Hobgood, standing just behind ANTIMONY, tapped him on the shoulder and whispered.

"This is what is going to kick the Kraut's butts, not old, useless relics like you and me."

ANTIMONY nodded. *Indeed so, Colonel, indeed so.*

After an hour or so, the noises ceased. With chains stowed, the refueling complete, *Atlantis's* tanks topped off and hose stowed and lashed on the fore deck, the hatch opened. An officer stuck his head in and spoke. "You may all now come back onto deck, please, and finish with your bedding."

"Thank God. This hell hole is stifling," came a universally felt comment from somewhere in the crowd.

Atlantis had pulled away, about seven or eight miles to the west, towards the South American shipping lanes in search of more victims. Good-bye, good riddance, and bad luck seemed the general consensus of all who stood on deck staring at their attacker with various states of bitterness and hatred. By sunset, the makeshift cotton mattresses had been finished and moved below. The baggage had been stowed in a cargo hold by a group of volunteers under the direction of the habitability committee headed by a Brown University man.

"I hope they let us have our things soon. I'm beginning to smell gamey after two days in these clothes," said one of the men leaning against the bulkhead, puffing on a cigarette, the last one from a pack hastily shoved in a jacket two mornings earlier.

"Hear, hear," came a reply from across the deck.

"Smart ass," muttered the unwashed passenger as he turned and tossed his cigarette butt into the water below.

A man with a huge stomach looking terribly well-fed, passed around to each *Zamzamer* an enamel bowl, an aluminum cup, and a spoon. The refugees became very acquainted with this nonthreatening and friendly enough fellow. As the ship's purser, he had responsibility for feeding the refugees. Dinner that night consisted of a rice soup, two pieces of crusty sour bread and tea. ANTIMONY marveled at the abundance of tea, both on the Atlantis and Dresden. The U-boat problem had made it almost a luxury item in Britain. He later asked the chatty purser where it came from.

"It comes in from India on neutral ships to the South American ports, usually in Chile or Peru. We purchase it in Brazil and always offload some to the raiders as we pass by them on our way home to Germany," he responded with apparent pride.

Cotton from Mississippi, oil from Venezuela, and tea from India, our own bloody Empire! A black, ugly cloud gathered in his mind as he contemplated this horrific irony—the German war machine being supplied by the same countries that they fought, soon will be fighting or might eventually be swallowed up by the expanding Third *Reich* Empire—a cruel irony at best.

After dinner, the refugees returned below. The two lights flicked off even before everyone had a chance to stake their claim to a decent spot. A few embarrassing moments occurred as people bumped into each other in the dark, but thankfully, no one got hurt. Number Two Hold had only one exit and it had been securely shut for the night. In spite of this being a merchant, it became clear that the captives would be treated much like prisoners of war rather than guests and would not be given free rein to wander about. Two galvanized steel buckets placed by the wooden staircase served as toilets. In the darkness, those daring to use these meager facilities more often than not missed the foul-smelling and sloshing buckets. This situation prompted a remark from the witty ambulance driver that at least they had a pot to piss in.

Unbeknownst to the refugees sleeping fitfully or not at all in the cramped, wet, dark holds, their immediate fate had been determined that night. For several minutes, the telegraph key bounced back and forth as *Dresden* reported her position and disposition. An hour or so later came the response. In the dimly lit, tiny wireless room, Jager, the first officer and the unusual tenth sailor, SS *Sturmbannführer* Karl von Donop, received Berlin's orders. She would loiter in the area until she received the signal, then make her way into the North Atlantic, then on to an as yet undesignated French port to offload the refugees. It would be at least a month before she would be allowed to make port. Bad luck thought Jager as the radioman read aloud the decoded message from Naval Headquarters, Berlin. The orders, it said, came from the *Führer* himself. Double damn thought the captain. The quiet SS officer merely smiled. The authors of the orders, Himmler and Goebbels, the *Reich* propaganda minister, had been contacted in the middle of the night before, but neither had dared to awaken the *Führer*. They had ordered the transfer of the refugees from the *Atlantis* and had presented their plan to Hitler at the morning audience. They would allow the British to announce that the *Zamzam*, carrying over a hundred Americans and overdue in Cape Town, had presumably been sunk by a German raider or submarine. At that time, the Germans would counter with the passengers, boarded at fine hotels along the French coast, safe and sound. The captured, compromising Admiralty message would then be produced, proving that the sunken ship sailed, in fact, not as a neutral but as a belligerent, thus dispensing with the otherwise ticklish diplomatic issue—a brilliant riposte and Goebbels at his best. The priceless piece of paper left by the indiscreet master of the *Zamzam* and now safely locked away in Captain Jager's safe, awaited its moment in the sun.

CHAPTER 16
WALTZ ACROSS THE ATLANTIC

On a cool, damp London day, clouds hung gray and puffy promising more rain followed by a misty overcast, followed by drizzle, followed by more rain, and so on. What a wonderful day! The *Luftwaffe* bombers would not come today. The door opened with the usual low frequency hum. Fleming hurriedly entered Room 39 and fairly flew over to his desk by the door to Room 38.

"Ian, the old man was asking after you," said his compatriot sitting opposite his desk.

"Thanks, Ted. Are they all there?"

"With rings on their fingers and bells on their toes. Even Stephenson. He got in early this morning from Halifax. A bit crotchety, I should think."

"Good. This will warm him up." Fleming waved the dark brown envelope in the air. He had spent the last two hours in the Code Room at the Foreign Office waiting for this message to be deciphered. The latest message from the "mole" in the German Foreign Ministry contained explosive details relative to the Verdi operation. He had received a call from the watch officer at the Foreign Office just after 0500 that morning and had raced down to Whitehall, barely shaving and brushing his teeth. He had that bitter aftertaste of one too many cups of over-brewed black coffee. The FO boys thrived on it. *How did they get so much coffee with the U-boat problem? Damned civil servants. Probably have some high-level source in South America who slips tins of it into the diplomatic pouches. Well, it kept them awake on those long night watches in the Code Room.* Hundreds of messages a day arrived from various diplomatic posts around the world not yet sucked into the vortex of war, especially in South and Central America.

"You'd best take off those boots, Ian, old sport. You know how the old man hates having his carpets mucked up," laughed Ted Merritt from the opposite desk.

Fleming looked down at his sea boots, filthy with a gooey, light brown mud from the bomb-damaged street outside—a wasteland of mud, loose bricks, and mortar. "Thanks, Ted," he answered, settling down at his squeaky desk chair. He slipped on his more official regulation shoes, stood up, pulled down the hem of his uniform blouse and knocked twice, firmly.

"The weather is definitely better in New York, gents," observed *INTREPID*, balancing a tea cup on the delicate Spode saucer and standing by the window looking out over a swampy, wet Horse Guards' Parade.

"What about those horrid, wet humid summers and all that snow in winter. It's the extremes that get you, Bill," retorted Godfrey.

INTREPID pondered this for a moment. Manitoba born and bred, the winters did not bother him. The hot, humid summers, well, the Admiral had him there. "Very well. Let me revise that. The spring and autumn seasons are far better and it is a glorious spring this year."

Fleming entered and quickly took his seat at the conference table. He plopped the brown envelope in front of him. INTREPID turned away from the rain-spattered window and sat in the leather side chair by the window.

"Good morning, Ian," said Admiral Godfrey.

"Admiral. General Menzies. Mr. Stephenson. I have the latest from the Foreign Office. I feel we have a clearer picture now of the tactical situation. It isn't good, but it may not be getting worse and believe me, gentlemen, it could be much, much worse."

"Since INTREPID has just arrived, I think it best if you review the entire events of the past two days. Does anyone disagree?" Godfrey looked around the room. "Commander Fleming, it's your show."

"Yes, sir." Fleming stood up and pushed the chair back away from the table. "There are really two levels of activity going on here. Let's call them a macro and a micro level. On the macro, we have the physical conditions of the operation—where the players are and what is influencing them. On the micro level, there is the question of the undercover aspects. Let us review the macro and how we heard about it." He paused and took in a deep breath. "We know from signal traffic and HUFF DUFF analysis that the raider *Atlantis* is operating in the area. The central South Atlantic, that is. HUFF DUFF intercepted and fixed its position precisely ... here." He strode over to the navigational chart of the South Atlantic with *Zamzam*'s track laid out in blue and the positions of the *Atlantis* marked in red. Fleming picked up a wooden pointer and lightly tapped the chart as he spoke. "*Atlantis* sent a lengthy report to Berlin night before last—most unusual and thereby indicating some occurrence of great significance."

"Excuse me, Commander, do we have any report of shipping losses in that area recently?" broke in Menzies.

"No, General. From subsequent traffic intercepted, but not broken, and because she has not checked in with her company operations office, we speculate that the *Zamzam* might have been sunk early on the morning of the 17th."

"Just as you were sending a warning message to Braithwaite about this ARMAGEDDON chap," grumbled the General, much distressed by the entire situation.

"I fear so, Sir. Admiralty transmitted in the blind to *Zamzam* under the code name MEMPHIS using an operation called Plan Green."

"Well, the bloody bastards got their way. The Germans found it and sank it all right," spat out Menzies bitterly.

"It would appear so, Stewart," added Godfrey in a soothing voice spoken over the rim of a steaming cup of Ceylon tea. He, above all, must keep calm and rational. All is not yet lost. "Proceed Commander."

Fleming cleared his throat and moved around to the other side of the chart. He ran his finger down the east coast of South America until he found a small dot. "We also believed that the *Zamzam* survivors were transferred to the armed merchantman *Dresden* yesterday. The latest intelligence we have from shipping movements on her is that she was last sighted leaving Santos, Brazil on 21 March, bound for Germany with a cargo of lumber, oats, cotton wool, and oil."

"For the raider?" asked INTREPID, hitherto silently sipping his tea.

"Presumably, Sir. We speculate that *Dresden* is one of the raider's supply ships. We also speculate that the passengers were offloaded onto *Dresden* for transport to some neutral port or to Germany herself."

INTREPID stood up stretching his legs. His calves still throbbed and ached from the long, energy-sapping night flight. It felt good to stretch occasionally. "You keep saying speculate, Commander. Is there some change in your intelligence?"

"Yes, Sir, there is. I shall get to that shortly. It rather ties this entire package up neatly." Fleming, the showman, had to build up the proper anticipation. "HUFF DUFF has identified *Dresden* as being within an area of forty nautical miles of the known position of *Atlantis* as of midnight GMT on the 17th. Within a few hours, she was also transmitting to Berlin using long narrative. Again, it is a new code, and we cannot yet read it." *Now is the time, Ian. They are sufficiently whetted appetite-wise. Now is the time for the piece-de-resistance—the envelope lying unopened on the table.* "And then, this came in last night's diplomatic pouch from Stockholm. It confirms everything we have suspected to date regarding the fate of the *Zamzam* and her passengers."

Until now, there had only been speculation and conjecture and a rapidly diminishing hope that the strange activities of the two German ships had had nothing to do whatsoever with the Egyptian liner, and that she still jauntily made her way to Cape Town over sun-washed, balmy South Atlantic waters. Now, Fleming confirmed their fears. The bleak, damp weather outside could not match the somber cloud of dismay that now settled over the room. The fire in the grate crackled and puffed ever so slightly. No one spoke for several seconds, each digesting the news and anticipating the scope of the tragedy.

"That's the FO traffic, then? More from that chap CHARLEMAGNE?" quizzed Godfrey, leaning forward and pointing at the innocuous envelope.

"It is, Sir."

"For brevity's sake, why don't you read it for us, Ian."

"Certainly, Sir." Fleming laid down the pointer on the polished table top and picked up the envelope. He popped the wax seal, which he himself had affixed, ran a finger under the gummed flap and removed a flimsy paper. It seemed to pop as he shook the top of the page. Tree leaves crashed up against the window, flailing helplessly against the unforgiving north wind. Fleming felt a bit like that tree branch, fighting forlornly, losing against the awful power of the wind.

"EGYPTIAN SHIP ZAMZAM SUNK BY RAIDER ATLANTIS EARLY MORNING 17 APRIL. TWO REPORTED CASUALTIES, AMERICAN WOMAN AND A DUTCHMAN. ABWEHR AGENT PRESUMED TO BE DUTCHMAN. ABWEHR CONSIDERS OPPORTUNITY TO LOCATE SOUTH AFRICA SPECIAL WEAPONS PLANT LOST, WILL NOT PURSUE VERDI LEAD FURTHER. REFUGEES TRANSFERRED TO S.S. DRESDEN ON 18TH. FINAL DISPOSITION UNDETERMINED, BUT MOST LIKELY

WILL LOITER IN NORTH ATLANTIC FOR 15 TO 40 DAYS, THEN DE-
BARK PASSENGERS AT PORT IN OCCUPIED FRANCE. WILL ADVISE."

Fleming laid the paper down on the table. A cold, stabbing feeling started
at the base of his spine and ran the entire length up to the base of his skull,
then back down again as if icicles lanced into his back every few inches, twist-
ing and wrenching into his flesh—the feeling of defeat. He had never known
this feeling. Not even during the retreat from Europe, during Dunkirk, or
the horrific blitz of the previous autumn had he felt the pain of defeat. Perhaps more personal this time, the Verdi operation had been his baby. He had
set it up; he had gathered the players; he had served as intermediary between
the disparate interests, and he had made them see the importance of this
mission, not only for Britain, but for the future of the world. It had been his
passion for the past month, and now, it had come unglued. Nay, it had been
exploded by the accidental meeting on the high seas of a bloodthirsty German killer ship in search of prey and an unarmed, helpless little disgrace of
a ship and the damnable meddling of some fool upstairs trying to tempt the
Germans into making the same gargantuan blunder that they had made in
1915, hoping for a similar result. That part of the plan had certainly worked.
Those responsible surely knew that the raider operated in the area that the
Zamzam would transit. They had accomplished their mission. Fleming's lay
dead in a piece of flimsy paper lying on a highly polished, antique mahogany
table on a rainy, dreary London morning.

"This chap doesn't seem to know about our friend von Donop." Menzies'
analytical comment broke the almost narcotic lethargy that had settled on
the morose group of men.

"Quite right, Stewart. I concur. Anyone else have a thought on that issue?" added the Admiral.

INTREPID had been leaning back in the side chair, eyelids partially shut,
apparently from the exhaustion of the trip. In reality, he had screened out
all external distractions, the hissing fire in the marble fireplace, the rapping
of the tree branch outside, even the aromatic smell of his tea. He had been
dwelling on every word of the German's message, analyzing, concentrating, digging for hidden meaning, listening, and analyzing again. A thought
formed in his mind borne out by months of intelligence work on the harsh-
est of terms in the face of a devastatingly powerful enemy. There is an answer
in the message. There is a way to salvage the mission if ANTIMONY is still

on the job unharmed and with his cover intact. On that presumption, they would not abandon him to the Nazi wolves. *What is it about the message that flickered a spark in his subconscious mind? What is it! France. France! Bloody God-awful France!*

"Ian, where did you say *Dresden* was bound for?"

"I didn't, Sir, but, let me see. Oh, yes. The Consulate in Rio de Janeiro reports her as sailing for Lisbon with no arrival date given. Security reasons, I'm sure."

"But the CHARLEMAGNE traffic referenced Occupied France," INTREPID interjected, his eyes now blazing with intensity.

He's on to something thought Fleming as INTREPID strode over to the table. "Yes, Sir, but it is not certain."

"What if we presume that the Germans intend to bring the *Zamzam* people into a French port? Let us assume that this von Donop intends to snatch Verdi. Killing him is his last option short of letting him go, but, as long as the passengers are landed in Occupied France, they can hold him indefinitely while they set up their plan. An outright kidnap is just not on. After the sinking blunder, they will be very careful to stage something to make it look like a defection. The good Italian scientist realizes his error and returns to the Motherland, the true Fascist son and all that rot. That will take a few days to set up. I doubt it can be properly done on the *Dresden*. He doesn't have the resources or the coercion ability. I certainly would not try it.

No, the cards are playing von Donop's way and he knows it. He can bide his time and wait for reinforcements. So, gents, we do the same!" he shouted slamming a fist down hard on the table.

Tea cups rattled. They had never seen INTREPID quite so animated.

"Pardon me, but I'm not quite sure I follow. We do the same?" queried "C" now thoroughly confused.

"Just so, Stewart, we do the same. Remember, there are two factors that we must count on here. First, that ANTIMONY is still in the game and operating. Second, that von Donop will not be able to seize Verdi straightaway especially with American consular officials crawling all over the place." He would ensure that the men from the State Department would be doing just that regardless of where Dresden made port. "We shall have a window of opportunity of perhaps only a day or so, but enough to counter any Nazi plan and to send in our men to extract both Verdi and ANTIMONY."

"And, if the Germans release them both as repatriated American nationals ... ?" injected Godfrey.

"Then, Sir, we win. The mission is accomplished. I, for one, am not willing to bet that the Jerry will simply let them go."

"So, Bill, what do you propose?" asked Godfrey, suddenly interested in the possibilities.

INTREPID had retaken his seat by the window. The tree limb no longer slashed at the window. "I'll arrange for ... two ... yes, two will do, of the best SOE men from Camp "X" to be airlifted into the area to extract them by force if necessary right from beneath the German's noses. All the better if they are in France where we can utilize the Resistance for logistic and intelligence support. It's a dicey show, but I believe the risk is worth taking. Can you support that operationally, Colin?"

Nodding and general agreement came from around the table.

"We should never have let the blighter get on that ship," Gubbins snarled, shaking his head.

"Well, it happened. It really was not our place to interfere, but having happened, we damn sure are going to clean up the mess. Our first line of offense is the American diplomatic corps. Regardless of where they land those people, they must be insistent that everyone is accounted for and sent home straightaway. They must not give von Donop's people time to make off with Verdi. If they do, we must be ready to step in. That is the essence of our redefined mission."

The chill had gone. Fleming warmed with the fever of renewed activity. The mission is back on! It had a chance to succeed. He would be vindicated, and the world might take one step further back from the abyss.

Early the next morning on board *Dresden*, guards again opened the hatches and ordered the passengers up on deck. People rotated limbs or did deep knee bends—anything to work out the kinks of the dreary night. Buckets of cold, salt water came out for washing, but none of the refugees had soap, towels, or even fresh clothes. Still, it felt good to remove some of the crustiness of two days and nights.

Shortly after breakfast had been cleared (an odd concoction soon referred to as "billboard paste"), Captain Jager called for the passengers' committee to come up to the Pilot House. He addressed the group and again offered his heartfelt apology for the inconvenience. "This may be a long voyage and you will be obliged to do a great many things for yourself. I have neither food nor quarters to support nearly four hundred people including my crew comfortably. You must expect some hardship, but I promise you we will do everything we can." The first part of his position appeared straightforward and clear. He seemed genuine and concerned. The passenger committee, satisfied with Jager's stand, accepted it. In a few minutes, he appeared on deck and addressed the crowd in a loud, but edgy voice. He made his second position quite clear. "I will stand for no monkey tricks from behind. My orders are not to fight this ship or try to run away if an English warship should intercept us. This is for your protection. I shall let you off first in boats and when you are safely away, I shall scuttle this ship. I have enough bombs already placed to sink her in two minutes. I have plenty of rifles and machine guns and grenades also. Remember that if you have any funny ideas."

Clearly, Jager anticipated that the *Zamzam*ers would attempt to take the ship. One simply had to count the numbers. He had a crew of sixty with the additional ten sailors to the over 200 male prisoners. To emphasize the point, while he spoke two sailors mounted a machine gun on each Bridge Wing. There, they would set a watch to intimidate and it worked wonderfully. No passenger ever spoke the first word about a prisoner uprising. Jager had made the point.

By the third day, the refugees desperately needed fresh clothing. Smith presented this problem to Jager, who concurred, having gotten a good whiff of what came to be called "eau de polecat." About midday, Jager allowed the passengers to retrieve their baggage from the aft hold. The salvage crew had actually managed to recover an amazing amount of personal items. Two of ANTIMONY's bags had been rescued with all but one suit, all of his shirts and almost all of his toilet articles and underwear. A few small items had gone missing—no doubt now being put to good use aboard the *Atlantis*. The false bottom had not been discovered.

Buckets of hot, soapy water came up from the galley along with towels and face clothes. So many trunks, suitcases, and bags came out that it actually took two days to sort it all out. The genial purser supervised the opening of each bag like an overly attentive customs agent. He confiscated liquor, flashlights, matches, and cigarette lighters. The Germans feared the possibility of a passing ship being signaled. After this event, the routine settled down into a humdrum existence, boring and tense at the same time for day after successive day as the *Dresden* waltzed across the Atlantic.

The passenger committee aided by the *ad hoc* activities committee tried to make life bearable for the refugees. Utilizing the ambulancemen and the able-bodied men, the committees built a privy on the portside bulkhead in each hold, a mess table, and benches and shelves for each space below deck, an altar for the priests to conduct their services, and a shower. *Dresden*'s carpenter supervised the building projects utilizing lumber bound for Germany. In another cruel irony, one of the tobaccomen found stamped on a 2" x 4" board, the name Carston Lumber Company, Battleboro, North Carolina, his hometown. The ambulance drivers tirelessly washed down the decks with seawater daily and broomed them down before every meal. At mealtime, they acted as mess sergeants. Below decks, Chief Engineer Burns supervised security.

The diet, somewhat well short of *haute cuisine*, kept everyone going. As the days passed, tea became less and less tea and more tinted water with a little sugar ration. It is amazing how people come to treasure the mundane under conditions such as this. ANTIMONY craved a really good, strong cup of tea with lots of sugar and fresh milk. Hobgood fantasized about pork barbecue and hush puppies much to the annoyance of those not yet initiated to its marvelous succulence. At one point, he walked over to ANTIMONY after a delightful lunch of macaroni, bread, and tea and stuck his hand out over the rail. It shook violently.

"Are you all right, Colonel Hobgood? Let me fetch the doctor," ANTIMONY said putting a palm on his forehead testing for the telltale fever.

"No need to, Mr. Prince. They can't do a thing for it. It's called barbecue withdrawal, stage five. I should point out that this condition is terminal when it reaches stage seven, so, let's convince the Huns to turn left and head for Wilmington. What do you say?" They both turned back towards the sea and laughed heartily.

For the first few days, the Germans kept the sexes segregated, a great cause of grief for the families. Finally, the captain allowed husbands, wives and children to meet on the Promenade Deck daily between 1000 and noon. The men came moping back to the lunch mess line after those meetings.

Dresden sailed in circles, obvious to everyone who had been to sea. One morning, the sun would be off the port side, the next, off the starboard. No one could explain this until at the beginning of the second week, Jager announced that they would soon rendezvous with *Tamesis*. Early the next morning, the low, sleek outline of the raider came into view. Jager announced that they intended to take on more food, especially canned milk for the children—canned milk carried off the *Zamzam*, but no one brought up that fact. The passenger committee drafted a strongly worded protest to Captain Rogge demanding that the passengers be transferred to a neutral ship or be offloaded at the nearest neutral port. It said that the Germans had no right to put neutral Americans in double jeopardy by attempting to run the British blockade of European ports. Rogge greeted it with surprisingly good grace and advised the committee that he would order *Dresden* to sail north into the usual trade lanes to try to locate a neutral ship or failing that, head for a South American port. The passengers became ecstatic over the news, but not ANTIMONY. He knew the enemy too well. Having blundered, the Germans held the aces now, so long as they had the refugees and the Admiralty message. He kept silent. That evening, *Dresden* turned north away from the scene of the crime.

The inevitable occurred—dysentery. The sanitary conditions and diet made it almost a daily routine with at least a dozen or more people completely bedridden. It only added to the sanitation woes and general misery. The ship's fouled bottom restricted her to only ten to twelve knots at full speed. As she approached the windless equator, the stifling heat became almost unbearable. Those without hats or shoes passed out on the blazing hot deck, many weakened by illness. Soon the neutral ship myth became apparent. As sailors placed bales of straw around the Pilot House, always a sign of possible action, the ship continuously steered north by northwest towards the North Atlantic. As the neutral shipping lanes and the coast of South America faded off to the southwest, the passengers became nervous and acrimonious. Fights broke out over the least significant thing—a presumed affront, an unintended bump, a verbal slight.

Above all this, ANTIMONY kept calm and aloof. He constantly oversaw Verdi to ensure no inadvertent slip of the tongue. *The mission—maintain forward momentum. The mission must be accomplished.* All the while, he kept his eyes on the strange sailor. A pattern had developed. ANTIMONY observed the various watches. Not surprisingly, the odd man neither stood machine gun watch nor came on deck to supervise exercise periods or take part in boat drills or other routine ship operations. During odd times—in the mess line or during the hosing down or showers on deck—he would appear on the Bridge Wing, lurking, hunched over the rail, his burning eyes staring at nothing in particular, yet everything in general. Other passengers noticed him as well. Refugees dubbed him "The Vulture" for his strange, watching manners. Once or twice, a bold passenger asked one of the English-speaking sailors why this man never stood watches. The answer always came back as a stern mind your business and carry on with what you are doing. At one point, a rumor spread of his being *Gestapo* there to keep everyone politically in line. It made sense and the rumors died down. ANTIMONY continued his vigilant watch. He sensed that this strange man would play a great role in his destiny, and by extension, that of Verdi. He would observe and note. The hunter would become the hunted, the watcher, the watched.

As the ship pressed north, the weather and the attitude changed. Summer comes slowly to the northern seas and the sunny, balmy days of the South Atlantic turned bleak, miserable, and wet. A flu epidemic spread like a dry prairie fire in the confined spaces of the holds. ANTIMONY and Verdi both went down hard for several days.

12 May.

"Do you see them, Fritz?"

"*Yawohl, Herr Kapitan.* Bearing 280 degrees. Many of them!"

"Right 30," shouted the captain. "Ahead full, maximum revolutions!"

The helmsman rang up the bells with a loud clanging. Oily black smoke belched from the stack. The ship heeled over hard to starboard as the 30 degree angle of the rudder caught the water violently rushing over it. ANTI-MONY raced to the port rail. Off to the west, barely visible on the horizon, specs, like great insects, crawled across the water in a vast formation. *Convoy! A convoy and Dresden had just blundered into it.* He gripped the rail. Verdi raced over.

"British convoy," ANTIMONY whispered, not wanting to alarm the sailor standing a few feet away supervising morning showers.

"Did they see us?"

"I don't know. Pray that they did."

They did not. The two escort destroyers, neither with a reliable radar, had not detected *Dresden* hidden in the brilliant, blinding early morning rays of the rising sun. She resumed her course. At noon the following day, *Dresden* turned again. At 43 degrees north latitude, she turned east, headed for Occupied France and the safety of *Luftwaffe* air cover. The hopes and fears of the passengers, which had swung between each pole of despair and exuberant optimism, now swung down into despondency and depression. The daily services given by the missionaries and attended by most regardless of faith, provided some consolation. Several musicians, particularly the priest who had so reveled in his swing music so many nights before on a warm, starry South Atlantic night, provided music for the hymns.

On the 18th, *Dresden* made Cape Finisterre off the coast of Spain. For two days, she weaved in and out of Spanish territorial waters around every headland, avoiding lurking Royal Navy submarines. On the 20th, three destroyer escorts came alongside the ship. At dawn, *Dresden* came alongside the breakwater of St. Jean-de-Luz, the French port near the coastal resort city of Biarritz. The "season" had begun, but the only tourists this first spring after the disaster of 1940 wore *Wehrmacht* gray, *Kriegsmarine* white, and *SS* black.

*Zamzam*ers lined the rail as the German Navy pilot took command of the ship to bring her in. Harbor piloting is an acquired skill. It takes many years of apprenticeship to master the unique features and quirks of each harbor. One does not do so in a few months by reading harbor charts. The inevitable happened. The pilot ran the *Dresden* aground. It took the embarrassed Germans three minesweepers and several hours to free her from the sandbar to the consternation of Captain Jager and delight of the *Zamzamers*. Perhaps some little justice provided this spark of retribution. No matter. In thirty-three days, the refugees had traveled almost 5,000 miles, endured foul weather, a flu epidemic, dysentery, and the uncertainty of not knowing their fate. Their spirit had not been broken. The words painted on the bulkhead in Number 2 hold by the witty ambulance man captured the essence of their defiance—"THE ZAMZAM WANDERING AND WONDERING SOCI-ETY, SOUTH ATLANTIC CHAPTER."

As ANTIMONY stood on deck with hands in his jacket pocket clutching the key ring with the choking wire, he could only speculate as to what his fate would now be. On the enemy's turf now, there would be new rules to play by. The game board had changed, but not the objective. Verdi, linchpin of the effort to perfect an atomic weapon before Nazi Germany, must still be saved—saved and repatriated. The mission had not changed; it had only become more difficult. He must be strong. He must not fail. In the little French seacoast port of St.-Jean-de-Luz, the waltz of the *Dresden* ended; the band finished its tune. Now, a new orchestra would play and all must dance to it.

CHAPTER 17
BANGERS AND MASH

The three uniformed officers strolling down the Strand attracted little attention. Everyone seemed to be in uniform of some sort these days. They turned the corner and headed north along Aldych Circle towards the theatre district. A brass bell hung in front of the establishment with the old ship's name still visible—*Mary Swanson*, Liverpool, 1872. No one knew for sure what happened to the good ship *Mary Swanson*, but her bell adorned the entranceway to the popular Bell and Clapper Pub, much to the annoyance of the locals. In spite of its height, which prohibited the run-of-the mill patron from ringing it, the King's College lads made it a point of pride to mount on each other's shoulders and ring the bell at the oddest of hours. The publican who owned the place loved it. After all, he lived in Chelsea. It never bothered him and it made for good publicity.

The three men entered the dark, smoky pub, which always had the heady aroma of freshly baked crusty bread, stale beer, old wood, and brass polish—a warm, cheerful place even in wartime and a popular lunch destination for the officers fighting the war from down the road at Whitehall. Brass spittoons, candlesticks, sconces, and lanterns adorned the place. Salt-worn gray block and tackle hung from the ceiling; decaying fishing nets strung from the walls and paintings of ships, boats, and sailors surrounded by the memorabilia of the publican's thirty odd years as a merchant seaman adorned the interior—a comfortable place.

The three officers sat near the door. They would have preferred a booth, but at this time of day they had done well just to get a table. A white-haired waiter with apron squarely tied about his bulging mid-section and walking with a noticeable limp parked himself over the table with notepad in hand and pencil poised.

"What'll you 'ave, Sirs?"

"Ah, two bitters and a stout, please, and," looking all around as he spoke, "one bangers and mash and two bread and cheese plates," replied the senior officer.

"Right. Be out with your beer in a sec," he nodded as he hobbled off.

The man who ordered wore the black uniform with wavy gold braid of a lieutenant-commander of the Royal Navy Volunteer Reserve, complete with his customary fleece-lined sea boots—not strictly regulation, but this is wartime and strict uniform policy was a peacetime luxury. The second man wore a khaki uniform with three pips on his shoulders and the red, white, and green diced Glengarry bonnet of a captain in the Canadian Black Watch Regiment. The third man, also in khaki with three pips, a captain of the Royal Welch Fusiliers with the unique ribbon flash on the back of his collar, completed the trio.

The drinks came. For the Fusilier, the heavy, pungent stout hit the spot. He much preferred it to the lighter, thinner Canadian ales he had had for the last six months as a special operations instructor at Camp "X." The Canadian, in London for the first time, tried a bitter. Fleming ordered a second round. This is a work day. Two's the limit. They dove into the sausages and mashed potatoes and the crusty bread with Cheddar cheese, fresh butter, and a garnish of tomato and onion.

"Pardon me, Sir. Would you be Lieutenant-Commander Fleming?" asked the plain, but friendly barmaid.

"Yes, I am," responded Fleming.

"Telephone, Sir. It's your office. The gent says it's urgent. Telephone's there, over behind the coat rack, Sir." She pointed out the call box hidden in the corner.

"Thank you. Do excuse me. Let's see what's up."

"Fleming here."

"Ian, the show is on."

"Right. I'll see to our guests. Expect me within the hour." *The show is on!* He hurried back to the table where the waiter had just brought the second round of drinks. "Bottoms up, lads. We're on." He raised his pint high in the air in a salute. "Here's to a successful outing."

"Here, here!"

The two officers raised their pints and clinked them together. Tomorrow would not be quite so congenial. Fleming rushed the two men back to the SOE safe house just off Leicester Square, nestled among row after row of drab townhouses. Watched and guarded from intrusion, SOE used it as a jumping off point or temporary bivouac for agents fresh from Camp "X" departing on missions. McElroy, the Canadian, spoke French and German and handled demolitions and weaponry. Gwyath, the Welshman and an instructor in the martial arts, small arms, insertion, and extraction, spoke passable French but excellent German. The very best INTREPID had to offer, they had been fitted out and readied to fly into Occupied France to bring out, one way or another, Verdi and ANTIMONY. Despite U.S. State Department contentions, that, as American nationals, the Germans would release both immediately upon debarkation into the custody of the consular representatives standing by in Paris and Spain, the British knew better. Donovan concurred and convinced President Roosevelt of the same reality. The Verdi operation working group had decided to conduct an extraction and to hell with the possible diplomatic flap. Let the FO boys worry with that one. So, at the SOE safe house, the two officers prepared themselves for the mission as Fleming hailed a cab back to Admiralty.

"Gentlemen, it's time to activate Operation Cavalry."

What an appropriate code name. Fleming had chosen it. He rather liked the image of the cavalry charging over the hill to rescue the beleaguered wagon train. He probably had read too many western pulp novels, but Godfrey let the name stick. The DNI moved over to the shroud covered map on the easel.

"General Menzies will not be in attendance. He is preparing the logistics for the mission." Godfrey lifted the cloth covering the map of France. Divided into sectors, large block letters delineated the code name for each of the SOE operational areas. "We know from this morning's latest traffic that

Dresden is making for St.-Jean-de-Luz ... here." He pointed his forefinger to a spot on the southern end of the Bay of Biscay only a few miles from the Spanish border.

Fleming already knew every word of the DNI's brief. Mostly his own staff work, he had developed the brief for the benefit of INTREPID, who had just returned to London and General Gubbins under whose authority the mission operated. Fleming's thoughts drifted back to the night before. He had been so wrapped up in the whole Verdi affair for so many weeks that he hardly had any time to relax and unwind. The stress wore on him. *How had Commodore Braithwaite held up? Is he even alive? If so, is his cover intact or is he in the ship's brig bound for a Gestapo prison when they landed.* Damn it, he just didn't know and it ate him alive from the inside out.

"St.-Jean-de-Luz is in the *Scientist* network area. We've had relatively good luck there, chaps."

Gubbins' brief followed Godfrey's introduction. Fleming drifted in and out of the briefing. He had gone out on the town the previous evening or as much as the town could offer during the Blitz. Though darkened in the streets, behind the heavy blackout curtains, London still meant life—wonderful, exuberant, ecstatic life! He needed a good dose of it.

"The primary mission of the French Resistance operation in that area is threefold. One, to escort any of our people fortunate enough to make it that far over the Spanish border. Two, observation of military and merchant shipping operating in and out of there and the coast of Spain. And three, protecting fugitives. The *SS* and *Gestapo* are not quite as active there as, say, in the *Prosper* network around Paris, so it is a relatively safe haven. We do not encourage sabotage or attacks there—too damned risky just yet and it would bring down the squareheads' attention on our escape operations there. In fact, the Huns couldn't have picked a better place to bring our lads in given our in-place resources."

Fleming now became totally oblivious to the brief. He had found the club recommended by a Spitfire pilot from Biggin Hill. So why not give it a go on his first R&R out of uniform in some time (not since his trip to New York weeks earlier). *God, how he hated the ride over and back. How in the world did INTREPID stand those constant overnight flights? Dimly lit, the place smelled like a good beer hall. It reeked of sweat, cigarette smoke, watered down perfume, and sex.* His thoughts drifted in a haze, caught between memory of the night before and the reality of the brief.

"The leader of the *Scientist* group in that area is a most extraordinary young lady, one Eliana Descartes."

The young lady had met him at the entrance and escorted him to a small booth near the bandstand.

"She is a former barrister and practiced in Marseille before the war. Now her cover is as a legal assistant to one of the town's magistrates, a very pro-Vichy type. Her cover is relatively safe since she was known to be quite conservative in prewar politics. Not Communist-leaning by any means, this gives her some credibility with the Vichy crowd. Or, so they think. She is first and foremost a French patriot."

"Cigarette?" the young girl asked.

Fleming had none. "Sorry. Fresh out, Love."

"Not to worry. I smoke too many of them anyway," she motioned to the waiter, a huge, ungainly obese man, who obviously had not suffered ration-wise during the food shortage. He set down two glasses of whiskey. Ian hadn't even ordered. He didn't care. The whiskey is all right.

"She operates a unit of ten men and three women, all relatively well-placed in the local establishment."

The local establishment—not for locals, but for the thousands of lonely young airmen, soldiers, sailors, and marines ripped from the gentleness of home and family. For them, it's a release—emotional and sexual just as it would be for Fleming.

"Miss Descartes has an excellent wireless operation, so we can remain in touch throughout the rescue operation."

The girl, barely twenty if that, had a North country accent. Newcastle, he guessed.

"She speaks superb English, so communications with our chaps will not be a problem."

"Do you speak French," she asked.

It startled Fleming. *What did that have to do with anything?* "A bit. Why do you ask?"

"I thought so. All of you well-born gentlemen must speak French. It makes you a member of the bleeding 'igh society, don't it," she said, not disdainfully,

but rather winsomely, as if impressed at the elegance of it all. She leaned over the table and kissed his forehead—a long, loving, watery kiss leaving smudges of ruby lipstick behind as a telltale token that she had been there.

"We shall insert the team by air—Lysander of the Moon Squadron—tonight. It's best to be in place when *Dresden* docks tomorrow, but not long enough prior to risk detection. The Navy will conduct the extraction. HMS *Tribune* will perform the mission."

"Are you a pilot?" she asked.

"No. Navy," he stuttered, still overcome by the suddenness of the passionate kiss.

Gubbins turned to a small detail map of the St.-Jean-de-Luz/Biarritz area. A few kilometers south of Biarritz, a small promontory jutted out into the Bay of Biscay near the village of Bidart, roughly halfway between St.-Jean-de-Luz and Biarritz and just off the main coast highway. "Here. The local Resistance calls it Point 'Hope.' We've used this place for extractions before. It has excellent observation from the head of the promontory and is a steep dropoff down to a sandy beach below. Just the sort of thing the Navy lads like to land on. The water is very deep so a sub can get in quite close to lessen the time in the water for boats, thus their time on the surface. That also makes them happy."

Chuckles came from all around.

She had chestnut brown hair, the fine kind you love to run your fingers through in a caressing sort of way, and pale brown eyes, almost the color of a nut brown country ale. Not very tall, she seemed more so than her actual measurements. Perhaps the length of her legs that seemed to reach to her armpits. Maybe the slinky red silk dress she wore, slit up each thigh, made this so. Warm and delicate, her hands felt soft to the touch.

"This is the latest photograph of Miss Descartes taken last year, I believe."

"I'd go to France for her," came a rude remark from the back of the room followed by the expected chuckles.

"Yes, she is rather striking, and terrifically intelligent, bold, resourceful and aggressive. She's one of the best we have behind the Jerry lines. Our two men are in good hands."

She placed her fingers in his cupped hands. He closed his bleary eyes, tense with exhaustion and compounded by a serious lack of sleep. She sensed this and gently stroked his fingers. In spite of his exhaustion, a fire burned within him, one he had managed to submerge in an ocean of work and missions, brief-ings and analysis, day after day.

"How do we alert the partisans that an operation is imminent, Sir?" "Very simply. This evening, at precisely 1630 hours, there will be a reading of a poem on the BBC World Service followed by a specific musical piece. The poem alerts the Resistance to stand by to receive wireless traffic and the specific music designates the precise partisan cell. The actual transmission details the operation and instructions and is keyed at 1730 hours. The trick is to not let Jerry know which cell is being contacted by which musical number. This could betray them even if the coded message cannot be broken. This information is, of course, highly classified."

The house band began a slow melodic tune—"Moonlight Serenade." They weren't bad, this little bordello quintet calling themselves the Bill Stuart Five. What a strange combination of instruments for a big band number, but it sounded wonderful. The lights went even dimmer while blue filtered spots came up. The smoky room took on a dreamy, surreal landscape. Dancers tightly clung together; all swayed gently in the shimmering, hazy light. Flem-ing breathed in deeply. Her perfumed hair cascaded over his chest; her cheeks pressed tightly against his shirt. He felt as if he would pass out but no, the slowly flowing strains continued on. The pungent, sweet-smelling air stung his nostrils as he squeezed her hand. It seemed as if electric sparks arched around him and the young lady of the evening. He didn't care who she had ever been with. She would be his for a few lustful, all-releasing hours.

"The Lysander departs Tempsford tonight at precisely 2200. They should arrive at the designated landing zone not later than 0100 hours. It is at the maximum range of the aircraft even with auxiliary fuel tanks, so the land-ing zone must be prepared and ready on time or they will have to abort the mission. Lieutenant-Commander Fleming has been seeing to our two chaps. Are they ready for the mission, Ian?"

In the clean, crisp, cool air outside the club, they had shared his great coat. She snuggled up under the sleeve. Her metal tipped heels clicked on the pave-ment as they briskly walked away from the club through deserted Soho streets.

"Commander Fleming. Have you left us?"

He left her flat that morning in the early dawn light before she awakened, leaving a ten pound note on the dressing table. He felt refreshed, alive, reinvig-orated and ready to answer all bells. It is time to kick Fritzes' arse!

"Sorry, Sir. I was pondering the ... the lady, Sir. Most extraordinary. The SOE chaps are ready and eager. They're at Leicester Square packing their kits just now."

"Excellent. Are there any questions?"

Dozens followed. How this, why that, why not another. The meeting formally adjourned at just past 1600. Fleming headed back to the safe house to retrieve his charges. He would take them to an early dinner at the Savoy Grill, still a fine dining experience despite the bombing, then escort them to the airfield at Tempsford. Hidden in the Bedfordshire countryside, miles from London and the threat of German bombers, Tempsford appeared to be a simple rural farm. But, known to RAF pilots and SOE operatives as "Gibraltar Farm," it served as the base for the Westland Lysanders and other aircraft of the Special Duties Squadrons, known as the Moon Squadrons, who regularly flew SOE agents in and out of Occupied France in support of the growing Resistance movement.

At precisely 1630, the announcer's voice vibrated through the speakers in a thatched hut high up in the hills several kilometers from Biarritz. The French shepherd had tuned in the radio minutes earlier as he did every day at this same time, just before he went down the mountain for his dinner. He leaned back in his chair puffing on the one precious bowl of tobacco he allowed himself each day.

"Good evening. This is the BBC World Service. And now, for our friends abroad, today's poetry selection is from 'The Love Song of J. Alfred Prufrock' by the American poet, Mr. Thomas Stearns Eliot." The reader's deep melodious voice reverberated across the tiny cabin. " ... in the room, the women come and go, talking of Michelangelo ... "

The shepherd ceased his casual puffing on the treasured pipe as he sat up in his chair and leaned forward. He nearly bit the pipe stem off as his teeth clutched tight in anticipation of what would come next.

"And now, a musical interlude. Our first number is by the American jazz and popular music composer, Mr. Irving Berlin, with the BBC swing band performing 'Where Will I Go.'"

He leapt out of the chair. Not waiting for the singer to finish the number, he clicked off the radio set, grabbed his crook and a battered wool cap and raced down the mountainside followed by three yapping, excited sheepdogs. Dinner would have to wait tonight.

2154. Three figures strode briskly out across the grassy field towards the stuttering noise of an aero-engine idling in the distance. Dressed completely in black, two had their faces blackened with smudged burnt cork. The third wore a naval officer's reefer with no cap. The two black-suited men each carried black canvas rucksacks. As they approached the airplane, they ducked low to avoid the wing.

"Right lads, hop aboard then," shouted an unseen face from inside the Lysander of No. 138 Squadron above the engine's drone.

They tossed their rucksacks up into the open cockpit then turned to Fleming, each extending a gloved hand.

"Best of luck, chaps. Give my regards to the Commodore." Fleming grinned, shaking each man's extended hand.

They only nodded. These men, now prepared for a dangerous mission and with their concentration complete and focused, had little room for pleasantries in their narrow world this night.

Fleming cleared the plane and jogged back towards the flight operations building. The airplane, a modified Lysander model, had one purpose—to airlift in and out the men and women of the SOE. Small and light but sturdy, it could carry a large load of passengers and gear. The plane could make up to 200 knots and though not fast enough to outrun a fighter, it relied on low altitude and camouflage for safety. Dull black and made largely out of balsa wood for weight consideration, it did the job nicely. The powerful Bristol Mercury radial engine revved up just as Fleming reached the building. He turned. Even as close as he stood, he could barely make out the silhouette as the aircraft wobbled down the grass runway and into the cool, damp night air.

Over the Channel and into France flying at barely above treetop level, they avoided the night fighters that operated at a much higher altitude searching for the stream of RAF bombers. They flew around any area suspected or known to have a German troop concentration and headed to the torchlit field in southwestern France where Eliana Descartes and her team waited.

"What's that down there," the gunner spoke into the

intercom as he tapped the pilot on the shoulder and pointed down towards the ground.

The pilot banked left to get a better view. It appeared again—a tiny streak of electric blue as flame shot out of the engine exhaust pipe from some unburned fumes. Still thirty kilometers from the landing strip, the Lysander bore on right on schedule. The pilot of the *Messerschmitt* ME-110 *Zerstörer* night fighter angled over and dove towards the blue flame coming from the Lysander's engine. The German dove past the starboard wing. The RAF pilot began immediate evasive maneuvering, but to no avail. The telltale blue flame shot out even further as he went to full throttle for more air speed. The night fighter pulled in behind the defenseless Lysander. After two short bursts from the nose guns followed by a longer third burst, the *Messerschmitt* peeled off, fearful of running up the tail of the slower plane. But, his marksmanship had been true. Flames burst from the engine and under the fuselage. Shards of wrenched metal and torn wood showered the pastures below. The Lysander lost altitude and stalled into a death spiral to the hard earth below. The *Messerschmitt*, low on fuel, turned away and headed for home satisfied that the enemy plane had spun down to its death. The *Luftwaffe* crew did not need to see it hit the ground. It had been a most unusual training flight in an area not generally known for any excitement—quite the story for the squadron mess at breakfast. The ME-110 roared off into the French night.

PART III
DEATH'S PIROUETTE

CHAPTER 18
PHYSICS 101

"Ladies and gentlemen. Please. Please, your attention, please." The harried German officer attempted to line up the passengers and crew in a somewhat orderly fashion. After several minutes, the straggly line marched out of the building along the cobblestone street and back into the pier area. It looked like the same drill as weeks earlier onboard *Atlantis* separating the groups, only this time, far more ominous. The British and Canadians now had the designation "Prisoners of War," not neutral refugees. Inside the Harbor Master's office, two officials checked and verified passports, identity papers, driving licenses, and anything else that established identity and nationality. Hovering over the two men stood a drab-suited man. He spoke very little, but watched every face that came in and every piece of official paper. ANTIMONY recognized the *Gestapo* man right away. Not the local one, this one had been sent down from Berlin to personally supervise the debarkation operation. Unbeknownst to the *Zamzamers* standing for hours in the hot, late afternoon sun, the world already knew of their fate.

The diplomatic game of move and countermove, of perception and deception on a grand world stage had already begun. On the day before their arrival, His Majesty's Government announced to the international press that the overdue ship had presumably been sunk on the high seas by a German warship—a calculated propaganda effort. The impact of the loss of over a hundred American lives to the barbarous Nazis would be immense. The news represented the lead story of many newspapers that spring day. London could have softened the embarrassment that the government would suffer, but dared not. To inform the press that Admiralty knew the whereabouts of the refugees and their probable destination would at worst compromise the source. At best, he would cease sending reports and data, which amounted to the same thing in practical terms. In this game of international one-upsmanship, the British government would have to suffer a severe case of egg on the face, a condition dubbed by Fleming as the disease *Omeletitus Britannicus*. The day that *Dresden* sailed (or rather grounded and limped) into St.-Jean-du-Luz, the German government informed the American embassies in Berlin and Paris and the Consulate in Marseille of her arrival. The missing Mrs. Avery would be easily glossed over since of course, no record of her passage existed back in New York.

The officials divided the refugees into five distinct groups—Americans, other Europeans, non-European crew, European crew, and British and Commonwealth persons. A great many tears and sad handshakes erupted as the various groups boarded buses for transport to different sites. Captain Smith and Chief Engineer Burns went with the British and Commonwealth passengers. As they loaded the dusty green and blue bus, ANTIMONY stood cold and passionless, staring into the windows of the British bus at nothing in particular and everything in general. He had preserved his cover as Edward B. Prince, businessman from Albany, New York, but in his heart he wanted to lash out and strike down the captors especially the malignant *Gestapo* man with the clipboard checking off names as each person stepped onto the landing. But, his head made him hold his wrath. On the bus, with faces blank and listless, each dealt in their own way with the terror of captivity. Some wept. Some simply placed heads in hands or stared out the windows. Captain Smith, last to board, shook hands with First Officer Fiedel, said something inaudible to ANTIMONY standing fifty feet away, turned and stepped up into the bus. ANTIMONY would not see any of these people again.

All of the other groups had been taken away when two men from the American Consulate in Marseille arrived, tired and dusty from their hurried trip over bad roads. The Germans refused to turn over the American passengers. Not just yet. The senior diplomat protested, but to no avail. The smiling *Gestapo* agent assured the State Department men that it would only be a matter of a few days to properly process everyone and offload their baggage, nothing more. The diplomats did not know that the *Gestapo* hack had been ordered to keep the Americans under his control for at least five days. The order had been given to him personally by his supreme boss, *Reichsmarshal* Himmler himself. More buses arrived, newer and better than those for the previous groups. Not surprising. The Germans seemed desperate to ensure good treatment for the Americans. They did not allow anyone to talk to the press even though a few enterprising reporters had managed to race over from Paris, Marseille, and Madrid to cover the *Zamzam*'s arrival.

The bus bounced over the bumpy streets into Biarritz. Ah, Biarritz, the gem of the Biscay coast. ANTIMONY had been on holiday here in his youth those oh so many centuries ago. The town had not really changed all that much. He noticed a few more modern hotels than he remembered, but all in all, it had not lost its charm, its beauty, its little resort-by-the-sea ambiance. But it missed the revelers, the families on holiday, the young lovers walking hand-in-hand on the streets or engaged in romantic conversation in the bistros, impervious to the world around them. The place looked now like a German Army recreational center, which, in truth, it had become this first season of the Occupation. The holiday crowd would eventually return, but not this spring.

The first bus clanked to a halt in front of the hotel. The naval officer who had served as the combination shepherd and master of ceremonies, announced that everyone should remain seated. The leather seats felt cool and comfortable after the hard, sterile holds of the *Dresden*. Many had simply nodded off on the forty-minute drive from the port to the hotel and didn't really care much either way. Five buses in all pulled up to three separate hotels all along the same strip of waterfront playground. The Germans had spared no expense to host their unwelcome guests. The third bus carried ANTIMONY, Verdi, and Hobgood—no accident. The Germans had made no attempt to assign specific people to particular buses or hotels. The put upon port personnel had been content just to let the Americans sort themselves out, and as long as each bus left full and each hotel was used—fine by them. Once ANTIMONY realized this fact, he had nodded to Hobgood, who had been keeping an eye on his British friend. The colonel strolled over as if to engage in idle conversation and to light up a smoke, his last one saved for this occasion. ANTIMONY had whispered discreetly.

"Stay close. There could be trouble."

"Right. I'm a shout away."

The German officer stood in the landing area beside the sullen driver, a former French Army sergeant and bitterly resentful of the German conquerors. But, he had a family. He kept his mouth shut and did what they told him.

"Ladies and gentlemen. This is the world famous *Hôtel du Palais*, the former summer home of the Emperor Napoleon III and Empress Eugenia. It will be your home for the next few days. On behalf of the *Führer* and the *Kriegsmarine*, let me welcome you to Biarritz. We hope you enjoy your short stay. For purposes of security, however, we ask that you not leave the confines of the hotel without an escort. There will be several *Wehrmacht* personnel in the lobby at all times for your convenience. Thank you for your kind indulgence and patience with these arrangements for your safety and security." The threat wasn't very subtle, the delivery not very convincing. Hobgood leaned forward in the seat behind ANTIMONY and whispered. "We're still prisoners of these Kraut bastards."

ANTIMONY could only nod his head in agreement. Once again, he had limited freedom of action. As they stepped off the bus one at a time like a group of foreign tourists carefully shepherded by the underpaid, but still obsequious tour guide, the passengers finally started to smile, the first genuinely happy grins in weeks as the pallor of the entire episode lifted at last. *Damn! Have to be bloody careful. Must be as happy and cheerful as the rest of the group and not stand out.* No one about to be freed from unwanted captivity is gloomy. A frown captures the entire essence of mood far more than a thousand words. Standing on the sidewalk in front of the hotel just off the *Avenue de L'Imperatrice*, he looked up and down the nearly deserted street. Wide, as French avenues tended to be in contrast to the typical European urban street, and with a tall row of hedges fronting the side opposite the hotel entrance with a small park beyond, the *Avenue de L'Imperatrice* offered cover either as a quick hiding place in the event of an escape or for quiet observation. A low stone fence bordering the wide sidewalk provided potential cover in case bullets started flying. A major intersection just beyond the adjoining Carlton Hotel, where he had stayed as a young man, gave three routes for escape, thus complicating any pursuit (providing he had a sufficient head start). He had an idea of an escape plan, but he suspected that the boys in London had already developed one. *Chapter Twelve—situational awareness is critical.* Any one or more of the blank, staring French faces watching them from a distance or from behind awning-covered building fronts might be part of the plan. He must be patient. They would contact him in good time. Perhaps, just perhaps, the Germans would let Verdi go simply as an American. No, they wouldn't. They had tipped their hand on that dark, misty cobblestone street in Recife. It would be agonizing, but he must be patient and wait—wait for aid to come to him. After a few minutes, he had memorized all he needed to know. He prepared to wait and recalled the section in his treatise—*"nothing can betray the man in the field faster than impatience. It can call attention to oneself, or it can motivate action that is either premature, not well thought out, or simply rash and reckless."*

The crowd moved into the hotel in a loose gaggle. The lobby had that overwhelmingly opulent, late 19th century gilded look with reddish marble, scrolled Ionic columns, and magnificently carved ceiling panels. A wide, curved Grand Staircase, truly fit for a French emperor, led up to the higher floors, an important consideration in making a rapid running escape. People oohed and aahed at the hotel's splendor. At the main reception desk, an impervious concierge ruled over his kingdom of bellboys and baggage. He meticulously copied everyone's name into the register and, with a snap of his gloved fingers, jostling, scurrying bellboys rushed to the desk for instructions. The luggage had not yet arrived and would be sorted out and deposited at each hotel lobby later in the day. More than one embarrassing moment occurred as the guests fumbled for tips for the bellboys; many had nothing. They needn't have been concerned. Each hotel staffer had been briefed on these odd tourists and paid a handsome gratuity by the Germans, who would not tolerate any sort of disturbance or discontent, a fact made very clear to the army of hotel employees.

ANTIMONY's fourth floor, ocean side room, had a wonderful view of the Bay of Biscay with highly ornate, very enameled, very gold-leafed, very, well, very French furnishings. He preferred the simpler, cleaner lines of Queen Anne or Regency furniture. *Never mind.* A fresh, salty breeze wafted through the open window causing the delicate Belgian lace curtains to flap ever so gently. The luxurious carpet felt good under his feet. A proper toilet, a water closet with a carved crystal pull handle, a bidet, and an oversized iron bathtub with feet in the shape of lion's paw and clean, sweet swelling linen made this new prison much more acceptable. He collapsed in an armchair by the open window. Would that he could simply relax and enjoy and dream all the weight of responsibility away. He closed his eyes, but only for a moment.

He felt the stab of danger in the back of his head. His eyes shot open. Some-where in this elegant, blissful, forget all of your cares and woes resort, some-one plotted his downfall—someone malevolent. Someone who had every-thing to do with this ordeal. The sailor off the Atlantis perhaps—the one who never seemed to be a proper crewman. ANTIMONY could not help but feel that his fate somehow revolved around that odd man, yet he could not tell why. The room had one feature of importance above all. It shared a bath with the room next door occupied by one Dr. Enrico Verdi, American, Professor of Physics at the University of Chicago. They could communicate without the notice of the diligent soldiers on watch in the hall. His eyes went fuzzy; eye-lids slowly crept shut. The physical and mental turmoil of the past few weeks now took its due. Exhausted, he needed rest and a clear head. He slept sitting upright in the armchair, cooled by the gentle sea breeze. The sun slowly be-came an orange orb, deep in the western sky just above the horizon.

Two swift knocks at the door startled him out of his deep, trancelike state; in a brief moment of panic, he reached down, still half-asleep, for the weapon in his jacket pocket. *Where the devil is my . . . ! Wake up! No gun. It is somewhere in Davy Jones' locker. Maybe this is not a problem.* He reached into his jacket, the now shabby and worn gray flannel one, and took out the very dangerous pen. He cradled it in his palm.

"Come in."

The brass door handle turned abruptly. The door opened slowly and a chambermaid entered. "Towels, *Monsieur*," she said as she shut the door be-hind her and lay them on the edge of the bed.

Striking, with deep auburn hair and dark Gallic eyes, she had a slender but powerful-looking figure. Above all, he noticed her eyes—not the sad, tired eyes of an overworked hotel chambermaid exhausted by a whole bevy of new guests, who anxiously awaited the end of her shift. No, these alert eyes searched the room for treachery, for a man concealed behind a curtain or in a closet or the least little thing out of place. Satisfied, she turned to-wards him and whispered, almost too low to hear.

"ANTIMONY, INTREPID sends his regards. Do nothing yet. We will be in touch."

ANTIMONY, who had sat motionless clutching the deadly pen, nodded. She turned and left the room. The cavalry had arrived.

Ring, ring. Ring, ring. Ring, ring. Ring, ring.

"Yes," croaked a bleary-eyed Fleming. He had not even turned on the table lamp. In fact, he didn't even remember stumbling over to the telephone table. He intentionally placed the phone some distance from the bed so as to allow for wakeup time before he answered. Still half-asleep, he wasn't so sure about the logic of that just now.

"Ian, it's Ted. Are you awake?"

"Yes, Ted. what's up?"

"We've lost them. You'd best get in. I've alerted the old man."

Fleming clicked on the lamp and looked at the clock on the end table by his bed. Barely 0500. He had only arrived back in London from Tempsford at two that morning. After a stopover at the office to brief the night watch and to ring up Godfrey, he had staggered home, half-dozing then. He felt like hell, but the tension in Ted Merritt's voice told him that something had gone terribly wrong. "I'll be in as soon as I am able. And, Ted, brew up some of the marsh water you call coffee."

The walk down the long, narrow dimly-lit corridor, seemed even more claustrophobic than normal. His vivid imagination conjured up the symbolism. As the attempt to protect Verdi unraveled, so the walls of this dark corridor seemed to close in on him. Whether the mad ravings of a complete lunatic or the adrenaline-stoked exhaustion of a man on the edge, it didn't matter. The operation appeared to be coming unglued and him with it.

"Morning. Please note the conspicuous absence of the usual adjective 'good,'" he grinned, trying to put on the best face possible.

"Ditto, old sport," responded Merritt, the offgoing night watch. His watch officially ended at 0800, but like everyone else, he would be there for the duration of the crisis. First light poked its way into the windows of Room 39 overlooking the sparkling fresh dew on the clipped grass of Horse Guards Parade. Merritt shut the door firmly behind him. Fleming slumped down into the high-backed wing chair, his favorite, but one usually cornered by someone more senior during the briefing and planning sessions. The room seemed decrepit and sad this morning.

"What have you got, Ted?"

"Not good at all, I'm afraid," he said as he rattled the paper. He switched on a desk lamp on the secretary next to the Admiral's desk and read the report, paraphrasing as necessary. "SOE received this wireless message at about 0400. They had it decoded and over to me by 0500. That's when I rang you up. I did contact the Admiral first. After that, I reached INTREPID. Gubbins, of course, got the word from his own people. It seems that the Lysander was intercepted by a *Luftwaffe* night fighter—probably just a million to one chance meeting and probably on a routine training mission."

"They still carry live ammunition," interrupted Fleming.

"Quite right. The Lysander was badly shot up, but the attacker hauled off before finishing the job. Probably low on fuel, I should think. Our plane was afire, but the pilot kept it aloft."

"Where were they?"

"Thirty bloody kilometers from the landing field, less than eight minutes flying time."

"Damn!"

"Yes, quite right. The pilot had no instruments, but the fire died out, so he decided to try to make the landing site on visual. Those Resistance chaps usually make an "L" pattern with their lights, so he was able to make it out fairly clearly"

"Couldn't they jump for it?"

"Not according to the Resistance report. He was only at 100 feet—couldn't get any attitude and losing power, so given that, as long as he had a compass fix, might as well take her all the way in," Merritt shrugged.

"I suppose so," sighed Fleming.

"They made the landing site only three minutes behind schedule and he brought it in." He paused. Fleming looked up at Merritt, then looked at the floor, ready for the ax to fall. "They cracked up on the landing field; it killed the pilot."

"What about our lads?"

"McElroy is in a bad way. He has multiple fractures and is unconscious. Gwyath is ambulatory, but badly broken up. It will be days before they can be moved. The Resistance people plan to take them into Spain when they can travel."

"At least they are alive. The RAF accomplished the mission. They got them there. Damn the bad luck!" He jolted up from the chair and paced the floor.

Godfrey's desk phone rang. Merritt answered. "Yes. Right. Right. Yes, I'll pass it on to him straightway. Thanks." He turned to Fleming as he lay the phone back down. "The old man, "C" and Gubbins are going to brief the PM at 0800. I'd hate to be in on that. Winnie can be in a foul mood early in the morning, but especially with something like this."

"Yes, and especially after we sent two Force H cruisers on a wild goose chase that came to nothing but a lot of wasted fuel oil."

"Yes, but Admiral Somerville has them back, and they might—might mind you— have just bagged Atlantis. It was worth the effort, Ian."

"So what about me?" Fleming asked. He had stopped pacing and stood, hands locked behind his back, staring out the window.

"Yes, you. You are to meet INTREPID in an hour at Kew Gardens, main entrance."

"I see. I should have thought he would be in the meeting with Churchill."

"Three schoolboys are plenty for the Head Master to chew on at one time. No, you and he are to plot a revised operational plan."

Plot an operational plan indeed! The rescue team out of action. Verdi in German hands and ANTIMONY cannot make any overt move. Damn it all! A planning session?

Merritt read Fleming's troubled mind. "Well, Ian, old lad. That's why we all work for the man, isn't it?"

Technically, the Service agencies answered to their own chain of command. Practically, INTREPID, as head of BSC and *de facto* in charge of all British wartime intelligence, counter-intelligence, special operations and espionage operations in North America, had the final word. Yes, they all worked for the energetic, brilliant Canadian from the plains of Manitoba.

The sun sat well up in the eastern sky as Fleming stepped out of the taxi and handed the driver an overly generous tip. Kew Gardens, that magical botanical tribute located in the southwestern suburbs of London begun centuries earlier by King George III, provided a respite in a time of great trouble. Fleming noticed a stately Bentley with two, not so discreet men sitting in the front seat, one reading the *Times* and the other holding a cup of some steaming liquid. He walked into the Gardens. Lilacs bloomed. Life from death, beauty from ugliness. No wonder man reveled so much in spring's coming. The roses of June would soon be here.

Fleming spotted INTREPID, who extended a hand in greeting. Without a word, both men strolled through the manicured patches of blue, yellow, and white flowers, a tall, lanky man in black naval uniform and a shorter man in a brown herringbone suit. It seemed to both as if the weight of the world lay squarely upon their shoulders.

Finally, INTREPID spoke. "A bad business last night, Ian."

"Indeed, Sir. This rather puts us out of the game, doesn't it?" No reply. They kept walking.

"Directly, yes. Indirectly, no. We still have the Resistance cell and they are damned fine people. Gubbins may be a bit anxious about putting them in jeopardy though. That is his main conduit for bringing out our downed flyers through Spain."

"I understand his concern."

INTREPID leaned over and picked up a fallen tree limb. He cracked off a small twig and tossed the branch behind a row of boxwood bushes. He examined the twig intensely, then tossed it into a clump of flowers as if the twig had helped make up his mind. It generally didn't take INTREPID very long to decide on and then implement a course of action. He strolled on. "ANTIMONY is the key. He's come this far, and, as far as we know, he's still in the game, albeit, hampered in his choice of options. I believe we should, as the Americans say, stick with the starting quarterback."

"What about the Resistance people?"

"We've already endangered them far beyond prudence by the wireless reports they have been sending and cleaning up the crash site. No, we should go with ANTIMONY. If possible, they may provide him some discreet logistics support. I'm sending another signal for them to relay to ANTIMONY. HMS *Tribune* will be on station at midnight day after tomorrow as arranged. He will have to get Dr. Verdi there."

So there it is. The decision, made with the savvy and confidence forged in the fires of adversity, had been made. Trust your man in the field to do the job, otherwise, why send him out to start with. Hopes now lay squarely on the shoulders of a middle-aged retired naval officer, but one far more capable than even he gave himself credit for. They walked past a row of roses with tightly wrapped buds just waiting for the right moment of warmth to spring open and shine.

"I have read ANTIMONY's war record from the last one. He never failed in a mission, no matter how difficult or daunting the opposition. The truth is, Ian, I don't believe that the Nazi bastards are a match for the old boy. If I didn't believe that, I would never have allowed him to go on this little romp. He's there. He'll find a way."

The two men walked in silence through the early morning, dew covered grass of Kew Gardens amidst the blooms and fragrances of a May day.

ANTIMONY leaned over to tie his shoe. He propped it up on the old oak chest in the corner of the room. More for decoration than anything else, it didn't quite seem to go with the remainder of the decor. He didn't really care what the room looked like after a month in the *Dresden's* hold. At any rate, the chest seemed like a convenient place on which to tie a shoe, the same ones he had worn every day since the morning of the attack. When he left New York, they had the burnish of a well-turned shine and looked every bit the handcrafted fine pieces of workmanship. Now, scuffed and mashed, laces frayed, they looked more like the shoes of a less than successful door-to-door salesman having a bad season. He had other shoes rescued from the wreck of the *Zamzam*, but considering the ticklish situation of the moment, he needed the security of the contents of the heels of these particular shoes. A short rap came at the door. He tensed and turned towards the door several feet away, but didn't go and open it. In case of attack, distance gave him maneuver room. On the other hand, he had locked the door. That is, except the previous afternoon when he had dozed in the side chair by the window. *Very bad form.* A locked door forced a visitor to speak and identify themselves.

"Come in," he said, ready to react.

A key rattled in the lock. The regular chambermaid had already been in and made the bed. This woman, the contact with London, again had towels. If this kept up, he might go into the linen trade after the war given the surplus he had now collected.

"Fresh towels, *Monsieur.*"

"Yes, of course. Thank you." He looked towards the open window and the ocean beyond. He kept it open to make sure that any roving eyes would not get suspicious about closed drapes while all others stood wide open allowing in the cooling morning sea breezes. Nonetheless, he made sure to stay in the line of fire for no longer than necessary. The woman went into the bathroom with no windows, thus she could speak. ANTIMONY sat down in a side chair, this time well away from the open window.

"Two men arrived from Berlin early this morning. They are scientists of some sort, *Monsieur.* They are here to speak with Dr. Verdi."

"When will they be here?" he asked only loud enough for her to hear.

"They have ordered a luncheon to be brought up to Dr. Verdi's room at one p.m. precisely."

He looked at his watch—just past 0900.

"They are being briefed by the *Gestapo* now, so I would not expect them before noon."

"I understand."

She came back into his room and made a curtsey in the old fashioned servant's way. She played this role exceedingly well. "If there is anything else you require, *Monsieur*, please do call on us."

ANTIMONY smiled. "Thank you. You have been most helpful. Good day."

She curtsied again and left the room.

Damn! This could be bad. What were they up to? He hadn't much time, but an idea had already formed in his mind. He stepped into the bath and knocked on the door to Verdi's room with the prearranged signal—one short tap followed by three more. Verdi opened the door. Well away from the window, they could speak without being observed from the beach.

"Yes, Mr. Prince? Something important is in the air.

I can tell. Are we found out?"

"Probably not, but we may have some trouble."

Verdi sat on the edge of the bed, gripping a bedpost. ANTIMONY sat on a chest, a mate to the one in his own room.

"You must be completely candid with me. I realize that I am British and you are American, but we are in this row together. I need some information that may be classified by your government."

Verdi hesitated. *Could this Englishman be a plant, a fake all along to generate trust, then pry open the secrets of his research work?* It had already occurred to him. The attempted kidnapping in Recife could have easily been staged. What is the evidence that Van Eyck wasn't who he said he was, simply a Dutch diamond merchant. But, there are always a thousand what ifs and only one concrete fact. Verdi's reading of this man with whom he had endured hardship and turmoil for the past few weeks told him that in spite of all the uncertainties, he must trust this Englishman.

"What has happened, Mr. Prince?"

"The chambermaid just came with some distressing news."

"Yes, I heard her whispering from the bath. I couldn't make out the conversation though."

ANTIMONY stood up and leaned forward, staring Verdi directly in the eyes. "How much do the Germans know about your work?"

The direct question caught Verdi off guard. He turned pale, but quickly recovered. So it came down to this. The enemy is closing in. "Not much. Not much beyond the theoretical. Though to be honest, their own physicists have perhaps progressed as far or surpassed my own work."

"But they don't know that, do they?"

"No, I suppose not."

ANTIMONY rose and paced, rubbing his temples. His head ached with the tension and pressure of the crisis. "But with your knowledge and skill, combined with theirs and their research to date, is it possible that the Germans could produce a practical atomic weapon before either of our two nations?"

What a question of tremendous magnitude! All through the crisis—the assault in Recife, the capture by the raider, the wanderings of the *Dresden*, and now this stately prison—this had been the underlying question. ANTIMONY had never asked it, and Verdi tried to submerge it to the simple task of survival. But there it is, real and horrific in its implications.

"Yes, Mr. Prince. That is not outside the realm of possibility."

ANTIMONY took in a deep breath and let it out slowly. "You have been frank with me, Sir. Let me be frank with you. Van Eyck's probable mission was to follow you to South Africa. Some months ago, we planted a rumor through a double agent that we have a "special weapons" facility in South Africa. There was no connotation of atomic research. It was merely to confound Jerry into spending his resources going after that and leaving our real facilities alone. When they found out about your visit, the *Abwehr* seemingly assigned Van Eyck to follow you figuring you were actually visiting the facility and would lead him there. I have no hard evidence of that; it is merely speculation. Were I Admiral Canaris, though, I would certainly do the same. So, I suspected that there was an *Abwehr* man on board. I just didn't know who he was until just before Recife."

"That certainly makes sense, but why the attack in Brazil. I don't understand."

"Neither do I, unless there is someone else involved beyond the *Abwehr*. It may well have been Van Eyck behind the Recife attempt, but I doubt it. I smell the malignant odor of the SS in this. I fear they want you for your knowledge of atomic physics, not just for weapons plant intelligence."

So it finally came clear, even though both men had suspected the truth for weeks, they had mentally sublimated it. Now they had to face it. The throbbing in ANTIMONY's head stopped. He knew what he had to do. Clearing the decks for action, his mind sharp and clean, he stood ready. "Can you teach me enough atomic physics in three hours to make them believe that I am you?"

"You must be joking. Why? I don't follow you."

"Simply this. At about one this afternoon, two physicists from Berlin will be here to speak with you. That was the message from the chambermaid. She is French Resistance and in contact with London. I suspect that their mission is twofold. One, to be certain you are the true article and two, to see if you might be persuaded to come to work for them—sort of a patriotic appeal to your Italian heritage."

"That is behind me, Sir," he shot back with a tone of bitterness and anger.

"I understand that, but it is a tack I would also take."

"So what do you propose?"

"A switch."

"A switch?"

"Yes," he paced again, his mind racing in a thousand directions, running through all of the possible defenses. "I shall be you. If they are simply here to talk, so much the better. If, on the other hand, they are here to snatch you, I need to be convincing enough to fool them until you are well on the train to Lisbon and on the flying boat back to New York."

"What would happen to you, then?"

ANTIMONY jolted. *What would happen to him? Death, execution, horrific torture at Gestapo hands.* He didn't have the little pills normally issued, the ones with the bittersweet, almond-smelling potassium cyanide. He blocked it out of his mind. *The mission. The mission must succeed in spite of the risk.* He had risked death before. He would do so again.

"I will be all right. Not to worry. You must be on that train."

He lied.

"What is your scientific training?"

"Several chemistry, mathematics and physics courses at Eton and then again at Oxford, though I took my degree in Modern History. I have been an avid reader of science, though, so I should say a fair working knowledge of theory and application.

"It will have to do then. Let's get started."

"Let's hope that neither of these Hun bastards have met you."

For the next two and a half hours, they drilled over and over again. Years of theory and research refined to its essence, compressed into a Millerand of time in the history of the world. They delved into protons, neutrons, and electrons and atomic particles and their properties. They dissected the Einstein's theory of relativity and the recent work of Bohr, Fritch, and Pierls and, of course, Verdi's own handiwork. And finally, they honed in on the theory of nuclear fission, the process of splitting the atom and producing millions of electron volts of energy—energy that could topple empires and devastate cities or armies.

At the end of the session, ANTIMONY changed into one of Verdi's suits—a bit loose, but the scientist had roughly his same height and build. In spite of his age, ANTIMONY made it a point to stay fit and strong and his well-toned, athletic frame resulted. Verdi, working in the lab or the classroom all day, had not done so and weighed perhaps ten pounds heavier. Barely fifteen minutes after they exchanged rooms, two men in dark suits appeared at the door, smiling. Behind them stood two less friendly looking thugs—*Gestapo*.

"*Professorri* Verdi?" queried one of the men in mangled Italian.

ANTIMONY hadn't considered this. Fortunately, many pleasant days in Italy during his tours of duty with the Mediterranean Fleet made his knowledge of Italian passable. He replied in German. "I speak reasonably well in German, Sir. Please, do come in." He motioned them in.

The speaker appeared noticeably relieved at not being required to speak in Italian or English. Only the two scientists entered the room. The *Gestapo* men stayed in the hall.

"I am Doctor Otto von Schnabel and this is Professor Fritz Bose. We are from the *Kaiser Wilhelm* Institute in Berlin."

"I am pleased to meet you." He shook each one's hand in turn. "Please, do sit down, gentlemen."

The two Germans placed their hats on the bed and sat in the wing chairs. "We are both great admirers of your work Dr. Verdi, and have come all the way from Berlin just to discuss it with you," offered Professor Bose, somewhat timidly.

"I am honored. Have I met either of you distinguished gentlemen professionally?"

"I fear not, Sir, but we have read all your research publications."

ANTIMONY merely nodded. He had not probed Verdi about research titles.

A loud knock at the door interrupted the uncomfortable pause. Von Schnabel shot up in his seat. "That will be our luncheon. You will forgive me, Dr. Verdi. I took the liberty of ordering for us. It is a simple, light affair appropriate to the weather. I hope you will approve."

"Of course, *Herr Doktor*. Very kind of you."

The Germans' attempts at being accommodating and pleasant came across as almost nauseating. They tried too hard to be affable and the two physicists did not seem to be much of a threat, unlike the men in the hallway. The waiter rolled the cart into the room and uncorked the wine.

"I ordered a *Chablis* for us. I understand that is your favorite."

A trap? Christ Almighty, what wine did Verdi always order at dinner? Think man! Hours of scientific details drilled into him only to be uncovered by a bloody bottle of wine. Chablis. No. No, not Chablis. White Rhine wine. That's what he always ordered! "Actually, I prefer a good white Rhine wine with a light meal, but a *Chablis* is perfectly fine."

"Pardon, *Monsieur*, but this is a white Rhine as you ordered," said the waiter, cradling the bottle with the label up; he had learned enough German to follow their conversation. So many of the patrons these days were the hated *Boche*—not like the old days.

Von Schnabel's face flushed with embarrassment. "I'm so sorry. I'm not really a wine expert. Please forgive me."

ANTIMONY's tension eased. The crisis passed. Not a trap. *Herr Doktor* von Schnabel proved to be simply the absent-minded professor, nothing more. The lunch—crusty bread and butter, cheeses, fresh Spanish fruits, jams and pastries—turned out delicious as expected, particularly after weeks of *Dresden* fare. *But how did von Schnabel know to order a Rhine wine in the first place?*

They spent the rest of the afternoon in tit for tat conversation. ANTIMONY dodged and wove his way around certain issues and even impressed his interrogators with some facts that even they had not been aware of. He had to be as general and nonspecific as possible. He had to disguise the fact that he could not even begin to discuss either the equations and formulae of atomic physics or the current state of research. To succeed, he had to obfuscate and deceive so as to create the impression that he would not divulge any facts about his research, his depth of knowledge, or the state of the American and British research programs. Eventually, they raised the question of defection, though obviously, it embarrassed them. Scientists, not politicians, they offered him the finest in research facilities and resources, both human and physical. They spoke of great comfort, wealth, and resources far exceeding a simple research professor's means. They dangled prestige, a high rank in the Party, and all sorts of attractive inducements. ANTIMONY politely told them that he must decline the offer.

The two scientists departed late that afternoon convinced of three things. One, they had spoken with Dr. Enrico Verdi. Two, that the American atomic research program actually remained in a primitive state far behind their own, which accounted for his reluctance to discuss any point of substance or to delve into the physics of atomic energy, and three, that this same Enrico Verdi had no intention of voluntarily working for the Reich. As they prepared to board the special SS airplane for the short flight back to Paris, they placed a phone call to Reinhard Heydrich in Paris to report their conclusions. As the SS plane took off, another phone call went out, this one from Heydrich to a quaint seaside hotel a few kilometers down the coast from Biarritz.

CHAPTER 19
MILANESE PHOTOGRAPH

The knock on the door came quick and rude, not casual and friendly as one would expect from the hotel staff. "*Herr* Prince?"

"Yes, can I help you?"

The officer wore the *SS* uniform, jet black from the bottom of his polished boots to the silver trimmed top of his peaked cap with silver coil embroidered Nazi eagle over the breast pocket. The uniform, meant to impress and to frighten, did both. "I am SS *Sturmführer* Schilling. You are most cordially invited to dine this evening with *SS Sturmbannführer* von Donop at eight sharp in the dining room. Simply ask for the von Donop table. We can expect you then, *Herr* Prince?"

How sublimely subtle these Germans are. The friendly, smiling offer of a fine dinner at a marvelously extravagant hotel while most cordial indeed, hid the undercurrent of a threat. This is not an invitation at all. It is an order delivered by an officer in black, more so to emphasize the gravity of noncompliance. "Yes, of course. I'd be honored. Eight sharp, you say?"

"*Jawohl, Herr* Prince. The *sturmbannführer* will be most pleased. Good day, Sir." The *SS* man turned.

"Oh, by the way Mr. Schilling, is it? I don't believe I know an officer by the name of von Donop."

The visitor smiled broadly and slyly. "He knows you quite well, Sir. Good evening."

ANTIMONY closed the door, but kept his ear pressed to the panel. As he suspected and feared, the next knock came at Verdi's door. *The squareheads must have figured it out. No, maybe not. His performance that afternoon had been spectacular. Perhaps after the war Lew Grade would give him a job in the cinema. No, if Jerry knew what's up, then why muck about? Why not simply arrest him? Why the formality of a dinner? Something is not quite all there. The enemy knows something, but needed something else as well.* He raced to the window. Though forty feet up, he had already scouted out and planned a dangerous, though potential escape route. But with only one way to the ground, it would not work. Three *SS* men stood beneath his balcony as if they knew where the escape point would be. He raced back to the door in time to hear the officers' final words to Verdi, the same he had spoken to ANTIMONY only moments earlier.

"The *sturmbannführer* will be most pleased."

Indeed he would be! ANTIMONY checked his watch—almost eight. The opponent is damned clever. He had issued the challenge with the ferocity of a charging rhino leaving no place to run to, no place to hide, no time for another plan. *Damn! Why had he not come up with an alternate escape route?* Never organize a single escape plan said the treatise. Always have multiple options available. In the frenzy of the ruse with the German scientists, he had not planned a different escape route. *No choice. They must play out the hand dealt. Perhaps this SS man is simply on a snipe hunt with nothing definitive. Perhaps they could bluff their way through yet another assault.* He ran to the door connecting the shared bath. Verdi waited on the other side, about to knock on ANTIMONY's door as the Englishman burst into the room looking left and right to ensure security, then putting his hands firmly on the man's shoulder. He looked the scientist squarely in the eyes. He saw strength and courage. He saw the integrity and gumption that had made the man able to turn his back on his homeland to make a point about freedom. *This man is up to it.* He could read his character.

"We're up against it, aren't we, Mr. Prince?"

"Quite possibly, Doctor, but we must play out the hand." He noticed Verdi's nod towards the open window. "No good. The bastards have figured that out. They've posted men at the point where we would have to come down. I have seen *Wehrmacht* men at the fire escapes as well. No, we will have to tough this one out. I know you are up to it. Don't volunteer anything more than you have already. Don't let this von Donop throw you. He might be only fishing. Let's hope that the two from Berlin have departed. Maybe the SS sent him to try to get something on you. I don't know. Just be careful."

"Does he know who you are?"

ANTIMONY bit his lower lip and raised his eyebrows. "I don't know. We'll find out. Whatever happens to me, don't cave in. You are an American citizen and they have their hands tied diplomatically, so they must be very careful." ANTIMONY looked at his watch again—two minutes until eight. "We'd best be going. You go first. I'll follow a minute or so later. Good luck, Sir." He extended his hand. The Italian's handshake seemed firm and strong. *He will do fine.* ANTIMONY pulled the door to Verdi's room shut as quietly as possible. He could not blank out the picture of a lovely smiling young woman in Milan, mounted in a silver frame. *Why did this bother him, this Milanese photograph? Van Eyck is dead. Why would this image not go away?* And the name troubled him. *Von Donop.* It conjured up an image of the past, the very distant past in a previous war, and, of another German named von Donop. And it conjured up another image of a sinking ship. Neither of these images faded as the elevator door clanked shut and the grinning, friendly operator pulled the handle down. *The picture and von Donop. Von Donop and the picture.* The hazy recollections and images would soon be cleared up. Of that, he remained confident. He walked across the hotel lobby and stopped at the *maitre'd* stand.

"Mr. Prince."

"Yes, Mr. Prince. The von Donop party. Dr. Verdi is already seated. Please step this way, *Monsieur.*" The *maitre'd* stopped at a table in the center of the dining room, well chosen by the German. Any overt, sudden action by ANTIMONY would be in plain view of the entire dining room. A bolt to the door meant weaving around or over several tables and chairs, thus maximizing the field of fire. He had already spotted several enemies. They sat in clumps at key tables about the dining room most looking uncomfortable in their ill-fitting suits pretending to be casual tourists. No women sat at the men's tables—therein, the tip-off. By the time he reached the center of the room, ANTIMONY had spotted at least seven plainclothes men and two more in uniform including the polite *SS* officer, who did have a lady present—a pleasant, pretty French woman. The privilege of rank, he mused. Verdi, already there, nervously fidgeted with a fork. Pale and with tiny beads of sweat forming under his hairline, a droplet rolled down his forehead onto his cheek. The *maitre'd* pulled the chair back for ANTIMONY. "The wine steward will be with you as soon as your host arrives." He bowed from the waist and retreated.

The ivory Belgian lace tablecloth, Waterford crystal, sterling silver place settings, and English Blue Willow china made for a most elegant setting. In the table's center, a pewter candelabra sputtered. ANTIMONY noted that the light level neither demanded nor needed candlelight. Another protection on the part of von Donop that prevented any swift moves masked by the suddenness of blown out candles. This man is good thought ANTIMONY, very good.

"Good evening, *Herr Doktor* Verdi, Mr. Prince. I trust that the hotel staff has treated you well."

ANTIMONY turned in his seat. Recognizing a vaguely familiar voice, he stared into the ice cold, cruel blue eyes of *SS Sturmbannführer* Karl von Donop. *It's him! It is him, damn it—the odd German sailor from Atlantis. The same face, the same squared-off face and closely cropped blond hair. The uniform is different, but it is clearly the same man. Why does the voice strike a familiar chord? Why?*

The *maitre'd* pulled back the chair for the German, who intentionally sat across the table from the two men. He could watch the actions of each without moving his head side to side, a practical as well as psychological ploy.

The wine steward arrived. "*Monsieurs*, allow me to recommend the *Chateau Lafitte Rothschild*, 1936. It is an excellent choice."

"Any objections, gentlemen? No? That will be good."

"*Oui, Monsieur.*" the wine steward strutted off, impressed with his self-importance.

"I have taken the liberty of ordering for us in advance. I trust my choice will be satisfactory."

"I'm sure it will, Major von Donop," said Verdi in a low, almost croaking whisper. Barely able to force these words out, the muscles in his neck tightened, choking his vocal chords. Von Donop noticed.

"Please do relax, *Herr Doktor*. You are perfectly safe here. Please tell him that, Mr. Prince."

"Of course, Enrico. Perfectly safe. We're American citizens and neutral. Mr. von Donop has only our best interest at heart. Am I not right, Sir?" ANTIMONY said as he lifted the cut lead crystal water glass to his lips. The candlelight caught the edge of the leaded glass and sparkled blue and silver. ANTIMONY watched for von Donop's reaction over the rim of the tumbler. None. *He is an ice man. Those eyes—so familiar.*

"Quite right, and, by the way, it is a small point, nonetheless important, *Herr Doktor* Verdi, my rank is *SS sturmbannführer*, not major. Major is, well, so common. I am a member of Germany's elite corps of warriors."

"What is it you do, precisely?" shot back ANTIMONY. From the treatise—when dealing with a stone cold character, ask him a difficult or compromising question when he does not expect it. Such questions can sometimes crumble the stout face of statues.

"I am a political officer actually, which is why we are here tonight." The face did not crack. The haughty countenance remained unbroken, indicative of a most formidable, very controlled man.

Also from the treatise—these types are usually flawed in one key area. They tend to have enormously huge egos. They may be narcissistic. They are skilled and they know it. Use it. It is a weakness to be exploited. Ego driven, overconfidence can lead to carelessness.

The wine steward arrived with the Rothschild. Von Donop tested it and pronounced it good. The steward beamed as he poured the wine all around. When he had left, von Donop leaned over the table and spoke conspiratorially. "The Rothschilds are Jewish are they not? Pity. They make an excellent wine." He leaned back. Neither ANTIMONY nor Verdi replied; they merely continued sipping the excellent vintage. For the next few minutes, von Donop did most of the talking—small talk, sort of I've been to New York, wonderful city sort of thing, and meant to disarm the tension. Verdi became visibly more relaxed as the minutes passed. The dinner came—an excellent *vichy sois* soup followed by rack of lamb, new potatoes, the Chef's special truffle recipe, and topped off with a delightful chocolate *soufflé*. Whatever trap von Donop intended to spring, he wasn't about to do so until after dinner. ANTIMONY ate heartily. He had no great appetite, but he suspected he might not eat again for some time. With the table cleared, the steward poured a fine liqueur.

"The British government must be rolling all over Whitehall with the news of your safe arrival, gentlemen. It was most embarrassing for them to announce that the poor *Zamzam* was overdue and presumed sunk at sea with horrendous loss of life only to have the *Reich* produce you safe and sound in a luxury hotel in Biarritz. Churchill must be livid," he chuckled.

"I wouldn't know," replied ANTIMONY. The roof caved in.

"Why not, ANTIMONY?"

ANTIMONY wanted to spring across the table and tear away the malignant grin on the evil face, and the eyes, the ice-cold eyes that sparkled in the candlelight. He wanted to gouge out the demon's throat, great handfuls of red, pulsating flesh flung asunder by his steely fingers. The second impulse said to run, to escape, to get far away from the black-suited tormentor. *No good. The enemy has planned too well.* ANTIMONY looked over at Verdi. The man's face had blanched as white as the Irish linen napkins. With hollow eyes, his lips moved up and down in a speechless twitch. Verdi dropped his dessert spoon. It glanced off the crystal glass, then spun out onto the floor. Several close-by diners peered over at the noise, then turned away, back to their own dinners and conversations. *No good.* ANTIMONY might make it to the door. Trained and well-conditioned, he could dive, roll, and dodge the inevitable hail of erratic gunfire from surprised soldiers caught fumbling for their weapons in unfamiliar jackets. Verdi, though, would not make it. He would be shot down instantly. *No good. A bad hand. Play it out regardless.* ANTIMONY loosened the tense grip on his bread knife. He had been fondling it when von Donop sprang the trap and had instinctively clutched it as a weapon. He loosened the grip. The knife clanked on the table.

"A wise move. I have ten plainclothes and two uniformed men in this dining room plus four more in the lobby. If you even made it that far, how many innocents would be killed in the melee *Herr* ANTIMONY?" Von Donop spat out the code name with obvious malice.

"Quite right, *Herr Sturmbannführer*. Quite right. Germans are not known for being overly concerned about the fate of innocents, are they?" responded ANTIMONY in a verbal counterattack.

"You British are a simpering race of do-gooders with your petite little gardens and your ugly dogs," he replied matter-of-factly. The enemy turned towards Verdi. "Were you aware that your traveling companion is a British intelligence officer, *Herr Doktor*," smirked von Donop, tipping his liqueur glass and letting the last drops roll down his tongue.

Verdi looked over at ANTIMONY in shock and confusion. ANTIMONY's face seemed to say no. Von Donop did not see it as he motioned the wine steward for a refill. "Ah … no … I didn't. You must be mistaken, *Sturmbannführer*. This is my friend Mr. Edward Prince from New York. I sailed with him on the *Zamzam*. Look at his passport. Surely you must know this," stammered Verdi, fumbling to make a convincing argument.

The wine steward poured the mahogany liquid.

"And did you know Mr. Prince before you sailed from New York, *Herr Doktor*?"

"Why ... ah ... well ... no, but ... "

"Then you can't say for certain that he is who he claims to be. He might easily have been planted by the British on the *Zamzam* before she sailed from New York."

"I ... uh ... suppose so ... but ... "

"Enough of this dancing about the maypole, von Donop. What is it you want?" blurted out ANTIMONY, ready to play the next scene. He would lose this engagement. Go to the next one where he might be able to work some advantage.

"I want him," replied von Donop pointing at Verdi.

"No!" Verdi stifled a shout, then looked down into his lap, a hint of defiance starting to well up in him.

"He's an American citizen. You can't touch him!" lashed out ANTIMONY in one last desperate attempt.

"I can if *Herr Doktor* asks the *Reich* government for political asylum. It would not be so strange. An Italian turns his back on Mother Italy to immigrate to the great Americas, only to learn that the America he lands in is putrid and rotten from the inside. So our wop friend does the only thing he can do to save face. He turns his back on America to return to the Fascist fold. It's really quite simple," smirked the German.

ANTIMONY leaned forward in his seat. The silk fabric crinkled with his movement. "And what, *Herr Sturmbannführer*, will cause him to do that?"

"I have something he treasures." Von Donop reached into his right breast pocket under the silver coil embroidered Nazi eagle, removed a dog-eared photograph, and tossed it on the table. The twinkling girl's face stared out at the two men. Below the smiling eyes read the caption penned in neat script: "To Dad, Love, Angela, Milano, Christmas 1940."

Verdi reached into his jacket pocket. *Angela's photo—gone! How. . .?* "You bastard, you stupid Nazi bastard. You can't get away with this," hissed Verdi in a low, powerful, angry voice. After the shocks of the last few moments, he had pulled together. The implied threat to Angela had driven away the fear and whimpering. He returned to the courageous, self-sacrificing, honorable man who had left behind his native land ten years earlier to protest the Fascists.

The eyes. The eyes. I know the eyes, the long sensual fingers, the slightly raspy smoky voice, the high cheekbones, the haughty matron. "Joan Avery!"

"Very good, ANTIMONY. You should have figured that out weeks ago. But, then, you weren't aware of a second agent on board that disgrace of a ship." As if to emphasize the point—no, to rub it in—he took out the silver cigarette holder that Joan Avery had used to taunt and excite the ambulance drivers. *A tall, elegant, sensual, unattainable widow. What a perfect disguise.*

"So, then, it was you rummaging in Dr. Verdi's cabin that night of the big band dance, not Van Eyck."

"Certainly. *Herr* Van Eyck—no, really *Hauptmann* Limken—was just another of the spineless traitor Canaris' buffoons. He couldn't fornicate his way out of a harem if his life depended on it. No, *Herr* ANTIMONY, that night I presume you saw me, thinking I was Van Eyck. I saw this little trinket in the good *Doktor's* cabin."

"So, you posed as just another passenger in the abandonment. Why not? In that confusion, who would know or even care," continued ANTIMONY, the entire story coming clear in his mind.

"Just so. Once on board *Atlantis*, it was easy enough to establish my identity with a few highly placed messages. I simply blended in with the crew. It would have meant immediate execution for any crewman to betray my identity to the prisoners."

"You enjoyed your cruise on the *Dresden*, did you?" replied ANTIMONY sarcastically.

Von Donop took a long draw of the Turkish cigarette and blew the smoke towards the ornately-carved ceiling with the glittering cut crystal chandelier. "Immensely. While your people subsisted on—what did you call it—glop and billboard paste, I dined out of the Captain's larder. There is a good reason why he is, shall we say, stout."

ANTIMONY shifted in his seat and stared directly into von Donop's eyes. "And Van Eyck conveniently lost at sea during the attack."

"Actually, before. The evening before the attack."

"I remember him leaving the bar with you that night."

"Yes, and the poor man's hormones were in overdrive. He became a feast for the fishes."

"Man overboard. He falls over in the middle of the night, too drunk to see straight having just left the ladies' cabin. Just bat your false eyelashes and who could challenge you. He would have died with a smile on his face, no doubt."

"Precisely, but we mustn't tarry. There are things to do." He motioned to the attentive waiter for the bill as he stubbed out the cigarette in the china ashtray.

Verdi had sat silent during the exchange between von Donop and ANTI-MONY. His anger welled up to the bursting point. "Where is my daughter?" he demanded.

"Over there." Von Donop motioned with a backward wave of the hand. Verdi looked over his shoulder across the cavernous dining room. By the entrance at a corner table between two very dour looking men, sat a frightened girl.

"You bastard!" scowled Verdi. As he turned back around in his chair, he started to spring forward. The Englishman's strong arm came across Verdi's chest, pushing him back down into the chair.

"You are a cold fish, von Donop," spat out ANTIMONY.

"War is heartless, Englander!" Von Donop's hand slammed down hard on the table. China and crystal rattled and clinked. The candles flickered. Around the dining room, startled guests turned and looked, then averted their eyes when they saw the seething, burning flashes in his blue eyes.

He is vulnerable. I know it. I must play on his ego, but I need more informa-tion. It is not yet time. The game is looking better now. ANTIMONY had just drawn to an inside straight. The waiter arrived with the bill and ceremoni-ously presented it to von Donop on a brass Damascene tray. With a flourish, he signed and presented it back to the attending waiter, who took it over to the *maitre'd.*

"Rene, take that trash out back and burn it. We will go out of business before I accept *SS* blood money. It probably is stolen from some poor Jewish bastard. Burn it," whispered the smiling Frenchman.

Von Donop rose, motioning ANTIMONY and Verdi to do likewise. "Stay here," he ordered as he went to the doorway to greet the officer sitting with the girl. "*Doktor* Verdi, you will go with *Herr* Schilling. I warn you in the strongest terms. There will be no outburst. You will remain calm. Believe me. My orders are to deliver you to Berlin dead or alive. I don't care which. Do you understand?"

"Yes, I do. There will be no outburst." He bowed his head.

"Now, walk to Schilling and leave the hotel. Your bags will be brought to you later. We're simply taking you to a safer hotel—the Grand, I believe—a most pleasant spot, I'm told."

"A more secure prison, you mean."

"As you wish. Now go."

Verdi walked over to the door. He nodded to his daughter, who managed a weak smile. She too had been warned of how tenuous their lives could be at this moment. There would be plenty of time for embraces and kisses later at the new hotel.

"So, ANTIMONY, you will come with me. Walk ahead. Go straight through the lobby. Do not even look left or right. Go out the main doors. Attempt nothing. I shall be right behind you. You are an enemy agent. I can shoot you with impunity. Do you understand?"

"Indeed I do." He walked slowly amongst the tables and chairs.

His hand brushed the fountain pen with the stiletto blade safely tucked inside his jacket pocket. *Maybe von Donop would miss it. Maybe.*

As the Verdies passed hurriedly through the hotel lobby, sitting in a wicker settee under a palm tree, a Spanish-looking gentleman read *"Le Monde."* As the two captives followed by the *SS* men trooped past him, he carefully folded his paper, donned his cap and walked behind them at a discreet distance. As they got into the Mercedes Benz staff car, the Spaniard eased into a waiting Renault.

"Do you like my car? I'm very proud of it. *Herr Reichmarshal* Himmler himself gave it to me," von Donop beamed as he motioned ANTIMONY towards the front seat of the 1935 Mercedes Benz 500 Special Roadster convertible with cream-colored doors and burgundy wings. The black leather upholstery, buttery-soft to the touch, heralded the maximum in pre-war automotive grace and elegance. A young soldier, barely twenty if that in an *SS* uniform, sat stiffly behind the wheel. Von Donop settled into the cramped passenger seat behind ANTIMONY, who sat next to the driver. As the hotel doorman shut the door, von Donop motioned to the driver. The click of von Donop's Luger P08 hammer told ANTIMONY that any attempt to escape meant certain death.

"Go."

The smooth engine hummed as the roadster pulled away from the curb. *One thing about these Germans—they do make magnificent machines.* They rode in silence out of town and up into the hills. *There is more to this man than he is telling. What is so familiar about him? Something from the past—*

the very distant past. Some ugly memory keeps jumping up and shouting, but what is it? Von Donop. The name is so familiar. What is the connection?

"What plans do you have for Dr. Verdi?" ANTIMONY shouted above the whistling night air.

"Oh, the best. He shall be taken to Berlin. Trotted about so all of the world's press can see the prodigal son returned to the true fold. I'm sure Dr. Goebbels will make a good deal of it, then, he will begin to work on our own project. It's really very simple and precise, isn't it?"

"And if he doesn't cooperate?" probed ANTIMONY already knowing the answer.

"Then there's always the question of his daughter. She will, of course, go back to Milan to finish her studies, but under the careful eye of the *Gestapo*. Then she will simply join her loving father at his new home in Berlin."

"Won't this all frighten the Americans into intensifying their own development program? Aren't you defeating your own aims?" he asked in a last desperate chance at reason.

"Perhaps so, but we have their primary resource. This defection will set them back years. America's Day of Doom will soon be at hand Englander," he chuckled gleefully.

Day of Doom. Day of Doom! He jerked as if a Heavenly-tossed lightning bolt hit him. His mind reeled, turning over and over like a man falling off a high building. *Day of Doom. ARMAGEDDON!*

"You are very good, ARMAGEDDON."

The German only smiled as if it had no impact—as if he expected the recognition sooner or later. "Quite right, Commodore Braithwaite. I believe you knew my father in the last unpleasantness," he hissed as the grin became demonic.

There it is — von Donop—the German naval officer from the SMS *Aachen* in East Africa -- ANTIMONY's first mission as a Naval Intelligence field agent and who died with that doomed ship. What goes around, comes around. Now, years later, here sat his son, his cruel, fanatic son. Only this time, ANTIMONY didn't have the upper hand. How coincidental it all is. "I knew your father." *It is the eyes, those cold, blue eyes. The man's father had those same eyes.* ANTIMONY should have perceived the phony Mrs. Avery once he saw those eyes, but a lot of rust had to be shaken off first. *Pray God it is still not too late to recover the situation.*

"I barely knew my father. He died when I was only seven, but I knew of his great work for the Fatherland. Be assured, *Herr* Braithwaite, that I am many times better at this little game we play than was my father. You are old and worn out and you have lost to a far superior force," he chortled gleefully.

That's it, then. The weakness is there. His ego makes him think he has won, that ANTIMONY has nothing left. Let him think that. It will make him careless and inattentive. There's the advantage. Use it. From the treatise—while the enemy is still alive and in the field, he is dangerous. Never let down your guard. Never assume you have won until the threat is totally eliminated. Never let pride or ego cloud your caution. Obviously, *SS Sturmbannführer* Karl von Donop had never read ANTIMONY's treatise on the intelligence officer in the field.

The Mercedes pulled to a halt by a shabby shepherd's cottage in the middle of a pasture, high in the hills overlooking Biarritz. It had to be eight to ten kilometers inland, a good hike down at any rate. Two *SS* men snapped to an alert attention as the roadster stopped. A dim light came from within.

"*Heil* Hitler," snapped the two men in unison.

Von Donop returned the salute. A guard opened the door and motioned ANTIMONY out. He stepped down into soft turf, damp from a recent rain. That might be significant. It might slow down a normally swifter pursuer. He would remember it. In the distance about thirty yards from the cottage, sat a black Mercedes military staff car. The raised hood indicated that the *SS* men had been servicing it. *Good. That will distract at least one of them.* He looked around the exterior. The cottage had no telephone wires or any indications of a wireless set anywhere near. *Very careless, von Donop, you egomaniac.*

"Inside, please," said von Donop, prodding from behind.

ANTIMONY walked towards the cottage and stopped in front of the roughhewn door. An *SS* man opened it and nudged him in with the handle of his *Schmeisser* MP40 machine pistol. ANTIMONY entered and turned his eyes away from the bright, glowing light of a single kerosene lantern. The one-room cottage had a loft and a single window opposite the door. *Excellent! This will limit the possible line of fire into the cabin from a gunman positioned outside.* The simple, crude furniture consisted of a camp bed and a chair with a rickety pine table. A shepherd's cottage, it had been built for shelter in foul weather. A Frenchman with dried blood caked on the side of his head where it had spilled out of the gash above his temple sat in the lone chair. The man looked up at the newcomer, but said nothing. His exhausted eyes merely acknowledged their presence and drooped down to the floor again.

"These bracelets are uncomfortable," whined ANTIMONY hopefully portraying weakness to the prideful German, who then motioned to the guard. *A woeful blunder, von Donop.* The guard unshackled ANTIMONY's hands, who rubbed them gratefully.

"You will have a wonderful time with your new friend here. He is a most uncooperative sort, just like you, *Herr* Commodore. Unfortunately, I cannot stay for your party. I have been summoned to Paris to brief Heydrich on our little escapade. My airplane departs within the hour so I'll leave you two. I shall be back tomorrow. Then we shall speak in earnest, *Herr* Commodore," he said with barely contained malice and threat.

Superb, you arrogant Nazi murderer. A monumental error. You have left the chicken coop guarded by the second string, to use American football terms. ANTIMONY's confidence rose with each passing event and enemy blunder. The door closed behind the *SS* man. ANTIMONY heard the sound of a bolt driving home, sealing them in their little stone prison. From outside, he heard the roadster engine revving up. He went to the window and watched it bounce out of sight, then moved to the edge of the window for a better angle. From that position, he could see the staff car. The *SS* man had put down the hood and started waxing it, an odd thing to do at night, but then these *SS* types seemed strange to begin with. The other guard, not in sight, presumably stood outside the door. He felt for the window bottom, grasped it firmly and pulled up with all his strength. It had been nailed shut from the outside, a wise precaution. The thick, crude glass panes and sturdy sash meant that even a chair slammed against it would probably do little damage.

"Greetings, *Monsieur*. Welcome to the *Bastille*," the wounded Frenchman laughed coarsely.

"Happy to be here."

"I am Jean Louis Gasperon. And you?"

"A friend."

"Very cautious. Had I been a bit more, I wouldn't be in this predicament, you see."

"And why are you in this predicament, *Monsieur* Gasperon?" queried AN-TIMONY as he continued to inspect the nooks and crannies of the cottage.

"I am, *Monsieur*, a member of the underground, the Free French Resistance."

"How did they catch you?"

"I don't know for certain, but I'm sure some slip or something I did or did not do properly. This is such a new game for us. Give us time, and we will perfect the art. It is still all so new."

The conversation continued for several minutes. Even though he spoke excellent French, ANTIMONY let the Resistance man do most of the talking, with ANTIMONY listening intently like a man unfamiliar with the language. He listened for details about the guards, about von Donop, about the Resistance fighters—anything of use that might be missed in a two-sided conversation. ANTIMONY sat on the edge of the bed listening intently. The man already knew his identity. That verified his authenticity since he gave details about the operation that the Germans presumably would not know. Had he divulged this to the Germans? No. He would die first. And, so it went.

"It was very clever how you foiled *Monsieur* von Donop in Brazil. Very resourceful," the man droned on.

Action Stations! Action Stations! All hands to Action Stations. ANTIMONY jerked slightly, imperceptibly. *Brazil! How could this man know about Recife?* Only he and Verdi, and of course, von Donop, knew about the foiled kidnap attempt in Recife, figuring it had been the SS man and not Van Eyck behind it. The man must be a plant, a traitor at worst, a careless actor at best, but most assuredly a ruse. Only von Donop could have told him about Recife. *Why would he do so? It had been a monumental embarrassment. No, he would only have told this man so as to make a point about how resourceful this Englishman is, so watch one's step. Well, this Frenchman had just misstepped.*

ANTIMONY stood up as if to stretch his legs. He walked around the room listening to the man chatter on. As he rounded the table, he looked out the window. The second guard still polished the staff car. He stood behind the man now and slowly reached into his pocket, carefully feeling around some coins, a handkerchief and the object of his search—the key ring. He gently pulled it out. The man kept babbling on totally impervious to the assailant behind him. *Yes, you do have a lot to learn!*

"These Nazis have very good ways to make us talk. I hope we can be strong enough to resist them."

ANTIMONY pressed the latch on the metal ring and slowly, silently pulled out the thin strangling wire to its full length. He coiled each end around his hands to get full control of the deadly wire. The man prattled on. ANTIMONY stepped in closer behind the chair. *Now!* The wire flipped through the air over the top of the man's head and down. It caught him in the middle of the neck just at his Adam's apple. ANTIMONY yanked on the ends. In a microsecond, the wire tightened around the Frenchman's throat. He tried to scream, but no air would come through. ANTIMONY pulled harder. The man's eyes rolled; blood vessels in his temples bulged. *He is close to losing consciousness. Now is the time.*

"Listen to me, Jean Louis Gasperon. Listen very carefully. You will answer some very easy questions and I'll let you live, otherwise . . . . Do you understand? Raise your right hand if you do."

The fingers of his right hand trembled as he weakly raised it in the air.

"Excellent. I'm going to release the pressure, but if you scream or run, I'll kill you in an instant. Understand?"

Again, the trembling right hand raised. ANTIMONY backed off the pressure just enough to allow the man to breathe. He coughed and sputtered and clutched at his ravaged windpipe.

"Now, think before you answer. A simple yes or no will do, otherwise, short answers, please. We haven't much time."

He shook his head.

"Is your name Jean Louis Gasperon?"

"*Oui.*"

"Are you a member of the local Resistance?" "*Oui.*"

"Were you put here to get information from me?"

"*Oui.*"

"By von Donop, or is he working with someone else?"

"No. Alone. Just the soldiers outside."

"What did he offer you to do this?"

"Money. And my life."

"How much?"

"A thousand *francs*."

"What did you tell him about me?"

"Only that your code name is ANTIMONY and a physical description sent us by London and that you were posing as Mr. Prince from America."

"Why did London tell you this?"

"They sent in two men, two agents to take you and Dr. Verdi out."

ANTIMONY turned pale. *Good God, there are more people in jeopardy now.* He tightened the wire just enough to remind the man of his precarious position.

"Think carefully before you answer. Remember, I will know a lie."

The man nodded frantically. ANTIMONY released the pressure.

"What happened to the agents?"

"They were injured. Their airplane crashed. They are safe, but they cannot be moved yet."

"Did you sell out your comrades?"

"No, *Monsieur* ... I ... "

The wire snapped taut. Tiny rivulets of blood from broken capillaries trickled out and down the neck. The man's arms flapped in desperation. *It is a lie.* ANTIMONY released the pressure.

"Try again!"

"*Oui! Oui!* I told him. I told him everything!" he cried as tears ran down his blanched cheeks.

"What did you tell him?"

"Names, *Monsieur*. Names, places where they could be found, where they lived, where they worked. Please! He was going to shoot me!"

"And, I won't? You sold out your friends for a thousand *francs* and your own useless life? You sniveling pile of rubbish. I ought to bloody well do you in right here and finish the job."

"No! Please, *Monsieur*. I beg you ... no ... please!" The man's whimper trailed off to a hoarse croak.

The point is made, the desired effect achieved. ANTIMONY had no intention of killing the man. Gasperon would lead him to the Resistance. Together, they would rescue the Verdies and then escape. *No, this pathetic man is too vital to the mission.* First, though, they had to escape from the cottage. That would be more than a simple task.

"Who did you tell this to? Who else heard?"

"No one. I swear by the Virgin Mary. Only von Donop was in the room. He is the only one who knows."

Good. It may not be too late. If he hasn't moved against the locals, they may still be safe. Von Donop is knee deep in the Verdi case. There is plenty of time to deal with local Resistance people. This mission is like a runaway freight train plunging down the track towards the yards with an imminent collision. ANTIMONY sensed it—the gathering moment of climax. The man sobbed uncontrollably. *Enough for now, first things first.* He flipped the wire back over the man's head. He halfway expected the Frenchman to bolt. He didn't. He merely sat in the chair, hands dangling at his side, whimpering in terror.

"What are you going to do to me?" he moaned as his eyes went wild and panicky.

"Shut up and you'll live." ANTIMONY looked around the room and picked up an old tattered shirt left behind by a previous occupant. Ripping off a piece, he stuffed the better part of the dusty cloth in Gasperon's mouth, wrapped the remainder twice around his head, then tied it off in back. That would ensure the man's silence. ANTIMONY looked out the window. The second guard had just finished his work and stood back admiring the car in the moonlight. Silvery light glinted off the finely polished black metal. ANTIMONY strode to the door and put his ear to it. He couldn't hear anything, but presumed the other man to be close. ANTIMONY lifted up a foot and clicked open the heel. Out fell a gray, putty-like substance onto the dirt floor with a plop. The Frenchman's eyes grew wider. Out of the other heel, he removed the detonator. Once the chemical fuse broke, he had five seconds before it set off the charge. He packed the putty around the door about where he thought the bolt should be. The force of the explosion would blow the door out and away from them making it more difficult for the Germans to enter the cottage. Sticking the detonator into the gray putty, he snapped it, then stepped back and pressed himself up against the wall as hard as he could. He whipped out the pen. With a loud click, the top fell away revealing the ugly, glinting steel blade.

Two ... one. Wood splinters flew about the room, several striking the Frenchman as the door blew out leaving a dust cloud. A shout came from outside then another from farther away. The closest guard rushed through the doorway, stumbling over shattered wood debris. *Now!* ANTIMONY lunged, the sharp stiletto out in front of him, racing towards the man in black. The startled guard whirled around in surprise. The blade caught him full in the chest, penetrating deep into his heart. He twisted and spun, ripping the blade out of ANTIMONY's hand. Deadly pain shot through the wounded man's chest. Eyes wide in shock and agony, he screamed wildly and spun around and around. His weapon dropped to the floor as he twirled wildly out of control then pitched forward and fell face down on the floor, made muddy by the blood gurgling from his savaged heart.

ANTIMONY lunged for the gun. A burst of bullets zipped by. *The other guard!* He rolled across the floor only inches away from the spurts of earth kicked up by the striking rounds. The guard fired wildly into the air, at walls, at the ground. He had panicked. ANTIMONY grabbed the fallen man's weapon. The kerosene lantern had been hit and clanked to the floor dousing the only light. Outside the darkened cottage, moonlight silhouetted the *SS* man. ANTIMONY leveled the *Schmeisser*, took careful aim, and squeezed off a short burst. That is all it took. The man lurched and staggered backward as his service cap spun off his head. A dead finger tightened on the trigger sending bullets into the ground, zinging and splintering into the stone walls and off into the trees beyond. It ended in just a few seconds. ANTIMONY's heart raced. He lay still on the dirt floor for perhaps a minute, then lifted himself up, carefully and slowly, while his breath returned.

Even with moonlight streaming through the bullet-racked window and shattered doorway, he could see nothing in the death cottage. He felt around the body of the dead German on the floor. *It must be here.* He had seen it hooked to the man's belt earlier. *There it is—a powerful torch.* The ribbon of light shot out and danced in an eerie, surreal ballet around the dark room. He pointed the light at the Frenchman. The top of the man's head had been blown off.

Damn! He needed this traitor. Just do without. He rolled the German over onto his back. The stiletto had broken off at the hilt burying four inches of blade in the dead man's gurgling chest. *Must tell the wizards at Camp "X" to use a better grade of steel. Gallows humor! No time to waste. Must get out of here. Other Germans may have heard the gunfire.* He pulled two extra clips of ammunition out of the dead German's belt, took the man's *Walther* P38, which he put in his jacket pocket, and slung the machine pistol over his shoulder as he ran outside. The other guard lay crumpled in a heap in the grass. He also had two extra clips. ANTIMONY put this second man's pistol in his belt in the small of the back hidden from the casual observer. *If there is to be a shootout, be well prepared.*

He raced to the highly polished staff car. The engine turned over and roared. ANTIMONY slammed it in gear and rolled off down the hillside, towards what, he could not say. He must find the woman—the not so ordinary chambermaid. She is the key now. Without the Resistance's help, he had a severe handicap. With them, he had a chance, a slim one, but a fighting chance nonetheless. That is the best hope he concluded as he roared off into the quiet night.

CHAPTER 20
A MATTER OF INTRICATE TIMING

The staff car jostled down the rain and wind rutted road barely more than a trail by which the shepherds brought the flocks up to the grazing meadow. ANTIMONY drove without headlights just in case any nearby police or German troops had heard the gunfire. He had hoped to take one of the *SS* man's uniforms to explain his possession of the staff car and allow him to roam at will in town in search of Verdi and his daughter. On second thought, as good as he looked for a 50-year old man, no one would believe him to be a genuine soldier, much less one of Hitler's elite corps. *Perhaps if one of the men had been a sergeant . . . Perhaps. No. It's a moot point.* His burst had caught the second guard full in the chest and shredded the tunic with bloody holes. The first man with the stiletto blade in his heart had completely soaked his uniform in blood. So, he removed the red, white and black swastika flag from the front wing of the car and shoved it under the seat. As he bumped and rattled down the hill, he considered his options. None looked promising. He had three imperatives. First, he had to locate the Resistance. What plans had London made for the escape? He had to find the chambermaid. Second, he had to locate the Verdies, and third, he had to somehow get them out of the grasp of Von Donop. *The first imperative—find the woman. The hotel is the key.*

He drove into the edge of town cautiously so as to attract as little attention as possible. There must be a safe place to stow the car and commandeered weapons. It took some searching, but he finally found the perfect spot. On the outskirts of town, about a mile from the beachfront hotel row, an unsuccessful garage owner had simply abandoned his business. The shop's roof sagged but seemed otherwise intact. Most importantly, the single bay garage, secure, safe, and big enough for the large automobile, provided shelter and obscurity.

The bay door runners had jammed. Rust, no doubt. Simple neglect. *There must be something around. Ah . . . there it is. A 2" x 4" board. Just the thing.* Making as little noise as possible, he banged on the rusted metal runner until it gave way. Dust and rusty flakes flew everywhere in a choking cloud. Trying the bay door again, it creaked and clanked, but opened. The air smelt of grease and old motor oil, which colored the dirt floor a deep brown. Here and there, casting eerie shadows on the gray, blank walls, hung mechanics' tools too heavy to cart away when the owner abandoned the property. No one observed the curious newcomer. Isolated from the town yet close enough for walking, it made an excellent hideout for the next few hours. He hopped back into the driver's seat and slammed the gear into drive. It rattled and clanked as he ground the gears. It hurt to injure a fine motorcar like this, but he hadn't the time to leisurely master the transmission characteristics. Cutting the lights and engine, he sat in the dark for several minutes, listening and waiting for the telltale noises of a curious passerby interested in a stranger with the fine Mercedes. No one appeared.

He slid out of the leather seat, hurried around to the rear and popped the boot latch. In the moonlight, he saw objects—very interesting objects. But first, he needed to shut himself off from intruders. Something had to be done about the rusty garage door. He flashed the torch about the garage. *It must be here. Ah . . . there in the corner—bright yellow container with paint peeling off in large flakes.* He sniffed and coughed from the odor of old oil left behind as useless, but good enough for the purpose. Holding the torch in one hand, he dabbed oil onto the rusty metal door runners with a paintbrush left on the floor. The garage door slid down the lubricated track like new, and more importantly, quietly.

ANTIMONY turned back to the open boot. With no windows and the bay door now shut, he could examine the contents without worrying about the flickering and waving of the torch. A large metal container appeared to be full of fresh water. Beside it lay several loose bottles of excellent wine, part of the Nazi "liberation" the year before. An army rucksack contained several tins of rations. He fumbled through them—sausages, cabbage, potatoes, the usual *Wehrmacht* rations. In a canvas bag, he found two loaves of crusty bread, a large hoop of cheese, and a crock of butter with a half-empty jar of fruit preserves, all in all, plenty of food for several men for several days. The implication seemed clear. The men and their prisoners in the shepherd's cottage needed to be self-sufficient and isolated. If von Donop had not lied about flying to Paris that night, then he stood a chance. Why would von Donop lie about it? It played perfectly into his ego to brag about a private meeting with such a powerful person as Heydrich. Why not gloat about it? No, Herr von Donop, well on his way to Paris, had removed himself from the picture for a few pivotal hours. It gave ANTIMONY the break he needed to regain the tactical initiative. Though not yet an advantage, it meant a chance to redress the balance. He no longer back-peddled in a hastily erected defense and now meant to go on the offensive.

He thought about the cool, soft to the touch, leather car seats. How easy it would be to curl up in the back seat and escape it all for a few blissful hours of wonderful sleep. His eyelids felt like iron doors ready to slam shut in a heartbeat. *No! Resist it! There will be time for rest later. The window of opportunity is counted in seconds and minutes. No sleep yet. Fight it!* The adrenaline pumping through his system from the past few hours had waned. His arms felt like weighted bags; his legs ached. Though exhausted, he must drive his body on.

From the back seat he grabbed a leather bag resembling a lawyer's brief case containing some military documents of no consequence and a pair of exceptionally good field binoculars. Locking the machine pistol in the trunk, he stuffed a Walther and several extra clips into the bag with the field glasses to complement the weapon in his waistband. He would appear on the streets as a harried, overworked *petit bourgeoisie* bureaucrat headed home from a long shift at the office. He still had his American passport, but this might do little good if stopped by a *gendarme* or any suspicious military policeman. Therefore, he prepared for a firefight. At least he would take a few of the buggers with him to join the three bastards lying in a shot-up cottage on the hill.

He walked briskly through the town centre weaving hurriedly, but not too conspicuously, among the crowd of mainly German and Spanish tourists. Late night street traffic had picked up, many headed for the Biarritz Casino. His goal, the *Hôtel du Palais* and the chambermaid, lay ahead. In the streetlight, he noticed a spot of blood on the front of his jacket. ANTIMONY could do nothing for it now. Perhaps anyone seeing it would think a meatball had gone astray at dinner. Along the avenue, the sea with the moonlight catching each cresting wave, made a sparkling light show of a thousand bright stars. He heard the soothing dull roar of the surf as it rolled up onto the pebble beach, then pulled away in a bubbling, foamy wave.

Across from the hotel, the park lush with foliage provided cover for concealed observation. Fortunately, the wrought iron gate remained open all night, a boon to lovers looking for a quiet place amidst the bustle of beachfront strollers. He headed for an expansive shrub overlooking the hotel's main entrance across the avenue. If the woman came out of any entrance on this side of the hotel, he would spot her and follow. He took up his position lying prone in the manicured grass surveying the building with his newly acquired field glasses. An hour passed.

There! There she is standing in the entranceway. She seemed to be looking for something or someone. Her head bent from side to side as if checking to see if anyone waited to follow her. Satisfied, she turned right and headed down the street past brightly lit bistros serving late night suppers to revelers and lovers, mostly soldiers on leave with newly-acquired French girlfriends. It is her, unmistakably her. She had the same full head of dark hair and the precise, measured, aggressive stride as the chambermaid who twice had spoken to him about INTREPID and London. He must catch her. He must make contact. She is the last hope. He started to raise up. The gun barrel felt chilling and hard against the back of his head.

"Please. Do not move," came a calm but authoritative voice. "Stretch your arms out in front of you. Hands out. Fingers extended."

He had been so intent on watching for the woman that he had violated a cardinal rule of the game—always be keenly aware of your environment. He had not heard footsteps as the gunman standing over him had crept up from behind. The man reached down and eased away the binoculars. He would not leave a weapon available to ANTIMONY. Gently, the man patted his sides and back, the muzzle pressed firmly into the back of his head to emphasize the point. ANTIMONY closed his eyes taut. He visualized a sailboat, a small one with a middle-aged, but still lovely woman at the tiller. The sails, now in irons, fluttered in the still, quiet air. He drew nearer to the bobbing boat. As he did so, he realized that Alice sat at the helm with a far off, distant, hollow look. He reached out to touch her, but only a listless small sailboat bobbed in the sea.

"Ah, here it is," said the man as he lifted ANTIMONY's jacket hem revealing the pistol tucked into the trousers at the small of his back. The man put the gun into his own belt. ANTIMONY opened his eyes, snapped back to the here and now by the tugging on his belt. "Please. Stand up very slowly and turn around. Keep your hands in the air or I shall shoot you. Now get up."

ANTIMONY had no choice. He lifted his hands off the grass. He had clutched a handful of freshly cut grass and as many pebbles as he could scratch up.

"Please. Hands open. Fingers extended. Palms down. No tricks, Monsieur."

This man is good. He had stepped back several feet, close enough to put a bullet through ANTIMONY's forehead, but far enough away to counter any sudden, violent moves. ANTIMONY stood up slowly, hands turned down, and faced the man. He did not look or sound like a German—short, with dull hair and a closely cropped mustache, dressed like a fisherman in black knit shirt, loose fitting coveralls, and sea boots. ANTIMONY should be able to overpower the man, if he could get close enough. Even so, he had lost the trail of the chambermaid. With every ticking second, his window of opportunity closed. He must act soon.

"You will kindly walk onto the Avenue. I shall be a few paces behind. Do not attempt any sudden moves. I am very quick. Now move." The man waved the weapon to emphasize his instructions. ANTIMONY walked through the iron gates to the wide sidewalk, then across and over to the front of the brightly lit hotel. No one recognized him. The gunman stayed several paces behind him, his weapon concealed in the folds of an oilskin slung over his arm.

"Turn left," the man whispered from behind.

Taking the same route as the chambermaid had minutes earlier, at least it represented the right direction. They walked silently for several minutes past the *bistros* and shuttered shops, the low hum of voices coming from the canopied tables, their speakers intent on each other, not the two men out for a night stroll, one a local and one a middle-aged tourist. They reached the end of a block of row houses, quiet and locked up for the night. He could only hear his own footsteps and those of the man following. *There must be a place to turn on him, somewhere. The man can't be that good.* ANTIMONY's eyes darted back and forth looking for anything, any opportunity, any bit of physical geography that he could use to turn the advantage his way again. He thought of the stiletto blade broken off in the dead German's chest.

"Turn right and walk to the car."

He saw it up ahead barely visible in the dark alleyway and well-shielded from the bright lights of the nighttime avenue. He approached the car, battered and decrepit, painted a dull gray and much in need of waxing. He stopped several feet from the side of the Renault.

"Please get in."

ANTIMONY turned towards the follower. The gun came out of the oilskin and pointed directly at his chest. The man would not allow an attack in the dark of the alley. ANTIMONY turned to face the car with no choice but to play out the scenario. *Perhaps in the confines of the vehicle.* He put his hand on the chrome handle, flaking and crusty with age and salt air corrosion, pulled open the squeaky door and hoisted himself up and into the worn leather front seat. It crackled as he sat back next to the figure in the driver's seat.

"Good evening, *Monsieur* ANTIMONY. You have been trying to reach me, no?" said the chambermaid.

He looked back at where the gunman had stood. *Gone!*

"That was Charles. He keeps an eye on the hotels along the Avenue for us. We suspected you would be back there looking for me if you were able to escape, that is."

She reached down, pulled out the choke button and pumped the accelerator while turning the key. The engine sputtered and wheezed, kicked to life, then settled to a low, powerful hum. Impressive! So the shabby appearance is only that—an appearance. She drove the car onto the Avenue, turned right to head out of town and sped up. Once clear of the town's center, she gunned the engine. With a lurch, the power kicked in as they sped through the night, the town of Biarritz receding behind them.

"We thought we had lost you this evening," she said matter-of-factly, never taking her eyes off the road.

"I had a minor disagreement with the Huns. How did you find out?"

"I came to give you another message that we would take you, Verdi, and his daughter out tonight at 2100 and to be prepared. Obviously, the *Boche* got to you ahead of me. We were ready to intercept you should you return."

"Do you know where Verdi is? They took him somewhere with his daughter."

"*Oui*, they are at the *Hôtel Grand*. It is further north along the avenue and quite popular with the Germans on holiday. They give them the best service. Dr. Verdi is more secure there. We were able to follow them there, but we lost you. That SS officer's car is very fast and we feared giving ourselves away."

"It's also more important to get Verdi out rather than me."

The woman sat silently, carefully steering the car around the curves and turns. "We all understand the rules of the game, *Monsieur*. The mission is most important. You understand that."

"Yes, I do. Well, I'm damned grateful you found me, anyway."

As she drove through the night, she explained the situation with the downed SOE agents and the details of the mission. Along with the minimal information London could send by wireless, these Resistance fighters had a pretty fair assessment of what they had to do now. At all costs, Dr. Enrico Verdi must get onboard that British submarine in just under twenty-three hours. All are expendable—Eliana Descartes, ANTIMONY, and the Resistance cell. Verdi must be on that submarine. The sane world had no other option.

"Where are the SOE men now?"

"They are safe, several kilometers inland at a very anti-Nazi village. They must heal first, then we can take them across the mountains into Spain."

"What about the airplane wreckage? What if the Germans find that?"

"Not to worry, *Monsieur*. A farmer conveniently burned brush from a field clearing where the plane caught fire. As to the broken parts, well, who knows what German engine they might end up in some day," she grinned.

She had said enough. The Germans would not locate the plane or the makeshift landing field. These French Resistance people are thorough.

I must tell her, he thought. *She must know. They could all be compromised.* "You have been betrayed."

She jerked her head over and stared at him, the first time she had taken her eyes off the road. He detected the first hint of terror in those dark eyes. That word is the foulest in the language for the partisans. It implied cowardice and greed or fear and supplication. It heralded an uncertain future. "How?" She turned back to the road, knuckles gripping hard on the wheel.

"Your man Gasperon. He was at the cottage where von Donop took me. He was there for a purpose to get me to say something compromising, but he did that himself. He knew things only von Donop knew about me—things von Donop would only tell a man in his confidence, not to a hated enemy. I interrogated him myself. I believed what he said. He was in terrific fear for his life. He told the truth. Now von Donop knows of your network and how to ferret you out. I am confident of that."

"Then we must see to *Herr* von Donop as soon as he returns from Paris."

"You know where he is going?"

"Of course. The mechanic who works on the German airplanes at the aerodrome is a brother of one of our fighters. He lets us know these things and he overheard the *SS* officer bragging to the crew about his meeting with Heydrich in Paris today."

Ego. The man's ego is his undoing. It made him leave ANTIMONY unguarded save by two hapless *SS* guards and a cowardly Frenchman. *Bad mistake, old sport.* And it made him leave his captives out of reach for a full twenty-four hours, an even graver mistake. ANTIMONY beamed. Not only had he regained the offensive in the see-saw game of move, counter-move, strike, counter-strike, but he finally had an advantage. He had an edge. *Ego, simple human ego.*

"What about Jean Louis?" she asked, almost timidly.

It had to happen. He had to tell her. "He is dead. The Germans sprayed the cottage with fire trying to get me. They got him instead. I'm sorry."

"Don't be. He was a coward and a traitor. He merely got what he deserved, Monsieur."

ANTIMONY could not help but see the tiny bubble of moisture running down her cheek. It glistened in the moonlight, then fell off into nothingness. "Were you close?"

"We were lovers, Monsieur ANTIMONY."

"I'm sorry."

"It is over." She pulled into the courtyard of a stone farmhouse. Armed men in the yard hid discreetly behind hay wagons and a stone fence.

"We are here. You must be exhausted. You must rest. Then we plan an escape for your Dr. Enrico Verdi, no?"

As they walked to the house, ANTIMONY spoke in a fatherly manner with compassion in his voice. "*Mademoiselle.* This is very dangerous work. Do you not fear for the safety of your family? Won't your activities put them in danger if the Germans catch you?" he probed, very carefully avoiding the use of the phrase "loved ones."

She stopped and looked him directly in the eyes. Her Gallic eyes shining in the moonlight showed sadness but also a fierce determination. "*Monsieur* ANTIMONY. France is my family. She is in danger. No, I have no one close in the country. My mother perished in an accident years ago and my brother died defending the Republic last year in the invasion. My father fled France to Canada after the Occupation. He teaches at the University of Laval in Quebec. He is quite safe there."

They turned and went inside.

He slept—wonderful, blissful sleep. He did not even remember dreaming, unlike the nervous, agitated, tense, nightmarish sleep of recent days. Why, he could not say. It must have been that in spite of the dangers ahead, he felt for the first time since that morning of the sinking, that he had the upper hand. He slept peacefully. ANTIMONY's window of opportunity decreased with each metallic click of the watch on his wrist. But, he knew that fatigue can be as great a threat to the man in the field as the enemy himself. He must be rested to joust with the foe. At midnight this night, a Royal Navy submarine would surface off the coast twenty kilometers to the south. He must be there with Dr. Verdi. He must sleep and be alert.

Eliana awakened him at 0800. He had slept for six hours. It would be enough. Outside, hidden in the barn sat the staff car. One of the Frenchman had gone into town to the garage and had driven it back to the hideaway. It would be needed in the assault on the hotel, the magnificent prison called *Hôtel Grand*. The *SS* men and the wretched traitor Gasperon would be left alone for the time being and disposed of later in an "accident." For the next several minutes the group briefed ANTIMONY on the escape plan they had devised while he slept.

"What if the watch commander insists on a verbal confirmation from von Donop before releasing the prisoners?" ANTIMONY asked.

"That is easy—Claude," interjected Eliana, turning to the ruddy-faced, balding man at the end of the table. He nodded.

"I am a switchman for the telephone company. In fact, I rewired that hotel just last year. I shall slip into the cellar where the junction box is located. It is difficult to access, so it is unlikely that anyone will stumble upon me. I will intercept any outgoing or incoming calls by this," he beamed, holding up his headset of the type used by telephone lineman to break into phone lines for testing and a box with a single amber light and a spin dial. On the phone, a readout of ten numbers could be coded into the device for intercept. ANTIMONY saw the hand of SOE's mad scientists. "I shall make sure the man on the other end is our friend *Herr Sturmbannführer* von Donop."

"How can you be sure the watch commander will think it is Von Donop?"

"Because I shall be him," spoke up the goateed man in a pinstriped suit known as the Professor in perfectly correct German. "As well as teaching languages, I am an amateur impersonator. It is a hobby I have enjoyed for years. I shall show you my Winston Churchill someday, *Monsieur.* Perhaps after the war is won, eh?"

"Perhaps the watch commander would like to hear Mr. Churchill this evening," responded a grinning ANTIMONY.

The laughter about the table relieved the tension.

"We will strike as soon as we get the signal from the aerodrome that von Donop's plane has landed. That is at least a thirty-minute drive to the hotel. During that time, he will be out of touch by telephone or wireless. The Professor will ring the watch commander and inform him that *Oberst* Finkel, aka ANTIMONY, will arrive shortly to take custody of the two Americans," added Eliana.

"What if von Donop stops along the way to ring up, say, to let them know he is coming?" asked the man with the black eye patch, courtesy of a German bullet the year before.

"That's a risk we run, but it is minimal, I think," responded Eliana. "We expect that he will go straight back to his hotel along the coast road. He will be tired and will want to go directly to his room. We hope. If not, and he calls the watch commander or heads for the *Grand,* then the Professor will ring up again as von Donop and say the plan has changed and to expect *Oberst* Finkel instead. ANTIMONY should be well clear of the hotel by the time von Donop actually arrives. We have only half an hour in that case. Should von Donop ring up, then the Professor will convince him that he is the watch commander. We have been observing the personnel for weeks and are confident that an impersonation will work. The trick is to never let the two actually speak to each other. If he uses wireless, we are out of luck, but again, it is an acceptable risk. There is no need to use wireless when the telephone is more accessible."

"What's next?" asked ANTIMONY, nodding his concurrence with the plan thus far.

"The documents. Being a major conduit for downed airmen out of France into Spain, we have become expert at document forgery," responded Eliana, handing him a very official looking packet identifying the man in the yet to be taken photograph as a *Wehrmacht* Colonel, *Oberst* Hans Finkel, attached to *SS* Intelligence in Paris.

"It's excellent work."

ANTIMONY smiled at the fake identity paper. Part of his liaison duties at BSC had been the coordination of fake passports and identity papers
for SOE agents operating in neutral countries such as the United States and
Central America. He recognized first rate work. No *Wehrmacht* junior officer would dare challenge an imperious colonel with these documents. He
handed the identity papers back to the forger.

"There's one other thing we need—a driver," he said.

"A driver?" grimaced Eliana. "That is highly dangerous. Any one of our
people who speak German well enough might be recognized if not on the
spot, then perhaps later by one of the guards. No, *Monsieur,* that is too risky."

"I have an excellent candidate. We just need to spring him from his refined captivity at the *du Palais.* I refer to one Colonel Frederick Hobgood,
U.S. Army Signal Corps, retired. He said if we need him, he is willing, ready
and able. He is also a consummate professional."

"Very well then. Hopefully the guards at the *Grand* will not recognize
him. We can bring him out the same way we had previously planned to bring
out you and Dr. Verdi."

"And take him back in?" quizzed ANTIMONY, fearful of endangering
his friend.

"*Oui.* And back in. There is a passageway from the pantry in the kitchen
to the street in the rear. The Germans do not know about it and post no
guard. We have watched this. The hotel owner despises the *Boche* and will be
more than cooperative," replied Eliana.

"There is one problem. He is rather large and strapping."

"That is not a problem, *Monsieur,*" chimed in a man standing in the corner, the cell's "tailor." "We have a sergeant's uniform from just such a man
in Marseille. The poor sod was on leave there and his hotel room . . . . Well,
the local *Gendarmes* were simply unable to find the thief who made off with
his money, his identity papers, and his uniform while he was in a drunken
stupor. And they never did locate the young lady who went up to his room
with him that night," chuckled the tailor.

Eliana grinned broadly.

"Then let me send him a note," said ANTIMONY. He scratched on a piece
of crumpled paper, folded it, then handed it to the chambermaid.

"Let me try on the uniform," said ANTIMONY rising. He walked into the
next room with the tailor. The Wehrmacht colonel's uniform fit moderately

well. The previous owner, about the same height as ANTIMONY, had quite a bit larger girth. The decorations identified the man as a veteran of the First World War, thus likely about the same age, and also newly decorated presumably from the battles of the previous two years. ANTIMONY had a healthy professional respect for the man who had owned this gray uniform. After all, the politicians started all wars. Wasn't it Carl von Clausewitz, the Prussian theorist, who had said war is merely an extension of politics? The professional warriors had to only fight and die, not make policy. Nonetheless, the man is an enemy and his uniform now became an instrument in the fight against his nation's politics.

"Do not worry, *Monsieur*. I am tailoring the tunic to fit you like the kid glove," said the tailor.

"Just reasonably comfortable will do. How did you get this uniform?"

"It wasn't hard, *Monsieur*," came the strong but feminine voice from behind him. He turned towards Eliana.

"Colonel Finkel may have been a great soldier, but he was also a man of the flesh. He was a great customer of the ladies of the evening in Paris just after the Occupation. One of them shot him with his own gun. We found out about it and raided his quarters before the *Gendarmes* or the Nazis could get there. This was what we were after ... uniforms and identity papers to be used in other parts of the country. Who would notice that one of three or four service uniforms was missing," she shrugged her shoulders.

"What happened to the prostitute?"

"Who knows. Executed, I'm sure. The Nazis do not like such things happening in their happy Ayrian Empire."

"Then we'll make good use of it."

A crisp knock came at the door. Hobgood jerked. He had been sitting by the window day dreaming with the curtains closed and the room in semi-darkness. At the door stood a chambermaid carrying towels. "Extra towels for your bath, *Monsieur*."

"Sorry, the other maid already brought plenty. You must have the wrong room, Ma'am. Thanks anyway," he smiled as he started to shut the door.

A foot thrust into the door jamb. "No, *Monsieur*. There is no mistake. You need these towels." The woman pushed her way into the darkened room and turned towards the startled man with the gaping mouth.

"But. . .I. . . ."

She raised her finger to her lips. It cut him off in mid-blubber. "I have a message for you, Colonel Hobgood. Please keep your voice low."

"Okay, I'm game, what's up?"

His expression became somber and concerned as she handed him the crinkled paper pulled from her brassier. Hobgood unfolded the message and read: "BARBECUE, I NEED YOU. COME WITH THIS WOMAN."

Hobgood looked up at the chambermaid and back down at the note. He chuckled at the greeting: "Barbecue." Very good! ANTIMONY had even used the more traditional Piedmont North Carolina spelling with a "c" rather than the more common "q." It served two purposes. If the Germans intercepted the Frenchwoman and found the note, there is no linkage to Hobgood unless the Krauts beat it out of her. Even then, he might be protected by his neutrality. More importantly, it identified the message as legitimate. Only someone who had been sitting at the table that day on the Zamzam would understand the significance of the word "barbecue." What a singular piece of fieldwork—simple, but effective. Damn, that limey Braithwaite sure knows his business! "Is he all right?"

"Oui, Monsieur, quite safe."

"You Resistance?"

"*Oui, Monsieur.*"

"I understand. When do we leave?"

"Immediately, Colonel. I shall leave first. Follow me by one minute down the back stairway to the main lobby. Just to the right of the Concierge Desk you will see a bronze, hinged door with a round window. Go through that without being noticed. I shall be waiting on the other side. Good luck, Colonel." She turned to leave the room.

"Oh, Miss. You forgot to leave my towels," he smirked, an impish grin on his broad face.

"Indeed, *Monsieur*. My apologies," she chuckled as she handed him the set of pristine white towels.

"It's a great plan, John. I hope like hell it works or we will both have our butts in a sling."

"It's got to work. Von Donop arrives in a couple of hours. The man is unbelievably good, but he has made some fundamental errors, old boy. We shall drive a lorry, or should I say, his own staff car right through them."

"Damn! Joan Avery! Damn! Well, he made a great looking lady, that's for sure."

"Makeup and stage presence, that's all it is."

"Shit, John. He fooled the hell outta you!"

ANTIMONY could only smile. ARMAGEDDON had fooled the hell out of all of them. Van Eyck had only learned that too late. The German sergeant's uniform fit Hobgood barely, but adequately. No colonel, be he *Wehrmacht* or *SS*, would have driven such a car himself. There would always be an enlisted driver. Hobgood looked the part of the career army sergeant—a "lifer" probably in his twilight tour, but closely attached to his colonel, and with a bit too much of the schnapps, sausages, and potatoes under his belt. Hobgood's last military assignment had been in the code breaking section of Army Signals Intelligence. He spoke German like a native and had the presence to carry off the part.

The Resistance mole called from the aerodrome. With the plane due in on time, the plan started in motion. It all came down to the next few minutes. The mission devolved into a matter of intricate timing. ANTIMONY popped the gray service cap on his head and adjusted the angle.

1741. They climbed into the staff car, Hobgood behind the wheel and ANTIMONY in the back seat looking impressive and authoritative. As they got in, Hobgood stood to attention and saluted the red, white and black Swastika flag fluttering above the wheel well. He then gave another salute well known in the U.S. consisting of the middle finger proudly protruding in the air. ANTIMONY laughed. With tension building, the gesture proved a great reliever.

"Good luck, *Monsieurs*. We will be a few hundred yards behind you. Claude and the professor are already on station in the hotel cellar. *Viva la France!*" shouted Eliana, her slender hand extending over the top of the door, shaking ANTIMONY's.

"Luck! Hell, we'll knock 'em over with our charm and good looks," grumbled Hobgood in the front seat. He slid off the handbrake and put the car into drive, grinding the gears. "Well, okay, so it's not a Ford."

The car lurched down the hill as Hobgood got accustomed to the car's precise transmission. It would soon smooth out. 1745.

Von Donop's plane would land at precisely 1800 right on schedule or even a few minutes early thanks to a tailwind according to the pilot's check-in. From that point, it would take approximately fifteen minutes for him to debark and climb into his waiting roadster. The youthful *SS* corporal, his foot propped up on the running board and enjoying a last smoke, had arrived at 1730. In that period of time, von Donop could ring up the hotel to confirm that everything is well, which he would do, and of course, all would be well. The commandeered staff car would arrive at the hotel by 1815. If all continued to go as planned, the prisoners would be on the way out by the time von Donop could get to another phone, or have made the drive to the hotel. Timing was critical with little room for error—delay, fatal.

The amber light on the phone handset blinked twice indicating the line to the hotel's central switchboard from which the operator could connect the incoming call to any phone in the building. Claude flipped the toggle switch to activate the intercept. He put his lineman's extension to his ear. The Professor crouched near to his head to hear the voices on the line.

"*Oui, Hôtel Grand.* May I help you?"

"This is *Sturmbannführer* von Donop. Connect me with the watch officer."

"Right away, *Monsieur*," replied the now tense operator.

"*Ya*, watch officer."

"Von Donop here. How are our guests this evening?"

"They are very well, *Herr Sturmbannführer*, very comfortable and quiet," he replied.

"Excellent. Make certain they stay that way." He had a vaguely threatening tone to his remark.

The watch officer ignored the implied threat. He had twenty men in and around the hotel mainly to protect the high ranking muckety mucks who had come down for the season. *Where were the prisoners going to go? Typical SS arrogance!* "Do not worry, Sir."

"Good. What is your name?"

"*Hauptmann* Kluge, *Herr Sturmbannführer.*"

"Well, *Hauptmann* Kluge. I am at the aerodrome. I will be there in precisely thirty minutes."

"Very good, *Herr Sturmbannführer.* I shall expect you then."

The men in the cellar looked at the Professor's watch. 1750. Damn the bad luck! The plane must have arrived early. They counted on that thirty-minute window where von Donop would be out of communication. With the plane's early arrival, though, von Donop might well arrive with ANTIMONY inside the hotel and no way to reach the Resistance people in time. The men in the cellar could make outgoing calls by patching into the hotel's trunk line, just as they could intercept incoming and outgoing calls, but could reach no one to warn them. Even should they get through to the farmhouse, the people at the receiving end would be at least a quarter of an hour behind the staff car. A speeding car attracted a lot of attention. No good. They had not accounted for the plane arriving earlier than expected. Damned German efficiency! The escape must be aborted. There is no other choice. 1751.

"I'll go up and intercept them at the intersection," said the Professor.

The telephone man shook his head. The intersection up from the hotel would be the logical place to head them off at the narrow street where it joined the broad avenue. The men in the Mercedes could not help but spot him as they cruised by even if he made no overt attempt to flag them down, which he wouldn't for fear of attracting undue attention. The Professor stood up. The amber light blinked twice.

"Wait," said the telephone man, putting his hand on the Professor's jacket tail. The Professor crouched back down.

"*Hôtel Grand.* May I help you?"

"This is *Sturmbannführer* Von Donop. Connect me with the watch officer again."

"Oui, Monsieur. One moment please." The operator transferred the call to the front desk where Kluge still stood, conversing with the sergeant of the guard.

"Watch officer."

The trip to Paris had been an emotional high to be sure. He had been running on adrenaline for the past twenty-four hours. In the past two hours or so, ARMAGEDDON's body had come down from the mountain of self-induced energy and momentum and into the pit of exhaustion. He could not relax, though—too near to the finale of one of the greatest intelligence operation coups in history. To snatch the Western world's top nuclear physicist right out from under the Americans' noses, and with the meddlesome, but ineffective British interference, amounted to a feat of monumental proportions. Even the egomaniacal Heydrich had been impressed, so much so that he wanted the status of the operation briefed firsthand before he returned to Berlin, hence the critical, if inconvenient trip to Paris. Heydrich promised ARMAGEDDON that his promotion to Oberststurmbannführer was assured and that he would be presented the Knight's Cross by the *Führer* himself. Yes, indeed, quite a coup. He needed a release from the tension, the anxiety, and the strain. His muscles ached. His head pounded. He knew of only one cure, one release for the megawatts of energy coursing through him.

"*Herr Hauptmann.* I shall not be coming to the hotel. Not yet. I shall be going to my hotel, the du Mont, to freshen up. Do you have the number?"

"*Yawohl, Herr Sturmbannführer.* Just as you left it."

"Good. Ring me up at any time should there be any problem or the slightest . . . inconsistency. Do you understand, *Herr Hauptmann?*"

"*Yawohl, Herr Sturmbannführer.* Completely."

"Good." He replaced the telephone handset in the cradle and walked away from the control tower. The SS corporal held the roadster door open. ARMAGEDDON sat heavily in the passenger side. The soft leather rolled around his form encompassing his tired, but electric muscles like the welcoming arms of a lover. It felt wonderful after the hard, unfriendly seat of the *Luftwaffe* aircraft. 1755.

"The *du Mont*, Werner. We have needs to see to."

"*Yawohl, Herr Sturmbannführer.*"

The roadster roared off into the night, heading south, away from the town, the *Hôtel Grand*, and the Mercedes staff car heading into the northern outskirts of Biarritz.

1800. ANTIMONY checked his watch. *The bugger should be landing about now. On schedule.* All going well, he thought as he gazed out at the ocean.

1816. The staff car pulled to a halt before the canopy-crowned hotel entrance with wrought iron *fleur-de-lis*. Neatly manicured potted trees lined the sidewalk on either side. Two uniformed guards stood at the entrance with another in a red and white striped sentry box across the narrow street under the columned arches. This set up a crossfire problem should they have to flee. He felt for the machine pistol tucked out of sight under the seat. *Pray God we don't have to use this.* A doorman in hotel livery eagerly swung open the door of the staff car, then sprang to stiff attention. In better times before the war, there would have been three such doormen—one to greet, one to handle the door, and one to carry luggage.

"Welcome to the *Hôtel Grand*," he exclaimed with a forced smile.

ANTIMONY grunted and stepped down onto the pavement. The two sentries on either side of the entrance sprang to an alert present arms. ANTIMONY returned the salute, gloves in hand, in the leisurely fashion of a man used to high responsibility and weary of the accompanying formality. In the front seat, Hobgood gripped the wheel, feet ready to pounce on the clutch and accelerator, alert for the possibility of a hurried getaway. Above the waist, though, he exhibited the relaxed, self-confident, mature demeanor of a professional veteran comfortable with his place in life. Underneath, his heart pounded. He gently reached down and flipped the leather holster safety flap. A subtle nod towards the sentry in the box across the street indicated to ANTIMONY that should a firefight erupt, he would take out that man first.

"*Jawohl, Herr Oberst?*" sputtered the surprised corporal behind the lobby desk, who had the duty of greeting all guests above the rank of *Hauptman* and ensuring that they received the utmost care and courtesy.

"I'm *Oberst* Finkel. I've just arrived from Paris."

"I'm terribly sorry *Herr Oberst,* but I was not informed of your arrival. We have no more rooms, but I'm certain we can find you a most delightful suite in one of the other hotels."

ANTIMONY cut off the struggling man with a hand raised in the air. "I am not here for a room. Notify the watch officer that I wish to see him immediately," glowered ANTIMONY only adding to the sweating man's discomfort. *So far, so good.* His German may have sounded somewhat stilted and formal to the typical German much as does an Oxbridge accent to the average Briton. *Never mind. It's good enough, if I add enough impatience and bravado.* He had the upper hand. He must stay on the offensive. The watch officer appeared, nervous, but in control.

"May I help you, *Herr Oberst*?"

"You are holding an American and his daughter—Dr. Enrico Verdi—are you not?" The man grew pale. *You are not to discuss the presence of or any facts regarding the Americans.* Those are the standing instructions of the arrogant and frightening *SS Sturmbannführer.* The watch officer almost gagged.

Strike now! You have him on the run! Thrust! "You may freely answer, *Herr Hauptmann. Sturmbannführer* von Donop works for me. I have just arrived from Paris with him. Did he not mention that I would be arriving?"

"Why, no, *Herr Oberst.* He has rung up twice, but there was no word of your arrival. I'm sure that if . . ."

"No matter," ANTIMONY snapped. *Cut the man off. Keep him off balance.* "I am here to take the two Americans. You will release them to my custody immediately. My car is outside. Please bring them down after you have cleared the lobby of all unauthorized personnel."

The man rocked back on his heels. The shock of the demand totally unnerved him. He needed reinforcements. He had none. He gulped hard. "But, *Herr Oberst*, you realize that I must have authorization first from *Herr* von Donop. You must understand this, Sir?" pleaded the frightened man.

The moment of truth. The entire mission turned on this one episode. ANTIMONY took a deep breath. *Press on, old boy. This is what His Majesty's government pays you for.* "Of course. You must have authorization." ANTIMONY reached into his tunic and produced the altered *Wehrmacht* identity documents, completely authentic other than the new photograph of a sour-looking career army colonel. The watch officer handed them back to ANTIMONY. His hand trembled ever so slightly.

"With your permission, *Herr Oberst*, I need to speak with the *sturmbannführer.* You understand that I need to verify your authority in this matter."

"Of course," ANTIMONY replied. He thought of the two Frenchmen crouched in the cellar. They had better be as good as they said. The watch officer reached into the breast pocket of his tunic and pulled out a crumpled piece of paper with the telephone number of the *Hôtel du Mont and* dialed.

1823. As before, the amber light flashed twice. The telephone man pressed the handset hard to his ear, listening for the voice on the other end to answer as they had expected. Then it came, loud and clear.

"Hôtel du Mont, may I help you?"

The toggle switch flipped, intercepting the call. Now, rather than at the *du Mont*, the call terminated in the cellar in the linesman's device. The operator would assume that someone had dialed a wrong number and merely hung up without speaking rather than be embarrassed. It happened all the time. On Kluge's end, he heard a faint, barely audible click. He now spoke to the French Resistance.

"I wish to speak with *SS Sturmbannführer* von Donop, Suite Number Two, please. *Hauptmann* Kluge calling."

The telephone man handed the device to the Professor, who had listened intently to von Donop's voice pattern. He could replicate it all, at least to the satisfaction of the watch officer. He took a deep, long breath.

"Von Donop," he said, an octave too high.

Lower! The voice should be lower.

Kluge hesitated. *"Herr Sturmbannführer* von Donop?"

"Ja? Is this Kluge?" he demanded.

"Jawohl, Herr Sturmbannführer." Damned Froggy telephone system. Not like a reliable, good German system.

"What is it, *Herr Hauptmann?"*

"There is an officer here—*Oberst* Finkel—who says he is your superior from *SS* Headquarters, Paris and he is here to collect our special guests. I thought it best to confirm this with you, Sir."

"You were correct. Is this man tall with slightly graying brown hair?"

The German looked up at ANTIMONY taking note of his hair. *"Yawohl, Herr Sturmbannführer."*

"Good. Ask him the name of the code room wench in our office with the convenient flat."

"Yawohl," replied the grinning officer, who posed the question to ANTI-MONY, who in turn grinned.

"Fraulein Gelher, *Herr Sturmbannführer."*

"Correct. He is *Oberst* Finkel. You are to release the two Americans to his custody."

"I understand. I shall do so at once," replied the German as he put down the telephone, beaming with self-pride that he had done the right thing. "Please come with me, *Herr Oberst.*"

ANTIMONY walked to the man's left side, taking note of the physical layout of the place. Not out of the forest just yet, he had to be prepared for a quick escape should something go awry. Down in the cellar, the Professor dropped the instrument. His breath came in short bursts as large drops of sweat formed on his brow. *He had done it, by God. He had done it!* The telephone man put a hand on his shoulder and shook it in glee, bursting to shout for joy, but daring not to in case they might be heard. There would be time for celebration later. It wasn't every day that they could tweak the *Führer's* nose.

"*Herr Doktor*, you and Miss Verdi will accompany *Oberst* Finkel. Please gather your belongings."

Verdi almost gave away the game. When he opened the door, there stood the man he had trusted and relied upon for weeks wearing the uniform of the enemy. *Is it possible that he had been deceived all this time? Had he been set up by the urbane, smooth Englishman posing as an American business-man? No, that isn't the case at all.* As the watch officer spoke, the taller man standing behind him in the uniform of a *Wehrmacht* colonel winked that sort of "play along like nothing is amiss and we'll pull it off" wink. It is truly amazing how much can be conveyed by the simple physical twitch of an eye.

"Yes, of course. We are ready to leave now," he said, turning towards his daughter.

"No, we will not! We are American citizens! You have no right or cause to hold us. I demand that you release us and phone the Embassy this minute!" hissed Angela in controlled anger, striding forward to the door, facing the watch officer and staring him coldly in the face.

"Miss Verdi, I'm sorry but . . . . "

ANTIMONY cut him off. He must regain control of the situation. Verdi had apparently not briefed her on the situation. Either that or the feisty young lady was a tremendous actress. Either way, her indignation endangered the operation. She must be calmed down. "*Herr Hauptmann*, please leave us. I shall discuss the situation with Dr. and Miss Verdi. Come back in two minutes," he ordered sternly.

"*Jawohl, Herr Oberst,*" replied the officer, retreating back into the hallway.

ANTIMONY stepped into the room and closed the door solidly behind him. The timorous Kluge would not dare to listen at the door; nonetheless, just to be sure, he put his finger to his lips to indicate silence.

"Colonel, you must either . . . ."

"Angela!" The stern authority in Verdi's voice had not been heard in such a fashion by Angela in many years. It stopped her cold. "This is Mr. Prince. He is a friend. He is British. He is here to rescue us. Now be silent," he whispered.

She stared at the tall man in front of her. She sensed truth in her father's statement. The man did have a certain nonthreatening aura about him. Her father must know. She would trust him. She would go with the man in the *Wehrmacht* uniform. They gathered their belongings quickly. There wasn't much, but it made for a good appearance. It would all be left behind, of course, in the custody of the French. They would literally escape with the clothes on their backs and what could be stuffed in pockets. It did make the transfer seem legitimate to have luggage, though. In precisely two minutes, Kluge returned with two strong-backed privates to carry the bags. ANTIMONY asked for five more minutes to finish the packing, which suited the watch officer. They could ill afford the lost time, but too hasty a departure would raise suspicion. Therefore, they must risk that extra five minutes.

1830. If von Donop came straight to the hotel, he would arrive in just a few moments. It would be tight. They needed to be out of town by then. Fortunately, the aerodrome lay inland to the east so they would not pass the red and cream Mercedes along the escape route.

"Carry their bags and hop to it. I haven't all night," snorted an indignant *Oberst* Finkel.

The two soldiers hoisted up the several suitcases and followed the party down through the lobby.

"You! You there. Come here now," shouted Hobgood, feigning irritation.

The teenager blanched as he realized that Hobgood pointed directly at him. The sentry raced over to the driver's side of the car and snapped to attention again. "*Jawohl, Herr Feldwebel*?"

"What is your name?"

"Goetz. Hermann Goetz, *Herr Feldwebel*," sputtered the frightened man.

"And your commanding officer?"

"*Herr Oberleutnant* Sturm."

"And what, Goetz, do you think that *Herr Oberleutnant* Sturm would say if he realized that you stood guard at this grand palace, complete with all manner of high-ranking guests, with the top button of your tunic unbuttoned?" he growled, adding emphasis by punching out each syllable.

The soldier turned pale as he felt for the top button. He quickly fumbled with and re-buttoned it. "*Danka, Herr Feldwebel*."

"Hmmm, of course. Now resume your post and be more careful," grumbled Hobgood.

The German sprang back to his post by the entrance just as ANTIMONY and the Verdies exited the hotel. The man popped to a crisp present arms, to which ANTIMONY returned a casual salute. Hobgood leapt out of the car and opened the back door as the two soldiers turned porters loaded the luggage into the boot. Dr. Verdi and Angela sat in the back seat. The physicist could not entirely suppress a grin. He recognized the German "*Feldwebel*" as his sometimes bridge partner in the Dining Saloon oh so long ago. Hobgood raced around to the driver's side as ANTIMONY stepped up on the running board.

1833. "Let's move. Fast," ANTIMONY whispered.

Hobgood gunned the engine as the car wheeled about.

"What was that all about with the sentry?" asked ANTIMONY as they cruised away from the hotel.

"Oh, I just wanted the lad to look his best when the *SS* shoot the entire lot for letting you get away with this scam," chuckled Hobgood.

In the cellar, the amber light flashed. The two men looked at each other, terrified. Surely the escape must be complete. They had heard no shouting, no telltale gunfire. Should they answer or leave it? What if it is von Donop. No time. Do it! The telephone man flipped the intercept toggle switch.

"*Hôtel Grand.* May I help you?" he answered in a bored, laconic, end of shift tone.

"This is *Sturmbannführer* von Donop. Put me through to the watch officer."

Hail Mary full of grace. What do we do now?

"One moment, Sir," he said as he clicked the switch for hold. "He wants to speak to the watch officer. Can you do him?" the lineman asked without panic in his voice, but definitely great consternation.

"I'll have to . . . no . . . wait . . . let me think," said the Professor, squeezing his eyes shut, concentrating to the exclusion of all else. *No. He couldn't do him, not Kluge. That needed work. What else. Yes. The phlegmatic little lieutenant that he had seen earlier. What was his name? Boset? No Bose, Leutnant Bose. He would pass himself off as this man. They had to do something fast. It must be done now.*

"Watch officer."

Pause. Silence on the line.

"This is *Sturmbannführer* von Donop. You are not Kluge. What is going on there?" he demanded.

"Nothing wrong, Sir. I have merely relieved *Hauptmann* Kluge for the evening. He has left for his quarters, I suspect. May I help you, *Herr Sturmbannführer.*"

"Who are you?"

"*Leutnant* Bose, Sir."

"What do you look like, Bose?"

Think! Von Donop must have seen Bose. He might even know him. Think! "I am short with dark hair and I have a limp from a combat wound." He remembered the limp.

"Do you hold the Iron Cross, *Herr Leutnant* Bose?"

Damn. What are his decorations? He had seen the man's medals on his tunic, but what were they. A fuzzy recollection, but he could see the silver and black cross. "*Yawohl, Herr Sturmbannführer.* Iron Cross Second Class."

Von Donop seemed mollified. "Did *Hauptmann* Kluge pass on to you my orders?"

"*Yawohl, Herr Sturmbannführer.* He was most explicit."

"Then you know precisely what to do then?"

"*Yawohl.*"

"Good. I called to tell you I shall be there at precisely 0800 in the morning. Have our American guests packed and ready to travel at that time."

"It will be done, *Herr Sturmbannführer.*"

The SS man clicked off the line. The Professor's hands trembled. It had been the finest performance of his career. The staff car sped out of the town, headed north. They had done their job in the dark cellar.

1838.

ANTIMONY reached the cottage with his refugees. There had been no incidents. Their ruse had not yet been discovered or if so, the Germans did not know where to look for them. With Verdi and his daughter safely in the cottage, Angela began a rapid fire questioning. A bright, articulate, and brave young woman throughout the ordeal of her arrest in Milan and through the incarceration and the escape, she had maintained a defiant calm. Once in the cottage, though, she became the inquisitive youngster, wanting to know everything, every detail, and the eternal why, why, why. This is good thought ANTIMONY. There would be several tense hours before they could make their break for Point "Hope," and they still had to pass back through town to get to the rendezvous where HMS *Tribune* would be waiting. The busier the Verdies stayed during this time, the better.

Hobgood changed back into his civilian clothes. The tailor handed him the German sergeant's Iron Cross as a souvenir of his escapade. It would be treasured. ANTIMONY walked with Hobgood down to the Renault that would take him back to the *Hôtel du Palais*. The Englishman extended a hand, which Hobgood grasped firmly. The American's eyes twinkled accompanied by an impish grin.

"Enjoyed the little frolic, John," he said, shaking.

"Thanks for your help, Fred. I wish we could return the favor."

"Not a problem there, Limey. When you get back to New York, hop the flyer down to Durham and I'll treat you to the finest Carolina pig-picking ever witnessed."

"Thanks, old sport. I'll take you up on that."

The mood turned suddenly serious again.

"Good luck ANTIMONY."

ANTIMONY nodded in acknowledgment. Hobgood stepped into the Renault. The commodore stood at the edge of the gravel road watching the car bounce down the dark, bumpy drive.

They would stay at the cottage until 2315 when they would again drive out and down the coast road towards Point "Hope," some twenty kilometers away. They would use the staff car and ANTIMONY would remain in the uniform. Hopefully, there would be no manhunt and if so, they might bluff and bluster their way out of a jam. The rest of the Resistance people, including Eliana Descartes, would stay in town to determine if any alarm had sounded meaning that the ruse had not worked. They would stay there until 2300, then make their way south to the rendezvous point. Should German activity indicate that ANTIMONY had been found out, then they would head to the cottage straightaway with the warning. It would be a tense few hours for all.

PART IV
RESURRECTION AND REVELATION

CHAPTER 21

THE CAVALRY IS
UNEXPECTEDLY DELAYED

Von Donop sprawled in the settee, his bare feet propped up on the wicker coffee table. The silk dressing gown had fallen away off his naked legs and dangled on the floor. The vintage cognac tasted especially sweet this evening. Taking a long drag from a Turkish cigarette, he methodically exhaled the grayish-blue cloud. A breeze created by the slowly circulating overhead fan caught the rising smoke rings and whipped them away to oblivion. Outside on the terrace, a gentle breeze occasionally flapped the canvas awnings as the light of a full moon rising caught the gentle waves in the harbor, blinking on and off the tops of the waves like the candlelight reflection through a thousand crystal goblets. Small boats swayed and rocked back and forth to the gentle roll of the waves. The German sipped the brandy as his eye caught the steady winking of a buoy light. He had that self-satisfied smugness of a man savoring a monumental triumph. Like a sportsman on the verge of winning a championship, he stood ready to lift the figurative trophy high in the air. Von Donop chuckled in delighted self-satisfaction.

The ringing telephone momentarily jarred him out of his previctory trance. Hesitating for a moment, he debated whether or not to answer. Then, spurred on by the energy caused by months of frantic, deadly attentiveness to every stimulus about him, he stood up and shook off the alcohol-induced stupor. By the third ring, his hand clutched the handset. He took a long, deep, steady breath.

"*Ja?*"

The watch officer on the other end, taken back by the forcefulness of the unexpectedly harsh answer, hesitated a moment.

"Uh . . . *Herr Sturmbannführer* von Donop?"

"*Ja*, this is von Donop."

"*Herr Sturmbannführer*, this is *Oberleutnant* Schickel at *Wehrmacht* HQ St.-Jean-de-Luz. I . . . uh . . . have standing orders, Sir, that you are to be informed if there is any unusual activity, day or night."

"*Ja*, what is it?" Alarms triggered. Intuitively, von Donop knew that something had gone wrong, something he had not accounted for. His pulse raced. The veins in his temple throbbed. His fingers tensed in a kind of spastic motion. No longer *SS Sturmbannführer* Karl von Donop, he again became ARMAGEDDON, master agent, now alive and alert, primed for action.

"We just received a sighting report. An E-boat on patrol sighted what it believed was a British submarine running on the surface, just off the coast. The captain initiated an attack, but lost contact before they could put a weapon in the water. This occurred at 2245 hours."

"And what is unusual about that, *Herr Oberleutnant*?" ARMAGEDDON now played devil's advocate.

"Well, Sir, we have never had a submarine sighting here. At least, not since I arrived. We don't have enough major shipping traffic, military or merchant, which would cause the British to post a submarine off our harbor."

The revelation struck ARMAGEDDON like a full quiver of arrows shot from many bows all striking simultaneously. The world collapsed and he did not know why. "Very well, *Herr Oberleutnant*. You were correct in ringing me. I'll be sure to inform your commanding officer of your careful attention to your duty."

"*Danka, Herr Sturmbannführer!* Good evening, Sir," beamed the junior officer, grateful for praise.

"Good night!" ARMAGEDDON slammed down the telephone and flung the brandy snifter across the room. It struck a still life and shattered causing the painting to droop to one side, dangling from its hook. *It might be nothing. Perhaps an overzealous subcommander just wanting a "look see." No!* Every instinct he had developed over the years screamed danger. ARMAGEDDON stood in the moonlight trembling with rage. On the verge of his magnificent victory, suddenly, a new unaccounted for circumstance emerged, which he could not control. But, to such people, there is only response. Action—rapid, decisive, straight for the heart action. He snatched up the telephone and rapidly dialed the number, impatient at the amount of time it took for the dial to revolve back to its starting point.

"*Hôtel Grand.* May I help you?"

"This is *Sturmbannführer* von Donop. Put me through to the watch officer immediately!"

"*Oui, Monsieur.*" *Filthy German pigs. They have no manners, no couth. It's do this, do that, and be quick about it.* The operator did not especially like the peacetime British tourists, but at least they tried to be polite. *Filthy Germans! At least they still paid his salary.*

"*Jawohl*, watch officer," answered *Hauptmann* Kluge.

"This is von Donop."

"*Jawohl, Herr Sturmbannführer?*"

"The American and his daughter—are they still there?"

There is a moment of truth in many person's lives when a seemingly matter of fact question, which requires a simple yes or no answer, suddenly implies disaster for that person. Kluge blanched. "Why . . . uh . . . no, *Herr Sturmbannführer. Obest* Finkel took them into his custody several hours ago."

"What!"

"*Jawohl, Herr Sturmbannführer.* He had proper identification. He is your senior officer."

"My senior officer is in Paris you fool!"

Kluge recovered his composure. Now he became angry. The colonel did have proper credentials. He would stand his ground against the overbearing *SS* officer.

"*Herr Sturmbannführer*, you authorized the release. I spoke with you myself, by telephone!"

"Impossible!" The rage built in him, but not aimed at the hapless watch officer. He had apparently done his job. Rather, ARMAGEDDON fumed at his own carelessness and the arrogance that could have allowed such a catastrophe to happen. He gripped the telephone receiver so tightly that his knuckles turned chalky white.

"*Hauptmann*, where did the *Oberst* Finkel take the Americans?"

"Why, Sir, he didn't say. I presumed it was to fly to Paris."

Enough! Insults! Lies! He had been made a fool of. ANTIMONY! ARMAGEDDON—cold, cruel, calculating, merciless ARMAGEDDON had been cuckolded! He slammed down the phone.

"ANTIMONY!"

The acridness with which he uttered the hated word would have melted tempered steel. There is a reason why men like ARMAGEDDON thrive.

They rarely fail because they respond to changing circumstances. They are able to redefine the battlefield and force an advantage to overcome the "fog of war." In short, they are flexible and cunning. ANTIMONY, just such a man, had outmaneuvered ARMAGEDDON. Maybe, just maybe, he could turn the tables. As the seconds passed, his mind whirled. *Even ANTIMONY is not foolproof. What is the flaw, the potentially fatal flaw? Find that and you find ANTIMONY. He has a few hours' lead on you. What is the fatal flaw!*

Overhead, the gently turning fan whirled in low harmony blowing the warm night air. Underneath, the German's white hot mind considered option after option, scenario after scenario. He squeezed his eyes shut, tightly shut to keep out all other stimuli, all other distractions. His eyelids snapped open. The muscles in his taut, hard face now released and relaxed.

"The submarine. The Goddamned submarine!" He snatched the telephone once more and furiously dialed *Wehrmacht* headquarters. *Why would a British submarine be on the surface this close to land in enemy-occupied territory? Had he been forced to surface due to mechanical difficulty, he could not have crash-dived when the E-boat spotted him. No, there is only one explanation. A rendezvous. ANTIMONY is going to take the American wops out by sub. And the only place that a sub would dare to surface at is the precise rendezvous location!*

"HQ *Wehrmacht*, St.-Jean-de-Luz. *Oberleutnant* Schickel."

"*Herr Oberleutnant*, this is *Sturmbannführer* von Donop. Where did the E-boat spot the sub? Where precisely?"

"One moment, Sir." He paused for a few seconds. "Off a small promontory about halfway between St.-Jean-du-Luz and Biarritz, Sir. That is near the village of Bidart on the coastal highway."

"Thank you, *Herr Oberleutnant*." Click. A malevolent grin crept across his face. The roles of hunter and hunted had once again switched in the battle of wits. ARMAGEDDON had chosen this small hotel in this tiny harbor town for the quiet enjoyment of his impending victory. Now, more importantly, it sat already halfway down the coastal highway from Biarritz. ANTIMONY would be forced to drive slowly and carefully so as to not attract unwanted attention. ARMAGEDDON, on the other hand, could race there. He knew the place from previous scouting. In all likelihood, he would beat them there. ANTIMONY would not dare to travel down the coast road until the last minute, timing his arrival at just the precise moment. A rendezvous is not likely to occur before midnight, especially on a brightly lit night. There is still time, but not much. 2305.

"You are dead, ANTIMONY!" The guttural howl of rage and victory that followed must surely have awakened and terrified the residents of the quaint seaside hotel. But, *c'est la guerre*, and strange things happen in wartime. The sudden appearance of the almost naked man standing in the doorway, moonlight fluttering over his body startled the corporal and the pretty, young French prostitute. She instinctively pulled the silk sheet up above her breasts, but not out of modesty. God knows, after the animalistic goings on of the three just a short two hours previous, the young girl had no modesty left to conceal. No, this was a reflexive, defensive reaction to the appearance of the wild man, whose ranting and shouts in the next room over the previous couple of minutes chilled and terrified the soldier and the prostitute. ARMAGEDDON flipped on the light switch. The brass lamp cast a warm glow across the two bodies on the bed.

"You! Get out of here. And take this French slut with you!"

"*Jawohl, Herr Sturmbannführer.*" The young man slinked out of bed, afraid to make eye contact with the raving lunatic. Both threw on enough clothes to be decent and crept out of the room. Impervious to their departure, ARMAGEDDON darted around the room. *Action! Action! Move fast!* He threw on his uniform, not buttoning his tunic—time for that later. *Extra ammunition!* He yanked open an armoire drawer and took out four clips, opened his holster and pulled out his pistol. With his right thumb, he popped open the clip lock switch. It slid out with a metallic clunk. *Good.* Jamming the clip back in, he raced out the door towards the 560 Roadster parked in the alleyway. The groggy night concierge sensed only a blur of black as it shot past his station. *Crazy Boche!*

The Mercedes roared as ARMAGEDDON gunned the engine. He had intentionally parked the car facing the main road for a fast getaway without the time-consuming delay of backing out. In this game, even seconds could be vital. He slammed it into second gear as the Mercedes picked up speed heading south to the rendezvous point only a few kilometers down the coastal highway. The idyllic, moonlit harbor scene became a blur. On a single, all-consuming mission, all else became extraneous. Except perhaps, that he steered with his left hand while buttoning his black tunic with his right. He knew that the next few minutes could be vital to his world, his new order.

He would face the enemy proudly as an officer of the *Führer's* elite personal corps. He shifted into fourth gear as the needle moved steadily clockwise across the face of the speedometer.

Agony! ANTIMONY glared at his watch. They had been on the road for forty minutes and had made only a few kilometers. Even on the sleepy coast, the Germans appeared alert and everywhere, no doubt due to the presence of the *Zamzamers* or more specifically, the horde of officials constantly arriving from Berlin. He looked at his watch again as they passed the little seaside village of Chaya and the pretty little *Hôtel du Mont*. ANTIMONY sped up once outside of town. He looked at his watch for the third time in less than a minute. 2330.

"You really must calm down, Mr. Prince," spoke up Verdi. "Your constant attention to the time is most unsettling."

ANTIMONY nodded. The physicist is right. Nevertheless, if they missed the rendezvous, they would be in deep trouble. The submarine would only surface three times—first to put the raft in the water with the rescue team, then just before midnight, and again to recover whoever came out. The final surface would be at 0200 and they still had several kilometers to go—plenty of time, but little margin for delay. He backed off a bit on the accelerator. It wouldn't do anyone any good to be killed in an auto accident on these winding coast roads. At several points, ANTIMONY thought he saw taillights up ahead where the highway leveled out in a straightaway.

"Prepare to surface, Number One."

"Very good, Sir."

HMS *Tribune* broke the surface at precisely 2350 still a mile offshore with plenty of depth beneath the keel to crash dive if necessary, but still close enough for the small, rubber dinghy to return from the beach in a minimum of time. Black water drained off the conning tower as the hatch seal broke. A whoosh of wind rushed out as stale, musty air got sucked out by the lower outside air pressure. Crisp, fresh night air poured back into the metal cavern. With the precision born of a thousand drills, the gun crew clambered up the hatch onto the deck and made the gun ready for action. Commander Peacock had done a periscope horizon sweep prior to surfacing, but saw no sign of the E-boat that had spotted them on their last surface to launch the landing party.

Peacock and the First Lieutenant scanned the horizon, 360 degrees, with binoculars.

"Looks clean, Sir."

"Concur." The outline of the beach, two thousand yards away, could be seen in the moonlight. "I would have preferred a blackened night for this sort of adventure." Peacock raised his head and nodded towards the full, lustrous moon back over his shoulder.

"Those intelligence chaps are all werewolves anyway, Sir. That's why they prefer a full moon," responded the first officer bringing chuckles all around.

"Captain," called the conning officer from below.

"Yes?"

"Lieutenant Chesterton reports beach all secure, Sir."

"Very good. Stay in touch with him, if you will."

"Aye, Aye, Sir."

Red light poured up from the conning tower. The watch officer stuck his head up the hatch once more. "Captain, signal from the beach. Lieutenant Chesterton believes he has landed off target. Signal reads "Heavier than expected wave action. Based on sightings and cross reference of landmarks, believe we are approximately 1.25 miles north, repeat 1.25 miles north of landing zone. Now moving to proper spot."

Commander Peacock took a deep breath and let it out slowly. He looked at the chronometer. 0000. Midnight precisely. "Very well, tell him to expedite."

"Aye, Aye, Sir."

"Keep a sharp eye for that E-boat, Number One."

"Very good, Sir." As Morrison peered into the night, he shook his head. *Well, that was a damned unnecessary order.* He began another 360 horizon scan.

On the beach, four black-clothed Royal Marine commandos jogged along the surf, the breaking waves just making it up to their toes. They hoisted the rubber boat over their heads and moved along silently, in unison, through the firmest part of the beach sand. The only noise came from the rhythmical clink of metal as the Sten guns strapped over their shoulders bounced off rubber wet suits. At their current pace, they would reach the rendezvous point in 15 minutes—at precisely 0015.

The beach at Point "Hope"—wide, level, pebble-strewn, gently sloping—made the perfect spot to whisk refugees off the beach to an offshore submarine. Overlooking the sand below, a cliff, carved out by millions of years of wind and water erosion, stood fifty feet high with a severe drop off. Two trails switch-backed across the base of the cliff leading down to the beach below. The road turned sharply inland roughly a hundred yards or so beyond the path to the cliff and disappeared behind a great granite rise, a gaunt survivor of some prehistoric volcanic upheaval. ARMAGEDDON eased the Mercedes to a halt, off the road and concealed behind the granite monolith, hidden from view of anyone coming along the highway. Nervous perspiration made his palms clammy and moist. Wiping them on the tails of his tunic, he stepped out onto the gravel roadway. Out of the holster came the Luger. Feeling along the face of the granite, he made his way to the edge several yards from where the road angled sharply. Hearing nothing but the sound of the surf, he thrust his head out, and simultaneously, the gun. *Still nothing.* Crouching down, ARMAGEDDON sprinted across the highway and ducked down into some low bushes.

2350. He had not been down these cliffs before, but had been briefed on them by the local *Gestapo* representative, as a possible spot for the local partisans to receive seaborne supplies. Neither the *Gestapo* nor the army had the manpower to patrol the area routinely. Just as well thought ARMAGEDDON as he crouched in the bushes. He didn't need any *Gestapo* clowns interfering with his triumph by stumbling in and scaring off the quarry.

Satisfied that no one had arrived yet, ARMAGEDDON sprang out of the bushes and jogged to the crest of the cliff. In the full moonlight, he saw the wide, pleasant beach below. Looking left, then right, he spotted a ribbon of grayish-white sand indicating one of the trails down the face of the cliff. He sprang over to it and half-walking, half-jogging, made his way down. The night wind off the Bay of Biscay had freshened. Beach grass swayed jerkily. All the better he thought. Movement at night is easier disguised with the distraction of moving plants and the roaring sea wind. It would mask his movements and ensure the vital element of surprise. *After all, most likely, ANTI-MONY has picked up some of the French bastards for protection. He must take them out as well. There won't be many. Too many bodies attract attention. No, two, maybe four at most. Not more than a carload.* He reached the bottom of the cliff. A few yards beyond the entrance to the beach, a small alcove, cut into the rock hundreds of years ago by some industrious local fisherman for protection from the elements, provided cover. ARMAGEDDON positioned himself inside the alcove and out of sight from the beach. He, on the other hand, had a perfect moonlit view of the beach.

Anyone standing there with the moon behind them would be perfectly visible as if lit up by a huge stage spotlight. 2355.

"*Merde!*" whispered Eliana.

"Shall I take him out?" The Resistance man had already taken a bead on the German.

"No!" Eliana placed her hand on top of the rifle and gently pushed it down. "No shooting. We can't arouse the whole garrison of these bastards."

2330. They should have already been at the rendezvous site by now securing the beach with the landing party of Royal Marines. Instead, here they sat, not yet out of Biarritz, hiding in a cellar, while two German soldiers pawed and fingered their Renault. Bad luck. Eliana had picked up the two men in the hotel cellar. For some reason, though, the Germans had chosen to set up a new checkpoint on this road leading south out of town. The Germans are nothing if not regular and predictable. The checkpoint on this road was always on alternating nights due to manpower considerations. Tonight, though, they had altered their cycle and two sentries blocked access to the coast highway. Fortunately, Eliana had spotted them in time and screeched to a halt. The four Frenchmen piled out of the Renault and tumbled pell mell into the cellar of the nearest house. One of the sentries had heard the approaching car, wandered over, and started investigating the suspicious vehicle. The Frenchmen could easily take out the sentries, but a missed hourly radio check would rouse the garrison. They did not need this tonight or any other night. The repercussions of two murdered German soldiers would be disastrous. They would have to figure out something else.

"Heinz!" The German corporal looked up. His companion stood several yards away, motioning. "Time to move."

"Ja." The German kicked the right rear tire. *Oh well, it was probably one of those amorous French couples out after curfew about to make another French bastard. Anyway, nothing ever happened in this town, even with the Americans and all the attention they had generated of late.* He slung his rifle back over his shoulder and walked towards the checkpoint. The four Frenchmen looked at one another, not speaking. A minute later, the *Volkswagen* headlights bounced by the parked, silent *Renault* and disappeared down the street.

"A random alternating checkpoint. Right, let's move," ordered Eliana.

The four sprang from their hiding place and leapt into the car. Without turning on the headlights, she raced off into the night. With any luck, they would make the rendezvous site only a few minutes late. She cursed softly to herself. Pray to God we have not ruined this escape she thought, pushing the accelerator to the floor. 2340.

ANTIMONY could see a long straightaway in the bouncing headlights. He slowed to a crawl. This must be it. He pulled to a stop off to the side of the road. Gravel crunched under the tires. He turned around in his seat. Verdi held his daughter with her head in his chest. What a strong woman ANTIMONY mused. The exhaustion of the three perilous days manifested itself, but she had held up against the strain. Now, she simply wanted to be close to the father she had not seen in two years.

"Not to worry. I think we are here. I just need to confirm that. Don't get out of the car." He opened the door and stepped onto the gravel, which crunched as if walking on icy snow. Across the road on the far side, he again checked his watch. He had to angle it to catch its face in the moonlight. Plenty of time if this is the place. He scanned the panorama from the vantage point atop the rise. Always know your escape route. Know it like you know yourself. How could he have been so careless as to not scout out the escape route already? Never mind! That is a useless distraction. I really am getting too old for this work. It is for the young and stupid— those young enough to do it and stupid enough to not realize the risks. So here it is, nonetheless. 2358.

He silently recited his directions. Look for a long straight road, several hundred yards in distance. At the end sits a large granite rock. The road makes a left bend around the rock. Overlooking a wide beach is a cliff with two pathways down to the sand below. Go down to the beach. We will be there. So had said Eliana Descartes. This must be it. The description is perfect. And then he saw it. First came a moment of panic, then calm, then exhilaration. Unmistakably, a mile or so offshore, silhouetted against the moonlight, sat the shape of a conning tower—the conning tower of a Royal Navy submarine! ANTIMONY's heart raced. He ran back to the car and leapt into the driver's seat. Dr. Verdi bolted upright.

"Trouble?"

"No. We're here. I can see the submarine offshore." He snapped off the parking brake, threw the car into gear and eased out the clutch. The Mercedes rolled down the road of freedom. ANTIMONY intended to take the car down to the granite rock. As he approached the cliff, however, he decided against that action. It would be better now to simply park it off the highway. The Frenchmen would drive it back to town at any rate. Time is precious. Why waste it hiding the car only to have to walk back down the road. He had no evidence of pursuit. He pulled the car onto the shoulder overlooking the cliff and turned to his passengers.

"Right. Here we are. Follow me. Hold hands. This cliff path is quite steep and tricky. Let's move!" ANTIMONY thought as he leapt out of the car and grabbed the rear door handle that he had not had this much energy in years—perhaps the thrill of being back in action or perhaps just the emergency of the moment. He felt energy surge through his muscles. He felt the electricity of action. The three raced across the road to the cliff's edge. ANTIMONY spotted the path straightaway. Holding hands, the fugitives delicately made their way down the treacherous path back and forth across the face of the cliff to the sandy beach below. They found no sign of the Frenchmen, only the sound of the tide rolling in, the low rush of the sea wind, and their own heavy breathing. ANTIMONY held up his hand. The Verdies halted and froze. ANTIMONY strained every sense of hearing and sight. *Something is wrong here—something dreadfully wrong.* Very slowly, almost imperceptibly, he reached for the pistol still holstered at his waist. His instincts cautioned against any sudden movement. *Nothing must be done to panic an adversary if one lurked in the shadows.* His hand felt the black leather holster just as he heard a crunch of sand under foot from behind him.

"Descartes?"

"Yes."

ANTIMONY spun around on his heels. The hobnailed leather sole dug into the soft sand almost throwing him off his balance.

"Good evening, *Herr Oberst.* ANTIMONY." The German stood twenty feet behind them. In the moonlight, ANTIMONY saw the muzzle pointed straight at his chest. "I should leave your weapon where it is." The venom in his voice chilled the refugees.

"ARMAGEDDON!"

"Yes, appropriate to your present situation I should think."

The moonlight sparkled in the man's hard blue eyes. "Forgive my lack of manners, *Herr Doktor.* Miss Verdi."

"ARMAGEDDON." Verdi replied, coolly masking the panic he felt.

ANTIMONY felt the trauma of defeat. Here, on the beach, with rescue in sight, he had lost. The German had somehow outwitted him, had been one important step ahead. *How had he found out about the rendezvous? Is one of the Frenchmen a traitor? How?* It didn't matter just now. ARMAGEDDON held the upper hand and the gun.

"Dr. Verdi, you and your daughter will come to Berlin with me. Your unfortunate accidental death will, of course, be reported to the American Consulate in Marseilles. Something about a late night drive up the coast in a borrowed auto. And as for you, Englishman, your Royal Navy friends will find your bullet-ridden body on the beach. Who knows, maybe a burial at sea with honors will take some of the sting out of your defeat."

What monumental conceit! What incredible ego! This German is actually delaying the final solution. Shoot! Damn it! Never give your opponent what he desperately needs—time! You are giving me a last hope. Time to conjure up a reaction, a plan to turn the tables. Keep talking, Nazi blowhard. Think, man. This arrogant bastard is acting just like the egomaniac villain in oh so many Hollywood dramas. He's bragging about how he's going to kill off the hero and how he . . . Hollywood! That's it. That's the key! Somewhere in the recesses of ANTIMONY's mind he remembered a scene from a not so great, but certainly thrilling movie. *What was it? No matter. On a beach such as this. What did the hero do? What did he do? Yes!* ANTIMONY fell down on his knees as if in surrender and defeat. The movie bad guy had gloated in premature victory. And all the while the hero cradled sand in each hand preparing for a last desperate attempt—a play as old as man had been dreaming up action adventures and as basic as it is, it just might work.

ANTIMONY lowered his eyes. The suddenness of this action momentarily startled ARMAGEDDON. He quickly recovered. The SS man moved towards them. Even better. The German now stood only ten feet away. ANTIMONY must seize the initiative before the enemy discovered the plan. "I am undone, ARMAGEDDON. You are the victor." ANTIMONY dropped his head. Both hands touched the sand below. *Play to his ego. That is your trump card.* "You have been one step ahead of me the entire time. Please don't harm the girl. She has nothing to do with any of this."

"On the contrary, Herr ANTIMONY. She has everything to do with this. She is the key to . . . ."

Now! Move! Two fistfuls of grainy sand shot up from the beach like pellets from a scatter gun, random and not aimed, striking out in all directions. *Spring! Now! His throat! Go for his throat!* ARMAGEDDON reeled. The suddenness of the explosion of sand unhinged him. Von Donop lost his balance as he threw a hand up to shield his eyes from the onrushing particles. As he staggered backwards, his rage exploded. Two flashes of lead streaked across the beach. One found its mark. It hit ANTIMONY just above the right kidney at an oblique angle. Blood poured from the wound staining the gray *Wehrmacht* uniform. But ARMAGEDDON had staggered, falling backwards two or three steps. Even the wound could not stop ANTIMONY's onrushing mass. Every muscle, every fiber, every molecule of his body surged forward towards the throat of the malevolent Nazi. His fingers, free of their sand weapon, extended out. He didn't even feel the jolt of the wound.

ANTIMONY reached the German just as the man recovered his balance. He hit him hard, as hard as he had ever struck a human being before. Ten fingers clutched the evil throat just above the silver *SS* flashes glinting in the moonlight, providing the perfect aim point. His thumbs pressed home. *Shut off his air! He must react to that! It is your only chance!* Two thumbs found the Adam's apple and pressed in with all the strength he had. A gag and sudden rush of air whooshed from the target, who thrust his arms up in a desperate attempt to break the thumb grip. His tongue rolled out of his mouth with saliva flying. *Now!* ANTIMONY, his right knee spattered with his own blood, thrust it hard into the man's groin and felt him buckle as they fell backwards. *Now!* In the sand, he would lose his advantage to the German's superior strength. *Too late!*

With the thrust to his groin, ARMAGEDDON had spastically dropped the pistol, arms flailing as he desperately tried to break the death lock on his throat. The pain rose up from his midsection. *Forget it! Forget the pain. Take the initiative. You are stronger than this old man. Slap him to the ground.* He started gagging. *No air! Must have air!* Blood welled up from broken blood vessels in his ravaged throat. *Falling, we're falling. Good. I have the advantage on the ground. Must break the maniac's grip!*

The two men hit the sand. The impact did what ARMAGEDDON could not. It jarred loose the grip on his throat. The German regained the advantage. ARMAGEDDON lashed out with his left foot. The boot tip caught ANTIMONY in the calf—not a great blow, but enough to throw the Englishman off balance. ANTIMONY now felt the wound in his side. He would lose if the battle continued. He had to do something. He raised his right hand into a fist, struggling to regain pressure on the German's throat. *Not enough!* He had allowed the enemy to recover his breath. ARMAGEDDON threw his arm up and deflected the blow. At the same time, he brought his left knee up sharply into ANTIMONY's midsection. The grip on the German's throat loosened. He grabbed the enemy's elbow and with a tremendous thrust, pushed away the killer thumbs—away from his ravaged throat. With the other hand, he struck his assailant on the side of the head, enough so that ANTIMONY tilted over to his right. Von Donop could see the opponent's eyes shut hard in a wince from the last several blows. *The old man is spent!*

He lashed out hard into ANTIMONY's chest causing an explosion of air. The German's bleeding throat ached. Forget it. I have won.

ANTIMONY's eyes popped open. Must . . . must forget . . . the . . . pain. Strike him! In spite of the fierce body blows, he still had the German pinned to the ground. He could seize the advantage. Ignore the burning pain! ANTIMONY never saw it coming. ARMAGEDDON, spreading out his arms to gain leverage in an attempt to push the man away first touched, then clutched a stone sharpened by the wash of a trillion waves. The stone came crashing down on ANTIMONY's left temple. Blood spurted out and spattered over the prostrate German below. For a brief moment, the world went black. ANTIMONY lost his bearings. Neither up nor down, he just tumbled. ARMAGEDDON thrust his chest up, propelled by two strong arms anchored in the sand. The Englishman went limp, crouching on hands and knee, shaking his head to and fro, desperately trying to recover his balance and his senses while attempting to get to the weapon still holstered at his waist. ARMAGEDDON stood up as he regained his balance. The German still held the stone. He raised the weapon high in the air and above the enemy's head, much as an executioner would his ax.

The first round struck between the shoulder and the rib cage causing a sickening crackle of crushed bone. Blood from a severed artery pulsed out over the black tunic. The stone fell as ARMAGEDDON dropped to his knees. His mouth gaped open. Slowly, excruciatingly, he stood up, arms dangling limply at his side, and turned to face his assailant. Five feet from him stood his executioner, Angela Verdi. She held the Luger with both hands. Spent powder smoke rose from the muzzle. Shot with his own gun by this Italian bitch! How? Angela saw the wild-eyed hatred and contempt in the German's eyes. She pulled the trigger two more times. ARMAGEDDON's body flung backwards with the impact. One bullet entered his chest below the heart and another into his lower abdomen. He uttered a deathly, primeval scream as his limp body thrust backwards and down into the blood-soaked sand. From his throat came a rumble, a hideous gurgling death rattle. Dead. The monster is dead.

CHAPTER 22

AS IGNORANT ARMIES
CLASH BY NIGHT

A NTIMONY vaguely perceived some presence hovering over him. The loss of blood had taken its toll. He had passed out, but now sensed someone sponging his forehead with a wet rag—a salty wet, cloth moistened with sea water. His head cleared. Around him clustered a gaggle of Royal Marines and French Resistance partisans.

"Commodore Braithwaite, I'm Lieutenant Chesterton, Royal Marines. Are you able to stand, Sir?"

"I believe so."

Strong, young arms extended to help him up. As he stood, he felt woozy from a combination of the blow to the head and loss of blood. ANTIMONY looked over at the figure of Karl von Donop lying in a crumpled heap on the sand, eyes still open—the menacing, cold blue eyes. In a sort of fetal position, he had died clutching his abdomen in the dark sand stained by the man's lost life blood. The enemy's bullet had passed through ANTIMONY's midsection near the right kidney, but had struck no vital organs. Despite the considerable loss of blood, it caused no life-threatening damage. It hurt like hell, though. ANTIMONY winced and grabbed his side.

"Will you make it, Sir?"

"Yes. I'm fine, Lieutenant."

"We'd best be shoving off, Sir. Shouldn't want any attention from the local Huns." The officer's subtle remark meant to hurry the party along. One does not wish to dally on an enemy beach any longer than necessary. ANTIMONY saw Verdi for the first time in several minutes. The old man looked drawn and worn from the excitement of the past few minutes. In his hand he held a German service pistol—a pistol, ARMAGEDDON's weapon. He had taken it from Angela. The trigger guard wrapped around his index finger,

Verdi let go of the grip. The handle swung towards the ground, barrel in the air. He extended the ugly weapon forward toward ANTIMONY.

"A memento of the occasion, perhaps? Who would have known that my daughter was such a good shot with a pistol?"

ANTIMONY reached out and grasped the gun. He nodded. He had been vaguely aware of Angela's action. "Why not. Thank you, Doctor. Thank you for my life, Miss Verdi."

"Oh no, Mr. Prince. Thank you for mine. And my father's."

"I have been a foolish, sentimental old man. This trip was—how shall I say it—ill-advised. Thank God you were here to save me from my disaster," Verdi exclaimed unashamedly.

ANTIMONY nodded again and motioned to Eliana to come nearer. "Miss Descrates, I fear you may have a traitor among your men. How else could ARMAGEDDON have known about this place?"

"No, *Monsieur*. Only these three and myself knew the exact details of the rendezvous. We have all been together since. No one has had access to a telephone or wireless during these hours. No, my friend, this German was a very clever devil. He had to have figured it out by some other means, though I don't know how. Do not worry, Sir, we will dispose of this German filth. We shall arrange for a convenient accident for him and his two companions at the shepherd's cottage. The local *Gendarmes* can be notoriously lax in their investigation of these matters. And the Prefect of Police—well, he likes his ladies without his dear wife's knowledge. Do not worry. We will not be compromised, *Monsieur*."

"Yes, thank you again."

ANTIMONY took two more agonizing slow steps forward supported by a Royal Marine on either side. There is a certain honor among warriors that transcends any culture, nationality, or ideology. Despite ARMAGEDDON's cruelty, his venomous hatred, and his destructiveness, he did what he did for his country and cause—no less than ANTIMONY to his or the Frenchmen to theirs. ANTIMONY looked back at the crumpled heap on the sand. The disposal that Eliana proposed is not deserved. ARMAGEDDON needs better than that in spite of himself. He had lost the battle. Let him have an honorable ending.

"Lieutenant, do you chaps have a German ensign onboard?"

"Why . . . uh . . . yes, I believe we do. In the Signal Locker."

"Good. Bring along the German officer if you would."

The Marine crinkled his brow questioningly. "Sir?"

"Yes. The man will at least have a proper burial at sea. See to it please, Lieutenant."

"Yes, Sir."

He nodded to two Marines, who ran back up the beach to ARMAGEDDON, lifted his corpse and manhandled it to the dinghy. Eliana nodded.

"We will take care of his disappearance."

"Miss Descartes. In my jacket at the cottage, sewn in the lining, are several gold coins. Use them for your work. You have my unequivocal admiration. Good luck. Good hunting," whispered an exhausted ANTIMONY.

On the beach, Eliana and her men snapped to attention and saluted. As the rescued and rescuers rowed through the surf, ANTIMONY heard from the beach a cry of defiance—the cry of victory.

"*Vive La France!*"

All had gone below except the commanding officer, the first officer, and ANTIMONY. In spite of his painful wound, he wanted to stay topside for a while longer. In the moonlight, the huge granite monument could be seen as HMS *Tribune* gently rolled in the sea. He thought of a line from a poem read in his youth—a Matthew Arnold poem, "Dover Beach." The line came to his conscious mind: "as ignorant armies clash by night." He let out a deep breath, partly from relief, partly satisfaction. Mission accomplished. All had now been revealed. He was indeed up to the task. Self-doubt had plagued him ever since the tennis match with INTREPID so many eons back. No more. This was his revelation. And now, ANTIMONY had been resurrected.

"Number One, take her out and prepare to dive."

"Very good, Sir. Helm, come left, steer 285 degrees," he shouted down the brass voice pipe.

The sleek, gray hull gracefully slid through the water as white, frothy bubbles danced up from her sides. In the distance, ANTIMONY saw the winking and flashing lights of Biarritz receding into the darkness.

"It's going to be a long, nasty war, Commander Peacock."

"It is indeed, Sir, it is indeed. Take her down Number One."

"Aye, Aye, Sir."

THE END

AUTHOR'S NOTES

The story of the *Zamzam* is true. The unfortunate sinking of the neutral, Egyptian vessel created an international diplomatic crisis in the late spring of 1941. When Time-Life Books published their World War II series (Barrie Pitt and the Editors of Time-Life Books, *The Battle of the Atlantic*, 1980), in the volume on the sea war in the Atlantic, they included a piece entitled "Zany Saga of the Zamzam." Intrigued by the story of the ship and its odd crew and passengers, my concept for the story soon formed. My brother Larry Carpenter, had earlier proposed the concept of a World War I field agent resurrected for service in the Second World War and suggested the title Resurrection of ANTIMONY. The mixture of young, adventurous, hearty American volunteer ambulance drivers, a bevy of youthful RAF wives who hadn't seen their husbands in months, a hard-drinking batch of North Carolina tobaccomen, all combined with a shipload of missionaries on a derelict liner with a disreputable polyglot crew steaming through dangerous waters provided a witch's brew to make a Hollywood screenwriter mad with envy. By adding in the fictitious Commodore Braithwaite as ANTIMONY and the malignant SS agent von Donop as ARMAGEDDON, both on a mission of immense importance to humanity's future, the *Zamzam* story proved an irresistible setting for a World War II action-adventure, espionage thriller.

I had read widely on Allied wartime intelligence operations, including INTREPID, OPERATION FORTITUDE SOUTH (D-Day operational deception), "the man who never was" (Sicily deception) and British Naval Intelligence as well as Ian Fleming's James Bond series and have always been fascinated with such topics. By mixing in real persons such as Sir William Stephenson, Ian Fleming, Rear-Admiral John Godfrey, Captain Bernhard Rogge, Colonel William Donovan and Captain William Gray Smith, the story of ANTIMONY, the middle-aged former field agent, came alive. I have attempted to be as true to the real personages as possible and many apologies to their memory where the need for drama resulted in fictional conversations and actions. Since the overarching theme is the race to develop an operational atomic weapon, readers will easily recognize that the Enrico Verdi character is a thinly-disguised Enrico Fermi, the émigré Italian physicist who achieved the first atomic chain reaction in 1942 at the University of Chicago as part of the American Manhattan Project.

For the reader interested in the historical context of the *Zamzam* adventure, let me provide a brief summary of the main points of interest in what truly is the "zany saga of the *Zamzam*."

Zamzam began her seagoing career as the SS *Leicestershire*, a Bibby Line freighter, in 1909. Built by Harland and Wolf of Belfast, Ireland, the same shipyard that built the RMS *Titanic* and her sister ships *Britannic* and *Olympic*, *Zamzam* displaced 8,059 gross tons with a length of 467.2 feet and a beam of 54.3 feet and had a 31.7 foot draft. With twin screws and a speed of fifteen knots, *Leicestershire* represented the state of the art in pre-World War I shipping. Launched on 3 June 1909, her maiden voyage from Birkenhead (England) to Rangoon (Burma) commenced on 11 September.

In August 1914, as World War I swiftly enveloped the European powers, the Indian Colonial Government requisitioned *Leicestershire* for troop transportation. She carried the 17th Lancers to Marseilles (France) for duty on the Western Front and subsequently transported Indian and Burmese colonial troops for Middle East service. The British government again requisitioned *Leicestershire* as a troop transport in 1917, carrying troops from Plymouth (England) to Bombay (India), British troops to Archangel (Russia) for service against the Bolshevik "Reds," and American "doughboys" to England. After the war, she transported Australian troops home to Freemantle, Melbourne, and Sydney. Many ships of her class did similar duty in the conflict, a fact pointed out to Captain Rogge on his visit to England in 1937 as a naval representative at the coronation of King George VI. This factor later played into the attack in April 1941 according to Rogge's testimony. His Royal Navy host informed him that the Bibby Line ships of the same class as *Zamzam* had been used as troop transports in World War I.

Returned to her owners following the Armistice, *Leicestershire* underwent a conversion from coal-burning to marine fuel oil propulsion as well as other modernizations. The coal bunker, converted to cargo holds, greatly improved the ship's hauling capacity. In 1930, the British Expedition Company, Ltd. purchased the ship, renaming her *British Exhibitor*. But, a victim of the worldwide depression of the period, the company went bankrupt and in 1933, the Egyptian Company for Travel and Navigation purchased the vessel. Renamed SS *Zamzam*, she carried freight and passengers and for two months of every year, transported Islamic pilgrims back and forth from Mecca. In 1934, *Zamzam* ownership transferred to the *Societe Misr de Navigation* (or MISR Line) of Alexandria (Egypt) for the passage of religious pilgrims.

In 1939, in great need of maintenance and repairs, the company laid up the ship in Alexandria where she received damage to the stack, captain's quarters, and Pilot House in an Italian air raid. Once repaired and under the command of a new master, William Gray Smith, in December 1940, she set out to transport passengers and cargo on the Alexandria-Cape Town-New York run. To minimize wartime risk, she sailed via the Red Sea, Indian Ocean, South Atlantic, and Caribbean to Boston. However, the return run to Alexandria took *Zamzam* to South America and across the South Atlantic where she encountered the *Atlantis*.

At this point, I slightly altered the routes and dates for dramatic effect. In the story of ANTIMONY, *Zamzam* sailed into New York and stayed only long enough to take on cargo and passengers. In reality, she arrived from Boston on 24 February 1941 where she remained much longer due to a law suit from a stevedore in Hoboken, who claimed that he suffered a skull fracture while working aboard the ship. Upon posting a bond, the company was allowed to sail the *Zamzam*. Accordingly, on 20 March, *Zamzam* pulled in all lines and departed Hoboken (New Jersey) bound for Alexandria with projected port calls in Baltimore (Maryland), Trinidad, Recife (Brazil), Cape Town (South Africa), and Mombasa (Kenya). With a crew of 141 composed of several nationalities, the ship also carried 202 passengers of which 137 were Protestant and Catholic missionaries bound for various spots in Africa. Additionally, she carried the six North Carolina Tobacco buyers and the two dozen young men of the British-American Ambulance Corps headed for North Africa. A contingent of Royal Air Force wives bound for Egypt to join their husbands along with several odds and ends British, American, and Canadian businessmen rounded out the passengers. Many of the missionaries had brought their families, thus the manifest included several children and women.

Arriving in Trinidad on 30 March, the ship received Admiralty orders to sail a preset course to Cape Town under blacked-out condition. Captain Smith protested due to his neutral status and the presence of women and children aboard. Denied the request, the crew painted the glass portholes black during the transit to Recife, where they departed on 9 April. Additionally, she sailed without lights or national ensign and in radio silence.

Hearing the distress call of the Norwegian ship *Tai-Yin*, Smith changed course a number of times before returning to base course once he felt safe. However, *Atlantis*, the notorious Raider 16, disguised as the freighter *Tamesis*, still lurked in the area. At 0500 on the morning of 17 April, she opened fire on the supposed British armed cruiser. The first rounds knocked out the wireless antennas, so chief wireless operator Anwar's SOS did not transmit. Though many of the boats had been damaged in the shelling, every passenger and crewman made it safely aboard the German raider. The following day, all passengers except the badly wounded Ned Laughinghouse, Dr. Robert Starling and Frank Vicovari transferred to the freighter *Dresden*, which simply circled in the area for several days. Laughinghouse eventually died of his brain injury aboard *Atlantis*.

Dresden finally sailed north towards Occupied France and evaded both a British merchant convoy and the Royal Navy blockade. She arrived at the port of St.Jean-de-Luz on 20 May, a day after the British government announced that *Zamzam* was overdue in Cape Town and presumed sunk by the Germans. Germany, taking full advantage of the timely arrival and relative safety of the crew and passengers, claimed that the ship, though neutral, carried contraband war goods and by sailing in a darkened-ship condition with no national ensign, had violated her neutral status. I took the situation quite a bit further to create the dramatic tension of having the ship used as bait to create an international incident, a situation that some historians have accused the British Admiralty of having done with the *Lusitania* in 1915. Nonetheless, the incident with the message hidden under the blotter actually occurred. German sailors found the Admiralty message that Captain Smith had attempted to conceal. He did manage to drop the code book over the side before their arrival. It was this message that the Germans produced and based their claim that *Zamzam* sailed under Admiralty orders and thus represented a legitimate target. As to the issue of whether she was bait, one can only speculate. However, in a moment of candor a year later, Anthony Eden, the British Foreign Minister and future Prime Minister, commented to photographer David Scherman that: "You chaps on the *Zamzam* were quite a disappointment to us. We expected the incident to bring America into the War."

The American nationals went to the resort city of Biarritz and to several of the grand hotels under the supervision of the American Consul at Bordeaux (France), Henry S. Waterman. Passengers and crew of nations then at war with Germany went by sea to Bordeaux and then to various prison camps in France, Germany, and Bulgaria. Many remained interned until the end of the war; however, most of the women and children were exchanged for German women held in Allied countries.

Meanwhile, American diplomatic personnel arrived from various posts in France and Spain to coordinate the evacuation. On 31 May, at the Franco-Spanish border, the Germans released 119 Americans to U.S. custody. These *Zamzam* refugees were taken by train to Lisbon (Portugal) for embarkation. On 9 June, the first passengers arrived in New York at La Guardia Field Marine Terminal via the Pan American Flying Boat, including *Fortune* magazine editor Charles J.V. Murphy and *Life* Magazine photographer David Scherman, who had embarked at Recife and whose photos of the sinking of the ship and the epic journey appeared in the 23 June and 15 December 1941 *Life Magazine* articles and the later Time-Life Books article. Throughout the summer, in gaggles, passengers arrived in New York aboard various vessels.

A photo of *Atlantis* taken by Scherman proved invaluable to the Royal Navy. Using the picture for identification purposes, the County-class heavy cruiser HMS *Devonshire* sank Atlantis on 21 November 1941 off the South African coast. Many of the crew and captives, including Captain Rogge, survived the sinking as prisoners of war. Frank Vicovari survived and after two days in the water, a German U-boat rescued him and several *Atlantis* crewmen. Eventually exchanged in a prisoner swap, he returned home in 1944. The remainder of the surviving crew and passengers were eventually freed as Soviet and Allied armies overran the various internment camps. The last passenger was finally freed on 27 April 1945, just days before Germany's surrender. Thus ended the "zany saga of the Zamzam."

The German raider *Atlantis* started her career as the freighter *Goldenfels*. Built by the Bremer Vulkan shipyard in 1937 and operated by the Bremen-based Hansa Line, she was converted to a commerce raider and recommissioned as *Atlantis* in November 1939. At 17,600 tons displacement, she carried a 349-man crew, and an array of armaments, including 6–150 mm guns, 4 torpedo tubes, and two Heinkel float planes. In March 1940, she sailed for the South Atlantic with the mission of hunting down and destroying Allied merchant ships and disrupting trade with Asia and Africa. After her sinking, most of the crew eventually made their way back to Germany through various routes. Capitan Rogge and Lieutenant Mohr both survived the war and wrote accounts of the *Atlantis* and her career as the most successful of the German commerce raiders of World War II.

Many of the central characters and locations in ANTIMONY's story are real. A short history might be interesting to some readers.

Rear-Admiral Sir John Godfrey had commanded the battle-cruiser HMS *Repulse* in the late 1930s and was awarded for his service with promotion to flag rank and the post of Director of Naval Intelligence (DNI) in June 1939. Naval Intelligence Division (NID) operated out of Room 39 in the Old Admiralty Building in Whitehall, described as a dreary, uncomfortable, large space with institutional beige walls and overlooking the garden of 10 Downing Street, St. James' Park Lake and Horse Guards Parade. Described as tall and imposing with pale, blue-gray eyes and a domed cranium, Godfrey managed the world of naval and maritime intelligence gathering with great skill and tenacity. Although the DNI did not control field agents directly (the role of the Secret Intelligence Service or SIS), Godfrey oversaw the Operational Intelligence Center (OIC) at Admiralty. Buried under twenty feet of steel and concrete, OIC tracked shipping movements and particularly the activities of enemy warships, commerce raiders, and submarines. Clandestine activity, which DNI had previously managed, was turned over to the Special Operations Executive (SOE) in 1940 under General Colin Gubbins or "C."

Lieutenant-Commander Ian Fleming served as the Personal Assistant (Code 17F) to Admiral Godfrey. The admiral personally recruited Fleming (then a subaltern Black Watch reserve officer) at the start of the war. Commissioned as a Royal Naval Volunteer Reserve (RNVR) lieutenant, he was promoted eventually to commander. Section 17, the DNI's personal staff, served as the NID "brain trust." Fleming, a former Reuters reporter and stockbroker before the war, relished his role as wartime intelligence officer and personally supervised many NID operations. Following the war, he enjoyed a career as the author of the James Bond novels. But, probably due to his heavy drinking, womanizing, chain-smoking, and hard-living lifestyle, he died at the age of fifty-six. Described as dynamic, somewhat arrogant, extrovert, but very effective, he was the perfect action officer for the DNI.

Sir William Stephenson (INTREPID), hailed from Manitoba, Canada. A Royal Air Force fighter pilot and ace in the First World War, Stephenson proved a remarkable and successful businessman and was one of the founders of the BBC in the 1920s. Interestingly, one of his reputed twelve air combat victories before he was shot down and captured, was over Lothar von Richthofen, younger brother of the Red Baron, who scored forty air combat victories. Prime Minister Winston Churchill personally recruited Stephenson to head up all British Western Hemisphere intelligence operations (interestingly over the objection of General Sir Stewart Menzies, wartime head of all British intelligence operations). Traveling to New York in June 1940, Stephenson established the British Security Coordination (BSC) headquartered at Rockefeller Center in New York. Posing as a simple Passport Control Officer, he coordinated all hemispheric intelligence operations and became a personal representative of Churchill to President Franklin Roosevelt.

For those interested in the story of the raider *Atlantis*, I recommend Joseph P. Slavick's *The Cruise of the German Raider Atlantis* or Captain Bernhard Rogge's *The German Raider Atlantis*. For details of the workings of NID during the war, try Donald McLachlan's *Room 39: Naval Intelligence in Action, 1939-45*. For Sir William Stephenson and the activities of the British Security Coordination, see William Stevenson's (not related) *A Man Called Intrepid*.

Lastly, I wish to thank the General Manager of the Hôtel du Palais, Monsieur Jean-Louis Leimbacher, for kindly supplying me with extensive information on not only the hotel used as the setting for ANTIMONY's incarceration in Biarritz, but also on the history of the French resort city wherein Commodore John David Fairchild Braithwaite, RN, aka ANTIMONY, was resurrected.

CPSIA information can be obtained at www.ICGtesting.com
Printed in the USA
BVOW02s0203280916

463484BV00003B/19/P